PRIDE NOT PREJUDICE

VOLUME II

KERRIGAN BYRNE   PIPER HUGULEY   MIRA LYNN KELLY
CLARE REBECCA MCCARTHY   ROSALIND JAMES
CYNTHIA ST. AUBIN

OLIVERHEBERBOOKS

INVINCIBLE

KERRIGAN BYRNE

"By the pricking of my thumbs, something wicked this way comes."

— WILLIAM SHAKESPEARE, MACBETH

CHAPTER 1

Badb:

> "Sacred hate and ancient ire,
> By the wind, water, and fire.
> Reach through the souls now owned by me
> And pluck the one who shall be freed.
>
> A lover fair, a beauty bold,
> To ensnare a heart so cold.
> Force a King to his knees,
> And bring him to be ruled by me."

Wyrd Sisters:

> "As we will, so mote it be!"

*T*he Highland cave became as still as a tomb, and even the Wyrd sisters held their collective breath until one small bare foot stepped out of the nether, followed by a strong calf, long, sensuous thighs, and a body that would have melted the hearts of the most brutal of beings.

Pale, luminous skin glowed in the light of the nether, illuminating eyes the color of amethysts and hair as dark as midnight.

"Mistress," the shade spoke, running elegant fingers along bare flesh as though he couldn't believe what he felt. "What is your will?"

"Malcolm de Moray," Badb spat the name. "Bring him back to me, I haven't finished with him yet."

"Once we have the Druid King along with the Grimoire, the others will follow," Nemain drawled. "And since we are without Macha now, we'll need a third body to absorb the Magick we will claim from them."

That caught the shade's attention. "Me?" he asked hoarsely.

"Unless you'd like to spend another century in the nether."

"Nay," the shade stepped forward. "Nay, I'll do whatever you ask. Just don't send me back there."

"Seduce him," Nemain ordered, stepping to the man and running fingers through his thick hair. "Cripple him with lust and weaken him with pleasure."

Badb cackled at the idea. "Get him to trust you. Then his heart will be open and vulnerable for us to take. Then you'll say these words when he is at the peak of his pleasure, and all the power that is his, will be yours." She handed the shade a parchment with an ancient curse written upon it.

"*That* is when we'll strike." Nemain pulled a tattered, charcoal robe from her own shoulders and draped it across the shade. "A damsel in distress, I think, is just the tactic to disarm the King."

"But I am no damsel," the shade spoke. "I am in the body of a human...man."

Nemain waved that away. "The Druid King is the one sovereign in all of time who cares not for an heir or for his bloodline's legacy. He has only ever loved those of his own sex."

"'Tis common enough among mortals in their meat suits," Badb cackled. "Though they always find some reason to deny themselves and each other pleasure."

Badb spit into the cauldron she'd been stirring, and it hissed. "Malcolm de Moray will be sorry he ever crossed us," she snarled.

Nemain smiled, her amber gaze gliding down the lad's nubile body. "And sorrier still, that he ever laid eyes on you."

Malcolm de Moray's growl of frustration echoed off the stone wall of his laboratory. The looking glass he hurled shattered against it a scant second later.

By what ancient Magick had the Wyrd Sisters hidden the Grimoire from him? From *him*! The most powerful Earth Druid to be seen in a handful of centuries. The last potent Druid male of his kind. The King of the fucking Picts. And he couldn't get a simple scrying spell to work.

His enemies were close, he knew it. The trees shuddered at their evil, and the fields swayed with whispers of sightings, but nothing tangible.

He'd be damned if he sat with his cock in hand and waited for them to strike. Nay, he'd find the vicious bitches and send them to hell where they belonged.

"Have you eaten today, Brother?" Morgana, his younger sister, flowed into his laboratory carrying a tray of food. Though breakfast or dinner, he couldn't be certain.

"I know not," he answered shortly, eyeing the doorway for the inevitable following of his sister's Berserker mate. "What day is it?"

"Would it matter if I told you?" Morgana's blue dress shimmered like crystalline water as she made her way past candles, lanterns, shelves, scrolls, and herbs to set his repast on the table in front of him.

"Nay," he admitted, the word almost drowned out by the loud, hungry sound his stomach made at the scent of salted pork, rosemary roasted potatoes, and beets.

Morgana reached up and took his stubbled jaw in her hands, and instantly he felt a relief that only a water Druid could give another human with her touch. His aches and pains dissipated, his tense muscles relaxed, and the pricking of the headache that had begun to pound behind his eyes disappeared.

"Dear Malcolm," she murmured softly. "When is the last time you slept?"

He blinked down into a face the feminine copy of his own. Unruly russet hair, pale skin, prominent jaw. Though hers was delicate, and his defined. Other than the obvious difference in their sexes, the only other thing that set them apart was the color of their eyes. Morgana's were as blue as the ocean in summer, while his were a mossy green.

Elemental colors.

"Who can sleep with all these bloody Vikings invading *my* castle?" he groused.

Unruffled, Morgana patted his cheek. "They're not invaders, dear, they're allies. *Guests*. Two of whom are mated to your sister and cousin. So, they're family, as well."

Malcolm grunted. "That damned army of Niall's is picking our larder clean and planting bastards in all the kitchen maids."

"They've also pledged their swords and lives to help us defeat the Wyrd Sisters," she reminded brightly. "Now eat your supper, and I'll give you the gift that will make your search easier."

That arrested his attention. "What gift?"

The same mischief had lit her eyes for just over two decades now. Malcolm loved it, and he hated it. "Eat first," she ordered.

Malcolm took a step toward her, towering head and shoulders above her. "I am not a child, I am yer king," he said darkly. "I command ye to give me what ye have." No one had ever dared disobey him when he was in such a mood.

Morgana burst out laughing and lifted onto her toes to give him a quick peck on the cheek. "When has that ever worked on me?" she giggled. "Eat up."

Nostrils flaring, Malcolm stabbed at a chunk of pork and brought it to his mouth, chewing furiously while holding out his hand to his sister.

"Your vegetables as well," Morgana reminded him.

"Give it to me, or I'll do ye violence," he threatened. They both knew he wouldn't. First, because he loved his sister and would never lay a hand on a woman, and second, because Baelsar Bloodborn, Morgana's Berserker mate, would tear his limbs from his body and throw them in the tall grasses. Magick be damned.

With a gusty sigh, Morgana reached into her pocket and held up a piece of twine on the end of which the most perfect quartz crystal he'd ever seen reflected the light of the candles.

"Where did ye get that?" he breathed, snatching it away from her grasp.

"From a toad Bael and I met by the river." Morgana shrugged. "And you're welcome."

"What were ye doing by the river?" Malcolm asked idly, running his fingers over the smooth, clear surface of the spear-shaped crystal. It fit in the palm of a hand, and would be the most effective scrying tool of all time.

When he glanced up, Morgana's eyes were sparkling with that mischief again, and also with a lasciviousness that caused his belly to lurch with disgust.

"That's revolting," he spat.

"I said nothing," Morgana sang innocently, all but dancing toward the door.

"Ye didna have to," he complained.

"Now if you don't finish your supper by the time I return in an hour, I'll have Bael tie you up and shove it down your throat." With that cheerful threat, she closed the door to his workshop behind her.

"I'd like to see him try," he muttered to no one in particular.

Dinner forgotten, Malcolm retrieved the most recent map of his kingdom and uncurled it across his table. He murmured a Gaelic scrying spell as he sprinkled powdered mugwort, nutmeg, cinnamon, and yarrow onto the map. Licking his fingers, he let the crystal dangle over it and circle in the direction of the earth's rotation.

After a few minutes, the crystal stilled and skewered the map with its sharp point.

The Caledonian Forest. *Of course.* Within its ancient black depths any myriad of evils could hide. It was said that Fairy Magick still protected some of the forest, and that could be blocking each of the de Moray's attempts to find the Grimoire.

"Ha," he crowed in triumph. "I'm coming for ye." Grabbing his cloak and riding boots, Malcolm strode from his laboratory with vengeance lengthening his every step.

In his haste, he nearly knocked over his cousin, Kenna, when he rounded a corner on his way to the stables.

She jumped back into her mate, Niall's, broad chest and the man steadied her with gigantic, yet gentle hands whist glaring daggers at Malcolm.

"Malcolm," she exclaimed, her amber eyes glowing with genuine pleasure. "I haven't seen you in ages, you've been so isolated in your cave. Where are you off to?"

"The Caledonian Woods," he answered shortly, making to step around them.

"Going hunting are you?" she asked brightly, putting a fond hand on his arm.

"Aye."

"For game or for herbs?"

For evil. "I must be on my way."

"Of course." She kissed him on the cheek, which produced a soft sound of protest from her looming mate. "Ride past the west gate on your way out. My love and his men are erecting spear-tipped fence posts that would stop a war horse. It's really very clever."

Clever? Malcolm met Niall's light-eyed glare across Kenna's head and spoke to him in Gaelic. "My people were mapping the stars and discovering the mysteries of the universe while ye Nordic barbarians were still dragging your knuckles in your own people's blood and shit."

Niall's eyes narrowed even further with suspicion. "What did he just say to me?"

"They're just trying to help," Kenna answered back in the language of their fathers, putting a staying hand on her mate's chest.

"I should hex them all with a pox for making changes to *my* keep without *my* permission," Malcolm growled at Kenna, still in Gaelic.

"You've been locked in your laboratory for days," Kenna argued.

"Did he just threaten you?" Niall growled in their common tongue, taking a step forward with murder flashing in his eyes.

Malcolm made a fist, ready and willing to go to blows with the interloper.

"Oh... he said that you all are, indeed, quite clever," Kenna lied, sending Malcolm silent warnings of wrath. "*And,* he says *thank you* to you and your men for their hard work." She annunciated every word through gritted teeth.

The Nordic giant quirked a suspicious eyebrow. "That's not what it sounded like."

Kenna grabbed Niall's arm and guided him around Malcolm. "Oh, you know Gaelic, a rather harsh sounding language sometimes, isn't it? Let's go check on Ingmar and Bulvark, shall we?"

Malcolm watched as Kenna led her mate past him and disappeared around the corner in a hurry. He'd need to figure out what to do about these Berserker men. They weren't even properly married to his kin, and yet they'd begun living together as though they had been in an alarmingly short time.

Turning, he stalked down the corridor, his footfalls echoing off the stones. First, though, he needed to stop the impending Apocalypse. Everything else could wait.

Going after the remaining Wyrd Sisters on his own was reckless, he knew. But he had a secret vengeance to reap.

And if Malcolm was in a forest, he had more than enough weapons at his disposal.

CHAPTER 2

My *name is Sean.* It was all he remembered. Anything else had disappeared into the nether ages ago. His memories, identity, and humanity. He knew he used to be something. Someone. That he had loved, and had been betrayed. But even those details had begun to dissipate within the cold, dank void that had been his home for centuries.

When the madness set in, when he felt as though he'd fall through his prison that was as insubstantial as air, and yet as strong as iron, he'd press his cheek to the cold floor and chant the one thing he knew for certain over and over again.

My name is Sean.

His name remained the only thing the Wyrd sisters hadn't taken from his. The only thing he hadn't pledged to them. His last possession.

It seemed to be the purpose of the nether, to strip one's mind of all individuality. The longer one remained incarcerated there, the more of themselves they lost.

Though a thick mist shrouded the afternoon, and thicker trees blocked the sunlight, Sean blinked against the brilliance of the day. It had been precisely fifty years since he'd been called out of the nether that'd become his prison. Fifty years since he'd seen any light whatsoever, and before that it had been a few decades if he remembered correctly. In the hundred or so years he'd been incarcerated, he could count on one hand the number of times the Wyrd Sisters brought him forth to do their bidding. And once their objective had been acquired, it was back into the void with him. Alone and forgotten.

The dense forest shimmered with moisture. The leaves of trees, of which he'd forgotten the names, changed with the season, flaring into brilliant colors before they shriveled and fell to the earth. His eyes ached with the sight, but he didn't dare close them, for fear the beauty would disappear. He'd need this memory to hold on to, in case the Wyrd sisters didn't hold up their end of the bargain and sent him back once his job was finished. The beauty of this forest would keep him for decades, until it, too, faded.

The damp flora beneath his feet felt like a carpet of clouds. He didn't even care about the biting chill, and couldn't help but run the moss between his toes with a child's relish.

Even the wet, cold air that reached through his threadbare cloak until he trembled with body-tensing shivers felt better than the perpetual dry cold of his prison. It was *something*. A sensation and, though unpleasant, it was life-affirming.

Watching his hot breath puff into the autumn air, Sean drifted forward, ignoring the strange rustlings and noises of the forest. He only had one purpose, and the Wyrd Sisters' evil Magick would protect him from all else.

He must seduce Malcolm de Moray, and say the spell Badb had given him upon his release into de Moray's body. With it, he would take Malcolm's Druid Magick.

He approaches... the wind hissed with the voice of Badb, as she had dominion over the air. *Be ready... be ruthless.*

"Yes, mistress," Sean whispered just as trotting hoof beats drew near. Spotting a soft bit of ground beneath the corpse of a fallen tree, Sean threw himself down and made certain his threadbare trews hung low on his hips. He'd been dumped into this realm without so much as a sleeve, let alone any garment up top but for a rag who thought enough of itself to try a life as a cloak.

A damsel in distress?

As a dark shadow formed within the swirling mist and began to solidify, Sean moaned as piteously as he could.

"Help. Please sir. Help me?"

He didn't have to fake his open-mouthed gasp as the Shire steed obediently stopped, horse and rider peering down at him with nearly identical looks of astonished curiosity.

Malcolm de Moray, Druid King of the Picts, was nothing like he'd imagined. Indeed, Sean had expected an older king, grey-bearded, poxed, and portly from too much ignoble excess.

The man swinging down from his horse couldn't have yet seen five-and-thirty. He was tall and wide enough to merit such a giant steed, Sean could tell that even beneath the rider's forest-green cloak and kilt.

"Christ," he swore, hurrying over.

Sean couldn't make the assessments he needed, nor could he remember the plots and lies he'd worked on. The king's eyes were so mossy green and lovely in a face so raw with masculinity that the contrast rendered him speechless.

Locks of unruly russet hair fell over his braw forehead as he bent down to kneel beside Sean's prone body.

"What happened to ye?" he demanded, ripping off his cloak and covering Sean with it.

So much for distracting the man with bare skin. He'd have to improvise.

The reasons Sean couldn't answer him were two-fold.

First, because the cloak was fur-lined and sumptuous, retaining the warmth of his body and sliding across his cold, bare skin like a lover's caress.

Second, because his shirt was unfastened to his torso, and Sean could see the swells of his chest and the dark shapes of his nipples hardened against the cold beneath the thin linen.

He was lean in the way that wolves were lean. Long limbs thickened with power and sinewed with grace, but also clinging to his braw frame in a spare, hungry way that made Sean wonder if he ate enough to support a man of his size.

Sean didn't quite know what to do in the presence of such a male, let alone what to say, so he merely stared at him in an open-mouthed stupor.

"Are ye hurt?" The king made as though to put his hands on Sean, but then thought the better of it, studying him with shrewd, yet gentle eyes. "I doona see any blood. We're ye attacked?"

"I—I don't know," he answered shakily. "I don't remember anything. I just… appeared here." Lies were more believable when peppered with the truth.

"Can ye move yer limbs? Yer fingers and toes?" The king queried, still squinting at Sean alertly from beneath a cruel brow.

"Aye," he lifted his arm out of his cloak and wriggled a few digits.

"Were ye robbed?" he pressed.

"My head." Sean touched a hand to his forehead. "'Tis pounding, but I feel no pain elsewhere, and I have nothing of value to steal." Truer words…

"Perhaps someone came up behind ye," the king murmured. "May I?"

At Sean's nod, he reached out and threaded big, careful fingers in Sean's hair, probing his scalp with the expertise of an experienced physician.

"Are you a healer?" Sean asked, turning his head so his lips brushed against the skin of the king's arm.

"I have some experience with it," the sovereign hedged, pulling his arm away. "I doona feel a lump, though that doesna mean one willna develop. Do ye think ye can stand? I'll want ye away from here in case yer attackers return. There is much danger in these woods."

"I'll try," he said weakly, allowing the king to help him upright. Immediately, Sean let his cloak fall to the earth, unveiling the pale expanse of his slender form.

Then he swooned.

Malcolm de Moray caught him easily, and tensed as their bodies met.

"Do ye live here in the forest with yer...woman?" he asked uncomfortably.

"I live alone," Sean said against his chest. "I have naught but a cottage by the loch. Can I prevail upon you to take me there, sir? I don't think I can walk all that way back just yet."

Lifting Sean easily, he secured Sean on the back of his horse before bending to reclaim the wayward cloak. Swinging up behind, he wrapped them both in the fur, and pulled Sean back into the circle of his strong arms. "Lean against me, lad. Ye're like ice."

Sean leaned back, letting his head rest in between the grooves of a large chest. Pangs of guilt and conscience stabbed at his belly, but he brushed them away. Though he was handsome and gallant, Malcolm de Moray was still a man. Still weak and prone to temptation. He'd take what Sean offered, or maybe he wouldn't even wait for Sean *to* offer.

Men took what they wanted.

And so rarely gave.

Sean hoped he didn't hurry to the loch, though. The druid king's body fit so well against his own, and he soaked in the heat. He couldn't remember anything feeling so incredible.

Besides...he hadn't been warm in over a hundred years.

Malcolm did his best to keep his stallion's gait even. If the lad were concussed, jostling him overmuch could do irreparable damage. The mist seemed to thicken as they plodded toward Loch Doineann, which was more of a pond, in truth, surrounded by lush forest. He tried to keep his awareness on their surroundings in case brigands were about. If he didn't, he'd focus on how the willowy body fit against his, or how supple and tantalizing the grooves and etchings of his lean muscles stretched over long, elegant bones.

But the forest whispered warnings through the mist that unsettled Malcolm.

Beware. It said. *Enemies are near.*

If his enemies were near, then the Grimoire was too. The scrying stone had told him thus. So what was he doing escorting a peasant home when he should be searching for it?

"I've not seen you here in the forest before, how do you know where the loch is?" the lad asked, pulling his cloak tighter around himself and pressing his shoulders against Malcom's chest with a tremor of chill.

"I know every inch of these lands," he answered simply. *They're my responsibility.*

For some reason, he didn't want the lad to know who he was. Didn't want him to treat him with the deference he'd show the King of their Pictish people. For all he knew, Malcolm was a woodsman, doing another man a kindness. There was no Grimoire, Wyrd Sisters, Berserkers, or impending war. For just a moment, there in the mist, they were two men, making their way through the fragrant, loamy autumn forest.

"Do yer people hie from these woods?" he asked. "Do they live close by?"

"My people are all dead." This was said without much inflection. "I've been alone for many years."

It unsettled him how curious the man made him. He wanted to press, but knew the telling of a story would be painful. How did he come to be alone in these woods with nothing but a threadbare shift? Did his people die in the Lowland wars? Or by the hands of the English? Perhaps illness took them. Or plague. What family did he belong to?

Who had put the wounds and wariness behind his lovely, amethyst eyes?

"There." He pointed. "Just past that copse of trees."

Malcolm spotted the structure—if one could call it that—and frowned. Due to the lack of clothing, he hadn't expected much, but the rotting, dilapidated dwelling leaning against a few ancient trees was uninhabitable.

The roof, for lack of a better word, had rotted through and fallen on one side. The door was a bunch of green branches lashed together and propped against the entry.

Malcolm tensed as they approached, stopping on the narrow sandy beach of the loch and gaping in silent protest for several minutes. When the lad began to squirm, Malcom dismounted from behind him. "Stay here," he ordered. "I'll make certain no one is inside."

He nodded, his eyes growing rounder in his face, as though he hadn't considered intruders.

The interior was cozier than Malcom expected, but only just. The lad had been using the collapsed part of the roof as a chimney, with an old empty cauldron and cook fire laid, but unlit. A pallet of worn furs and a tattered blanket was the only protection from the chill of the dirt floor. A pestle, knife, tankard, wooden bowl, and a long-handled spoon were neatly lined up against the wall opposite the—well he couldn't rightly call it a bed, could he?

Forest fauna and the loch could sustain one person, he supposed, but surviving out here on one's own would be mighty difficult. Malcolm felt a pang slice through him at the thought of the poor lad shivering alone on the dirt floor at night. He had to be over five-and-twenty, but he was much too underfed.

A tender squeeze of his heart produced a cough Malcolm covered badly.

"I mean to mend the roof before winter sets in," the lad said from behind him.

Malcolm turned, unable to straighten to his full height in the cramped space. "Ye... *live* here?"

From the flash in his eyes, Malcolm could tell he'd said the wrong thing. "Aye, I live here, and it's a palace compared to where I was before."

At the words, his heart broke, but he tried to keep the pity from his eyes, lest it be interpreted as condescension. "I didna mean to offend ye. It's only that this place seems..." cold, dark, broken, not fit for a forest creature's den, let alone a delicate man. "Lonely," he finished. He didn't belong in this place, either. No one did. He prided himself on the prosperity of his people, upon the procedures he had in place to economically buoy those who were vulnerable.

"It does get rather lonely here." The voice lowered to a husky rasp of honeyed suggestion. "Most especially at night...in the dark."

The lad sidled closer to him, his cloak sliding down his shoulders to his elbows. Lavender eyes glittered like gems in the fading light against the dreary surroundings. Ebony hair gleamed like silk and velvet.

Malcolm's body's reaction was instantaneous. Suffused by lust and awareness, he hardened beneath his kilt. A spell seemed to make the evening darker, and the pale youth brighter. It was as though his body was no longer his own. He couldn't even swallow, let alone step away as a nobleman in his position *should*.

It was invitation he read in the uncommon eyes, there was no mistaking it. But something else lurked in their depths, a hesitancy, a vulnerability maybe, that kept him in check.

And pain. There was plenty of that.

Giving himself a stern cursing, he remembered that the man had been hit over the head not an hour ago.

"I want you lie down," he ordered gently.

The lad looked at him as if he'd grown horns. "You want me to—lie...with you?"

"Nay," Malcolm said vehemently, and at the sight of a puckered frown he amended. "Not, *nay*, just not... now. I mean, perhaps not at all. That is… I doona expect anything…but…" Christ, what was he, a pubescent youth? He clenched his teeth and tried again. "I want to examine yer head again, to make certain ye're not concussed."

The lad blinked a couple more times before replying. "I see."

Lowering to the fur, he cast his cloak to the side and stretched out on his back.

Malcolm watched peach nipples pucker against a smooth chest and give way to the shelves of his ribs, the length of a lean torso and the prominent bones of hips before legs that went on forever stretched beneath trews that didn't deserve the designation. To say his shape was fine would be like saying the night was dark or the December wind was bitter.

"You're staring."

Malcolm shook himself. "Apologies." Kneeling beside him, he reached for his scalp again. "May I examine ye?"

"I'm at your mercy."

Heat flared beneath the chill of the evening at the words, and Malcolm again reached into his soft tresses in search of a bump. Still finding none, he gently put his finger beneath each of the remarkable eyes and leaned in to check pupils for signs of inconsistency. "Is yer vision blurry at all?" he queried.

"Nay."

"Are ye nauseated or faint?"

"Nay."

Breaths mingled, and a strange kinetic kind of energy seemed to leap between their skin. "Ye should stay warm," he said, lamenting the husky note in his voice as he reached for his cloak to warm the lad again.

Malcolm found it strange that the man seemed perplexed as he tucked his cloak around his shoulder. He had to be chilly; it was colder than a sow's teat in autumn.

"What about yer headache?"

"It's better now." He shook his head back and forth as though to prove it.

Malcolm paused, his hand resting on a concerningly bony shoulder. There was naught left to do, and yet he didn't want to leave him here.

A soft hand snaked from beneath the cloak and covered his. "Is there... aught I can do to repay you for your kindness?" The lad reached out and ran a finger down the length of his stubbled jaw.

Malcolm had to force his next words around a throat gone dry. "Nay," he said. "I'd never take an offer like that as payment."

Lavender eyes flared. "Then what would it take, to get you to share my bed?"

CHAPTER 3

*S*ean thought Malcolm would hastily accept his invitation.
Instead, the king backed away and gained his feet,
knocking his head on the ceiling in haste. "I should... go." Moving
the door, he ducked out and replaced it with a final-sounding *thunk*.

No person he'd been forced to seduce for the Wyrd Sisters in a
century or more of confinement had *ever* turned him down. Not
man. Not woman. Not God nor demon. It seemed that the more
odious his charge, the more willing they were to take his body. His
beauty. There was not one thing odious about Malcolm de Moray.
The man was built as strong as the castle he lorded over, and had
features just as finely crafted.

Sitting up, Sean brought his knees to his chest and hugged them,
staring at the hovel's entry. Maybe the king could see past his
beauty, to the demonic creature he'd become after all these years.
Perhaps it drove him away.

Maybe his intuition was stronger than initially thought, or
perhaps the Wyrd sisters got it wrong he would rather lie with a
woman. And yet, a king his age and not married?

A rare thing, indeed.

Or maybe he *was* married. Come to think of it, the Wyrd Sisters had never mentioned it.

Sean considered every last one of these options before landing on his real fear. What if the king found him repugnant? Maybe the spark between them was one-sided and he was in a rush to quit Sean's company.

The question was, what difference did that make? Why was he so forlorn over a rejection?

He hadn't been sent to *fall* for Malcolm de Moray. His job was to get him to fall for Sean's charms just long enough to fuck.

Sean's intention to stay out of the void that imprisoned his soul for more than a century had gone past desperation, past madness, into a determined ruthlessness that drove him like nothing before. If Malcolm de Moray had to be a casualty of regaining his freedom, then so be it. He couldn't go back into that place, the dark hole where despair swallowed him in endless torment, and he couldn't even look forward to death as a release.

There was no release. No escape. Only this.

Running his cheek along his drawn up knees, he reveled in the warmth of the king's fine cloak.

He'd left it. Why? Pity? Because he was a decent man?

Most likely because he had a hundred more like it in his castle chambers and left this one to ease his conscience.

Well, it would be the perfect opportunity to see him again. Sean could request an audience at Dun Moray under the guise of returning it. The king would be more relaxed in his own home, less guarded, and easier to seduce. There would be beds, candlelight, and maybe he could get Nemain to craft a spell that would—

The collection of sticks that passed for a door moved again, stunning his thoughts to silence. Malcolm bent to enter, carrying a bundle of kindling and a few larger logs. "Yer wood pile is nigh empty," he chastised gently. "We'll need to remedy that."

Sean could only stare, as the king—*the king*— bent to lay a fire in the meager circle of stones that passed for a fire pit.

"We?" he finally ventured.

He stood again and left just as abruptly as before, returning with his saddle bags. Retrieving implements from within them, he bent to start a fire on some tinder striking the flint together blowing on the spot where sparks began to catch.

Sean knew he should be re-strategizing his approach, and he would, just as soon as he could tear his eyes from the way the man's back and shoulders stretched at the seams of his fine shirt, or how his kilt rested on his bent backside.

His legs were so long. Lithe and powerful. Sean's fingers itched to get at what was under that kilt.

For the sake of freedom, of course, he reminded himself.

Sean got the impression that Malcolm wasn't a man of many words. He worked quietly, absorbed in the task of building a fire, and didn't look up until the blaze was stable and throwing off a furnace of heat. That accomplished, he reached again for the saddle bags and extracted a cloth wrapped around some cheese, some bread, and a few slices of cured meat. Next came a skein of something, hopefully spirits or ale.

It had been so long.

"If yer not feeling peaky, ye should eat and drink something," he murmured. Taking a knife, he crouched down and cut a generous portion of the food, handing it to Sean without truly looking at him. "I retrieved water from the spring trickling into the loch, there. While ye eat, I'll restock yer wood pile." He frowned, motioning for Sean to take the food he offered. "I'll not leave ye here with no axe to pick through frosty kindling. I'd have to question my manhood if I did."

Sean thought of the member that had twitched and throbbed against his rump while they'd shared the saddle. No one in the history of the world would ever be able to question *his* manhood. Lord, but it was generous.

Blinking down at the offered fare, shock and something else entirely clouded his vision with moisture. Behind that was panic.

Where was this coming from? Why did he suddenly have a lump in his throat so big he was unable to form words of thanks? And just how in the hell could he seduce a man if he was a weeping disaster?

If he failed, he'd go back to the void. He needed to pull himself together.

Now.

"Why?" he whispered before he could stop himself, hating that his voice was tight with tears.

"Why, what?"

Sean didn't look up from his lap, keeping his eyes firmly fixed on his own knees. "If you want nothing from me, then why are you kind?"

De Moray's big, warm hand reached out to cup his cheek, his green eyes as sharp as cut emeralds and twice as brilliant in the firelight. "I'm kind because I am a Druid and yer king, and therefore kindness is not just my responsibility, but my way of life." He dropped his hand from Sean's cheek then, but his next words reached so deep, they seared to the very bones. "But make no mistake, lad, I want to take ye in ways that would wipe the word 'kind' from yer thoughts of me."

Sean's breath caught around a lump in his throat made of half emotion, and half elation. "Then, take me," he whispered.

"It wouldna be right," the king forced through clenched teeth, his eyes those of a warrior valiantly fighting a losing battle.

"I need…" Sean didn't dare say it. Couldn't put into words what it was he wanted. He *had* to lie with the King in order to take his powers, but this was the first time in a long time, maybe ever, that he truly *wanted* to.

Which made Malcolm de Moray more dangerous than Sean had ever considered.

Through with words, he rose on his knees, and undid the ties of his trews, letting them fall to the earth.

The king—Malcolm—regarded him from those jewel green eyes

like one would an approaching viper. Which was closer to the truth than Sean would like to admit.

His nostrils flared, and his fists clenched at his sides, but Malcolm de Moray remained where he was, obviously locked in a battle with his decency. His eyes devoured Sean like a starving man at a feast, but he didn't make one move in advance or retreat.

Decency be damned. Once the king realized who he was and what he'd done, he'd wish he'd left Sean in the woods to rot.

Firmly pushing that thought to the side, Sean reached for him, sliding his hands up corded shoulders to lock around his neck, pulling his head down.

Lips pressed, but Sean didn't have control of the situation for long.

Malcolm dragged him hard against his body in a deep, starving kiss. With a groan of surrender, he plunged his tongue into Sean's welcoming mouth with a thrusting rhythm that set his loins on fire.

Sean would have to try very hard to keep his wits about him. Already, his legs were beginning to fail, becoming weak enough that he leaned into the king. Once he felt that submission, he lowered them to the furs and stretched his hard body above Sean's yielding one.

He whispered a few unfamiliar words against Sean's mouth and the packed earth beneath their thin bedding suddenly became soft and fragrant with flora.

"Magick," Sean marveled aloud, wondering when was the last time anyone cared for his comfort.

"Like yer skin," Malcolm murmured, before claiming a kiss again. One moment his hot, silky tongue tangled with Sean's, the next he was nibbling and sucking, teasing with alternating pleasures.

Sean shifted so his thighs could split beneath him, cradling that swollen, needy part of him against his own sex. Malcolm's clothes still separated them, but they ground against each other instinctively, and Sean hissed at the intensity of the sensation.

Hungry for more, Sean lifted the hem of Malcolm's shirt and wordlessly demanded that he help peel it away.

The firelight threw shadows into the groves and valleys of his sinewed frame. The king was pale and fine, like the marble statues in the Roman ruins. He lifted himself to sweep away his kilt and boots while staring right back. His eyes traveled the length of Sean's form and latched onto the now throbbing cock sprouting from lean hips.

"I've never seen anyone of yer like," he breathed. "Someone so... open. So unabashed in their desires. Especially when the desire is becoming vilified as the Holy Roman Empire and their pyres of damnation keep pressing closer."

You need not fear those fires, my liege.

Sean's guts twisted with regret for a sin he'd not yet committed.

Malcolm de Moray was beautiful, as well. Not in the lovely way a woman was, but in a raw-boned, utilitarian way. Each swell and dip and angle fashioned for power and purpose.

And all that power was about to be unleashed upon him.

Within him.

Sean's breath sped to a pant, and he reached for Malcolm, suddenly feeling vulnerable stretched out and spread beneath him.

Malcolm settled against him instantly, hands roaming everywhere, mouth capturing Sean's with a wild possession. Finding the meat of his bare ass, Malcolm's fingers dug into the flesh there, pulling him firmly against his cock.

Sean would have liked to think he was not as affected with lust and wanting as Malcolm was, but they both shuddered with the intensity of their connection.

Keep your heart encased in ice, he warned himself. *Let your body burn.*

Malcolm's venturing fingers found his shaft, and they both moaned their pleasure. He was gentle, crooning things into Sean's ear as he kissed and licked the sensitive lobe. Dark words melted his core as probing fingers drove Sean higher than he'd ever imagined.

"Come for me, lad." The whisper threatened to undo him, but Sean held fast to his wits. To his sanity.

To the chance of freedom.

When teeth nipped down on his lobe, Malcolm's astonishingly smooth hand gripped and slid with equal parts insistent pressure and slow, torturous movements, just enough launch Sean to the stars with an astonished cry.

When one lived the majority of their years in a hole looking up to where the mortals walked, flying seemed out of the realm of possibility.

But fly he did.

And before he truly returned to earth, Malcolm was above him, positioning his legs then, with gentle, probing thrusts, he was inside, sliding torturously deep until he nestled against the curve of Sean's arse. His fingers reached beneath Sean's head, and threaded into the hair at his scalp until his rested in a large palm, secured and immobile.

"Look at me while I love ye," he said, and began to move.

For all of his easy confidence, Malcolm de Moray fucked like a doomed man, desperate for a safe harbor against the storms that loomed on the horizon. He fucked like he knew tomorrow was not guaranteed and he needed the pleasure to fill whatever hollow pain lurked in his eyes.

Sean could only see the wounds now that they were this close, nose to nose, sharing each other's breath. And flesh.

It was like everything slipped away. The void. The witches. Malcolm's Magick. Sean's lies. While his cock slid inside him, fitting as if he'd always done, it was as though he had truly melded together, somehow. With each thrust, he felt branded. Each moan and gasp was a wordless promise.

And the ecstasy, unparalleled.

Sean was too entranced to fight his second climax. It began at the base of his spine, ripping through him with all the power and inevitability of a tempest. He saw it on the horizon, flashing with lightning and threatening with thunder, but he was just as helpless to stop it as he was any storm. When the glorious gale hit, it locked him in its verdant clutches with arching tremors and pleas for mercy.

Malcom gave none, but followed after with thick, hot pulses of bliss and a roar of pleasure sent to the Gods.

Their Gods. Who used the powerful act of pleasure in their magick. Who expected their peoples to do the same.

Sean felt that magic spill inside of him, shimmer around him, pour from Malcolm de Moray's mouth with the perfect, treacle sweetness.

A sweet king. A gentle ruler. A hard man with a soft heart.

True hell would be knowing such a man existed, and having to return back to his lonely void.

Sean stared at the fire for what seemed like an eternity after.

He'd failed his charge. He'd not said the curse.

Malcolm dropped to his side between Sean and the wall, turning them both to face the flames. Tucking Sean's bottom against his hips, he wrapped strong arms around him and allowed them both to catch their breath.

His breath felt warm and strong, tickling Sean's hair and brushing skin with the purest of sensations. For the second time that night, Sean's eyes filled with tears.

"Ye're going to think I'm daft," Malcolm said against his hair. "But I like it here, with ye."

"In my lonely hovel?"

A soft chuckle brushed his face. "I truly didn't mean to offend ye," he rumbled, nuzzling through his hair and reaching the tender arch of his neck. "The earth in this forest is fragrant and soft. The night isna bitter, but chilly enough to enjoy the fire and yer warm body so close to mine." He pulled Sean deeper into the hollow he'd made with his frame. "It's different where I live, so much responsibility. So much always at stake. I oversee it all, and yet feel as though I control nothing. Here, the forest does my bidding and is simply happy at my presence."

"How can a forest be happy?" Sean wondered aloud.

Goosebumps flared on his skin as Malcolm's fingers idly ran over his shoulder and down the veins in his arm before dipping into his waist and flowing over the indent of his hip. Sean's tears overflowed his lids and slid down in a continuous hot path of pain.

"It's hard to explain," the king continued, unable to see the effect his touch had on Sean. "But I am a protector, a vanguard of the earth and her forests. They welcome me, because I bring good Magick and nurture life. Here, I am not but a Druid man and a creature of the earth."

Sean's breath caught on a sob, and his body jerked.

Instantly, Malcolm lifted to his elbow and leaned to peek over.

Sean hid his face, but not in time.

"Why the tears? Are ye hurting?" Malcolm asked, his voice full of concern.

Damn him. Damn him for being a good man. "Nay," he croaked. "I just...just..." He tensed with a hiccup, and then sobbed again. "Please don't think I'm touched in the head, I can't tell you why I'm like this." In truth, he couldn't. It had been maybe a quarter century since he'd even had the energy to cry. His despair had dipped below such displays of emotion.

Was Malcolm making him feel? Was he making him care?

Dear God, how much of this could he take?

"How long has it been since anyone's held ye?" Malcolm queried gently, rubbing his stubble-beard against the skin of his shoulder, then soothing the abrasion with a gentle kiss. "Since ye've been touched by another with affection?"

He sucked in a shaky breath. "It seems like... ages. Centuries, maybe."

He smiled against Sean's neck, and pressed a kiss behind his ear. "Did ye know that our bodies *require* human touch?"

Sean shook his head as Malcolm ran his fingers over their previous path, and back up again, seeking the places that caused him to arch and moan. Distracting from his tears.

"No matter how much ye feed a bairn, it willna thrive without the tender arms of a mother or nurse and will most likely die. Every caress, every embrace, every time our hands hold, like so." He traced Sean's arm until he laced their fingers. "It creates a substance within us that is vital to life."

"Magick?"

"Nay. It's just how we mortals are made. Call it what you will. Social beasts, souls in need of affectionate connection with another. Compassionate companionship." He released Sean's hand to cup his face, kissing the tear from his cheek. "'Tis a gentle thing ye're feeling," he murmured. "And I'm glad to be the one to touch ye. To ease yer loneliness. To liberate these tears of need." With utter tenderness, the king pressed his lips against Sean's temple, then his eyelid, then his cheek, and jaw.

Seized by raw emotion and instinct, Sean pulled away from Malcolm, urging the man to roll to his stomach. Throwing a leg over his shapely ass, Sean climbed atop him and thrust his hardening length inside the king of the Picts.

Next time. Next time he'd say the spell, but this moment was for Sean.

For Malcolm.

And what they could never have together.

"Give me yer name," Malcolm gasped, his hands fisting in the furs and moss beneath them, voice tense with pleasure and strain. "I want to know what to name to call when ye're inside me."

"My name is Sean," he said, then leaned in for a desperate kiss.

Now he knew the name of the demon he'd one day despise.

CHAPTER 4

*I*t never ceased to amaze Sean how quickly humans could drop off to sleep after sex. He'd barely climbed off of Malcolm's lean, talented hips before the king had collapsed onto his back, pulled Sean to drape over his body, and given up consciousness in almost his very next breath.

Sean had spent the last fifty years in a dark chasm, and thus didn't even like to blink, let alone fall asleep and miss one moment of freedom. Besides, the flutters of Malcolm's auburn lashes entertained him, as did the twitches of his limbs as he slept.

In fact, he reposed as though he and slumber were strangers. Perhaps he was as consumed with saving the earth as the Wyrd Sisters were with ending it. It would explain why he seemed so lean, hard, and stern.

It made the fact that he'd been nothing but gentle and patient with Sean that much more extraordinary. Here, on the floor of this hovel, he looked nothing like a king, but every inch the Earth Druid. The forest, indeed, seemed to welcome him.

Sean didn't know how long he watched his lover sleep. Long enough for the fire to die to glowing embers and the silver light of dawn to pierce the many cracks, holes, and weaknesses of the hovel.

He'd become accustomed to encompassing silence, so the sounds of the forest fascinated and lulled him. The rhythm of Malcolm's breath and the beat of his heart became the percussion to the forest's midnight melody, and the music transfixed Sean for splendid hours.

His body woke before he did, muscles lifting to press into him, and his manhood thickening beneath Sean's thigh as it rested in between his legs. His breaths came deeper, and more quickly, and when he shifted atop him, Malcolm groaned and stretched.

Now was the time. The spell of the night was broken, and everyone had to face the hard truths in the light of day. If Sean were to work the curse on him, this would be the moment.

Sean bit his lip hard, to cause himself physical discomfort that could match the sharp pang of guilt and sorrow.

"I'm sorry," he whispered. "There's no other way." He reached down to Malcolm's hard, throbbing sex, meaning to guide it inside and awaken him with the last bit of pleasure he could give...

Before he took everything.

The gentle nicker of a horse warned him a second before the entire hovel shook with the impact of the door being kicked in.

Malcolm shot up, his arms coming around Sean in a protective vice before he rolled him between the wall and the shield of his body.

"*Odin's bones*, Malcolm, your pale backside is the last thing I need to see this early in the morning." A dark masculine voice trembled with half amusement, half disgust.

Malcolm instantly relaxed, though his voice was laced with rage as he addressed the interloper. "Bael, if you doona get the fuck out of here, I'll forget ye're my brother-in-law and—"

"Malcolm you gave us a fright!" A flame-haired woman bent into the hovel, filling the poor structure to the brim. "What in the name of the Goddess are you doing all the way out—" She cut off when Sean poked his head above Malcolm's shoulder, her lovely blue eyes widening to the size of saucers. "Oh, my!" the lady exclaimed. "I thought... we assumed you were in danger... not...Oh my! Pardon us!"

Burning a bright pink, even in the dim light, the woman seized onto the dark-haired lummox next to her, and tugged at his arm toward the now ruined door.

The man relented, black eyes glittering with mirth. "My liege," he said in a strange, foreign accent before executing a mocking bow to Malcolm's back side, and ducking out of the hovel.

Their chuckles could be heard through the thin walls.

Malcolm's groan of frustration was more of a menacing growl. His morning erection still pulsed against Sean's thigh, and he'd yet to let go. "Sometimes family isna the blessing others make it out to be," he grit out.

Sean began to panic. What would he do now? How could he face the Wyrd Sisters after his failure? They'd know he'd lain with him, and that he'd chosen not to carry out his charge. "I... suppose you must be going now." Fighting to keep his voice even, he mentally berated himself for the weakness the king brought out in him. Was this the last morning he'd ever see?

"Aye," Malcolm sighed, pulling away and running his hands over his tired eyes. "Gather what things ye want to take with ye."

"What?"

Malcolm's jaw cracked on a yawn, and he reached for his discarded kilt and tunic. "I'll get ye home so we can finish what my sister and her husband so rudely interrupted." He kissed Sean's forehead, and pulled his tunic over his unruly auburn curls.

Sean gaped at him in absolute shock, frozen in place.

He pulled his kilt over his tantalizing backside and then turned as though to ask why he hadn't moved yet. Upon seeing his face, he crouched down to him and touched Sean's cheek, obviously taking his astonishment for outrage.

"I doona mean to offer ye the dishonor of being the kept lover of a king," he amended, green eyes sparkling with mischief. "I mean to make an honest lad out of ye."

He couldn't mean…

"What are you saying?" Sean breathed, his heart slamming against his ribcage.

"I'm saying I would bind with ye, Sean." He grinned before leaning in for a kiss. "Now get dressed, dawn is upon us."

Malcolm felt lighter than he had in months as he guided his steed over the moors toward Dun Moray. He ignored the silent, astonished glances of his sister and the smug, lifted eyebrow of his brother-in-law as they each followed behind him on their own horses.

He supposed he deserved both. Since Morgana had returned home from exile in England with a Berserker mate, he'd lectured both of them over the unwise speed of their union. He would reap what he'd sown, and try to keep a good humor about it.

Morgana was full to bursting with questions. Malcolm could feel them swimming inside her, but she wouldn't ask him until Sean was no longer clinging to his back in dazed silence. If nothing else, his sister was a lady.

And she'd always known that Malcolm had been born beneath the stars of two warriors. That he wasn't meant for progeny. Before, the Earth Druid had always been a woman, and he had that very strong, very female urge to create and nurture life.

He somehow always assumed he'd live life without a mate. That he was some sort of anomaly.

A mistake.

And yet, the moment he'd seen Sean trembling and wounded on the ground, something inside him had shifted. For so long, he'd been consumed by his work, by the responsibility of being the king of a proud and clannish people, and by the charge he'd been tasked with by the Goddess.

A de Moray Druid.

With his soft, bruised amethyst eyes and skin that seemed as though it had never been kissed by the sun, Sean made him feel like a man. *Just* a man. A creature of blood and bones and hunger and lust. Nothing more.

In truth, he could have stayed with Sean in that hovel and lived out his days roaming the forest, fishing the lake, and tilling the earth together. They'd tell stories, shape clay, weave baskets, and let the forest help them to forget that an Apocalypse loomed on the horizon.

"Is that Dun Moray?" Sean's question shattered his brooding fantasy as they broke over a rise and the Moray valley spread out beneath them. It shimmered like an emerald in the autumn sunlight, the village alive with activity.

"Aye," Malcolm answered, the mantle of obligation again beginning to weigh upon his shoulders.

"So, it's really true… You're King of the Picts." He said this as though the fact disappointed him, somehow, and that endeared the man to him all the more.

Most women of his acquaintance chased him with the vigor of a pack of wolves. His crown being the prize rather than his heart. "Do ye think ye could take to being my Consort?"

"That remains to be seen," Sean whispered, and pressed his cheek to Malcolm's back. "Why would you want me? I know naught of your world. I have no family. I'm nobody… nothing."

The forlorn words were made all the more bleak by his tone. He truly believed that about himself, which was a tragedy. Malcolm planned to spend the rest of his life changing Sean's mind.

"To me, ye're about to be everything," he insisted, hoping Sean could hear the raw truth in his tone.

"How can that be? You don't know a thing about me. I don't know a thing about you. We've only just met."

A wise and careful man, his lad. He liked that. "I know that ye're practical and resilient, which I appreciate. Ye know what ye want, and ye go after it." He was glad Sean couldn't see his lips twitch with the memory of how he'd persuaded him into bed.

Not that it took much in the way of persuading.

"I know that ye're proud and lonely and that ye carry around a painful secret that ye doona want to share with anyone, least of all me."

The gasp was audible. "How do you—what makes you think that?"

"I'm more perceptive than yer average man, lad," he tossed a smile over his shoulder as they began to descend the hill into Moray Valley. "And we all have secrets."

"What are yours?" Sean asked after a pause.

Malcolm considered putting him off, perhaps until they knew each other better, but something about the open vulnerability in the question pushed him to answer it.

"When my father was killed, everyone thought I was in exile while Macbeth ruled, but in truth, I was in the hands of my enemies."

"The English?" Sean asked.

"Nay. Druids. Dark Druids. Women who have taken the powers of the Goddess and twisted them for their own evil purposes."

Sean was quiet behind him. Offering no words of sympathy, no empty platitudes, and somehow that prompted him to continue.

"I had no concept of time when I was in their clutches. They held me for months, but it felt like an eternity..." His hands tightened on his reins as the memories washed over him, spilling chill bumps over his flesh. "The worst of it is, I would have been able to break any chains wrought of iron or prison of stone, but... they didna imprison my body, they invaded my mind, held it captive with their black Magick."

Sean's arms tightened around his middle, offering him more comfort than any words.

"They tried to rip me from myself. To bring me to their side.

And when they failed to do that, they used... terrible means to trick me into giving up my Druid powers to them."

"Obviously, they failed," Sean offered, his voice tighter than he'd yet heard it.

"Aye," he ground out. "But their attempts they... changed me... and not for the better." Bit by bit, Malcolm had felt his heart grow colder, his thoughts more bitter. He'd nearly lost himself in that place, in his own head, and the abyss he found within frightened him more than any physical pain he could imagine.

Even more than death.

"You ask me why I'm taking ye home," he murmured, placing a hand over the soft arms banded about his waist. "It's because when I'm with ye, I feel like myself for the first time in ages, and that is the most precious gift anyone could give. And I promise ye, all that I have to give is yers."

Sean's breath had sped behind him, and he gave a few suspiciously rapid sniffs. It melted his heart that the man was touched on his behalf. "Aren't you afraid they'll come for you again?"

"They will," Malcolm shrugged. "They already have. But we're all stronger with someone by our sides to remind us what we're fighting for. I see that now." He cast another look at Bael and Morgana, who were locked in a conversation of their own a way off.

"You... know what they're after?" Sean asked.

Malcolm realized that this was a lot for a lad to take in, and that he'd likely just given him cause to fear for his life. The best thing he knew to combat fear was information.

"There is a prophecy in the de Moray Grimoire that says that when four elemental de Moray Druids cast behind one gate, they are fated to bring about the Apocalypse," he explained. "We are only three. My sister, Morgana, my cousin, Kenna, and I. As long as one of us are behind castle walls, we are able to ward them off, for now. 'Tis why Kenna didna join the search for me, I expect."

"How do you know the Wyrd Sisters cannot come for you?" Sean queried, adjusting in the saddle as if he'd never ridden astride in his life.

"Because my castle is warded."

"Warded how?"

"Do ye see the symbols carved in those stones?" He pointed to the incredible standing stones at each side of the gate to Moray Village. "They're placed all around the valley, and are strong enough that neither the Wyrd Sisters nor their minions can cross—"

With a cry, Sean's arms were jerked from around his waist as he was thrown from the horse and into the grass by the invisible barrier that protected these lands.

Malcolm slowly turned his horse, meeting Morgana's wide, blue eyes before he could bring himself to look at the man who stared up at him from the ground.

A cold, bitter fury built in his gut as he realized, he'd never told Sean the names of his enemies, and yet he'd only just called them the Wyrd Sisters.

Because he was in league with them.

CHAPTER 5

*S*ean turned his shackled wrists this way and that, testing
the security of the iron and his ability to slip out of it. Of
course, it would figure that Malcolm's chains would hold fast, that
his dungeon would be as absolute as the void had been. It was
almost worse, because Sean could mark the passing of time through
the narrow-barred window at the top of the tall stone wall. The
sunlight crept in a moving square across the floor, and every
moment it passed was a moment he could mark his failures.

It had taken some considerable reworking of the wards to allow
him into the castle, and still keep the Wyrd Sisters out. The power
of the de Moray Druids was nothing like the dark workings he'd
seen from his captors. Their spells were lyrical chants and prayers
and even songs. Their runes pulsed with light instead of darkness,
and their Magick was fortified with love rather than hatred.

But the wrath in Malcolm's eyes had been terrifying.

Lethal.

More frightening than any of the atrocities he'd witnessed as a
captive of the Wyrd Sisters. In fact, it was the dark-haired, black-
eyed Berserker, Bael, who'd shackled Sean and whisked him to the
dungeon.

Because Malcolm couldn't bear to look at him, didn't trust himself to touch Sean without causing him harm. He'd said as much.

And who could blame him?

The irony weighed on Seans chest like a load of bricks.

As the shadows grew long, and the meager light from the outside began to dissipate, he fought an encompassing, paralyzing panic. His chains became heavier, the stones colder and more unforgiving. The scuttles of vermin, unseen or just imagined, were more frightening than the complete isolation of the void.

You've failed us, Sean. Badb's voice hissed on the wind. *We're coming with the Grimoire, and if you don't take what we bade you when we break the wards, then you'll be returned to the void for eternity. But first we'll make you watch as we toy with your lover, and slaughter everyone he loves...*

"No," he whimpered, dropping to his knees. Even in this dungeon he wasn't safe from their evil. The darkness always found him. That was his curse. He'd traded his soul to it, and now had to live with an eternity of tormented regrets.

The sound of the heavy bolt and the scrape of the door against the stones brought Sean to his feet. Never let it be said that he faced his fate on his knees.

Never again. Not even before Malcolm de Moray.

The king's climb down the dungeon steps was long, as though he didn't want to reach the bottom. Golden light from his torch spilled over the stones from the entry a moment before his wide frame filled the archway.

Sean's heart leapt into his throat and stayed there, rendering him mute, as he watched Malcolm mount the torch in its sconce.

Gone was the gentle, patient lover of the prior night. Gone was the noble, beloved ruler of the Pictish people. The man who stalked into the prison trembled with a fury that covered wounds. Wounds that Sean created. Scars he'd ruthlessly ripped open.

As Malcom loomed, a creature of cold rage and hot blood, one word ripped from his lips that surprised them both.

"*Why?*"

The question encompassed so much, and yet Sean didn't know where to start. Malcolm had such control, and such power. Sean realized now that the Wyrd Sisters, as potent as their dark Magick was, underestimated this Druid.

"You have no right to ask me that," Sean answered, cursing the tremor in his voice. "My reasons are my own." And they were many.

"I have every right!" The king exploded, the stone walls of the prison trembling with the force of his emotion. He captured both Sean's shoulders in a brutal grip, and pulled him closer so his eyes burned down with the wrath of a thousand forges. "I wasna asking why ye're a minion of those evil hags." He gathered a cold, lethal calm back into his voice. "I was asking *why* I still desire ye as desperately as I do. Even after everything ye've done."

Sean didn't have time to process the question as the king crushed his lips to Sean's in a punishing kiss. He didn't plunder or explore, didn't give time to respond, but instead kissed him long enough to bruise his lips and then ripped their mouths apart with a snarl of aggravation.

"Damn ye," he forced through gritted teeth, and bent to claim another.

"No!" Sean cried out, chains scraping the earth as he lifted his hands and pushed against his chest. "Damn *you*," he spat. "Damn you for making me care!"

They circled each other like suspicious wolves, but the shackles restricted much movement. Emotions swooped and flew about them like bats in a cave, blindly searching for a safe place to rest, but finding none.

"You know what it's like as their prisoner," Sean appealed to the empathy he knew the king possessed. "Can you blame me for doing anything they asked to escape their wrath?"

"Ye could have told me!" Malcolm roared. "I would have protected ye."

His words both touched and angered Sean at the same time. "How can you be so arrogant? They threaten me even now, within these walls. I am not their prisoner as you were Malcolm, I am their *possession*. They own me, body and soul."

Malcolm froze in place, his eyes daggers of emerald fire within the sharp planes of his masculine face, his chest lifting and falling as though he'd run a league at full speed. "The only way that could be is if ye…"

"*Yes*," he hissed, a bit of his soul flickering and dying like a candle in a storm at the disgust and disbelief in Malcolm's eyes. "Yes, I made a deal with them. I sold my soul, more than a century ago, and I became one of their *minions*, as you call it."

Malcolm took a step toward him and looked as if he was about to be kind, but Sean backed away, holding a hand up.

"Don't you dare ask me why," he warned. "It doesn't matter anymore. Just comfort yourself with the knowledge that whatever happens here tonight, whether you win or lose this battle, I'll be thrown back in the dark void that has been my personal hell for the rest of eternity." His voice wavered on that last sentence, so he kicked his chin up a notch. "You'll be done with me forever."

"I'm not done with ye," Malcolm de Moray growled, eyes glinting with a familiar fever. "I'll *never* be done with ye." Tearing off his shirt, Malcolm tossed it to the stones. This time he stalked Sean like a predator, reaching out and dragging him against his hard, corded torso with punishing force. "Ye've bewitched me, somehow," he accused, giving him a shake for emphasis. "Ye canna belong to them, Sean, because ye are *mine*."

Oh, if only that could be true.

Even if his soul were to be set free, Sean would instantly die. "Malcolm—"

Malcolm's fingers pressed against his lips. "Doona speak," he commanded as his lips descended once more.

He had to know, Sean lamented quietly. The tension in Malcolm's muscles, the bruising desperation of his lips told him that the king realized the futility of their connection, but refused to accept it.

It was the anger of a man who was a Druid in his spirit and a King in his land. He was used to controlling his environment. To bending others to his will.

But Sean was something he could neither control nor possess.

With a frustrated groan, Malcolm shoved his tattered trews down his waist, allowing Sean's cock to spring free. In an astonishingly graceful maneuver, the king turned him to the bars, forcing him to cling to them.

His own clothing hit the floor.

Malcolm's body was a muscular mass of coiled strain behind Sean as strong hands gripped ass with bruising fingers. He spat into his hand in a coarse gesture, then maneuvered his erection in place.

Sean panted as alarm and shock heightened the blood and lust racing through his veins. Malcolms growl of possession drowned out his whimper of submission and he surged forward with a powerful stroke.

Pleasure/pain rocked Sean forward, flooding his limbs, and he threw back his head with a moan.

"I'm sorry," Sean gasped, as he thrust forward again, harder this time. Deeper.

"Shut up." Malcolm wrapped Sean's hair in his fist and secured his neck in place as he shoved inside with such force, Sean's teeth clacked together.

"Forgive me," he panted.

"*Never.*" Malcolm thrust forward again and again, his hips bucking against Sean's ass with jarring force.

Sean braced himself against the bars, the task leaching him of strength. His arms trembled and burned with the effort, and sweat bloomed on his skin.

Malcolm thrust so deep, he evoked sensations Sean never before experienced. His body wanted to thrust back, to seek release and to meet his need. But his relentless rhythm was too brutal and too fast, so Sean helplessly took what he gave.

The king's growls became groans as the friction intensified to unbearable.

"Come for me." This time it was a command, as he pulled on Sean's hair in a way that caused his inner muscles to clench with a spiraling pleasure. "Scream my name, traitor, as ye knew it all along."

Sean obeyed. Treacherous pleasure seized him in its unrelenting hold and Malcolm's name poured from his lips again and again. First as a plea, then as a prayer. And at last, a worshipful gasp as wave after wave of bliss pulled him from the void and lights exploded even in the darkness behind his eyelids.

When the climax began to fade, the Wyrd Sister's cruel threat permeated his pleasure with a raw pain.

We'll toy with your lover, and slaughter everyone he loves...

Inside him, Malcolm grew impossibly thicker, hotter, his breath speeding with his approaching climax.

Conjuring his courage, Sean squeezed his eyes shut once more and whispered the words Badb had made him memorize. Three times. He had to whisper them three times and it would be over.

His life would be over. Freedom beckoned.

"Blackened blood and tainted soul, from this Druid Magick pull.

Into the nether set it free, then by darkness grant unto me—"

Malcolm's strong hand clamped over his mouth as their movements became jerky and frenzied. The entire castle seemed to tremble with the strength of his roar, and for a long moment, Sean feared that the stones would bury them both.

Maybe that would be for the best.

Lightning singed the air and screamed through the night as it touched down close by.

Malcolm withdrew with a groan and lowered his head to rest

between Sean's shoulder blades as their breaths exploded into the silent aftermath.

They'd just entered the eye of the tornado, and neither of them had an anchor.

"They're here," Sean whispered, dropping his own forehead against the cold bars, his lungs seizing with despair. "They've come for us both now."

CHAPTER 6

*M*alcolm gripped Sean's delicate shoulders and turned him so they faced each other, his eyes searching for a truth he was almost afraid to find.

"Before I face them… answer me this. Why didna ye do the spell last night in the woods when we made love over and over again?" His guard had been down. He was embarrassed to admit to himself that the lad would have been successful.

Sean's eyes dropped to his chest. "Because I'm a fool," he gave a harsh, humorless laugh. "I'd planned to. But you touched me and everything…changed." He blinked up at Malcolm as though trying to understand it, himself. "And I've given up my soul for a *man*, a second time."

Malcolm seized upon that bit of information. "What do ye mean?"

Sean hesitated, but Malcom shook him as though doing so would rattle the answers loose. "Tell me what happened," he demanded. "Help me make sense of this before I go to face my fate."

After a long moment, Sean nodded.

Malcolm released him and took the moment to dress as Sean gathered both clothes and his thoughts, He couldn't stop watching the way the firelight threw gold and blue hues into his raven-black hair.

"More than a century ago, I fell in love with a War Chief named Kenneth McManus," Sean began.

Malcolm instantly hated the man, though he realized the bastard had been dead a few decades, the jealousy that swirled within him was unreasonably violent.

"The McManus and the Gregor were at war," he continued. "And at the time, the Wyrd Sisters were summoned by the Chieftain of the Gregor and paid for their dark Magick to help win the skirmish. The price, was the soul of an enemy."

He paused then for such a long time, Malcolm wondered if he was going to finish, until he finally gathered enough resolve to continue, his forehead crimped with bemused pain.

"I thought Kenneth was so brave. That he was a man who could unite a warring people. I was proud that he chose to love me, when all the lasses chased him. But when he fell into the Wyrd Sister's clutches, he told them to contact me. Do you know why he did that?"

Of course, Malcolm knew, but he wasn't about to say it.

Sean turned to him, eyes filled with such bitterness and self-loathing it surprised even him. "He *knew* somehow, that I was weak and gullible enough to make such a stupid offer. That I would give my soul in his stead. That I loved him almost as much as he loved himself. And when it was done, he promised to find a way to liberate me…"

Unable to stand the sadness and pain radiating from Sean, Malcolm went to him, enfolding his arms around the slim shoulders with a new sense of compassion. "He couldna find a way?" he asked.

Sean shook his head, a tear falling from her cheek to his bare chest. "He never even tried," came the tortured whisper. "He married a—a lass, and forgot about me."

Malcolm held him even tighter, cursing the man's name. "If it makes ye feel better, the Gregors decimated the McManus, and took their lands."

He gave a short laugh, and then a sniff. "It does help a bit," Sean said fondly, pressing himself closer. "Since I've been in the void, Malcolm, I've suffered every form of madness imaginable. I've prayed to every God and Goddess known, and they've all abandoned me to the darkness, just like Kenneth did. And so, you see, I made a vow that if I ever had the chance to escape the void, I would take it, no matter who became a casualty of the circumstance."

In that moment, Malcolm not only understood his choices, he sympathized with them. His anger drained away, and he was left with a helpless sympathy that unsettled his very soul.

"But ye didna, lad," he murmured. "Here I still am, in command of my people and my powers."

Sean made a bitter sound, but didn't pull away. "Like I said, I'm a fool. I promised myself that I would never again sacrifice my interest for a man or his cause."

"I doona blame ye." Malcolm stroked his hair, thinking that he ought to take the shackles from around Sean's wrists. He didn't deserve them. He'd been imprisoned enough.

Sean lifted his chin and rose on his toes to press a kiss to his jaw, lips seeking Malcolm's own mouth. Malcolm tilted his head down to comply. The kiss was soft and achingly sweet. Malcolm drew his lips over Sean's again and again, the tenderness passing between them blooming to life against his soul.

It was Sean who pulled back, lovely eyes shimmering with unshed tears. "I lied," he whispered. "I lied to myself."

"How do you mean?" Malcolm brushed hair away from the pale perfection of his cheek. Such a beautiful creature, this man. Almost ethereal.

"Your cause is to save humanity from the Apocalypse. That is a cause worth giving my soul for."

"Sean, *no*." Malcolm panicked, clutching him with the strength of a desperate man. "Doona do anything foolish."

A tear slid down Sean's cheek, but his features were disturbingly serene. "And you, Malcolm de Moray, are a man worth the sacrifice, because it's one you'd never ask me to make."

Malcolm gasped his name, but in the next instant he was only clutching the thin, empty garment as the manacles that had once shackled Sean's wrists clattered to the stones.

The inhuman sound that ripped from him shook the entire castle and brought his family storming into the dungeon.

"Malcolm!" Kenna gasped, her amber eyes wide with astonishment. "What's happening?"

Malcolm turned to them slowly, shaking with the force of his rage and loss, trying to summon the cold wrath of which he knew himself capable.

"Arm yourselves," he ordered his Druid family, and their Berserker mates in a dark voice he'd never heard before. "We're going to war."

Even Bael and Niall stepped out of Malcolm's way as he stalked toward the stairs, aiming to make preparations for the battle to come. First, he was going to defeat the Wyrd Sisters and stave off the Apocalypse. Then, he was going to fetch his lover, even if he had to claw his way through the depths of hell to do so.

CHAPTER 7

*S*unset turned the Berserker knights and their Viking comrades into dark silhouettes against the flaming sky. Loch Fyne glimmered like a lake of fire as it buffeted against the western side of the castle. Thirteen men, including Bael and Niall, stood bravely in front of the fence of wooden stakes, angled to impale an advancing enemy. Across the expanse of the Moray Valley, a vast army crested the rough Highland peaks and began a syncopated march down toward Dun Moray and the village.

Ingmar—a general of Niall's who would have been a jester but for his voracious bloodlust—turned to address Malcolm and his small garrison of kilted countrymen as they approached the Vikings from behind. "You should stay behind your wards, King Malcolm, and let *us* battle your enemies," he said smugly. "You've marched to the front lines with no armor, flanked by women and mostly naked men, which, in my opinion, should be the other way around." He hit his leather jerkin with his shield. "Leave us the glory of plunging into battle and bloodying our armor. It is what we are bred to do."

"I believe we shall," Malcolm replied absently, as he scanned the approaching army for the Wyrd Sisters. They were yet too far away to make out distinct features, but Malcolm knew they were out there. The distinct stench of evil flowed on the Highland breezes, and demoralizing threats whispered on the chill winds.

"Who are they, Colm?" Morgana touched his elbow and squinted into the gathering shadows that seemed to follow the endless swarm of the advancing enemy. "They wear no colors."

"I think it's an army of the damned," Kenna drew up to his other side. "Badb said that she had countless souls at her disposal. I think she's unleashed them all upon us at once."

Souls like Sean. Some innocent. Some malevolent. All desperate to do whatever it took for the promise of redemption. Or maybe just for the release of death.

"Do you think he's out there?" Morgana whispered, the compassion in her eyes cutting Malcolm to the quick.

He knew to whom his sister was referring.

"Nay. The Wyrd Sisters know Sean wouldna march against me. 'Tis why they took him from me." Malcolm fought to keep his composure and reminded himself that a village full of women and children relied on his protection.

The future of humanity, itself, relied on the strength of his principle and power.

How would they feel if they knew he was tempted to sacrifice it all for someone he'd met yesterday?

Tempted.

But he couldn't shirk his duty.

Even for love.

"I expect the village bard will be writing lyrics to our valor and ingenuity," Ingmar still taunted. "If there are any men left after this.

"I told ye *not* to touch my castle grounds weeks ago. Not to cut down trees to make yer fences," Malcolm replied slowly.

Niall turned, ignoring the warning look from Kenna. "What would your people have done without our fortifications?"

"What if the army breaks through the line?" Ingmar asked smugly. "Not that it's likely," he added. "But Dun Moray would have been defenseless if not for us."

Malcolm made a slight gesture to his men, and the forty archers spread out, making enough space between them to reach the edge of the loch.

With a whispered spell, Malcolm stretched his arms out, palms up, and lifted them from his sides. As he did, the earth trembled beneath them, and then separated, lifting him, Morgana, Kenna, and the entire line of archers above the slack-jawed Vikings, and their wooden fortifications, on an impenetrable rock wall thrice as high as Bael, the tallest Berserker.

Standing on the corner of the wall, he wrapped the structure of stone around the village, using the edge of his wards for a guide.

As preoccupied as he was with Sean, with revenge, and with the inevitable battle, Malcolm enjoyed a victorious moment over the Viking's rare, awe-struck silence. "You see." He lifted an eyebrow. "Your fortifications were not needed. And I would *never* leave my people unprotected."

"I'd like it to be noted that *I* never doubted you." Bael twirled his axe and winked at Morgana, his dark eyes glittering with anticipation of bloodshed.

The army of souls began to run forward as they reached the edge of the loch, their weapons raised. The Vikings drew their own weapons and clustered into a shield formation. Bael and Niall growled their pleasure as *Berserkergang* overtook their bodies, their eyes turning into black voids, promising a quick death to their enemies.

If they were lucky.

"I can feel the Grimoire," Malcolm told the Druids on either side of him.

"It's close," Kenna agreed. "They're close, but I can't see them."

"Do you think they can die?" Morgana worried. "This army of souls?"

Malcolm watched them advance, his hand clenched around the staff made from the sacred Ash, a relic of the de Moray Earth Druids that transcended written history. He drew strength from it, the strength of patience, and the strength of survival. "We're about to find out."

Kenna called for a torch that was handed to her by an awaiting warrior. With a flare of her powers, the flame rippled across the line of archers, igniting their arrows. "We are they who repelled the Romans," she said in their Gaelic tongue. "Protect the Viking army with your arrows, and slay our enemies." Upon her order, they let loose their first barrage, dropping the first line of the Army of Souls and igniting the flames of war.

"Malcolm, look!" Morgana pointed east, to the crest of the hill opposite the loch.

Four silhouettes appeared as statues atop their magnificent horses. The rise was far off, but the figures were unmistakable. They neither advanced nor retreated, but stood as sentinels, witnesses to the most important battle humanity had faced thus far.

The Four Horseman.

They'd come to watch him battle for the salvation of the world.

Malcolm sent a silent prayer to the heavens. It was a heavy thing to think that the fate of the eternities rested on the outcome of the day.

Malcolm found himself wondering which side The Horsemen were on. Did they want to bring about the Apocalypse? Were they expecting him to fail?

If so, they would be sorely disappointed.

Now was not the time. Not like this, by dark measures and blood Magick. The prophecy said that four de Morays would wield behind one gate and the Seals would be broken. Malcolm had always interpreted that to mean that four de Moray's would be born to *one* generation. He could not let the Wyrd sisters force the End of Days for their personal gain. There was still so much life left to be lived. So much progress and enlightenment and invention to discover. How could it end now when, it seemed, that the world was still so young?

A prickling of the fine hairs of his body heralded the notice of the Four honing in on him, even as the Army of Souls broke upon the Viking frontlines, and the fighting began in earnest.

Though the souls were neither alive nor dead, but some macabre version of *in between*, they still bled when Bael's axe culled a dozen down in one mighty sweep. They still screamed, and writhed when Niall's sword cut them navel to throat before kicking them off into the red-stained field. Their flesh sizzled and stunk as flaming arrows and bolts of Kenna's magickal fire decimated and illuminated the carnage.

Malcolm mourned for his lush valley, and for the souls of those he claimed as he used his magick to pull the black, sharp boulders from the earth and roll them through the advancing horde. The crunch was sickening, but the tactic effective, cutting neat swaths of blood and bone.

And still foes spilled from the gathering shadows of the night as new waves of enemies broke upon his walls.

"I cannot see the Wyrd Sisters, Malcolm." Morgana grasped his elbow. "Something's not right. Where are they?"

Turning to search, Malcolm noticed the Four Horsemen had begun a slow and steady advance down into his valley until they stood at the edge of the battle.

Apart from it, and yet an inevitable part *of* it.

Conquest, with his white stallion and silver armor looked like an archangel sent by a vengeful god. Whereas War, with his horse almost the same color as his blood-red breastplate resembled some kind of Hell spawn.

Next to them, Pestilence, his visage hidden in dark robes, perched atop his nightmare steed more regally than Malcolm would have imagined. And Death, his horse pale and dappled, his armor dark and antiquated, surveyed the carnage with a relentless power that could only belong to an immortal such as him.

"Ye will not have this day," Malcolm vowed at them, in a voice too low for anyone but him to hear.

Death's head turned slowly toward him, far enough away that Malcolm barely marked the movement.

The question is, will you?

The words were not spoken, and yet Malcolm heard them clear as day.

Death lifted a finger, and pointed to the edge of Malcolm's land, where Dun Moray's keep was buffeted by craggy Highland peaks. At first Malcolm saw nothing. Then a shimmer of disturbance in the air around his wards caught his eye the moment before lightning flashed, and two women straddling broomsticks flew through the air and pierced the protection of his magick.

"Nay," he growled. "How is this possible?"

"The Grimoire!" Morgana pointed. "They have it."

That *had* to be how they got through the wards. Cradled under Badb's left arm was the book filled with all the secrets of his Druid family since the beginning of time.

We're after you both now... Badb's eerie voice brushed past his ear on a chilling breeze. Even as he watched her hag's robes draping below her as she circled his keep on her broomstick, it was as though she whispered right next to him.

Fear sliced through him, followed quickly by a cold fury the likes of which he'd never before felt. Moray Village, full of innocent souls, separated the space between his walls and the castle. Could he get to them in time?

A sister for a sister... Badb's cruel winds hissed. With a deafening crash, she called down a silver fork of lightning. It struck his parapets and half the roof of Dun Moray gave a great shudder, and then collapsed.

With a harsh sound of strain and rage, Malcolm did all he could to keep the stones from crushing any of the inhabitants of the castle, but knew that from this distance, he had to have failed.

Come to us and we'll let the wee Moray babes and their mothers live...

Malcolm hesitated, though his heart bled. Of course, it was a trap.

One that, if sprung, could seal the fate of the entire world. And yet, what of his people? How could they make him choose between those whom he loved most dear, and—everyone who was or would ever be?

Bring Morgana, and we'll give you what you want, or should I say who you want...

Sean.

The thought of him locked away in their hellish void nearly drove Malcolm to his knees. The sounds of the battle receded into the background. Though Sean had been the one imprisoned all these decades, Malcolm felt as though he had found deliverance through him. He'd felt more wealthy in that hovel in the forest than he ever had in the halls of his own castle. A chance to be who he truly was. No pretenses, no expectations, and no barriers. He wanted nothing more from this life than to be given the chance to show him the same kind of freedom.

A love that never bound, but liberated.

Cursing the prophecy, the Fates, the Wyrd Sisters and the *fucking* gods, he turned to his beloved sister, a void of his own opening inside his heart.

"Keep me strong," he ground out a command and a plea in one breath.

She met his gaze with her soft blue eyes, clarity and determination sparking in their depths. "Nay," she murmured.

Malcolm flinched, and then glared a warning at her. "What are ye saying?"

Grasping his elbow, Morgana turned them both toward his keep, where Badb and Nemain touched down on the flagstones of his home. Lightning sheeted across the Highland sky, warning that their time was running out.

"We take the fight to them, Malcolm," Morgana said, closing her eyes and pressing her forehead against his shoulder as though gathering strength.

Gritting his teeth, Malcolm nodded, lowering them to the

ground on his piece of earth. "It's time we end this," he agreed. "One way or another."

"I'm going with you," Kenna announced, taking a moment to break from the line of archers. "Lower me down."

"Nay," Malcolm held his hand out to her. "Ye stay where ye are and help the Berserkers fend off the attack. They need yer fire."

Kenna stood upon the wall, her amber skirts flapping against her legs in the increasingly violent winds. "I know you could have loved him." Her eyes glowed with the fire of prophecy. "I'm sorry that you could not keep Sean and also your word as a Druid. But your decisions today will echo for millennia, one way or the other."

Her words affected Malcolm more than he could ever have expected. So much so that all he could summon for her was a nod before he turned with his sister toward Dun Moray. It wasn't sadness that welled up inside him as he stalked the thoroughfare of Moray Village toward where Badb stood, clutching her broom in one hand and the book in the other.

Rage. A helpless, impotent fury Malcolm had never had to grapple with in his entire life. He was a de Moray. The King of the Highland people. His family had held off the Vikings, the Romans, and the English with their might and magick.

How was it that this one crone and her coven were more dangerous than all the sword-wielding warriors who'd been after this isle since the beginning? How could it be possible that no matter which side won the day, the ultimate loss would be his? He'd always done everything required of him. Respected the earth. Studied his craft. Learned herbs, potions, incantations, leadership, justice, and mercy. Some of those lessons had been hard-won. Others came easily.

But after decades of sacrifice for his people and his Goddess, he was denied the only thing that truly mattered in this world. The one thing that would strengthen and solidify his power and allow him to become the man, the *King*, he was meant to be.

Love.

It was love that saved the souls of the mated Berserkers who now cherished and protected his kinswomen. Malcolm craved such love. The love of someone willing to sacrifice their eternal soul for his sake. The rare emotion that filled in the cracks of one's being and fortified the weaknesses with a power greater than any other.

Hatred boiled in the absence of that love, filling him with a dark power that surged dangerously just beneath the surface.

"Keep Nemain busy," he instructed Morgana. "Her fire is useless against your water. Draw from the Loch and drown her if need be."

"What are you going to do?" Morgana asked.

"Whatever is necessary."

The sky darkened as they stopped at the bottom of the stone steps to Dun Moray. The spires of his home now seemed sinister against the backdrop of the roiling clouds, occasionally illuminated with flashes of lightning.

Energy crackled in the very air between them. The ground was alive with it, and it sparked from the Crone's silver eyes as he approached.

"I've never understood you, King Malcolm," Badb spoke down at him from the top of the stairs, where she and the vicious girl/child, Nemain, blocked the entrance to the keep. "For a man of such power, you certainly lack vision."

"I'm envisioning ye in yer grave," Malcolm growled.

Badb's cackle sounded like the crunch of gravel beneath a boot. "To say such things to your family," she tsked.

"You're no kin of ours," Morgana said, her fingers twitching as she drew power into her hands and connected with the waters of the loch.

"I am a de Moray." Badb lifted the Grimoire, the wind flipping the pages of the ancient tome until it fell open. "There are four de Moray's behind one gate. The *Prophecy of Four* has foretold that we will be the ones to open the Seven Seals and bring about the Apocalypse."

"Ye know I'd never do that," Malcolm vowed. "I'd die before I succumbed to yer evil."

Badb's eyes flared, and she stepped forward, brandishing the book at him as she descended the stairs with the languor of a victor. "Evil?" she purred. "You men are always so short-sighted. You think there is only good, and only evil. You plant your flag on one side or the other and you fight to the death in service to the light or to the dark."

"I will *always* choose the light." He said this without hesitation, and still the crone laughed.

"It is easy for evil to take purchase in the soul of a good man." Badb stopped three steps above him, bringing them all but face to face. "Bliss can be found in a sin, and bitterness often follows a good deed, is this not so?"

Victorious cries from the wall heralded a triumph over the Army of Souls. Smoke curled into the sky, mixing with the dark clouds and reflecting Kenna's flames as though they licked skyward from the bowels of the Underworld.

"Your minions are defeated," Malcolm informed his enemies.

Badb shrugged. "What need have I of them when I have the two of you? Once I help our master rise from the deep and seize what is left after the Apocalypse, the Army of the Damned will be my minions, and I will rule them with unimaginable power."

"Ye're delusional," Malcolm spat.

"I'm a visionary," she corrected. "And I'm willing to share that power with you, King Malcolm. I'll give you a piece of my paradise when this is all over. And also, grant you what you desire most in this world, if you and your sister do what I want."

With a wave of her gnarled finger and a whispered curse, a portal opened up on the steps right in front of them, a window to the Void. There, naked and curled in on himself, was Sean, shivering in a hole of desolation and anguish, whispering his name as though it were a prayer to the gods.

Morgana's gasp seemed far away as Malcolm lunged for the portal, calling out to the man on the ground.

Sean's dark head lifted, sightless amethyst eyes searching blindly for his voice.

"Malcolm?" he choked as desperate tears streaked the grime on his face. Struggling to his feet, he put out his arms as if to reach for him, though it was obvious that he couldn't see in the pitch-black prison. "Malcolm, are you here? I can hear you."

Badb clenched her fist and the portal disappeared.

"He'll think you came for him," Nemain giggled. "How cruel."

Morgana lifted both of her hands, making an intricate sign with her fingers and commanded a pillar of water to rise from the loch and douse the small fire witch. "Silence, you vicious harpy, or I'll forget that I've taken a vow never to take a life."

"Let him go," Malcolm commanded, the ground beneath them trembling with the force of his rage.

"You know my price," Badb countered. "Cast with us, and open the First Seal. Help me unleash the Horsemen into this world and wipe out all the useless tribes of people who will only become like a scourge to this earth whom you love so much."

"We are not a scourge of this earth, we are her children, and I am her protector." They knew this, but Malcolm wanted them to remember that he had the power of the Goddess behind him.

Badb slammed the book shut, pulling it close into her robes. "Nemain has seen the future of this world. If we don't end it now, people will multiply until they spread over every continent and every land. They will build machines that belch poison into the sky and taint the rivers with their rubbish. They'll use everything the earth and the seas have to give and still demand more. You are not saving this world for anyone who matters. You can prevent all that. Join me now."

"Don't you dare!" Kenna threatened as she, Bael, and Niall drew up behind them leading none other than the Four Horsemen in their wake like giant, mounted sentinels.

They looked both mortal and inhuman, mounted on horses unlike any Malcolm had seen on this earth, their colors as vivid as the book prophesied, and their potency just as terrifying.

"I'll not believe your lies." Malcolm addressed the Crone. "Now hand over the book or I'll crush you to claim it."

"I'm not lying!" she screeched. "Ask her!"

Kenna jumped as Badb thrust a finger in her direction.

"Ask your seer if what I say is not the truth."

Malcolm turned to Kenna, whose eyes were filled with pain. "She's not lying… I've seen this in the flames, as well."

The image of Sean's despair flashed in his mind's eye. Could he carve out a life for them in this new world of darkness and subjugation Badb wanted to cultivate? Would it be any worse than the picture she'd just painted of earth's own future?

"You would be dooming poor Sean forever, and for what?" Badb pressed. "For a species bent on destroying themselves. They can't escape the inevitable, King Malcolm. Someday, somehow, the prophecy must be fulfilled. Why not now, when we can seize the outcome and turn it to our favor?"

Shame burned beneath the temptation, and Malcolm turned to glare up at the Horsemen, searching for answers in their inscrutable eyes. "You want this?" he asked them. "You want me to cast with them? To unleash you to wreak the bloody swath of your destiny on this earth?"

The pale horse stepped away from the line, and Death turned his dark head to survey the gathering Druids and Berserkers, poised on the brink of the End, ready to fight the final battle and finally put to rest the argument of destiny versus free will.

His voice evoked brimstone as he spoke. "If the Apocalypse begins this day, we will fulfill our final duties. And then, what is left for immortals such as us? What purpose will we have but to become agents of chaos and devastation? We will be what we are meant to be, and whatever is left after the End will be an unyielding temptation for the four of us... Think on that, Druid King, before you make your decision."

Death's answer chilled Malcolm to the very core of his essence. Badb's paradise could easily be turned into an unimaginable hell were these Horsemen to challenge her, or each other, for it.

Malcolm reeled as he cast his gaze about, to his family, to his enemies, to the smoke covering the sky, and to the faces of his people, who poked out from behind the village walls, awaiting his word to seal their fates.

A gentle hand touched his arm, and he looked down at Kenna as though she might be a stranger, willing his pounding heart to slow. "Dear Malcolm," she said quietly, her voice a warm flicker like a candle in the gathering darkness. "I have seen the shadows and suffering in the days to come, as the Wyrd Sisters predicted, but there is a reason I have not succumbed to despair, as you are about to do."

Despair didn't seem like a strong enough word for the bleak void inside of him.

"I've seen other things, as well," Kenna continued. "Sparks of transcendence from within the devastation. Marvels of ingenuity. I've heard poetry that would make your heart sing, and music that would cause the wounded to dance. There are those whose love will inspire entire generations toward change and hope. There is a limitless potential within us all, and how can we, in this very moment, take that potential away from those who would realize it?"

"Don't be a fool!" Badb scoffed, the wind blustering through the gathering with an angry hiss. "Humanity will always be ruled by fear like the sheep they are. They will be controlled with rhetoric and lies, and ultimately, their stupidity will be their downfall. Why prolong the inevitable?"

"The future is never certain," Kenna insisted. "But we owe the world a chance for redemption."

Malcolm stared down at his cousin with new eyes. She was right, *damn her.* He was wrong to be tempted by a future at the cost of humanity. How could he have even contemplated it?

Because the part of his heart he usually saved to encompass the entire world had been stolen by a raven-haired man and then broken by their star-crossed fate.

"We'll not cast." Malcolm addressed the Wyrd sisters with unyielding certainty.

"Don't be so certain." In a confusing flurry of robes, Badb hurled her broomstick on a powerful gust of wind. It impaled Kenna with such force, she was knocked from her feet and propelled backward before crashing to the stones.

Niall was at her side in a moment, his golden hair brushing her face as he gasped her name.

Bael ran for the Crone, but Nemain stopped him with an explosion of her fire, the strength of it knocking him to the ground, as well.

Reflexively, Malcolm lifted a flagstone from the earth and hurled it at Badb. She didn't counter in enough time to completely avoid it and her legs became crushed beneath its staggering weight, pinning her to the earth. The Grimoire went flying, sliding in a flesh-colored heap toward Nemain.

Badb tried to lift the stone with her powerful gusts of wind, but Malcolm used his magic to keep it in place, locking them in a battle of elements.

Nemain lashed out with her hands and a wall of fire crawled across the courtyard, effectively cutting Kenna, Niall and Bael away from the Four Horsemen and the four Druids.

Malcolm advanced on Badb, his hands out, intensifying the pressure of the stone crushing her legs.

Instead of shrinking in fear, Badb sneered triumphantly up at him, blood beginning to stain a few of her teeth that had been broken in the fall. "That makes three of us casting at once," she cackled. "Now Morgana must heal your cousin, or she'll die."

"Malcolm?" Morgana inched toward the fire. "I can't just do nothing. Let me heal her."

"You're running out of time, Druid King," Badb taunted. "How much are you willing to lose to save the world?"

The void in Malcolm's heart suddenly became a cavern, and all the loss, rage, and helpless fury rushed to fill it until his heart did slow, and his breathing stabilized as the answer to everything became startlingly clear. "Nothing," he answered coolly. "I'm done with sacrificing what is mine for the greater good."

CHAPTER 8

*I*t was a reckless risk, but he seized it. Whirling to face the Horsemen, Malcolm addressed Death once again. "This Druid has taken tens of thousands of souls from ye, including her own, and locked them in the Void."

Death narrowed dark, soulless eyes at Badb. "So she has."

"I doona think that ye want us to break the Seals." It was a stab in the dark, but something in the eyes of the Horsemen, in the way their steeds pawed the ground in impatience verified what he'd begun to suspect.

"We will unleash the might of the Underworld on this plane, whether we will it or not. Make no mistake of that." Death gestured toward the book, lying innocuously on the stones. "The prophecy demands it."

"Until then, it is yer duty to escort the souls to the Other World."

His statement was met with expectant silence.

"I could offer her to ye." Malcolm gestured to the Crone. "Ye could take her and the souls in her possession to do with as ye will."

"You can't!" Badb hissed. "Not in time to save your fire witch."

"Heal her!" Niall demanded of Morgana. "Now!"

"Wait," Malcolm ordered. "Doona cast."

"Malcolm, Kenna is dying!" Her blood was now running into the grooves between the stones, creating gruesome rivers in his courtyard.

"I am yer King," Malcolm commanded. "Ye will obey me for once."

The eyes of the man called Death were shrewd and unnerving as they narrowed on Malcolm.

"And what is your price for this trade?" Death inquired.

"One soul," Malcolm answered.

"The Fire Druid?"

"Nay." His throat tightened as he spoke her name. "Sean."

"Malcolm!" Morgana cried, tears running down her cheeks. "Malcolm don't do this!"

"I'll kill you *and* your consort if you let Kenna die," Niall threatened through the flames. "Your magic is *nothing* against my wrath."

Badb screeched, her powers flaring as she tried desperately to escape his hold. "I am immortal! I serve a master greater and more powerful than any of you! I'll return and my vengeance will turn the green Highlands into nothing but blood and ashes!"

Malcolm ignored them all, gazes locked with the man who eventually held all the souls in the world in his grasp at one time or another.

"I don't make deals," Death said evenly.

"This isn't a deal," Malcolm replied. "It's a threat. One that I don't make lightly. Give him to me, or I cast with them and force yer hand."

The time it took for him to draw his next breath felt like an eternity. Through the wall of flame, he could see Kenna twitching, her eyes beginning to flutter closed. His heart bled just as much as her body did, but he knew what would happen to her soul if she were lost.

She'd be taken to the Other World to wait until she was reunited with her mate.

Sean would be locked in a prison that not even Death could breach to set him free.

He couldn't let that happen.

A silent look passed between the horsemen, and then Death nodded. "Your descendants will pay the price, Druid King," he predicted, nudging his horse forward and up the stairs of Dun Moray.

Even Malcolm stepped out of his way as the harbinger of the Apocalypse swooped down and scooped up a spitting, cursing Crone before disappearing in a swirl of dark mist.

Bael used the distraction to leap through the flames, singing his dark hair, and beheading Nemain with a speed almost undetectable by the human eye.

Somewhere in the distance, a raven crowed.

And then...

Sean stood in the center of the courtyard, naked and trembling, his face wet with the evidence of grief, and his beautiful eyes wide with disbelieving astonishment.

Malcolm was only dimly aware of the fire disappearing. Of Morgana rushing for Kenna. Of the three remaining Horsemen turning and disappearing into the shadows.

He could see nothing but Sean's eyes. Those lovely irises such an unnatural shade of blue, they seemed purple. The color of Scottish heather in bloom. The color of Pictish royalty.

The color painted on his heart.

"Malcolm?"

His name on Sean's lips was the most beautiful melody he'd ever heard. It was better than rustling leaves, waving grasses, or shifting stones.

Sean's legs gave with a sob as he collapsed to his knees.

Malcolm flew down the steps, and seized his lover. Reminding himself to be gentle as he pulled Sean back to his feet and into his arms. The last time his hands had been on the lad, he'd been punishing.

Never again. He was a better man than that.

"You came for me," Sean whispered against his neck. "Tell me I'm not dreaming."

Dreams never felt like this.

"I'd have crawled into hell to come for ye," he said against Sean's hair. He left out the part where he'd nearly brought it to this world for him. He didn't need that weight on his shoulders.

"I like your Druid wars!" Ingmar interrupted, leading a band of battle-weary, but generally good-spirited Vikings into the court-yard. How they'd gotten over his walls, Malcolm could only guess.

The Viking general sent a leer in Sean's direction. "They always seem to end with explosions and nudity. What could be better?"

"Avert yer eyes, or I'll pluck them out," Malcolm growled harshly, ripping off his robes and spreading them around Sean's perfect skin.

With a few guffaws, the Vikings complied.

"Malcolm," Kenna croaked, pushing herself up on weak elbows.

Her blood still stained the stones, but through the blemished hole in her dress, new, healthy skin appeared. Morgana had been able to heal her, and Malcolm had never doubted that she would, even for a moment.

Shame settled in his gut, though not regret. "Kenna, I—"

"I forgive you," she interrupted.

"I don't!" Niall stood, his enormous shoulders taut and ready for a fight. "How dare you allow my mate to come to harm. I'm going to rip your limbs off with my bare—"

"Look at them, my love." Kenna admonished. Struggling to push herself up for a second before her mate leaned down and lifted her. "Would you not have done the same for me in such an instance?"

Niall's hard blue eyes softened down at his mate. "I'd slay every last soul alive if you asked me to."

Kenna rested her head on his shoulder. "Then how can you be angry?"

Niall's brows drew together, but he was silent as he studied Malcolm and Sean, as if restructuring a few things in his brain.

Bael took Morgana into his arms, as well, sharing a silent and desperate embrace with his mate. Keeping a hand locked with his, she went to the Grimoire and retrieved it, unsurprised that it was completely intact.

"You heard what the Horseman said." Morgana ran fingers across the pages. "It is our descendants who will be the prophesied Four. The de Morays who will… who will break the Seals."

Malcolm nodded. "I'll do everything I can to make certain that they are ready when the time comes, to defeat the Horsemen if need be."

"Is such a thing possible?" Sean murmured.

Malcolm blinked down at him, his heart too full for him to form any words for an answer.

He looked almost like the goddess, herself, swathed in his robes of green and gold, his ebony curls flowing over Malcolm's own colors.

He knew he looked like nothing more than an average man left in only his kilt and tunic. Stripped of all artifice, pomp, and duty, he could be only a man. A man who devoted his everything to Sean. A man who could give him what he'd given no other living soul. Could do what he'd done for none other.

Slowly, he bent his knees, lowering himself until they rested on the cold stones and he was kneeling at Sean's feet.

A King, and yet his loyal subject.

"Though I rule this land, I know it will not be thus forever." He took the trembling hand, his blood quickening at the adoration shining down at him from Sean's eyes. That indefinable spark passing between them as it had in the very beginning. "Our ways will die, but our line never will. Do ye ken how I know that?"

Wordlessly, Sean shook his head, as fresh tears spilled from glittering eyes.

"Because my worship of ye is the most sacred magic there is, and if de Moray progeny is raised in a home with such love, then they will have every chance to write their own destiny."

"As we have." Sean smiled.

"No, *mo ghaol*, my love." He rose and gathered him close. "Ye were always my destiny. And I'll not see that change. Ever."

ABOUT THE AUTHOR

Kerrigan Byrne is the USA Today Bestselling and award-winning author of several novels in both the romance and mystery genre.

She lives on the Olympic Peninsula in Washington with her wonderful husband, two Rottweiler mixes and a very cuddly cat. When she's not writing and researching, you'll find her kayaking, on the beach, eating, drinking, shopping, and attending live comedy, ballet, or too many movies.

Kerrigan loves to hear from her readers! To contact her or learn more about her books, please visit her website: www.kerrigan-byrne.com

THE SWEETEST CHOCOLATE DROP

PIPER HUGULEY

CHAPTER 1

*C*at Bennett looked damn good.

Even better than when he last saw her nearly ten years ago at the train station bidding him farewell on his way to bootcamp.

A frozen feeling haunted Mike in his fingers and he gripped the handle of the bucket he was holding and the sweat slicked up his hands. That was the time he had promised her, over and over he would be back for her.

He had never shown up again.

He had his reasons.

Now, Cat's beautiful beige features contorted with worry and pain. What a change from the love that shone through her as he boarded the train, leaving her behind for good.

"We came all the way across town," she said in her melodious voice, "And you don't have room?"

The nurse across from Cat said not a word but shook her head.

Then Mike noticed, away from Cat's barely aged face, untouched by time, the small person lying on a stretcher next to her. A little child. The feeling moved from his fingers to target the middle of his chest. She found someone else after he left her.

Well, what did he expect? Cat was a catch. Beautiful, dignified, a sharp dresser, even now in her difficulty, every inch the brown queen. Right out of *Jet*. Why should she wait for him, especially after what had happened? He gathered the few crumbs of courage the war had left to him.

"That room on the fourth floor just got empty." Mike stepped out from the pillar he had been hiding behind. Cat, so dignified, didn't betray anything. A flicker of recognition showed up in her eyes though, those Cat's eyes, the very reason he called her that name and not Cathy, as all of her brothers and sisters did. "Child went on to rehab, as I recall."

"Myron James." The receptionist said. "You have no business in this affair."

"Well, now. That might be and that might not be, Sarah. You see, I know these," and he turned to look at the small figure with two pigtails sticking out on either side of her head, hunched down in the bed, her large brown eyes shining over the covers. He knew well the call of the small, skinny twisted limbs reaching for help.

Something tugged at his heart. He knew the policy of the Crippled Children's home. He knew the customs.

He also knew the director. Who owed him a favor. And he owed Cat.

"These ladies. I might have to call on Mr. O to come on and let them in." He set the pail down.

"I could lose my job," Sarah bit out at him.

"Me too. But you lose me, you just have to clean up, lift, carry and all the rest around here."

Sarah bit her lips, and Mike saw Cat's back straighten. *Good. No time to give up now for your...child.*

He looked back at the little girl again, who in in all of this time, hadn't taken her eyes off of him.

"I'm going to get Mr. O." Sarah stood up and Mike could tell she really didn't want to, since her orthopedic shoes she was always complaining about, hurt her. And so what?

"You go on ahead and do that Sarah. I'll wait right here for both of ya'll."

They both watched Sarah hobble off toward the elevator. Mr. O'Brien's office was on the top floor four flights up.

The door of the lift opened and Sarah pushed back the inside grid of elevator doors, clanging them shut, as she got on the lift and, without a word between them, watched it go up.

Until Cat's child spoke.

"Mama. He's about the blackest man I ever saw."

The clear voice came strong from the small lump of a girl. Polio didn't touch her in her lungs, he guessed, wanting to chuckle. Still, Cat turned on the child with a wild ferocity.

"You better never let me hear you speaking like that again, Andie. Do you understand? I'll smack you into next week."

"Hey, hey now, Cat. This little chocolate drop is right. I'm used to that." Mike reached over to the girl and took her by her twisted hand and squeezed it a bit. "How you feel, honey?"

The child seemed startled by his touch, as did Cat. She turned on him with the same ferocity as she had with the girl. "Don't you touch her." She reached over and broke his hold on the girl and gave his arm a hard push. "Leave her alone. I'll find somewhere else to take her, somewhere you won't be."

Mike withdrew his hand, and folded it together with the other, trying not to show how her reaction made a sweet pain course through his limbs. He deserved that, every bit. But not the small lump of humanity beneath the sheets. "What's wrong with her? Polio?"

Cat nodded her head. The worry came back into her face. She didn't look so dignified any more, and his heart went out to her. "I'm sorry Cat. Truly."

Her eyes came up and flashed at him again. "We'll be alright. Just go on about your business."

"I'ma talk to my boss here. See what we can do."

"Nothing will be done, Myron." She knew it would hurt him to use his real name. "They won't have us up in here because we're Negroes. Or didn't you notice?"

"I noticed, Catherine." He let the name trip off of his tongue. "It's enough they have me up in here to work."

"As a janitor?"

Yes, he hurt her plenty. She kept on punching at him. He deserved it. "Let's say that's what I do, if you want."

"You had that bucket in your hand."

He looked at her again. A bright, fierce intelligence shone from her brown eyes.

"Not much getting past you, chocolate drop. I can see that." He smiled at the girl trying to calm her. "We going to get you a place to rest and start to work on your treatment."

Cat's gaze at him was wary. "I don't want you touching her."

The squeaky sound of the lift and proper voices upraised reached him and he laid a finger to his lips. Funny how he could always get Cat to silence herself by pointing to his lips. Might have brought back the memories of the good old days. It sure did for him.

John Casey O'Brien stepped forward to the little group as Sarah came around the back of her desk and perched herself at her desk, on watch again. Mike folded his hands. "Afternoon, Mr. O. These ladies here, need our help here at the home and I'm hoping you can be there for them."

"Well, now, Mike. It's all fine and good that they've come. But we don't have room just now."

"Well now, Mr. O. That's not quite it. Not sure if you heard that the Monroe boy got to go on home. His room is available."

Mr. O nodded. "I know. Saw him off myself this morning."

"Well, then, we can have that room ready for little missy here."

"You not working in administration here, Mike, you may not know we have a waiting list of children who have injuries from polio waiting to come over from Children's. No one can just show up here expecting to be admitted."

Mr. O dipped his head to Cat, whose eyes, tilted in feline grace, narrowed. She stepped forward with some papers in her hand and Mike took them from her. "You must not have seen these here orders signed by Children's. Wonder why they sent her over here, knowing that they know about the home."

He held them out to Mr. O.

John stepped back from them as if they carried some dread disease. Still, didn't take no reading or close notice to see what the papers were. "The home is very expensive here, ma'am. Only the finest care is provided here."

Mike loosened the tension of the room by laughing. "Well, now. Why do you think this beautiful lady has brought her daughter here? She knows that. We all know it working here like we do. We have all these patients coming here for help, seem like this polio done really spread this summer."

Mr. O turned beet red. "Your kind don't get polio the same way as others."

Angry words bubbled to his lips and there was time he would have spoken them. He knew better now. "I got to disagree with you, sir. Old wisdom, there Mr. O. Not true. And now, with this more recent wave, it's going to be children of all colors and races looking to come. Might as well start now."

Turning to observe the small lump of humanity underneath the sheets, his boss seemed to cave.

"Well, Mike, I'm sure your, friends here, must know how expensive this place is." He shifted to Cat. "Your daughter, she would be here for a long while, a period of several months to rehab."

Mike didn't disagree. He fixed a practiced eye to the child and he could see she was an especially bad case. Got it in all of her limbs. But that was no surprise. Polio was mighty hard to pin down, and in Negro children, it always got explained away as something else for a long time—until it was too late.

Cat spoke, "How much does it cost?"

Her full bottom lip, so red and rosy, began to quiver in a way that Mike didn't like. *No weakness. Stay strong, Cat.*

So, he did the unthinkable again and touched her. "We don't need to worry about that just now, Catherine. Mr. O and the center will take the finest care of this here chocolate drop."

Out of the corner of his eye, Sarah peered over her desk at the group, not liking the way the thing was going. She had a nephew here and didn't want him having to share a room with a Negro child. Good thing the one he suggested was empty.

Mr. O folded his arms. "Oh yeah, Mike? "

"High time, sir. Don't you agree?" He could use his deep voice to great effect many times. To soothe a child in pain, a baby to sleep, or to save a man's life in the heat of a war battle. It was the voice that Mr. O was most familiar with—the one that had coaxed him back to life.

The white man with red hair shifted and the beginnings of sweat shone through the armpits of his cream-colored linen suit. Yeah, Pittsburgh could get mighty hot in August. "There's that, Mike. But we have no room. I'm sorry."

"Sure. Still, wasn't so long some of your kind couldn't stay here." Mike regarded him with a pointed look. "In such a fine place. If it's that kind of problem and the room is taken, they can have my room. This chocolate drop is special to me."

Mr. O didn't look so uncomfortable anymore, but instead looked amused. "What now Mike? Who are these people to you?"

He edged over closer to Cat and grasped her by the hand. "This little chocolate drop is mine. She's my daughter."

CHAPTER 2

*H*er tongue transformed into her fast-beating heart at seeing that smooth Negro come stepping forward with a pail in his hand. The first thing in her mind was, "Praise God, he's come to save us."

Then cold water from the pail of reality came over her as the blood rushed forward to her face. *The louse.*

He stepped around the ambulance they had ridden there in, a low-set station wagon ambulance since Andie wasn't very big. He started ordering around the two white male drivers about how to move Andie from one conveyer to the other.

Once it was done, he turned to her, his beautiful teeth and lips gleaming. "Right this way."

Would her leg let her step forward? She tried. No. Was she getting polio? Dear God no. She was trying to recover from seeing Myron "Mike" James in this place at this time when her heart, her entire life was wrapped up in that twisted little body on the stretcher. She couldn't divide herself just now.

"You need help?" He held out his big hand to her.

"I do not." Her words whipped in the stillness as they proceeded into the home. She grabbed onto the cold metal of Andie's stretcher and willed herself. *Step forward. One at a time just as you've always been doing.*

A miracle occurred. She could walk. On her smooth brown pumps, she held herself upright and walked, as she always did. Could the same miracle happen for her daughter? Still as they pushed onto the elevator, it hit her.

How did he know?

There was only room on the small lift for Andie's bed, Mike and her. "We'll send it back down for you." Mike trilled in his deep voice and closed the gated doors of the lift himself in the faces of the director and the receptionist lady. He pushed his big body in front of her, next to Andie's bed and them into a corner. "Sometimes, you just gotta take things by the horns, right Cat? How's things?"

She could breathe again. He knew nothing. Joy and fierceness mixed in her veins. She bit the words out one at a time. "As you can see, Mike. Things are not going that well."

"Hard to see you've had such a time, Cat. You surely deserve better. But we are going to do what we can to get this little precious standing up again, running and playing like always."

Andie's brown eyes shone above the rim of the sheet that covered her and spoke from beneath the sheets because she was unable to lift up her chin, "Well, that's what we come here for, mister. I got plans for myself, just as soon as I can get out of this here bed."

Cat wanted to slink down next to the bed in horror at her daughter's forward response, but Mike seemed amused.

"What's that, chocolate drop?"

"I'm going to be Maria Tallchief. I'll dance in the Ballet Grand in a pretty white and pink tutu with garlands of flowers in my hair."

Mike turned to Cat and fixed her with a sharp look. Then he faced Andie. "Whatever you want honey. We are going to help you here. You going to get better. You don't have any more worries, Cat. It will be okay."

He reached forward in the small space of the elevator to take her hand. His white palm, crisscrossed with spiderwebs of brown intrigued her. That was not how his hand looked before. What had happened to him?

Maybe something had happened to him.

Was that why she never heard from him again?

He pulled his hand back from her and turned facing forward, letting them both get a good glimpse of his strong back. The same back she had clung to many nights in the summer of 1942, writhing, twisting, crying out underneath him in pleasure that bordered on pain.

The elevator bounced, matching the roller coaster emotions in her belly. "Don't worry ladies. This lift got a mind of its own, but I have control of it."

He pulled the gate back, then the doors, pulling Andie's bed off the lift by her feet. Cat stepped gingerly over the edge, not wanting to get a heel caught. "This way. She's going to be on the top floor in the penthouse suite."

Andie giggled from beneath the sheets. Giggle? Her daughter? Not since the horrifying morning when she complained she didn't feel like going outside to play, had Andie giggled in any way. Yet, here was Mike, the creator of the best and worst in her life, causing her to giggle.

She didn't know whether to laugh or cry.

Turning to look at her as he pushed the bed down the little narrow hallway, he said over his firm shoulder to her, "She's something, your little one here."

She pushed her pocketbook further up her arm. "Yes, she is."

"Smart too. Anyone can see that."

"Thank you."

"I was at the top of my class," Andie interjected without invitation. "And when I go back to school…"

"Hush, Andie." She spoke up loudly in the hallway so her daughter could hear her.

"We got school here, Andie. Bet you didn't know that. You probably smarter than all the kids here put together." Mike's deep voice rose over hers and caused her busy child to calm.

What was she thinking of? What was he? Should he even say that?

"Please. Don't cause trouble here."

Mike fixed her with a strong look. "It's not about trouble Cat, it's about truth."

"Well, all of these children can hear you. The doors are open."

"Hey, they know what it is when someone new comes in. Makes them stronger and up for the competition. And your child will be a fierce fighter, I know."

He stopped them in front of the smallest room at the end of the hall. "Here you are, my lady. Your suite."

Giggles again. "Thank you."

What was it about Mike that allowed him to have that way with females? It was better not to be with him. He did her the biggest favor leaving her on that hot August day, leaving her sobbing and clinging to his arm, his promises of returning to her echoing in her ears. It would be nothing but trouble to have to deal with a man who insisted on flirting with females, charming and schmoozing his way through life. She didn't deserve that.

Pushing the bed with Andie in it beside a saggy, worse looking bed, he pulled back Andie's sheet, and she could hear the sharp intake of breath from him.

Yes, her daughter's case was bad. Her small, skinny coal-black limbs were twisted and contorted. To make it worse, Andie suffered her summer rashes and so the crooks of her knees and elbows screamed bright blood red with inflammation.

Cat righted herself. No matter what, she didn't want his pity. Everyone had their cross to bear, and hers was Andie. She would protect her and help her no matter what.

"Got to move you to this new bed, chocolate drop. I'll lift you up and you let me know when you are ready."

"I'm ready, mister."

Gently, with great tenderness, Mike slipped his large hand underneath Andie's braids, cradling her neck, supporting it. His other hand rested on the underside of Andie's thin thighs, where no strength resided anymore.

How did he know?

How did he know the places where Andie could bear stress and strain?

She couldn't explain it, but he lifted her almost effortlessly and rested her in the new bed, with its dented in mattress. His bed.

"There. You alright?"

"That was great. Thank you."

He pulled the sheet over her once more, and Cat let out a breath. She didn't know she had been holding it in.

"You're most welcome. Your mama told you, I'm Mike, and anytime you need anything, I'm going to be right here to help you."

"Don't make the child promises you can't keep, Mike. I'm sure that you have a home and family to go back to."

Where did that come from? Her pain and hostility all together at once. She cleared her throat. Why did he have to affect her this way?

"No, no I don't Cat. I live right here in the hospital."

Andie piped up, "Why do you call my mother a cat?"

"Ahh, little one. Doesn't she look like one? Her pretty eyes, all tilted up like a cat? And just like she looking at me all mean now, just like a cat would. She look like she would pounce on me if she could."

Andie's sheets from around her mouth moved with her giggles and Mike lowered them for her, so that she could be clearly heard. "You're right. She does. I never saw that before."

She let out another loose breath and let the tension from her shoulders ease away. "So, you live here in the hospital? They let janitors live in the hospital?"

"I'm not a janitor here. Cat. I'm an orderly and night watchman both. Mr. O think he's running things up in here, but I know otherwise. Right, chocolate drop?"

"We call her Andie."

"Why you give your child a boy's name, Cat?"

"My name is Hannah. Mama just calls me that cause I'm always doing boy stuff. It's quicker."

"I think Hannah is a beautiful name. That was my mother's name, you know. Means grace."

"It does?" Andie's eyes got all wide. "I got grace, just like Maria Tallchief."

"Just in your name." He stood up. "You need to get some rest. I'm sure your Mama got other stuff to do with herself. Got to go home to your Daddy and fix his meals. Maybe got other children to take care of."

"No, no. I don't have no Daddy. She tried to get me one last year, but he was mean to us, so he had to go. There's no other children. Just the cousins. They're too little though, and got pulled away from me when I got sick with polio. So they don't get it."

Mike grasped onto the edge of the old bed Andie came in on. "That so? I got to take this downstairs back to the ambulance. I'll let them know you needing some lunch. You can say your goodbyes here."

He pushed the bed past her, but she couldn't read his expression at his obvious attempts to get information about her from her daughter. How low could a man get?

She stepped to the side of him and around to the small side of her daughter's bed, preparing to camp out just because he told her she had to go. How dare he?

"We'll be fine. Do your...duties."

"Thank you, Cat. And you need to get home and rest so that you can take good care of your child. Let us take care of her."

"I'm her mother. I know what's best for her."

He pushed the bed out of the room and she heard him retreat down the hall to the rickety elevator. The tiredness entered her body and infused her soul. Even as he left the room, Andie's long eyelashes, one of her beautiful features, slipped down to her face. She was tired too.

They both were. Tired of putting up a front. Tired of fighting. She slipped down into the chair next to her daughter's bed and slipped her pumps from her aching feet. She just needed to stop and think for a minute—for a while. What did it mean that Mike should give up his room for her daughter? Why would he bother doing that, when he slipped away from her without pain or regret on that August day and sent no letters, no communications. Nothing.

Her confusion reminded her of the heated panic that had resided in her body over her ten years ago when she knew that her period wasn't coming and that the man responsible had left her to fight in a world war.

CHAPTER 3

*H*is breaths came fast, deep and hard when he realized that his flesh was on fire.

Back in the war.

Back on the battlefield.

Back in France.

The same thing happened now as he walked away from the little room where he put Cat's daughter, knowing that she had a really bad case.

Hating himself for making more promises he couldn't keep.

When her daughter ended up crippled forever, she would hate him forever, if she already didn't.

He took the stretcher bed back to the ambulance drivers who looked really put out at having to wait a prolonged amount of time for it, but it seemed like the one was having a good time talking to the receptionist. And if Sarah could get a date to help her loosen up some, it would all work out, right? Cause she needed a man. Bad.

"Hey, there Mike. Come on back to the washroom a minute." Mr. O called out to him and he waved at him. Keep it light. Gotta keep it fun for the children. Always.

"Sure thing." Mike spoke up in a peppy voice, but right now, he wanted to be alone more than anything to calm the assault that his beating heart put on him.

Stepping through the old marble archways in the old part of the building, where it was cold, Mike went back into the washroom, mounded high with bed sheets and pillow cases. They didn't do the wash on the weekend, so it was empty and quiet.

"Hey. When you came on board, I thought you told me you were single and that's why you could save us some dough being the night watchman and an orderly."

Mike put his hands in his pockets and slouched on one of the pillars. "I wouldn't steer you wrong. I am single. I'm not married to her."

Right now, getting Cat's name past the developing lump in his throat was asking for too much.

"Ok, then so what's with the big reveal here?" His brown-red eyebrows came together.

Mike's ability to keep it light was fast slipping away from him. How dare this man, a man who wouldn't even be here on the earth if it weren't for him, question him about what he would do? He ran a hand over his wavy conk, hating the very words that he was about to say, but knowing that a little girl depended on him.

He laughed and moved a little closer to Mr. O. "We wasn't all innocent when we got to the big show over there you know. Less you was."

Mr. O's smile matched his own. "I know what you are saying, there Mike. No, none of us were."

"Come back, and this little honey want to know me better, so you know, me being a war hero and all. It wasn't hard to get a little piece of tail from time to time."

"Well, can't say as I blame you Mike. That one there, that mama's got some of the longest legs I ever seen on a woman."

"Remember how women was always asking for stockings? Cat didn't need none of that."

Mr. O elbowed him and it took everything in Mike to react the same way.

Keep it light.

"You rascal. How many of these kids you think you got out there?"

He smiled and spread out his hand. "Between my breaks from the war and when I got back? Who knows?"

"This one was born when we got back?"

Mike did some fast calculating in his head. "Yeah. That's what her mama said. You know, she's none too pleased with me just now. But if I can help her out in some way. Little Hannah's a smart little girl for her age."

"Oh, I could tell. And given that she's yours, we'll work it out somehow. Maybe one or two of the therapists you're friends with will be willing to help in her care and we'll cut the price of her staying here since she's in your room."

"I appreciate that. Yes, sometimes, these little slip ups do you right proud. Mighty smart for seven."

A frown appeared on Mr. O's face. He opened the folder in his hand and riffled through it. "Hannah Bennett? That's her name right? Got her folder here."

"Her mama named her after my mama. She's not a James, but she's close enough."

"Hannah's not seven. She's nine—according to these records here. Yes, Hannah Bennett. Born March 21, 1943. She's nine. Unless there's some discrepancy about it. Maybe you better go get the mother and have her explain…"

A flood of blood filled his ears. Hannah was nine? The vision of her pretzel-stick thin legs and arms invaded his mind and he couldn't think or hear. "Nine?" Nine. Nine. The word for no in German as well as a number. No. No. No.

He turned and ran as fast as he could out of Mr. O's office, hating he had sent Cat away from her daughter. Her daughter? His daughter? Named for his mother? As dark as he was? How else was it possible for light tan Cat to have such a dark child herself if it weren't for a dark father?

He just assumed, so wrong to think it, that Cat had moved on without him, just as the little girl said, that there were some other men to fill the void in her life. What man would be able to resist Cat of the long legs and the throaty voice that sounded like an angel when she sang? There had to have been someone else.

Times like these, when he was pressed to go fast, was when the pain came the most intensely and threatened to cut him into two. He wanted to stop, and take a breath, but she had left, probably for the streetcar stop and he had to find her, get her to explain this messed up math. Rounding the corner, he saw her, reach one of those gorgeous legs onto the platform of the street car.

"Cat! Wait!" He called out, and every breath was a ragged agony. The dirty air and soot from the steel mills just about a mile away didn't make things any easier.

Cat turned her beautiful face to him, but started up the steps.

How could she?

She saw him running to her as fast as he could. Would she pay the car fare and watch him struggle to reach her from the back window of the trolley? Would she be so cruel?

He had been that cruel to her once. It would serve him right if she left him, just as he had left her, emotionally spent. But, she came down off of the street car and stood back on the corner watching the car go past her, continuing on to its destination, well past her just as he reached her.

"What do you want? I'm going to have to wait another whole hour to get back now and they won't hold my job."

He laid his hands on her shoulders, not sure if she would twist herself away from him and his touch, but he had to know. "Cat, look, I need to know. Is Hannah mine?"

She tossed head back and laughed at him. She would have done better to hit him. Laughing at him just made him feel foolish. The pain of a hit would go away faster.

"Isn't that what you told your precious Mr. O so she could stay in there, where they don't want Negro children? Where I'm forced to leave my child and go back to work so she can be where people don't want her?"

"Woman I said, is she mine?"

"Of course, she's yours. She looks just like you. Same color as you, black as the ace of spades."

He had thought his heart was going as fast as it could go, but he was wrong. Looking down at his hands his pulse lived and became visible in his hands. "Dear God. Cat, why didn't you tell me?"

The look on her face was of stark terror. "I waited. I waited and waited. You said you were going to write me, so I could know how to get in touch with you. You were going to come back to Pittsburgh and you didn't. You never even introduced me to your family, so I could tell them. I was just someone off with you, wasn't I?"

"No!" Unexpected energy ripped the words from him. "No, nothing like that."

Cat stood there, a little smirk crossing her lips. "Well, you sure have a funny way of showing it, Myron."

"I always loved you, Cat, I wanted you. But the war. The war did things. Things you don't want to know about. Things that changed me. I couldn't come back to you. Not the way I was. Never that for you. It was better that you find someone else, someone to be strong for you. When I saw you, I thought you did and I was happy for you. Sad for me, but happy for you."

She tossed her head and her hat shifted a bit. "I tried to move on. It didn't work out."

"What was Andie talking about someone being mean to you?"

"I got married two years ago. He liked to use his hands on me and so I left him. Divorce came through a few months ago."

Praise God. Even though the knowledge lit a new fire in his belly. He would kill this man who dared put his hands on Cat. "Who was he?"

"No one you know. Why would you care anyway? If it wasn't for the grace of God, you would have never known, never cared about us."

He couldn't deny what she said was true.

What a mess of things he had made.

"Mr. O thought, after I said Hannah was seven, that your paperwork was wrong."

A confused look crossed her pretty features. "She's nine."

His heart sank all over again. So, she was his. "Cat, listen to me. On everything that's holy and right, I'm going to make this up to you. She's going to be alright, do you hear me?"

The look on her face was just like it was at the train station that day when he left her, ten years before.

"Do you think you are someone who should make promises Mike? After what you've done? Or haven't done? I don't want to hear you make me any promises, especially about Andie. I've had enough of it. I'm going home, even if I have to walk to get away from you."

He laid his hands on her to make her face him, and alarm crossed her face. Jesus, couldn't he do anything right? Especially after what she had just told him about her ex-husband? "Cat, don't go. I'm sorry. I truly, I'm sorry."

"Go back and take care of her. Rich isn't it? I've struggled all of these years to provide for her, care for her, love her. You go back and do it. I've had enough. I'm tired and I want to go home."

"Cat, I.."

He had to make her understand he meant what he said. Pulling her to him, he wrapped his arms around her and reached for her, feeling her soft lips on his, taking her sweet, sweet scent in, needing her to fill the empty space in his very soul, the space that had yearned for her for so long, but knowing he couldn't have her. Kissing her, ten years slipped away from them, and dear God, if only some magic force would compel them back in time to that train platform, where he could start over.

The stark, hard sting of her slap on his cheek made him know that it was 1952 and he was in just about the biggest mess of his life.

CHAPTER 4

*I*t hurt to slap someone. Cat knew it was true when she slapped Mike and the pain seared across her wrist. She wanted to hurt him, but ended up hurting herself.

The last time she was slapped by someone who loved her was when she told Mama Bennett that she was going to have a baby, her mind reverting back to that terrible day.

"You couldn't find no body better to get stuck with than that coal black you brought to church? Are you a fool?"

"No ma'am."

"Yes you are. Pack up your things and get up out of my house this instant."

A high time in her life. Thankfully, she was able to get by singing down at Wonderland under her stage name, Cat Benet. Until she got too big. Her brothers and sisters would come by to her little one-bedroom place over the club, sneaking food out of Mama's house so she could eat and nourish her baby, but there was no relenting from Mama.

After Andie was born on a warm spring Sunday, Cat showed her defiance to her mother by giving the baby the first name of Mike's mother and not her own. That's when Mama Bennett relented. But only a bit.

Her younger sister came to her door with a big basket on her arm and a hangdog expression on her face. May said, "You can give us the baby to take care of while you work."

Mama slapped her again. Just from really far away. "How does she know I would give up my baby to her?"

May shook her head. "She say you having too much fun working down in the nightclubs, getting soldier men to gawk at you like you was Lena Horne or somebody special."

She shrugged her shoulders. "That's why they hired me. They think I look like her. Even when I open my mouth and don't sing like her, it's okay by them."

"Right, but the baby don't need to be all up in that. Just give her to us."

Cat's eyes filled with tears. "When would I get to see her?"

"The clubs are closed on Sundays. You can come by then and see her while Mama's at church all day."

So she did it. She let her child get away from her, just like that. Because it hurt to look at her.

She slipped the little helpless black body into her sister's basket. May's face betrayed nothing, for no one betrayed Mama, but there was pain there too. May tried to give her hope. "Mama will let you come back home in a while."

"I don't think so." The tears got away from her hold on them. "I got to show this baby I'm worthy to be her Mama. I got to show Mama."

"That's right. She'll be fine." May reached out and squeezed her hand. "I'll see to it she'll be fine."

May kept her word. As did Mama. But Cat? No, she failed time and time again.

When the next trolley came pulling up close to the stand in the middle of the street where Mike had left her, bruising her lips with his well-planted kiss, she knew what she had to do.

No doubt, she looked like a wreck, standing in front of that receptionist with the snippy attitude. Still, she wasn't going to let anyone keep her from Andie. Not this time.

"She might be taking a nap now." The woman insisted.

"Do you know that for sure?"

"All of the children do at this time of day." The woman stacked some papers together. "It's enough that you've been causing multiple disruption to our facilities."

"Let me see Mike then."

"Myron? He's working with the children."

"But you said they were all napping."

Cat would have laughed, might have laughed back in the days when laughter was possible. Now, this woman just made her angry. Everything, her denial to be with her child, Mama slapping her, sending May to take her baby from her in a basket, was centered in this mean-looking woman with pursed up lips and an attitude as if she, Cat Benet, were less than nothing. She started to reach across the high counter and grab the woman by her severe gray dress, but Mike's hand, that indistinguishable touch of his, startled her back into her right mind.

He pulled on her shoulder and she turned around to him.

That louse had the nerve to look as if his dog had gotten hit by streetcar.

Lightness invaded her head and she slumped against him, just as she had when May took Andie away in the basket. Mike slid his strong arms up under her and cradled her to him.

"What's the matter with her?" the receptionist woman asked.

"She just, she's tired, Sarah. That's all. Like you ladies get. I'll take her upstairs. Come get the elevator for me."

"If you are taking her up to your room, I do approve of any funny business here in the children's hospital."

Cat closed her eyes against Mike's broad chest wanting to sleep, faint or something. The last thing on her mind was funny business with Mike, even if his arms held her firmly, yet gently as he might a China teacup.

"Woman, are you going to open the elevator or not?"

Mike's tone must have startled the woman, because she immediately went and opened the elevator and let them on it, sliding the gate shut with a particularly strong ferocity.

"You ok?"

"Yes. Thank you."

He squeezed her body and legs closer to her in his grasp. "I was ready to walk up all four of them flights with you in my arms, Cat."

Cat pulled her head back and regarded him. "I should have made you."

Laughter resonated throughout his body and she remembered, with some warmth, that he had crispy black chest hair. Was it still there?

"I would do it for you, Cat."

The elevator bounced up and down, and her stomach matched the bounce. Again. "I can walk. I'll be fine."

"I'll take you in on my arm."

"That's fine. I didn't have much breakfast today, I was so worried about getting her here."

"I understand." He put Cat down and she righted herself on her pumps. "I'll help get you some lunch too."

She put her hand in the warm crook of his arm and they walked down the long hallway together with the occasional voice calling out Mike's name. "Go on back to your nap. I'll be in to see you later." He called out to the children over and over again.

Wasn't that something? Mike was the last person she thought might want to be bothered, back in the old day. And now, here he was, beloved by these children as they recovered from this horrific disease. With their daughter as one of them.

He led Cat back into the small room and Andie's eyelashes blinked. "Mama, what are you doing here?"

"Came back to see about you, Andie. How you feeling?"

Andie couldn't tilt her head back. Not as she wanted to and not without pain, so she looked at Cat through filtered eyelashes and kept her chin very still. "Mama. If you don't go to work tonight, they be firing you. No more singing. You still got time to go get the streetcar and get on to work."

Cat could tell that Mike, despite his earlier promises of getting her something to eat, was completely riveted to this conversation. Riveted on the child in the bed. His daughter. "I'll take care of all that, sugar. You don't have to worry."

"If you don't get to work, they'll turn out all the lights as they did before."

Any other time, any other place, she might have snapped at Andie to stay out of her business. But Mike watched her. Why did she care what he thought? Every time he came into her life, he caused confusion and imbalance, but if he was able to make Andie walk again, she would do whatever, say whatever. She couldn't afford to have him be angry.

"Pet. Just go to sleep now. Mr. um. Mike here said he would bring lunch."

"When you wake up, it will be here for you. You need to get rest. When they come in to work with you, you going to need all of the energy you can get for them limbs to start working again."

"That's not going to happen."

Cat reached for her daughter's scrawny hand through the sheet. "You mustn't speak like that, Andie."

Mike had grabbed at the other. "'Specially since it isn't so. You just a little youngin', sound like you know so much, but maybe you don't know what you think you know. You come to a new place now. Things going to change."

Mike walked out the door and Cat swept the tears away with her sleeve. What would he do? How did he know? Did Andie have something to say to the big man who left the door? No. Andie's lashes fluttered down on her face and she was fast asleep. Again.

Weary, doubtless, from all of the burdens Cat had put on her.

She would do better by her daughter from now on.

CHAPTER 5

*M*ike shouldn't have promised Cat her daughter would walk again.

Andie's matchstick limbs looked like burned broken firewood at the end of a picnic. The ravages of the disease hit her in all places and tears sprang to his eyes after he pulled back the sheet on her little body. Her white cotton nightdress could do little to hide the damage.

He hadn't wanted to cry since the war had taken a toll on his own body. Now, even those tears were wasteful, self-centered. He had some life where he was able to walk around, had years of playing football with his brothers back in Alabama before the family had moved north to Pittsburgh for job opportunities. This child had nothing. She was only nine, and polio had taken all of that from her.

"What's wrong with you?" A clear determined voice broke into his thoughts.

Andie.

She might not be able to lift her own chin, but she had something to say for sure.

"Ain't nothing wrong. I'm going to help you get a jump on your therapy, is all. You are done resting miss. We going to work."

Her keen eyes regarded him. He started to look down away from her, but kept his gaze up. Who was the adult here?

"My mother told you not to touch me."

"How you supposed to get better if I don't?"

"Maybe I'm not supposed to. Put the sheet back."

"I'm not doing it. I'm taking you to the therapy room after you eat some of this breakfast."

"In the hospital, they said I was a goner. No point in eating breakfast."

His stomach sank into his comfortable soled shoe when he heard her refer to herself so casually.

"You been through the worst of it, chocolate drop. You had the fever and you come out on the other side. You're still here. It's what you do with it that matters." He pulled the tray of mashed cereal closer to her readying to feed her.

"It's Sunday. Nobody does therapy on Sunday."

"You haven't even been here long and you already know how the place works?"

"It's my business to know. I don't even know why I'm here, where nobody wants me."

Mike pulled the white sheet over her twisted limbs and pulled the cereal closer. "You a smart girl. You can decide for yourself. Work hard to get some function back. To make a life for yourself. Or lay there and die. Up to you."

"Told you what I wanted to do."

"Uhh. Huh. Except I don't think you mean it."

Big tears to match his own popped up in her eyes. "I want to be Maria Tallchief. A beautiful ballerina. I want to dance and dance. That's not ever going to happen. So, I don't see no purpose in it all."

Had he been stabbed? In his early bad days, he got knifed in his arm before and this is what that felt like. His flesh was knifed away at the thought that this child, his child, would never have, never be what she wanted.

He pushed the cereal closer to her and readied the spoon to feed her as he had to feed all the other bad cases. He always got these tasks with the polio children because no one wanted to touch them when they were at this stage, because of the foolish belief that Negroes didn't get polio as badly as white people, so he did it. Often, he taught them to feed themselves. Then the nurses could be bothered with them.

"You got a voice. Maybe you can sing pretty like your Mama."

Andie raised her black eyebrows. "Whoever heard of a crippled nightclub singer?"

"Whoever heard of a dark black ballerina?"

Now, he had knifed her. The pain boomeranged back onto himself. Clearly, this child had to be shaken from her daydreams if she would get a will to fight for some kind of function. "Open your mouth."

Her lips trembled, just the slightest little bit, but she did as he asked. Spoon by spoon he fed her the lukewarm Ralston, sprinkled with the slightest bit of sugar. Wasn't easy to get either. He could drink his coffee without the sugar. But he had gotten some just for her.

Watching her eat her cereal in silence, he was struck by the thought that Cat had to do these things for her when she was a baby. Feed her, change her, help her to walk. Andie occupied this space in Cat's life when she was a baby. Now, here he was, her real father, doing the same thing. Caring for Andie was not a punishment for his self-centered actions in leaving the sobbing Cat at the station. It was simply time to do these things.

When he had scraped the bowl of the last bit of sweetened Ralston, he pushed the tray back.

"Now Andie." He spoke loud in a voice, but not too loud to disturb the sleeping Cat who slept on a cot in the corner. "I'm going to help your muscles remember what they supposed to be doing for you."

"How will that happen?"

"Got me a little warmed up peanut oil here. Every day before you get into therapy, I'm going to massage these limbs of yours to get them to wake up."

"I don't want to smell like a peanut."

"No problem in that. Once we done with the massage, I'll wipe you off. Then you'll have exercises for today to do. I'll check in on you as I make my way around the wards."

He pulled the sheet back and took the oil into his hands.

Andie frowned. "No one ever touched me with no oil before."

"Got this idea from George Washington Carver. Know him?"

The little girl's eyes blinked fast. "I do. He was a famous inventor. Died the year I was born."

Mike rubbed a dot of the precious fluid into his hands. He had not even known that. So smart. "Well, Mr. Carver do a lot of things for himself. He was a dark black person like us. So, we can do a lot of things too."

Taking her thin arm into his hands, he used a gentle kneading motion on the limb, not wanting to hurt her, but knowing that was going to be impossible.

"You hurting me!" Andie boomed out with that strong voice of hers. Yeah, she got that from her mother.

"You want to wake up the whole place?"

"I don't care about them. Or you."

Mike did not stop touching her and kept kneading the little arm with his thumbs, going around the inflamed red place in the crook of her arm. "Every ouch you feel, every little pain is good. That's the limb saying, I'm alive and here I am. If you didn't feel no pain, that would be the bad news. Your job is to take it. Understand?"

She just blinked, since she couldn't nod. Yeah, he would have to work on that as well.

A rustling from Cat's cot told him she was awake. Cat clung to the end of the bed and watched him work on Andie, her face wreathed in concern and horror. "No one's done that before."

"No one's willing to touch her black flesh. I am. I'm going to bring these limbs to life. You watch what I do Cat. This is Sunday morning, when I got time to do it myself, I can help. You want her to get going again, you got to do what you can to help. You going to?"

"Of course."

Her dress was all rumpled from sleeping on the cot, but she had patted her hair into place. Waking up in the morning, she was so beautiful. He had thrown that all away. He didn't even know what he had.

"Good. Get on the other side of the bed and straighten out her arm. Get it ready for the massage. Watch what I do, with this warm oil here."

"I can't take the pain if you both working me." Andie moaned.

"Hush up, Andie. Do what he says, or I'll slap you into the New Jerusalem." Cat spit out.

"No need for all of that." Why did Cat speak so harshly to the child? Well, maybe for the same reason he had to speak to her just now. No need in letting her stay in her fairy tale world. Andie was going to grow up and be a Negro woman in the world, better get used to all of the harshness that life was about—sooner rather than later.

"Don't you tell me how to speak to my child, Mike James. A day late and a dollar short, coming up in here taking charge."

"Somebody got to. Somebody got to tell you, Cat. I have the right."

"Only because God above put you back into our lives. You wasn't looking to find us."

"You know this for sure?" Mike kept rubbing up the little girl's arm, applying pressure with his two thumbs ignoring the wincing looks on her little face too.

That seemed to shut her up. Anything to get her to stop her accusatory tone. He had his reasons. And he wasn't about to reveal them to her yet, until he gave her back her daughter—whole, complete, and uncrippled.

It was all he had to give her.

CHAPTER 6

*S*unday was the best day to go down to the nightclub and beg for her job back. Cat left behind a frowning Andie and an upbeat Mike so she could catch the slow Sunday trollies to go down to the Wonderland.

By the time she got there, it was near lunchtime and her stomach seemed to take on a life of its own. She never had to cook since she lived over the club, so she didn't have to buy food. She took part of her salary in the dinner the cooks made. The food was just palpable enough to eat so she could stay alive, but not lose her figure. Approaching the building from the alleyway, she knew well the sadness at losing her job. The emotion built up in her lower limbs, making them heavy and wooden with dread. All that lifted from her when she saw a familiar burnt orange couch being carried out by a strange man.

She ran.

Why were they taking her couch out of the apartment? Did losing her job mean losing her apartment as well?

"Stop that!"

The man holding the other end of the couch was her brother, Beansie.

"Beansie! What you all got my couch in the dirty alley for? I helped you get a job up in here and you taking my couch? "

Her skinny younger brother still looked eighteen, even though he was in in twenties like her. He gestured to the other guy to put down his end and he did. Cat did not recognize the other fellow. He had the nerve to look at her with his mouth gaping open like a fish. What was he staring at?

"You need to get my couch up out of these chitling entrails and take it back upstairs."

"Katie, you know nothing happen round here, but Miss Alice say so."

"She tell you to put my couch out?"

"They needing that apartment for the new singer. You didn't show up last night and you know what that means."

She knew. She had been there at the Wonderland for eleven years. A long, long run by any stretch of the imagination. Still, she had never thought it would end like this. "I was seeing to getting Andie set up in the home."

"I try to tell her that, but Miss Alice still say get this stuff out."

What had she ever done to anger the old woman? Well, Miss Alice wasn't that old, but she had thought of her as a second mother, when her own cast her to the side, and now this?

"New singer need the digs upstairs ma'am." The other guy gave her long, lascivious look of lust. "Your sister look more like Lena Horne than the new one do."

Well, what could she say to that? Thank you? That was the reason that Wonderland had hired her. She had been talented enough to pull it all off, she supposed, but the show was over now.

"Is she in there?"

"Counting up the week's receipts." The other guy pointed in the direction of the club's interior.

Cat stepped around them to see to Miss Alice, but Beansie pulled her arm. "How's Andie?"

"She's fine. I—Mike he works there. I couldn't believe when I saw him."

She would never forget the look on his face the longest day she lived.

"Well, Mama kill me for saying it, but we knew."

"You knew?"

Would her brother stop pulling down the world she knew bit by bit?

"Mama knew he was back in town. Knew he was on that side. You know how Pittsburgh is. You can lead a completely different life on one side of the river from the other."

"How long, Beansie?"

"How long what?"

"Don't act goofy. How long you know?"

"'Bout three-four years we knew. Mama don't want you with him. So, she tell us not to tell you."

The stench of rotting garbage in the hot August heat threatened to undo her. She swallowed hard. "I'ma deal with this later. I got to talk to Miss Alice first. Don't go anywhere. And put my couch back!"

Beansie told the guy to pull the couch end inside, but Cat didn't hear them taking it back upstairs. The power of Miss Alice was too strong. And Beansie needed his job here helping to run the club. All of those years, all of that time that he knew. Her closest relative and connection to Mama Bennett. What had she done to offend him?

Miss Alice sat at a table deep in the back corner of the room, where she had played for years and years. Day in and out except Mondays and Sundays. It all came crashing to an end. Seemed impossible, but what would happen for her now? She was—she gulped—thirty. What was there for her now?

"Miss Alice, may I have a word?"

"There you are, Katie. We was a bit worried about you."

"So worried you tell my brother to take my couch out to the alley?"

Miss Alice took the edge of her good Cross pen and stuck it in the edge of her pompadour. "I told him to pick a good clear spot and put the couch there. I knew you be coming back soon."

"Then you couldn't be so worried."

"Sit down Katie. You hungry? Got some roast chicken."

The hunger rumbling in her belly had disappeared completely in these new worries. She nodded and Miss Alice gestured to a young woman who was putting freshly ironed table cloths on the tables. The young woman had smooth cocoa-colored skin and avoided Katie's eyes as she followed Miss Alice's order to bring two plates of lunch for them.

"Lookahere Katie. My John, he's been wanting to go in a new direction for a while. The whole Lena Horne thing been getting a little old. When you didn't show up last night, it was like a sign from the Lord above. We can go in a new direction and you go on to a new life."

"You knew I had to get Andie into that home and it would take time."

"Did it work out?" Miss Alice had the nerve to look concerned.

"It did. But it took time. Since they don't take Negro children."

"How did you do it?"

"Mike, he…he worked there. Or maybe you knew that, too."

Miss Alice shook her head. "Andie's daddy? Well, that's something now isn't it?"

Cat still couldn't believe it herself. Pittsburgh was such a small village in so many ways.

"Well, see then. It works out. He helped you—high time he did. You deserve all the help with that child. It'll take time to help her get better and you won't have time for this club."

Miss Alice grasped her hand. "Look honey. We doing you a favor. Reason you singing in a club like this, is to find you a good man like I found John. You taking all this time, means other girls don't get no chance to find husbands for themselves."

The brown skinned girl put the plates down and went back to ironing the tablecloths.

Cat picked up a fork and started stabbing at the potatoes on the plate, willing herself to eat, but she couldn't hardly taste anything. The potatoes were a paste in her throat, threatening to shut off her voice for good.

Miss Alice didn't touch her plate, a reason she stayed a nice size despite her age. "It's time you were getting a father for Andie."

"I tried that last year, remember? And he beat on me."

"That don't mean you should give up. George was an idiot. Pretty woman like you, you still got looks a man could appreciate."

"I need a job, Miss Alice."

"You need to be married, sugar. Get yourself up out of this nightclub life. You need to be married and taken care of."

"Miss Alice, you work in the nightclub."

Miss Alice set down the tablet she was working with. "I'm here because this is John's club. I help my husband in what he do. You got to do the same. Both you and Andie get taken care of. That's what you deserve."

The chicken tasted like sawdust, but she needed her strength, so she ate it. How much more would God assault her? Mike, her brother, and now Miss Alice. How much more betrayal should she have to take in?

"I don't see it that way. I need a job to support us."

Miss Alice shook her head "The job is only to get you a husband to take care of yourself until the husband comes along. You already made one mistake. Don't compound it. You need a man with a lot of money to help you to take care of your crippled child."

"There's no need to insult Andie."

"What will happen on the other side of this Cat? You got to see reason. Look, we can hold onto some clothes for you in the upstairs closet, but you've got to move on. Why don't you go back to your mother in the meantime?"

"Miss Alice. You know I haven't spoken in her in years."

"Well, maybe it's time. Maybe it's us who's been keeping this hostility going and a family apart. Go on back to your mother and she'll help you until you find your husband."

Cat put her fork down. She had enough. For all sorts of reasons. She stood. "I'll make arrangements for a truck to get my stuff. Thank you for all of your help."

Miss Alice reached her hand out and although it galled Cat, she shook the older woman's wiry hand. "Let me count out a little to help you take care of Andie."

"I don't want any of your charity."

"Look, it's the least we can do to help. Call it leaving money."

Miss Andie counted out a hundred dollars and handed it to her. Cat took it. She wasn't no fool.

"Thank you."

"Go to your mother. Things are different now."

A hope surged in her heart. Did she dare think that for herself? Her mind went to Andie in her bed and Mike working on her ravaged limbs, working on her with patience and care. Was her life with her child now? Her head swirled as she took a last sip from a water glass on the table, and walked out of the club that had been her life for a third of the years she had lived on earth.

What would she do now?

CHAPTER 7

*F*irst thing. Buy a house.

Mike's mind wandered off after a busy day of tending to Andie especially. He watched everything the nurses did to help the other children and he would help her do her exercise on her braces. Still, after a child got out, she needed room and fresh air, not an apartment over a nightclub. Only a house would do that. He had a nice savings, since he was able to live in the home for the past three year. There had to be houses just down the hill in the Hill District—Pittsburgh's version of Harlem. Cat wouldn't mind living there.

He took another puff of a cigarette to relax him. He would work it out. What a difference just a little time made. A different man. And proud to be so. He had a purpose—something to look forward to.

But would Cat want it? What about the other Bennetts—especially that Mama?

A brisk cold river of fear washed over him and he took a deeper puff of his Chesterfield to help warm him. His fingers tingled as he remembered the one encounter he had with Cat's Mama.

It had been at church. The Bennetts practically held up an old church on the Northside of town—Allens A.M.E. Allens and the Bennetts had a deep long proud history of abolitionist tendencies. They had stepped out a few times, and Cat invited him to church one Saturday night.

Stepping foot into Allens people hovered over Mama Bennett's chair, seeing to every possible thing she wanted. A round, dumpy light skinned woman with sharp features, Mama Bennett looked like she might have been pretty at some point, but she wore a dress in a style that was from the Great Depression. The black dress washed her out, was too long and made of lace, but he guessed it was suitable for an older woman.

Cat asked him to sing with her on her solo, called "No Hiding Place but Jesus."

The entire church erupted into applause after the song and at the reception afterward, he helped himself to some rationed hard cookies. They were hard because they had no sugar in them. He overheard Mama talking to Cat.

"Let him go on back where he come from. You only twenty, you can do better than him."

"He deserves to be welcome to church like everyone else, besides, I was going to ask him to come to the house for dinner."

"No indeed, Katie. He don't need to be up in my house. Never had no one looking like him there, and won't start now."

The hard cookie dissolved to palpable mush in his mouth, but her words rang in his ears. He couldn't hear Cat's response, but Mama's next words hit hard.

"I don't have no cripples or darkies in my house. Ever."

Still, he put a mask on his face as if he was glad to meet her, but she kept her hands folded on her ancient purse in her lap. She would not shake his hand, as if the black would come off on her on her gold-colored skin.

He took a final drag on the cig. What had it been like for Andie to grow up in a house like that? Andie was as coal black as he was. With her body the way it was now….how could Cat hand off their child to someone like that?

A sleek car pulled up to the front doors of the home and he put the cigarette out. He approached the car to help the passengers out. Cat was inside, riding in style with a man.

Wasn't she fine coming up to the home where her daughter resided, in a car yet? The blood in his veins bubbled as if acid had just been pumped into him. How could Cat come driving up to the home as if butter wouldn't melt in her mouth?

His lips tight, he reached out to help her out. She had on a different dress this time, a black dress that was smaller in cut and didn't flare like the other brown one did. She had on a small hat was and a whisp of veiling stood up off it.

"Cat."

"Stop being so stiff, Mike. This is my brother if you remember him. Beansie."

He peered down into the car at the youngish looking man driving the car. "Nice to meet you."

"I remember you," Beansie said, his voice even.

Couldn't blame the guy. If he had met the man who left his sister in Dutch, he would punch him, so he was mighty lucky Beansie was too skinny and little to be the fighting type.

"You could park and come and see Andie." Cat yelled out to her brother.

"I'm afraid visiting hours are over, Cat." Mike informed her.

She reached in the back of the car and pulled out a small suitcase. Mike's heart leaped up. She meant to come. She meant to stay.

And then it sank in.

Because if she meant to come and stay, he would have to tell her about himself. The entire truth about himself.

"You want me to tell Mama anything?" Beansie yelled out to his sister.

"No. I don't have anything to say to her."

"Even though Miss Alice say to go to her?"

"Mind your own business, Beansie. Go on take this car back to Miss Alice. Tell her I'll arrange a truck to get my things."

They both stood in the doorway and watched the car go off into the August dusk.

"Why you need a truck?"

"I told you when I didn't show up last night they would fire me. They did and put me out of the apartment. I have tomorrow to get my things."

Something else to arrange. He had some idea about how to help her. The home had a large transport car and some space in the shed in the back.

He put an arm around her. "Cat, what was that talk about your mother?"

"They want me to go to her, tell her about Andie's care. Forget it. If she really cared about her granddaughter, she would have come down off of that hill and seen to her herself. I don't care what anyone says, I don't have to see her."

Mike squeezed her shoulders and hugged her to him. If he wanted to make a life with Mama Bennett's daughter and granddaughter, he had to make peace with her. And he wanted that life. More than anything right now.

Once he helped Cat up to his room and settled her in with Andie, who was wide awake, he went down to Mr. O's office.

"Can I speak to you about something?"

"Sure, Mike, what can I help you for?"

"Is there some room in the shed?"

"Haven't been out there for a while. Why?"

"Andie's mother, she lost her home. I need to have her in the room for a little bit longer. She's got to move her things quickly and she needs to put them somewhere else. For now."

"I don't see any problem with it. It's unfortunate. We're using every bit of equipment just now."

Mike knew that the home was filled with polio cases. If he hadn't offered up his own room for Andie, would she have been able to come for care?

"I know how it might appear, and I, well, I'm going to find a home for them, if I can have a few hours tomorrow."

"Are you planning to marry this woman, Mike?" Mr. O's smile spread across his face and he folded his arms.

"If she'll have me. I don't know that she will."

"You're a good man. Why wouldn't she?"

"I think you know. Woman wants a whole man. Not part of one."

Mr. O looked down at his trimmed nails and shuffled some papers. "I see. You're such a good man, we couldn't do without you around here. If she has a home, you might want to leave us."

Mike shook his head. "No. I want to help Andie and keep helping all of the other children here. Being here has given me some… purpose. I'll look close by here. In the Hill District. There'll be something for us there."

"Of course." Mr. O put the papers down. "And that isn't too far in case we do need you."

"Exactly." Mike warmed at the prospect of getting a home. When Andie got better, she could go to school and Cat could sing in one of the clubs in the Hill if she wanted to.

If she would have him.

Once he told her.

Everything.

Something grabbed him in his stomach.

It was enough to lose her once.

The answer was to convince her mother. If he could talk the old lady into forgiving her daughter, then maybe she would think everything was alright. He couldn't change his skin color. He couldn't change what happened to him in the war. But he could take care of his daughter. And his Cat. If she would have him.

Well, he was taking care of her right now. Caring for her made him feel mighty good as he made his way around the wards once more to check on his charges.

He whistled the song he and Cat had sung together in Allens A.M.E church. Nothing like a hymn on a Sunday.

CHAPTER 8

"*W*hy are you going house hunting?" Cat's question the next day came from pure curiosity.

"What's the reason people go house hunting? To get a house." Mike pulled back as he looked at her. She changed into a modest house dress, so that she didn't get peanut oil spots from Andie's massages on her black dress.

"What you need a house for?" Andie bit out.

"Well chocolate drop. I don't need a house. Your mother does. I'll take the van from the home and help pick up her things. We got storage space here back in the shed where you can put your things for a bit."

"Mike, all of that is wonderful. Thank you."

"Are you trying to marry my mother? Because if you are, you can stop it right now."

"Andie!" They both said at the same time and they laughed. It felt like bubbles to laugh for once over the past few weeks of trouble and heartache.

"I don't see what is so funny. You don't need to worry about getting married again, Mama. You had enough of that before, remember."

"Andie," Cat started out more gently, feeling funny under Mike's regard. "You're only nine years old. You don't need to be worried about these things. That's my job. I'm the adult."

Andie blinked faster. "Mama Bennett say you are going to hell in a handbasket anyway. It's your funeral."

Cat's hands balled up in a fist. What had she done to deserve her mother's harsh words come visited back on her in the form of this sick child? How much more would she be able to tolerate?

Mike put a hand on her fist. Their oily hands touched and a warm feeling came up her arm as if she were being massaged.

Mike scolded Andie, "Let grown folks do what they do. Sounding like your grandmother."

"Do you know Mama Bennett?"

"Not too well. Well, enough I suppose."

Cat couldn't help the smile that pulled at the corner of her mouth.

"Hey," Mike gestured to her, meeting her eyes. "I think we should go to see her."

The frozen feeling moved with lightning speed to her head and gave her a headache. "I don't think that's a good idea."

"I do. I want to tell her a few things. Will you do it?"

"You heard what Andie said, just now. Same thing applies to you."

Mike squeezed her hand. "I would die a happy man then."

He told her after they made sure Andie got her breakfast, they could go. A perfect time to get to the club, when it was quiet, to unload her things into the truck. She didn't have much, but still, it was all she had. She wasn't going to leave her things behind for some other heifer to have. She had worked far too hard.

So she was grateful. Yes, angry at Mike, but still, grateful that he was here now, driving the truck, ready to help her.

Miss Alice watched them pull up in the alley. "Good time to get here."

They weren't there to be helpful to her, but Cat kept that information to herself. Mr. John was there and he helped them to remove her things from the house. The most cumbersome items were her dresses, as some of them had many crinolines and were quite full, but they managed to get all of her clothes out, packing with relative ease.

Both the club owners seemed sad to see her go, and made repeated promises to come see Andie, but Cat's heart was hardened. She had thought of the nightclub owners as family. Now she could see that was a mistake. They were business people, making business decisions, just as she had made the decision to stay with her daughter that first night in the Home. So, when it was time to leave, there were no hugs, even though Cat could see they wanted to. Handshakes were fine.

"To see your mother?" Mike asked her when they reached the front seat of the van, ready to pull off.

Cat folded her hands. "She wrote me off when I was pregnant. I don't need to see her now."

"I need to see her."

"You won't be able to get up the hill in this van thing."

"I'll park it and we can walk the rest of the way."

Which is what Mike did. The city steps, embedded in the side of the hilly Pittsburgh terrain for ease of climbing, worked perfectly for them to climb up on. Still, Mike puffed up the stairs and despite herself, her heart tugged. What had happened to him in the war? He never said. Was he okay? Was he able to do all of these things for her and Andie? She had Miss Alice's one hundred bucks and a little more saved up. She could, she supposed, even if it the prospect made her curl her toes in her pumps.

They reached the top of the stairs and the Bennett home, which made the entire city of Pittsburgh at their feet. Cat loved this view. Sometimes, there was much to see, but not today on a hazy August morning.

"Ready?" Mike took her by her hand and somehow, her hands were still sticky, from sweat or peanut oil—she didn't know which.

"As I'll ever be."

Cat marched up to the door of her childhood home with confidence that she did not really have and knocked on the door. Her father answered the door and they embraced each other. Ten years did a lot to her father. He stooped a bit, but she was so glad to see him. Behind her back, as her father still held her, he shook Mike's hand.

"You don't know how I've longed for this day." Her father said to her.

"Mr. Bennett." Mike was respectful.

"We want to talk to Mama."

Her father pulled back from their embrace. "Maybe you can wait here. I'll bring her out, eh? How's that?"

"That will be fine, sir." Mike interjected.

Her father squeezed her hand and shut the door behind him.

"It's not fine by me." Cat pouted.

"It's August. A fine morning."

"Maybe, but it's having things the way she wants."

"You mean about not having any darkies or cripples in her house?" Mike tossed off to her and Cat turned her face to him, eyebrows pitched.

"How, how, did you know that?"

"I heard her saying it when I went with you to Allens AME. She meant for me to hear it, sweetheart."

Cat wanted to dive under something in embarrassment. "I'm so sorry."

Mike sat down on a metal chair covered in a thick rose point cushion. "At least I know where I stand with her."

"What do you want?"

Cat swirled around and faced her mother, standing, toe to toe. Mama was a little thinner than she might have expected, but the stern look of disappointment was still etched on her face.

"Far be it from me to think that you might want an update on your granddaughter." Cat pursed her lips.

"She got sick at your place. Picked up an illness from that den of sin you work at, no doubt."

Cat bit the skin of her lips. "I thought you might think that. Mike is the one who wanted to come. Remember him? The one you made everyone not say anything to me about? Andie's father?"

Mike stood to meet her. "Ma'am."

"Don't you ma'am me. You've done nothing but cause trouble here. It's why I don't like associating with your kind."

Her mother's boldness, took her breath away. Literally. For the second time in a few days, a lightheaded buzzing invaded her head, but Mike stepped forward and grabbed her by the waist.

"We don't want to stay long, ma'am. We just want to let you know. We'll be taking care of Andie from now on. You don't need to worry about her anymore."

"And what can you do for a child? After you abandoned my daughter?"

As if you didn't.

Cat couldn't stop the thought from invading her mind, but she didn't want to.

Mike kept on. "We'll be happy to have her visit her grandparents, but I'm purchasing a home for them both. If Cat will have me, I would be honored to live there as her husband, but if not, I fully intend to be in their lives."

The buzzing didn't stop. She turned around and stared Mike in the face.

Well, here it was. The very ending she wanted. The very thing she had dreamed of. He had come to save them, in all kinds of ways she hadn't expected. Yet, she didn't know exactly what to say.

Mama Bennett snorted. "Well, if she doesn't marry you, then she's no better than a prostitute."

What??? Did her mother never know where to stop? Mike's hold tightened about her.

"I was injured in the war. So I'm a cripple too." Mike bent down and lifted his pants' leg. The perfectly matched shoe held a leg of wood.

The growing horror was about to cut off the air in her lungs. When had that happened?

"So, I think Mr. Bennett's solution of meeting you on your lovely porch without having me, a darky and a cripple, step foot in your house is a perfect one. Thank you, sir."

Mike shifted his attention to her mother, glaring. "So, ma'am. You don't have to worry about having this darky darken your doorstep, ever. Literally. However, that goes for my daughter as well, given her dark skin color and her polio condition. You don't have to worry about seeing her ever again. She'll be well taken care of. I just wanted you to know. Cat, let's go."

Was she more shocked at his leg? Or at the way he just told off her mother? In the most respectful way possible? Maybe it was the stricken look on Mama Bennett's face. In her mother's face she saw pure love for her grandchild, reflected as pure terror as her eyes filled with tears.

She could never recall seeing Mama Bennett cry. Over anyone.

It almost made Cat feel sorry for her.

But now she knew what it was to be cast out.

Mike's hand held her up. Giving her the strength and permission to be held up. So she picked her way down her mother's front steps, down the city steps, with new strength to face the future and her heart filled with joy the further she went from her childhood home.

CHAPTER 9

*H*arder going down stairs than climbing up. Especially since the Pittsburgh city stairs were made of hard stone. The combination of the hot August day and the walk made the sweat pour down his face. He had thought he looked nice in his pressed beige pants and white shirtwaist with a tie, but by the time he got down to the bottom of the stairs and to the van, his shirt was soaked through to his undershirt with sweat.

"Are you alright?" Cat peered at him.

"This is exactly what I feared. When I told you about my leg, you would want to pity me instead of seeing me as a man."

"I'm not pitying you, I just want to know."

"It's pity."

He opened her door and went around to the other side, unbuttoning his shirt front as he did so and took off the wet shirt, stripping down to his undershirt.

Cat sat there with her hands folded in her lap, like a prim schoolteacher instead of the fiery throaty-voiced nightclub singer he knew.

"You acting like you seeing something new." Mike gripped the wheel. Couldn't a man even take off his shirt.

"Why are you talking to me this way?"

"I'm not talking to you in any way, Cat. I just. Listen. You never said anything about what I said back there."

"About?"

Have mercy. "I was talking about marriage back there."

She faced him, seeming ready to pounce. "You were talking to my mother. You never said anything to me."

"A man has to ask the parents now, right? That's what I was trying to do."

"Then the man had better come and ask me."

She rolled down the window on her side and he did as well. Just sitting there in the front part of the van, crammed full of her things, he supposed things were getting a bit close in there.

Why didn't she talk? Say what he wanted to hear.

She saw your leg. She don't want you.

There it was. The thing he had feared. Well, it was what he deserved. He left her on that train platform, crying. Never thought to write back to her, and he got injured. The oldest story of all time. And he understood from jump how her Mama was. She would never want him.

Now there was something different at stake though. Their little girl. He wasn't about to let anyone, not even Cat, treat that child as if she couldn't succeed. He said nothing and just started up the van and drove it slowly back to the Home.

"Do you need help?"

"Woman, if I needed your help, I would ask for it. Go inside where it is nice and cool, check on Andie and I'll take care of this here."

A hurt look crossed her face, but she stormed off into the inside, and went to wrangle with Sarah he supposed, before she went up to the room.

Mr. O came wandering out with his sleeves rolled up. "I've come to help, Mike."

"I know you got other things to do, now."

"Hey. A word of advice. Don't ever turn down help moving anything. There's a few fellows from the hotel next door who said they would help too."

"Why would anyone want to help us?"

"They know we're vets. We all have to help each other right?" Mr. O clapped him on the shoulder. "I'll be right back."

In a few minutes, Mr. O and the three hotel workers he brought with him had filled the shed with Cat's furniture and things instead of polio equipment. Soon, he hoped, the shed would be filled with polio equipment so that the children would be free of the terrible disease and Cat's furniture would be in a house of her own.

He would still be living here. Better than being homeless. Still, the thought of Cat living somewhere he wasn't made his stomach swirl. He promised he would take care of her. What was wrong?

You, you are what's wrong.

He wanted to hate Mama Bennett with everything that was in him, but that seemed foolish. As much of a fool as that woman was, she was a part of Cat and Andie. So, he couldn't hate her. No. Better to feel sorry for her. Because Mama Bennett was a fool.

So was he though. So, they had that in common, as much as she thought him an outcast.

He went to his room to get a new shirt and to let Cat know they were done unloading the van. He wanted to see if they could squeeze in some time to visit the real estate office in the Hill. They might not be able to look at anything today but at least they could let the agency know they were in the market for a home. Or he was. For her.

He owed her at least that much.

Still, when he reached his room and the bed was empty, the thudding began in his heart. He had been working in the Home for three years and he knew what that might mean. No. Mr. O had been out in the heat unloading furniture. How could anything happen to Andie and he wouldn't know it?

He grabbed a work shirt and took off his sweaty undershirt as he ran. But the sound of a popular song came from the recreation room. Cat and the children. Singing. Andie had to be with her, but how? How could she? He knew the rules of the Home. She was supposed to be in his room, not associating with the other children.

The rec room was on the third floor, so he had to go down stairs again. He opened the doorway to the stairs, following the golden throaty voice. He pushed open the doors to the rec room and every head, except Andie who was propped up in a bed, turned toward him. "Mike!" Several of the children shouted out to him.

He took time to greet each child with a touch or a ruffle of the hair, working his way back to Cat who sat next to Andie's bed with two nurses he knew. Cat finished the song and those who could, clapped. Cat clapped hard for those who couldn't, encouraging them.

She looked calm and fresh, as if they hadn't fussed in the van. Steady. Not afraid of the braces and illness that surrounded her.

"What's going on here?"

"Oh Mike." Mary Beth Kelly, one of the nurses, exploded. "We have had a lovely time getting to know your daughter and your future wife here. They are delightful."

"Really?" Mike folded his arms. He glowered at Andie. "You aren't talking about this child are you?"

"Of course they are." Andie burst out.

"What a darling child she is. A lovely voice to match her mother."

"And father," Rita Bauknight, the other nurse, put in. "How could Andie help but have a wonderful voice?"

"Truly. Even if she's a bit of a grouch."

Mary Beth waved a hand. "There's nothing wrong with her."

"I have polio," Andie chimed up.

"Well, that," Rita spoke out. "But we are going to work hard on that. Won't we?"

Andie actually smiled at the red-haired woman. Little minx. Like her mother. Cat stood up and went to him, reaching out her hand.

"We can look at houses tomorrow. I don't want you to get in trouble for too much time off."

Rita shook her head. "Mike's been our rock here at the Home. Imagine our delight in finding out he had you two. So close mouthed about it all."

Cat reached an arm around him. "Hard for him to know, when I didn't tell him. But we're going to make it good. Won't we, Mike?"

He swallowed hard. Overwhelmed by Cat's words, as well as the generosity of the two nurses, he didn't know what to say. He reached around and took Cat by her small waist. "We will. We're going to make it right. As soon as possible. If that's fine by you, chocolate drop."

Andie's eyes blinked very fast and she boomed out in her strong voice. "I want everyone to be nice to one another. That's all I ever wanted."

The thickness invaded his throat again and he reached over to her, patting down her braids and kissing her on her forehead. "Of course, sweet. Just because you want it, we'll all be nice to one another. Especially me and your mother."

The adults in the room laughed as did the children, who really didn't know what they were laughing at, but in their current condition, children always opted for laughter over tears.

"Cat, it was the worst day of my life when I left you. I'm sorry. I'll spend the rest of my life making it up to you."

A slow feline smile crept across her beautiful face. Then stopped. "I need time."

"I've got all the time in the world for you." He wrapped his arms around her neck, not minding the slow nervous laughter of the children or the shy laughs of Mary Beth and Rita. Everything he wanted was in this room, at arms-length. The sweetness of life had opened to him.

Finally.

ABOUT THE AUTHOR

Piper G Huguley, named 2015 Debut Author of the Year by Romance Slam Jam and Breakout Author of the Year by AAMBC, is a two-time Golden Heart ®finalist. and is the author of "Migrations of the Heart," a three-book series of historical romances set in the early 20th century featuring African American characters, published by Samhain Publishing. Book #1 in the series, A Virtuous Ruby, won Best Historical of 2015 in the Swirl Awards. Book #3 in the series, A Treasure of Gold, was named by Romance Novels in Color as a Best Book of 2015 and received 4 ½ stars from RT Magazine.

Huguley is also the author of the "Home to Milford College" series. The series follows the building of a college from its founding in 1866. On release, the prequel novella to the "Home to Milford College" series, The Lawyer's Luck, reached #1 Amazon Bestseller status on the African American Christian Fiction charts. Book #1 in the series, The Preacher's Promise was named a top ten Historical Romance in Publisher's Weekly by the esteemed historical romance author, Beverly Jenkins and received Honorable Mention in the Writer's Digest Contest of Self-Published e-books in 2015. A Champion's Heart was named by Sarah MacLean of The Washington Post as a best romance novel selection for December 2016.

Her contemporary romance debut, Sweet Tea, will be published by Hallmark Publishing in July 2021. Her historical fiction debut, By Design: the story of Ann Lowe, Society's Best Kept Secret, will be published by William Morrow in March 2022.

Piper Huguley blogs about the history behind her novels at http://piperhuguley.com. She lives in Atlanta, Georgia with her husband and son.

DIRTY DARE

A SLAYERS HOCKEY NOVELLA

MIRA LYN KELLY

CHAPTER 1

OFF-SEASON

TREVOR

"*S*ay it with me, little brother. No more jocks."

"No more jocks," I groan, turning left onto Old Wildren Road. Never again. And yeah, maybe I have a type, but whatever. I'll get over it.

The wooded country road twists and turns through another mile before splitting at the hand-painted sign for Little Lake Lane.

"Jesus, what am I doing back here?" My mom, sister, and I moved out of Wildren the summer after I graduated high school and started playing hockey for the Orators, Chicago's farm team down in Springfield. I loved it here, but after what happened when I left?

Maybe this was a mistake.

Tammy ignores the rhetorical part of the question and huffs.

"Getting out of Dodge so you don't have to spend the summer living in the same apartment with your cheating, asshole ex." She takes a bite of something crunchy, probably racing to get some food in her before the baby wakes up. "Retreating to a place where your life was simpler. I mean mostly. You know, except for *that*."

Right. That. Cameron Dorsey. The first jock.

First a lot of things.

"We're not talking about *that*." Ever.

She hums through the line. "You sure *that* isn't part of why you chose Wildren?"

Why I always crack and end up spilling my damn feelings to my sister I have no idea.

"Positive." It's ancient history, and if I had to guess, *that* is probably going to avoid me like the plague. *That* is probably married to a nice woman and has a nice life working in his nice family business just like he was always supposed to.

"Yeah, fuck *that*."

I grin. Okay, now I remember why. Two years older, Tammy's always had my back. And it's not like I've got anyone else to talk to about this stuff. No one else knows I'm a bi professional hockey player who, until a few months back, was in a relationship and living with a teammate for the better part of a year. A teammate whose professional jealousy and private insecurities drove him to betray me in a brutal way.

More crunching sounds through the car speaker, and then I hear the tiny squawk of my new nephew waking up from a nap. The crunching gets faster. Tammy gulps. "Anyone know you're back?"

"Not before today." I'd been planning to lay low. Hide out in the cabin on the lake and decompress after the roller coaster season I've had.

Figured when I ducked into the Sew Shoppe to pick up the keys my old athletic director left me, no one would remember the kid who only lived here a few years. But that's not how small towns work. "Cora Michaels was working. She says hi. Also, Danny Nobbs just bought his first house. Party tonight. Found out your ex, Tino, got Crystal Miller *and* Nora Jacobs pregnant three weeks apart—"

"Douche!"

I laugh. "Right? And I'm invited to dinner at my old English teacher's place next week."

"Not bad for a just-rolling-into-town, Trev."

"Guess not."

"I've got to go, little brother. Good luck getting all that peace and quiet you were after up there. And good luck with… *that* other thing too."

Not going to be an issue. "Love you, Sis."

I end the call and let myself *feel* being back here. Four years since I drove this road, and my heart's pounding like I'm eighteen again, heading to the party of the year. Only as my pickup rolls down the quarter mile of crushed gravel drive in dire need of grading, I know the place I'm heading isn't the same.

Last time I was here, we'd just graduated, and Finch, the athletic director at the time, was having his annual end-of-year bash.

All the varsity players from all the sports throughout the year were invited to his cabin for a barbecue dinner, swimming, and a bonfire at his beach. It was tradition, but with each subsequent year, he got more hands-off. My year… and as it turned out, his last in the role of athletic director, the man handed me the keys to his place about six p.m. and headed back to his house in town, leaving the cabin in the hands of the kids he knew would take care of it the way he'd taken care of us.

That night, everything changed. All it took was one dare, a joke that the two captains kiss, and this low, simmering thing in my belly turned to a boil. Cam blew it off like the pro he was. Didn't bat an eye. Didn't bother with more than a snort before taking off to use the head. But me?

Not cool. Because in a wink, I could see it. Me kissing Cam. The guy I was always drawn to in a way that was different than with my other friends and who more than once left me wondering if I wanted to get closer or push him away.

I could see it. And I liked the look of it so damn much that I had to make some bullshit excuse about getting a swim in to cool off before anyone noticed the way my body was responding.

I dove straight into the lake and swam my ass out to the far side of the floating dock, where I hung off the back side, shaking. Asking myself what the hell was happening inside my head.

Within a minute, I heard the *lap, lap, lap* of someone swimming out. And then he was there, powerful legs treading in place. The defined muscles of his arms and shoulders even broader than mine bunching and flexing as he slicked his hair back from those serious, soulful eyes.

And, *yeah.*

Sigh.

Now, I'm the only one here. From the looks of it, maybe I'm the only one who's been here since Finch broke his hip down in Florida two years back and decided to stay. The property's overgrown. The cabin's in need of repairs. And maybe it's exactly what I need. Maybe seeing this place looking nothing like the way I remember it is just the thing to get my head on straight before next season starts.

CAM

I'm running a sales report at the counter when the antique bell above the door sounds, signaling a customer. Or in this case, not a customer but my buddy Neil Watson. "Yo, Cam. You coming to Danny's tonight?"

I hate being the one who always says no to a party, but between work and water polo, more often than not, that's the way of it.

"Got practice, man. Say hi to everyone."

For anyone else, that would be the end of it. But Neil's that life-long friend whose default setting is *all drama, all the time*. Sure enough, his head drops, and he heaves an exaggerated breath before stepping completely into the store.

It's close to closing, so we're empty, and I've got time. But even if we weren't, it wouldn't stop him.

I close the laptop and round the counter to meet him by the fishing equipment where he will inevitably mix a couple reels of twenty-pound line in with the thirty.

"Hey, how'd it go with Judy last night?" He's been trying to date this girl since the third grade, but she's been in an epic on-again, off-again relationship with Harvey Pauls the whole time. At least up until a month ago when she swore it was over for good.

Neil grins. "Come to the party and see for yourself."

"So, the answer is good enough that she's letting you take her out again. Way to go, man."

"I'm not actually taking her." He shrugs. "She's already going with her sister. But we'll see each other there."

Uh-oh. My Spidey senses start to tingle. "Neil."

He shakes his head. "I know what you're thinking, but she's not stringing me along."

Yep. He knows exactly what I'm thinking. "I don't think she's doing it on purpose."

God help me if I suggest Neil's perfect angel might not be quite as perfect as his big, open heart wants to believe.

"Is she still talking with Harvey? Seeing him?"

It's the question Neil never wants me to ask. But I gotta. If for no other reason than to keep him from getting his head so far in the clouds that when he inevitably falls, it isn't quite so bad.

"Fuck you, man." He shoves a hand through his hair and walks farther down the aisle where he picks up a net and looks me in the eye... and then pointedly puts it back in the wrong spot.

Fucker.

But now I feel like a dick. "Hey, I'm sorry. I just don't want to see you get hurt." Again.

I know what heartbreak feels like, and watching my oldest friend race toward it scares the shit out of me.

He nods. Shakes his head. Then turns and socks me on the

shoulder to show we're good. "Fine. Make it up to me. Come to the party. See how it is with Judy. And who knows, maybe you'll even score some tail yourself."

Right. That's not gonna happen, and we both know it. "Look, I can't miss practice. I'm the captain, and we've got a match on Tuesday." I take the net and move it back to where it belongs. Wipe a smudge from the shelf and try not to think about Neil, alone, watching the girl he loves making up with her ex.

Shit.

"But how about I come by after."

CHAPTER 2

TREVOR

*a*n hour into the party, and I'm reeling. I knew it would be weird coming back and seeing everyone I went to high school with looking and acting more like grown adults than the kids they were when I left. What I wasn't expecting were all the ways it's the same.

Kelsey Pinsky is still hanging on Jerry Noble's arm, only instead of his class ring on her hand, it's a modest diamond.

Sue Humphries still has the most contagious laugh around.

Bill Waller and Dex Leighton are still manning the bar, but instead of the six-packs they sported when they played football, the guys look like they swallowed a pony keg apiece.

Gail Woo and Mary Trayner are still the go-to source for all things gossip around the lakes. A responsibility they take seriously, as evidenced by the way they cornered me the second I walked into Danny's small bungalow with the "Sold" sign still on the lawn.

"But it's just you? No family or girlfriend in tow?" Gail asks, not even bothering to disguise the fishing expedition.

"Nah, but Tammy's married with a baby down in Illinois. She's about halfway between Springfield and Chicago, and my mom has a place in the town over."

The women exchange a patient look, and Mary changes tactics.

"Are you going to be playing with the Slayers again this season? I bet you don't clear three games before the females start swarming."

They already are. But even two states away and surrounded by the people I spent a good chunk of my teens with, I'm not comfortable sharing all the reasons why I'm not interested... or even the most significant one.

Ironic, considering four years ago I was a stone's throw from laying it all out there for the world to see.

One night, and I thought that was it, I'd found what I was looking for, that missing piece.

One week, and I was ready to change my life.

Two, and it was over. After being ready to tell everyone, I blew out of town without a single soul knowing.

Hell, it's not like I'm besties with these women. I don't need to open up my soul to them. But yeah, there's this itch to go back to that time when I was ready to take the leap with both feet and just embrace who I was. Tell my friends that while I'm not dating now, until two months ago, I was in a serious relationship with a man I thought I loved.

Thing is, I'm so used to protecting Leo's secret that even all these months later and with everything that happened, I'm afraid that sharing my own might shine a spotlight on him.

At some point, I'm going to have to figure it out, but as of now, Leo's fear of people connecting the dots between us is enough for me to keep my heart to myself.

I take a swallow of my beer and search the crowd. Cataloging names and faces, I'm painfully aware of the one I haven't seen yet.

Gail must notice I've checked out and says, "Forget all that." Only, if I think I'm getting sprung from talk of my love life, I'm wrong. "Who knows, maybe you'll find a happily ever after right here in your hometown."

She juts her chin toward the front door, and I nearly choke.

Because that's Cam Dorsey holding it open. And holy hell, he looks good.

But once my brain slingshots back from taking inventory of the shoulders that somehow look even broader than they did when he was captain of the swim team, and the chest so built it ought to come with a hard hat warning... I realize Gail isn't pointing to Cam at all.

She's pointing to Laura Jansen, and the ridiculous flutter of nerves in my gut shifts into something uneasy.

"Laura's back, huh?" She was one of the few people I kept in touch with when I left. Or rather she kept in touch with me for a while.

"Uh-huh. And a little birdie told me she's excited to see you too."

Excited?

Laura is a great person. A sweetheart. I should be pumped to see her.

But there's a history between us. A will-they, won't-they past I was hoping four years apart would close the book on. But the gleam in Gail's eyes tells me she's hoping for a reunion on par with *Bennifer 2.0,* and that is not happening.

I look back to the door where Laura's giving Cam a big hug. Both are smiling wide.

It shouldn't make me jealous. It's *nuts* to be jealous, but seeing those two so natural and easy together when it won't be that way with me— for either of them —sucks.

Especially since one of them is the reason nothing happened with the other.

"Geez, stare any harder?" Gail sings as Mary nods enthusiastically beside her. "Trust me, there's *nothing* between Laura and Cam. I know you've been gone a while, but—"

"Gulls, man, no way!" a gruff voice bellows, catching the attention of most of the party. One of the guys from the hockey team, I think, but my focus is still riveted to the front door. To the former state champ with the still-damp hair, standing inches taller than anyone in the place.

Cam's head snaps up, his brows buckling as our eyes meet across the room. And yeah, that look is not screaming happy to see me. Figured he wouldn't be. I'm the asshole who knows his secret. But then he knows mine too.

Still stings.

Before I can even acknowledge him, a couple burly, inked-up arms wrap around me from behind, hoisting me off my feet. "Gulls!"

"There's only one fucker big enough to throw me around." I laugh past my constricted lungs.

"Just sweepin' you off your feet, Princess." Chase Caminski guffaws, setting me back on the ground and then hauling me into a bear hug.

"Chase, good to see you, man." The guy's been working construction and somehow managed to double in muscle mass over the past four years. "What the hell has Sandy been feeding you?"

I intentionally use his mother's first name, falling back on the teasing we used to give him about his being the hottest mom on the hockey team. "She still talk about me much?"

Rubbing a hand over his grin, he gives me a slow shake of his ash blond head. If we were sharing ice, I'd have all but guaranteed myself a trip into the boards for that one. Worth it, though.

We catch up a while, me doing my damnedest not to let on that I'm tracking a certain swimmer's every step, smile, and interaction. Waiting to see if he's tracking me.

Spoiler alert: he's not.

More guys from the team get in on the conversation. And damn, I'm surprised how much it feels like coming home.

Of course, Wildren isn't home.

It's a town I left years ago. It's nice to visit. But there's no going back to what this place was to me. Or even what it might have been.

Chase is still giving me a play-by-play of the Wildren high hockey highlights from last season when a head of light curls ducks under my arm and I'm caught in the feminine squeeze of Laura's hold.

"Trevor, what in the world!"

"Hey, thought that was you coming in," I say, hugging her back.

Chase juts his chin at me, flashing a wink before signaling to the group that they're all going for a beer and will be back in a few.

Wow. Not awkward at all.

"Congrats on graduation." I take a step back, still smiling. "What was it, accounting?"

Her eyes light up as she squeezes me again. "Holy buckets, I can't believe you remembered that! Or that I ever thought accounting was for me. I switched to early childhood education."

"A teacher? That's awesome, Laura. You got a gig lined up or still feeling things out?"

She laughs and rests a hand on my chest as she peers up at me like I just climbed a tree to rescue a kitten. "Same Trevor. Such a sweetie. I've actually got an offer for a full-time position in the fall over in Carver."

"Nice. Must feel good knowing you've got a spot." Not that I'm jealous. The fact that I don't know where I'll be is good. It means I've still got a shot at moving up. Playing between the Orators and Slayers is a good thing... even if it feels like there's no place I actually fit.

"Yes. I'm lucky." She wags her head. "I am."

There's obviously something else. "But?"

"But Carver's three towns over." She scrunches up her nose in that cute way she's always had. "I went to college thirty minutes from home. I don't know, I guess there's a part of me that feels like it might be fun to broaden my horizons some. Have a bit more *adventure*. Excitement. You know?"

"Sure. I get that." I also get that her hand is still on my chest and there's something in this prolonged eye contact that's conveying she wouldn't mind if that adventure happened with me.

Again I find myself searching out Cam. His dark hair still has that perpetually tousled look to it. His nose is still straight. And I'm guessing he isn't a guy looking for some adventure and excitement, because he hasn't even glanced over here since he walked in.

There's no ring on his finger— that I can see, anyway.

He came alone. Not that it matters.

Laura gives me a nudge and asks, "Right?"

Shit. She was talking.

"Sorry, Laura. Been a long day of driving. What were you asking?"

She laughs like it's funny instead of putting me on blast like I deserve. The least I can do is pay attention to what this woman— *this friend* —I haven't seen in forever is saying.

"No, nothing... I'm so sorry. I didn't realize you got here today! Uff-da. Are you even up for all these people tonight?"

She's sorry?

"I—"

"If you're wiped, I could drive you home." She bites the corner of her lip, peering up at me through her lashes. "We could have a beer. Talk and catch up somewhere... private?"

Ehh, shit.

CAM

For four years I've been wondering whether I made a mistake. If I should have trusted in something that felt like it was too good to be true instead of running away like the scared kid that I was.

A handful of times I've broken down over the years and scoured the Internet for any hint that Trevor Gulbrandsen's arrow might not be shooting quite as straight as everyone assumed... but I've never seen even a hint of him following through on that promise he made me out on the lake.

He said he wasn't scared.

That he didn't need to hide.

I know there have been women. I'm not proud of the sites I had to log into to find out, but even playing primarily on the farm team, Trevor draws enough attention to have some of his more casual encounters show up on the boards.

Not a lot. Hell, there were only three that I found, and they were all women without even a whisper of men.

But in case that wasn't enough, seeing Laura Jansen tucked up under Trevor's arm, her tits mushed against his side, and this epic eye-lock they have going clears it up for me.

I swallow hard and force my eyes back to Neil and Judy.

At least someone didn't get blindsided tonight. Judy might have shown up separately, but since I got here, she hasn't taken her eyes off my buddy once. And despite having been in love with this girl and captain of the SIMP squad for most of his life... he's not actually drooling or trying to snip a lock of her hair or doing any of the thousand desperate things I wouldn't put past the sad sap. He's just... having fun.

Something I'm not about to get in the way of just because I can barely fucking breathe knowing that Trevor is back in town. "Hey, man, thanks for getting me out tonight, but I'm beat. Are you cool if I take off?"

He legit can barely peel his eyes off Judy when he clears me to bail. It puts a smile on my face that holds up until I get to my truck. It's old enough it still needs a key to start and doesn't connect to a phone or any other device, but it's reliable and gets me where I'm going. While I wait for the engine to warm up, I look back to the house. And, just my luck, through the bay window, I see Trevor bow his head down to Laura's.

A proposition for her ears only? She tilts her head back and smiles before taking his hand and guiding him toward the door.

CHAPTER 3

CAM

J shouldn't be swimming in the lake tonight. My body was spent after practice, but after the party and seeing Trevor? The rhythmic cut of my arms through the water, more meditation than exercise, is all that's keeping me sane.

For all these years, I just sort of liked to think of Trevor as *out there*. A *maybe*. And tonight he went from a rare fantasy I try not to indulge in… to a hard *no*.

Because he's back, but he didn't call. He didn't reach out or stop by the store.

He didn't do anything but show up and put a smile on the face of a girl who has been waiting for him forever. So, good for her. Good for them.

My arms pull through the cool lake, my breath drawing every third burning stroke.

It doesn't matter that he's back. It doesn't change anything.

I swim through the darkness, listening to the water and my breath, the sounds of being inside my head.

Breathe, two, three. Breathe, two, three. Breathe, two, three.

Keeping an eye on the shore, I watch for Outlook Rock and then follow the inlet that wouldn't be visible without the light of the full moon. The water changes, calming, and I look up to find the ten square feet of floating dock that is my turning-around point.

In the mornings, I circle it once and head straight home, but tonight? Hell, apparently, I haven't had enough torture. So instead, I plant my hands on the weather-worn boards and propel myself up—

"Fucking wha—"

The startled shout followed by the rocking of the raft have me splashing back into the water mid-breath. I come up hacking so hard I'm probably only catching about a third of the profanities spilling from above in a stream so steady, my next cough turns into a laugh as I push my goggles off and try to choke out an apology.

"Jesus, *Cam?*"

Meaty shoulders and a head in silhouette come into view as a muscular arm thrusts out, locking with mine.

It's not him. It can't be him. Not here.

Except I know the deep timbre of that voice. And while the blond is muted by the night, there's something as familiar about the way the overlong mess falls around those heavy cheekbones as what's happening in my chest.

"Trev?"

That head above me starts a slow, disbelieving shake. "Holy shit, man, you scared ten fucking years off my life."

And before I can think too much about it, the grip on my forearm tightens, and Trevor hauls me up onto the platform like I'm some ninety-pound, top-of-the-pyramid cheerleader instead of six-foot-four of reasonably solid dude. It's nuts.

My ass hits the wood, and the balmy night air warms my skin.

I take a breath and man up, forcing myself to wipe the lake from my eyes and look back to see who else is on this derelict swim dock I've always thought of as mine, or *ours.*

Only there's no girl trying to keep decent, just the man who got away, standing a few feet back... looking more than a little uneasy.

Shit. "Hey, sorry, man. I didn't know anyone was out here."

What the hell is he doing here?

But then, I glance up at the house and see what I missed swimming in. The warm glow of lights cutting through the trees of a property that, to the best of my knowledge, has been unoccupied for the last two years.

"I— I rented it from Finch for a month this summer." He lets out a strained laugh and takes a step closer, which still leaves half a dozen feet between us.

"Cool. That's great." I grip the back of my neck, hating the way every awkward second is systematically stripping away a memory so precious to me, I can barely breathe through it. "Let me get out of your way, here." I swallow. "Now that I know you're here, I'll swim in the other direction."

I slide my feet over the side, the cool water doing little to ease the burn of too many things within me. I'm about to drop back into the lake when a warm hand meets my shoulder before abruptly pulling back.

"You don't have to go. Yet. I mean, you could hang out. Catch up a little." He takes a quick breath that has me slowly turning around. "Didn't get a chance to talk to you at the party."

Resisting the urge to ask what happened with Laura, I shrug. "Too many people for me after a long day."

He clears his throat and steps closer, and I swear there's a shift in the air around us. He gestures to my right. "Mind if I?"

"It's your dock," I say, aiming for light, but my nerves make it come off kind of dickish. So I quickly add, "But yeah. Take a load off."

There's a glint of his teeth like maybe he's smiling, and then that big hockey body that is definitely bigger than it was the last time I saw it— touched it —drops down beside me, leaving an ambiguous space between us.

It's not close enough to touch. Not a come-on, that's for sure. But not so far it feels like he's making a point either. He's just there, a few inches away, on the dock where we had our first kiss four— or maybe four *million* —years ago.

And that's got to be why he wants me to stay.

This spot is *private*. Safe. It's the perfect place for a pro athlete with a career on the rise to ask if I'd mind keeping that one time he dipped a toe into the rainbow under wraps.

When he opens his mouth though, it's not to beg for the privacy I'd give him whether he asked for it or not.

TREVOR

"How've you been, man?" I ask, going for casual like my heart isn't still giving me the Shake Weight treatment, and I wasn't just lying here asking myself if I'd made a monumental mistake coming back.

God, he looks good.

Like some kind of aquatic god with lake water running in rivulets from his hair. Poseidon... if he were twenty-two and wearing a criminally hot, thigh-cut Speedo with a pair of clear goggles clutched in his fist.

He also looks a little confused, like he might have been expecting me to say something else. But what are you supposed to say to the first guy who blew your mind and changed your life forever... then told you goodbye?

No idea, man.

But I try again, because he's here. Swimming right out of my damn thoughts.

And self-destructive or not, I don't want him to go.

"Heard you're still working with your dad." Yeah, I might have asked when I realized he'd left the party while I was letting Laura down in private. "You happy?"

He takes a beat and then relaxes into the question, leaning back on those straight, powerful arms.

"Yeah, I am. To both questions. I actually spent two years at the U and then moved to an online program when my dad needed a surgery."

"Oh damn, how's he doing?"

"It took him a while to get up to speed after, but he's good now, thanks. And he's got a shiny new hip out of it that we're hoping will last him through the back nine."

There's no bitterness in the way Cam says it, so I mean it when I tell him I'm glad to hear it.

I know he's close to his dad. Four years ago, protecting that relationship meant more to him than the freedom to be who he was. And, judging from the tone of his voice, there aren't any hard feelings.

No regrets. Not from his side anyway.

Me?

Hell, I'm just trying not to notice the moonlight contouring the lines of Cam's well-defined body in shades of silver and blue. Or how low his suit sits on his hips. How being this close to him settles something inside me, even while it turns so many other things upside down.

But Cam made it clear before I left, there wasn't room for *us* in his life. And so far as I can tell, he's good with how things have turned out.

So what am I doing here, practically begging this guy who just accidentally swam back into my life to stay a few more minutes?

I might have an idea, but before I can think too much about it, he juts his chin at me.

"I've gotta ask. What brings you back here?"

Makes sense he'd want to know. It's not like my roots run deep. We only lived here about five years, and while they were good ones, when I left to play hockey, Mom and Tammy followed.

"When I was playing in Springfield, didn't really mind sticking

around during the off-season. I had friends, a roommate." A relationship. "But uh… when I started getting called up"— I shake my
head, hating that I still feel it in my chest — "There was some jealousy. Lost some friends over it."

"Trev, I'm sorry."

I shrug. "Roommate was one of them. And until I know for sure
where I'll be starting the season— Chicago or Springfield —doesn't
make sense to find another place down south just yet."

"Crazy life," he mutters, staring out at the lake.

I nod. "Guess I had a lot of good memories here. One night last
month, my sister found Finch on Facebook, and everything kind of
came together from there."

"So you might be playing for Chicago now?" He turns, square
jaw resting on his shoulder. "Like a permanent thing?"

Wouldn't that be nice. "Not quite. Training camp plays into
things. But it sounds like management liked how I played while
Boomer was on IR. Enough that my agent's saying they might want
to try me for a couple games in Chicago, just to see. Doesn't mean
I'll stay there."

"Doesn't mean you won't," he says, like he knows something I
don't.

"True. Still. Lots of question marks." And no end to them in
sight.

Cam takes a deep breath. Even in the darkness, there's something thoughtful in the slope of his shoulders and angle of his head.
"It's got to be rough having so much uncertainty."

"Yeah, but I get to play." Damn, I need to stop staring. "And that
makes it worth it."

A smile. "Ah… the trade-offs."

"Always, right?" I expect him to chime in with a hearty agree-
ment, because if anyone should get it, I imagine it's him.

"Sorry about your friends, man. Sounds like you're better off
without them. But even so, that's bullshit and it's gotta suck."

I laugh. "That it does."

In ways I'm afraid to talk to even him about.

Instead, I ask about our friends from high school, wanting to hear the same updates I already got at the party, but in his words. His rich voice. I ask about the store and school and swimming, which is now water polo for him. I ask the polite questions old friends ask, skimming the moonlit surface between our lives without delving into the inky waters below.

Without telling him the things that really matter to me or asking him the same. Things like whether he's found love or if he ever thought about me the way I've thought about him. Because I don't want to risk crossing a line with Cam that might make him shut me out again.

We end up laughing about the time Randy Harris smuggled his new puppy into school and how all the teams came together to hide him.

"Football, band, chess, and debate." He's got that one arched-brow thing going, and combined with his crooked smile, it's taking everything I've got not to lean in and touch him. "Hockey, newspaper, and swimming. I don't even know who coordinated the effort, but we had that puppy daycare running out of the west bathroom for the better part of a week."

"Pretty sure we got busted on day three. Sylvia Cortez was allergic and had to go to the nurse with asthma and hives."

He snorts. "She married one of the Lacher brothers. Baby number three is on the way."

I let out a whistle. "Three? Jesus. I can't even commit to a dog."

He laughs and then slowly, the laughter fades into a silence that stretches and pulls at this thing between us.

This thing I know better than to give in to.

Him too.

"It's getting late." He leans back and rocks up to stand.

Shit, shit, shit.

He stretches out his shoulders beneath the moonlight, powerful arms swinging in a few mesmerizing arcs. "See you around, yeah?"

I get to my feet and nod too, looking away so I don't stare at his flawless body.

God, his ass in that suit.

He doesn't hesitate, just takes a couple fluid steps and does a shallow dive before popping up. I need to stop him. Say something.

"Hey, Cam."

He rolls to his back to face me, arms barely moving at the surface.

"I won't—" I clear my throat and try again. I can't let him worry about me outing him. "You know, I won't say anything about what happened with us. That last summer." It's too dark to read his features, but I— Shit, maybe I shouldn't have mentioned it at all. "Cam?"

"Yeah, I wasn't worried. But I won't either." He's pulling away, his arms slicing back overhead, one and then the other. "Not that it would make a difference if you did. Everyone knows I'm gay."

The dock rocks, or maybe it's just me. But suddenly my chest is doing something almost violent. "Wait, what?"

He stops with a short laugh, holding up a hand, because I'm balanced at the edge, a breath away from diving in after him.

"Whoa, Trev. Settle. Don't worry. You're secret's safe with me, man. Always was. Always will be." And he's on the move. One stroke, two, and then without breaking his rhythm, he rolls onto his stomach and swims off into the darkness.

CHAPTER 4

CAM

*R*unning my hands over my face, I listen to the chime of my phone alarm gently increase in volume. I don't want to get up.

I don't want to start another day knowing that Trevor is back in town. I don't want to be looking for him around every corner, thinking I see him in every crowd, and if it actually is him, making sure no one picks up on that weirdly intense vibe between us.

But most of all, I don't want to get caught in the same whirlpool of regret I lived in when he left after high school.

Because I had my chance.

He'd taken my hand that last day while the moving truck emptied the house he lived in with his mom and sister, and told me he was all in. That we didn't have to hide. Trevor wanted me. And anyone who didn't like it could screw off.

I'd thought about my dad. The store. Everyone I knew and the life I was terrified to lose... and then I told him I couldn't. I wouldn't.

The big, tough captain of the hockey team stood before me with tears in his beautiful blue eyes and begged me to change my mind. To give us a chance. He swore no one had to know. That if I wasn't ready, we could keep it a secret. He'd stay. Get a job. That we could find a way.

I wanted him. But I wasn't ready. I'd been too scared to trust. Him. Myself. The people I loved most in this world.

Turns out, most of my friends and family were pretty awesome when I told them.

But Trev? Okay, who knows what would have happened if I'd said yes that last night instead of getting in my truck and driving straight through until morning so there was no way I could get back before he left.

Maybe if I'd given us a chance, he would have been all in the way he promised. Or maybe he would have realized within a few hours or days that we weren't worth risking his dreams over—

Fuck. I press the heels of my hands against my eyes and rub.

This kind of speculation is exactly what I don't want to start my damn day with.

My life is good. It's everything I said I wanted. And his life just keeps getting better. I've seen him play. No way are the Slayers sending him back down.

And he's not out.

It's that simple.

All I need to do is stay away from him and both our lives will keep on going just the way we want them to.

Easy. Last night was a moment of weakness. Okay, more like two hours of weakness. Followed by another of sitting in the dark, watching all the Internet clips of Trevor I could find on my laptop.

I throw my legs out of bed, stretch the muscles that got twice their anticipated workout yesterday, and get ready for work. I'm already running late, so there's no time for coffee or breakfast, only a record-breaking shower before heading to the store.

I'm making a bigger deal of him being back than I need to.

Seriously, I need to turn my focus back to the here and now. The town I love. The natural beauty that is literally surrounding me with the deep woods and a lush canopy of maples, cedar, balsams, and birch so thick the warm, golden sun can only sneak through for a peek here and—

What the hell?

I slow as I approach the completely jacked hottie jogging shirt-less up my road. The man who isn't a permanent fixture in this landscape but fits in like he never left.

Trev's wide smile is directed at me. He waves and starts to walk, pushing thick fingers through a mess of untamed blond waves I really shouldn't be thinking about getting my fingers into. Sweat drips down the hard-packed terrain of his chest and layered abs, soaking into a pair of gray sport shorts that don't leave nearly enough to the imagination.

And as if all that mouthwatering hotness isn't torture enough, *he hasn't shaved.* And this man's morning-after stubble glinting in the early sun is like my personal Kryptonite.

I should keep driving, flash a smile, and roll right past. But glutton for punishment that I am, I pull to a stop beside him and lean out my open window with a grin. "I don't see you once in four years, and now this is three times in twenty-four hours. We've got to stop meeting like this."

For a minute, he looks like he's going to say something, but instead he takes a few seconds to catch his breath as he looks around. Then, "Pretty up through here."

"Yeah, it is." Even more so with him around for the next month.

"You a runner?" he asks with a jut of his chin, those blue eyes coming back to mine.

Only from you.

I grip the back of my neck, reminding myself not to get excited. It's not like he was going to ask me along or something. "Not really. I get my cardio in the pool."

"And lake." A dimple pops in his cheek, and suddenly I've got to shift in my seat.

Were these jeans so tight this morning?

"And the lake," I agree with a laugh that feels like it comes from some deeper place inside me than I knew I had. "I'm not much for land sports."

"Yeah." He scrubs a wide hand over that rough-cut jaw, and holy shit, the way he's looking at me, those hot eyes dragging from my eyes to my hair to my mouth... my chest.

It's almost like— No, that can't be right.

I swallow hard, looking at the steering wheel, the side mirror. Him.

Get it together, man.

"Seriously, though, aren't you supposed to be on break? I slept in to the last possible second this morning, forgoing my shot at a decent cup of coffee so I could get an extra ten minutes." And then I remember that I'm on my way to work. "*Oh shit!* I really did over-sleep. I've gotta go, or I'm going to be late."

Trevor steps back from the car with a grin. "Not on my watch. Get out of here."

Taking my foot off the break, I start to roll. "Have a good run."

He shrugs. "Basically done. Just saw you swim off this way last night and was curious where your place was."

It takes a second, but then the truck jerks to a stop with an embarrassing screech. "You were looking for me?"

That fucking smile. "Don't you have somewhere you're supposed to be?"

TREVOR

What the hell am I doing? Last week, I would have sworn the only reason I came back here was to hide out from the world and be alone. Now?

One glimpse of Cam and my heart started in on the aerobics.

A couple hours of talking, and all the plans I thought were rock-solid suddenly feel rocky instead.

A few minutes this morning and— well, no turning back now.

I shoulder through the front door of Dorsey Outfitters, looking up when an old-fashioned bell sounds above my head and then taking in the rest of the store with a growing sense of unease.

Not what I was expecting.

In all the time I lived in Wildren, I never had a reason to come in here. My mom didn't hunt or fish, so it wasn't how I grew up. All my time went to hockey. And while Cam worked here, we weren't the kind of friends where I'd show up at his job to hang out or make plans. So I'm not prepared for the sheer size of the place, the warm, lodge-like atmosphere, or that, thirty minutes after opening, it's already hopping.

But apparently Dorsey's is where the senior sect hangs out.

There are no less than a dozen old-timers ranging in age from I'm guessing sixty to ninety. They're parked on long couches watching some bass fishing program like the last episode of *Pam & Tommy* just dropped. They're pouring refills at a coffee station with a tray of mismatched ceramic mugs and a warehouse-sized canister of powdered creamer. Two of them are leaning against the counter shooting-the-shit style over a copy of what I'd bet is the *Gazette*. And behind the counter, in that torturously hot, fitted black polo with the store logo over the chest is Cam.

He's nodding attentively to this shrunken raisin of a man who looks to be telling some kind of big-fish story based on the slow-motion gesturing happening over there.

"Gullsy, that you?" A burly guy with a gray buzz cut slaps his knee from the couch.

Behind the counter, Cam straightens.

I raise a hand in greeting, and the old guy gives up a wheezing laugh. "Just this morning Missy was telling me that Cheryl heard from Pastor Craig you were back in town."

Face heating, I nod. "Yes, sir. Back for a month."

There's a chorus of croaked greetings and comments about my last game with the Slayers. It's nice but also makes me feel more than a little conspicuous.

Eventually, I make my way over to the counter where Cam's standing in a wide-legged stance, arms crossed over his broad chest, a curious smirk on his handsome, clean-cut face.

"So much for my plan to quietly drop some coffee by for you. Half the town's in here." I look back to where most everyone's attention has returned to fishing. "Didn't realize this was such a hot spot."

"That it is. Is one of those for me?" he asks, nodding toward the heavy paper cups in my hand.

Trying to be cool, I hold one out. "Felt bad about you missing your coffee window. Though I guess you've got plenty here."

The corner of his mouth twitches as he waves me in. I lean over the counter, and he meets me halfway. There's a wash of his breath against my skin, and I close my eyes against the sensation, afraid of what they'd reveal.

"It's *decaf*. They don't know, but we've been making both pots with the same stuff since before I was born. A deal Gramps made with one of the wives forever ago, and we've stuck with."

"Whoa." I pull back a couple inches, as far as I can willingly make myself go. "And you trust me with this state secret?"

His laugh is low and warm, the same one I remember from when we were paired up for biology lab in high school, the one that drew me in with a force I didn't understand. But made me curious just the same.

"What?" he asks before taking a sip and then rocking back on his heels with an almost pornographic moan. Or maybe it was standard appreciation and the fact that I haven't gotten any for damn near six months is starting to screw with my head.

"Just thinking about the first time I noticed your laugh." I say it quietly, but his brow still goes up and his eyes shift from me to the crowd behind us.

I know. *Careful.*

If I don't want people to know, I shouldn't say things like that. I shouldn't find reasons to be jogging by his house or bringing him coffee at work. But that's the thing… Cam makes me want people to know. He makes me want another shot at that thing we barely had a chance to skim the surface of the first time around.

But while I'm winding up to send caution into the wind, he's taking a step back from the counter.

That soaring feeling in my chest starts to sink until he holds up a finger for me to wait.

Ducking into an open doorway at the far end of the glass top, he clears his throat. "Dad? Can you handle refills on the coffee for a few? I'll hit inventory this afternoon."

There's a muffled response, and then Mr. Dorsey emerges from the back with a stack of paperwork and a laptop. There's no mistaking the family resemblance. The fall of straight dark hair and square-cut jaw, the broad build on a lean frame. "Where you off to?"

"Just out back. Come and get me if there's a run on the register."

His dad snorts and waves him off.

And then I'm following Cam through the back of the store and out to a narrow strip of fenced-in grass with a shaded picnic table in the center. It's private and quiet enough that the only sound I hear is the rustling of the breeze through the trees.

I rub the back of my neck. "Hey, sorry about showing up like that. I shouldn't—"

"I'm glad you did." He drops onto one bench and signals for me to take the opposite side. "Needed the coffee." He wags his head with one of those half-smiles I can't seem to look away from. "It's not bad seeing you again, either."

Heat floods my cheeks, and after a minute of studying my cup, I ask, "So everyone inside... knows?"

"That I'm gay? Yeah, they know." He watches me a second, running his teeth over his bottom lip. "But if you're worried they'll make an assumption about you showing up today, don't."

I nod slowly, thinking about it for a moment before meeting his eyes. "I'm not."

CHAPTER 5

CAM

"*Y*ou're not." He's not worried? What does that mean? Trevor must see the gears turning in my head. He sets his cup down and rests his forearms on the table.

"Four years ago, I didn't see you coming." He looks away, almost shy. "Yeah, I knew there was something about you. Even before that night, I couldn't keep my eyes off you. I told myself it was one athlete's appreciation of another. That the reason I knew the dip and rise of every muscle on your body was because I wanted that level of fitness myself. That the reason I gravitated toward you was because our ambitions matched."

"Trev." I stare, stunned by the unguarded words. But I shouldn't be— it's how he's always been with me.

He gives me a sheepish smile. "I thought the pull in my chest and gut was because I was just more comfortable around guys like me. And when I felt that pull even lower, I passed it off as teen horniness. I mean, I was attracted to women. I dated them, casually. So the reality of that attraction sort of snuck up on me. But once I understood it, it was a relief."

Christ, how am I sitting here with this man again? How is he telling me these things that tear at my heart and make it hard for me to breathe, that touch on a connection that feels as fresh now as it did then? These things that wreck me.

"Except I wasn't ready." I let out a humorless laugh. "It didn't matter that I very much understood my attraction to you. I knew I was gay. I was interested in dudes from the start. And the few girls I took out... well, let's just say I'm glad I'm not still trying to sell the straight thing." I shake my head and give him a truth I wasn't planning to share. "I wish that I'd been brave enough to come out about it sooner."

"You had your reasons. And coming here today, seeing what you were afraid of losing, I get those reasons even more now." His eyes meet mine. "But when I left, I didn't."

Even now, I remember the look on his face from that last night, the plea and pained disbelief when I rejected him. It still haunts me. "I'm sorry."

He shakes his head. "Don't. You have *nothing* to apologize for. Not a single thing. If anything, I owe you my thanks."

I raise a brow, and he shrugs one solid shoulder.

"You helped me figure out something pretty significant about myself. Something I hadn't recognized on my own. I mean it. And for a short time, it was just... Perfect. So, thank you."

I nod, but there's something I still don't get. "Can't believe I'm actually going to admit this, but I looked you up a few times."

The corners of his mouth twitch. "What were you looking for?"

"For an *out* hockey player." For the things he told me to be real. It's as far as I can go. As much as I can admit, because there's no way I'm going to tell him that if I found what I was looking for, I'd have hit the gas and driven straight through until I got to him. I'd have begged for a second chance.

Squinting off into the distance, he nods. "At first, I guess I was kind of torn up and confused. What happened with us felt like a lightning strike. I'd never experienced anything like it before, and it took a while before I could even think about anyone else. And then..." He squints at the sky. "Hell, I'd been so sure about us. And being wrong? It made me doubt things some. Wonder if maybe I'd been wrong about more. If maybe what happened between us was just a fluke."

I rub at the pain in my chest, the soul-deep scar I gave to both of us.

"So you went back to dating girls?"

He lets out a quiet laugh, staring down at his hands. "Let's say, I confirmed that I'm bisexual. I'm physically attracted to women. Been a few nights here and there. But when it comes to guys, I'm physically *and* emotionally attracted."

My mouth goes dry. "You've had relationships with men?"

"Two."

"I didn't see anything." My ears are ringing, and my chest feels like an anvil is parked on it.

"The first lasted a few months but wasn't meant to be. Different lives and directions. Probably a little too easy to let go. If it hadn't fizzled, I think we would have been open about it, but he wasn't big on PDA. So while it was happening, no one noticed anything more than a couple guys hanging out now and then."

I try to imagine it but realize I don't want to. Still, I have to know. "The second?"

"The second was almost a year. He wasn't out. Isn't out. He said maybe someday, but I went into it with my eyes open. Even so, pretending for all that time is rough, you know?"

But he'd done it. For almost a year.

If I'd believed him. If I'd trusted, maybe we—

I shake my head, because that's a train of thought I don't think I can afford to follow sitting right in front of him. "Is that why it ended?"

He looks away but not before I see the hurt in his eyes. I don't like it.

"There were a lot of reasons. But his not wanting our relationship to be public wasn't really one of them. His cheating on me though... definitely was."

"Trevor, man, I'm so sorry. When did you break up?"

"Few months ago."

About the time he was playing with the Slayers. I want to ask him more about it. But there's no missing the subtle shift in his body language, the way he closes off. Like he's still protecting this jerk.

So I stick to the only question that really matters.

"Are you over him?"

"Him? Yeah. *It?* I want to be, but that kind of betrayal has a way of sticking with you." A breeze blows through, tossing his hair around his face. "What really catches me up, though? The part that I resent the hell out of but can't seem to get past, is this concern that if *I* come out, it changes things for him. Puts his secret at risk."

"How do you mean?"

"Everyone knew we were friends. He's terrified if people find out I date guys, they might draw conclusions. That even if they don't exactly know... what if they ask him about me? About whether he knew? How he feels?"

"So now you... what? Feel like you can't come out?" I reach across the scarred wood and take his hand. I only let myself hold it for a second, just long enough to offer the smallest comfort before giving him back his space. "It's admirable that you want to respect his privacy, but I think you can do that and still live your own life. If anyone asks him about you... he can decide what he wants to say about it."

The look on his face says even if he thinks I'm right he isn't comfortable with it.

Spearing a hand through the overlong mess of his hair, he swings his legs out from the bench to stand. "You know, I've had a hard time making peace with that. Part of me felt like, without a good reason, what's the harm in giving him more time to put some distance between us? But maybe he's had enough time."

Abandoning our coffees on the bench, I rise with him. "What changed your mind?"

His eyes meet mine, and the air in my lungs catches behind everything I'm seeing there.

He steps closer, moving into my space so there's less than a foot separating us. Dappled sunlight plays across his brow, the crooked bridge of his nose, and those brawny shoulders, highlighting one perfect spot and then the next. Making me want to touch, to reach out and wrap my hand around the back of his neck, fist his shirt, and drag him in for a kiss.

Only I can't fucking move. I can't breathe as he searches my eyes with a helplessness completely at odds with his physical presence. "I saw you again."

"*Trev.*"

In what seems like some kind of slow-motion reality, Trevor reaches for my hand, the backs of his knuckles brushing lightly, tentatively… heating the nerves where our skin touches and sending tiny waves of static up my arm.

His eyes drift to my mouth, and whatever restraint I've built up for this man crumbles to dust.

I close the distance between us and graze his lips with mine in a kiss that's nothing like the heated desperation of my fantasies but somehow feels infinitely more potent. Our eyes meet, and this time, there's nothing helpless in his look. There's no question between us. Emotion I've kept buried so deep for so long surges up in an almost violent eruption, and we come together in a crush, chest to chest, mouths fusing, hands gripping and pulling and— Christ —there's not an inch between us. Not a breath we aren't sharing. Why does that feel more intimate than any sexual act I've ever engaged in?

There isn't a pause or beat or a single second of hesitation as we angle and open, taking and giving, our tongues moving together and sliding against each other. Each spearing thrust making me moan as sensation pierces through me in ways no kiss has before. Or at least not in the past four years.

Our feet aren't as coordinated as our mouths, and suddenly I'm staggering in a tangle of blind steps, Trev's arm locking around me as the outside wall to the stockroom meets my shoulders and his hard body presses into mine... all the way down.

Oh hell, yes. I can feel him thickening against me and—

zzz zzz

"Oh shit," I croak, breaking the kiss even though it nearly kills me to do it.

But my phone's on DND for work, and only one person's texts come through.

"Phone?" Trevor asks with a gruff, breathless laugh.

Our brows are still pressed together, our chests rising and falling like we've just finished back-to-back 1500 frees.

"Yeah, I— Sorry, my dad."

He nods without breaking contact.

zzz zzz

The corner of his mouth tips into a crooked slant that has the blood plummeting out of my head so fast I feel dizzy.

"You should check that." Slowly, he draws the hand that was in my hair down my neck, past my shoulder, over my lats where it rotates so his fingers lead the way, teasing lower to skim the rise of my ass.

My throat goes dry. That crooked smile is too much. Aching for another taste, I lean in, but Trevor matches my movement, drawing back.

"Your *dad*." He slides over my hip, and I can almost feel the phantom tug of him fisting my jeans, but instead, he works that big, slow dragging hand into my pocket and withdraws my phone just as it vibrates again.

Eyes still locked with mine, he hands over the device I'm tempted to use as a longbow target. "I should go."

Terrible idea. "Don't. Just give me a minute to let him know I'm leaving, and—"

His single-step retreat sinks my hopes of taking things back to my place and spending the next twenty-four hours or maybe twenty-four years in bed with this man.

"The store opened less than an hour ago. What's it going to look like when I throw you over my shoulder and skate out of here?"

Hot. Insanely so.

And while I've got Trevor by about two inches, there's zero doubt in my mind that he could do it. Easily. Throw me on the bed and be on top of me before I bounce. But the smile that fantasy conjures fades when the rest of his words sink in.

What's it going to look like...

"Right. Sorry, I wasn't thinking about people seeing us." I start my own retreat, only I'm already against the building and there's nowhere to go.

Trevor laughs, grabbing my hand and pulling me with him over to the bench where our coffees sit. Handing me mine, he leans in and drops a quick kiss at my jaw before stepping back.

"This might sound crazy, but in this moment... the only person I'm worried about is your dad. Part of me will always think he's the reason I lost you the first time."

I open my mouth, but he lifts the fingers of one hand in a sort of abbreviated stop signal.

"I know, there were a million more factors than him. And I get that he's supportive now. Hell, I'm thrilled about it. But I've been waiting four years to feel like this again. I don't want to risk your dad deciding he doesn't like me for stealing his star employee during work hours." He bites his lip, looking out from beneath the blond hank that keeps falling into his eyes. "Besides, I was thinking maybe we could hang out later."

I brush the hair back before I can think about whether it's really appropriate. "Tonight?"

"Yeah. Like a date, if you're into it. Or if you'd rather—"

"A date." I start nodding like a tool, and a nearly blinding grin breaks across his face. He texts himself from my phone and leans in like he's going to kiss me, but then sways back with a slow shake of his head.

"Better not risk it."

My phone starts to vibrate again, this time with a call. I pick it up. "Sorry, Dad. I'm on my way back in now."

CHAPTER 6

TREVOR

"*a* date? Like you're going out in public and holding hands through a candlelit dinner kind of date?"

"I don't know. That's the problem." I put the last handful of socks in the dresser drawer and stow my now empty suitcase in the hall closet. Has it seriously been less than a day since I got here? "I want to take him out, but I ran to the gas station this afternoon and I kid you not, it took forty-five minutes to get out of there. *After* I'd filled up and paid."

Tammy laughs. "I'm jealous. It would be so much fun to see everyone."

"Don't get me wrong. It is. But this is going to be *our* first date. I want to spend it with him, not fielding questions about my life without him."

"You should have stayed at the party longer last night. Then everyone would already be caught up."

Answering with a noncommittal hum, I prop a shoulder against the window and look out through the trees to the water beyond.

She might be right, but I wouldn't trade what happened for anything.

"Okay, little brother, here's what you're going to do..."

The hours creep by slower than the week leading to Christmas when you're eight. But eventually, I hop in the truck and drive up my lane and back down to Cam's. Our houses look like they were built about the same time in the same style, but where mine looks like it hasn't been occupied in two years and has the overgrowth to prove it, Cam's is neat as a pin. No branches touch the roof, and the gravel drive is evenly graded, ending in a wide turnabout. From there, a flagstone paver path circles the house with a split that leads to the front porch.

Nerves on par with the first time I stomped down the chute with the Slayers, I walk up to the door and knock. Waiting, I take in the thick, lush lawn with diagonal lines mowed into it and what appears to be a fresh coat of paint on the rail. This is what it looks like to put down roots. The thought sends an uneasy feeling through my gut, but then Cam's at the door, looking hot as hell in a dove gray button-down that hugs his impressive biceps and shows off the tapered cut of his torso.

"Hey, sorry, I'm running late," he says, stepping back with a wave at his neatly combed but not quite dry hair. "Delivery showed up as I was closing the store, and I got behind a few minutes."

There's a beat where it's clear he doesn't know what to do with his hands or quite how to greet me.

"No worries and no rush." And then because I'm trying to at least look like I've got some game when my actual *dating* experience with guys is next to nil, I reach for his hip and lean in to drop a quick kiss at his jaw. "You look great... really great."

And that hit of his aftershave mingling with the woodsy scent of his soap and product? *Damn*, it totally does it for me. And now I'm wishing I'd jerked off before I left because I'm at serious risk of sporting wood the whole night.

"Yeah? Thanks," he says quietly. "You too."

When his eyes come up and connect with mine, everything slows and the moment stretches. I feel that same sort of dizzying pull drawing me in, but somehow I manage to step back with only the smallest groan.

Based on the slant of his mouth and the color pushing into his cheeks, he hears it. And I don't think he's going to hold it against me.

"Umm, take your time getting ready. No rush. I'll be in the car."

I don't give him the chance to respond. Just spin on my heel and get the hell out before I do something crazy like back him against another handy wall and drop to my knees for him.

My fingers feel numb as I slide into the driver's seat and start the engine. If I'd hoped for a reprieve to get the situation in my trousers under control, I don't get it. Cam's out of the house within a minute, jogging down the couple stairs from the porch and stepping into the evening sun.

Gorgeous. Definitely should have jerked off.

He climbs in with a hesitant look. "Second thoughts? We don't have to go out if you're not comfortable."

This guy is amazing. But oblivious as to the source of my problem.

"My sister told me not to kiss you before our date." Jesus, I sound like an ass.

One dark brow pushes up. "Tammy? What's she got against kissing?"

"Nothing, if I thought I'd be able to stop."

"Sooo, you didn't think you'd be able to stop?" And the smile he gives me? Embarrassment totally worth it. He bites his bottom lip.

Is he doing it on purpose now?

He reaches across the cab and slides his fingers into the hair at the back of my neck.

Yep. He's definitely doing it on purpose.

I stop breathing, my eyes cutting back to his.

Doesn't Cam realize we're within caveman-hauling distance of his bed?

Don't. Think. About. Beds.

We *have* to make it to the restaurant, so I try to remember what we were talking about. There was something I wanted him to know... Right!

"I didn't want you to wonder"— I clear my throat —"if this was just a hookup. It's not."

"So no kissing at all then?" The way he says it, deep brown eyes dropping to my mouth, just a hint of disappointment in his tone, is killing me. "Not even one?"

The feel of his fingers against my neck is making me stupid. "I really want to take you out."

He nods. "You will. But since I've been thinking about kissing you again since the minute you left the store, maybe we risk it. Set a timer or something."

I've been thinking about kissing him again since I left too. And for the four years before that. Which is why, against my better judgment, I don't resist when he pulls me in. Our mouths meet in a firm press that feels so right, I just lean into the contact, savoring the connection.

He pulls back the barest breath.

"Hey, Google," he mutters. "Set a timer for sixty seconds."

And then we meet again, our mouths rubbing together in an unhurried kiss that makes my chest ache and my mind spin. We open to each other, our tongues teasing lightly from my mouth to his and back again. It's sweet and hot and all I can think is... *yes... this...* and *more.*

I want more than this kiss, more than the single month I'll be living here. Fuck, I want more than a life that can't accommodate anything beyond a career in flux.

Maybe it's that last thought that has my desperation ramping up, because suddenly I can't get close enough. Cam's seatbelt releases a second before mine, and we surge together.

The grip on my neck tightens as we groan into each other. And then I'm pulling at his shoulder while his other hand, wide and strong, slides up my thigh, higher, closer—

Chimes start to sound, and we freeze.

Painfully, I ease back as he turns off the alarm.

Cam's hair isn't quite as neat, but the hint of disarray is sexy as hell, and I can't help but reach up to touch it again.

He smiles, rubbing his hand over his mouth and jaw.

"So, are there any other cockblocking tips big sister bestowed?"

Falling back in my seat, I laugh. We both re-buckle, and I put the truck in gear.

"She told me not to make you dinner at my place for the same reason."

"You cook?" Cam's almost breathless the way he asks, and I make a mental note that our next date will be at my place.

"She told me to take you out of town, but to make sure you know it's not that I don't want people here to see us. It's because I don't want to share you with a bunch of awesome old friends who've been getting to see you on the regular since you were born. I don't want to risk someone mistaking our date as platonic and deciding to join us."

He nods, the corner of his mouth twitching with the smile he doesn't want to set free.

"Trev, do you actually think if they saw us at a table for two, with you dressed like this"— he runs a finger over my linen pant leg, up over my belt, and then flicks the silk of my light blue dress shirt, making me suck in a breath —"they'd think we were just a couple buddies catching up?"

Eyes focused on the road, I shake my head. "I don't know what they'd think. You're the first guy I've ever taken on a real date."

CAM

For having zero practice dating, Trevor Gulbrandsen is a natural when it comes to showing a man a good time.

The place he picked is a few towns away, situated on a lake with three walls of windows giving every seat in the dining room an open-air feel and spectacular view. He asks if I'm a "wine guy" and has the waiter help pick out something that will go with our meals.

It's comfortable. Like there's this crazy sense of ease that shouldn't be between us after all this time, with how things ended and the way our lives have moved on since. But I can't remember a conversation ever coming so easily or flowing so naturally from one topic to the next.

And damn, laughing with this man is something else.

He's beautiful to me. And I'm torn between never wanting this dinner to end and pretty desperately wanting to see where it goes next.

I've been on my share of dates. First dates and dates that have happened well into a relationship. But it's never felt like this.

Setting down my silverware, I watch as Trevor wipes his mouth and sets his napkin aside. It shouldn't be sexy, but... so sexy.

"Thank you for asking me out tonight."

He nods, looking adorably pleased. "I'm glad I did. And hey, four years later, pretty sure this place is way nicer than anything I would have come up with the first time around."

"I'm serious. When you came by Outfitters this morning, there was a part of me that wondered if maybe you came back because you thought I was still in the closet. And that if anything happened, you wouldn't have to worry about it getting out."

He jerks back. "What? No. Cam, I—" He shakes his head and tries again. "I don't know what I thought would happen with you. I — yeah, I wanted to see you. But I was pretty sure you'd be actively avoiding me the whole time I was here. And if you had, I wouldn't have held it against you. I swear."

"You're a good man, Trevor. And no matter what version of my life you walked into, I don't think I'd have a shot in hell at being able to resist you. But in this one, I don't even want to try."

Again he looks away, like he can take a hit from an opposing player on the ice in stride, but a compliment is too much. I'll have to work on that.

Only as soon as the thought crosses my mind, I check it. Because Trevor isn't here to stay. He's here for a few weeks. And then he'll be back in Chicago playing for the Slayers... because I can't believe for a second they'll let him go back down to Springfield.

And then like his thoughts were somehow echoing my own, he meets my eyes. "In this version of my life, things are pretty messy. The only thing I know for certain about my future is that I have four weeks in Wildren. But beyond that, I—" He searches my eyes, a pain moving into his. "I can't even make plans for myself. I don't know what city I'm going to live in. What team I'm going to play for. And the thing is, as much as that kind of uncertainty sucks, I've got to be grateful for it. Remember how lucky I am and how many guys would do anything to be in my place. This is what I wanted, but there are times when having it is harder than I expected it to be."

"Maybe that's why you came back. Maybe you needed a break from all the worry and waiting for answers. Maybe you just needed something simple for a little while."

I mean it to be reassuring but somehow it isn't.

Trevor nods but then drops his head for a breath. When he looks back up, that buoyancy I was feeling in my chest is replaced by something heavy, resigned. Because we both recognize the truth of it.

"Cam. The way I want you... I don't think this thing between us could ever be *simple*."

CHAPTER 7

TREVOR

$\mathcal{T}$he drive back is quiet. But somehow it's still not uncomfortable even after the truth of our situation became obvious. My thoughts bounce between the taste of Cam's kiss, the warm, free sound of his laughter, and what a damn fool I was for coming here when the only thing I know about my life is that this career I've been working toward forever is maybe, possibly, almost within my grasp.

That I nearly sacrificed my chance at the NHL once for this man… only to realize he didn't want me to. He didn't want me at all.

It was more than that.

It was.

I understand, but being back here, feeling myself falling again before I even realized I'd gotten close to the cliff—

Damn.

I should know better.

I should want to end this date as quickly as possible. Grab that bottle of tequila Lizzo's been saving for me and put us both out of our misery.

But even knowing better, *I don't want this to end.*

Wrapping my hands around the wheel, I hold tight so I don't reach for him.

Another mile, and my time is up. I take a left down his drive, my heart sinking as I pull to a stop in front of his perfect house.

I cut the engine and let myself out while he does the same.

Wind rustles through the trees, muting the rush of waves as we stand facing each other in the moonlight.

"Thank you." I swallow hard. "For letting me take you out and pretend for a few hours that my life was in a place where I could have something like this." Someone like him.

Cam nods, giving me a smile that hurts to look at. "It's nice to be reminded what a good date feels like. And nice to be with you. It's always been that way."

"It has." I lift an arm, inviting him in for a hug because I can't not give him one. And after tonight, there's no telling whether I'll have another chance. I'm supposed to be in town for a month, but the idea of living this close to Cam Dorsey and pretending I don't know what his mouth feels like on mine or how good we could be together if only both our lives and priorities were completely different? It's brutal.

He steps into me, wrapping one arm around my back while giving my shoulder a friendly squeeze with the other. *Ouch.*

I ought to be grateful he's able to be so cool about this, but it feels wrong.

Our chests linger in that half press, his head beside mine. Neither of us moving, like maybe he needs this last contact the same way I do.

Too soon, his hand leaves my shoulder.

That's it.

This is the end.

Except instead of letting me go, by some miracle, he pulls me closer, both arms coming around my back, his hands fisting in my shirt as he buries his face in my neck.

A shock of breath bursts free and then I'm clinging to him with a force that matches his.

"Trevor." He burrows impossibly closer, his voice as rough as I've ever heard it. "I get that it's not as simple as it could be, or even as simple as you need. But maybe... it doesn't have to be that complicated either."

I blink, unable to move or speak or breathe.

"Maybe," he goes on, "if we went into this with our eyes open and no expectations beyond this month—"

"Cam." However he's going to finish that has to wait. Because my fist is in his hair, and our mouths are slamming together in a demanding crush.

There's more tenderness in my heart for Cam than I have ever felt for another, but this kiss conveys none of it.

This kiss is desperate and hungry.

Deep and aggressive.

This kiss is *everything*.

His tongue is in my mouth, rubbing firm against the press of mine. Our chests and hips bump together as we angle and shift, needing to get closer. Needing more.

"Inside," he commands, fingers caught in my belt, tugging me with him as he backs toward the house.

My hands are on his ass, molding the hard muscle through his pants as he groans into my mouth. Then groans louder when I splay my fingers wide, bringing my thumbs together just hinting at a tease between his cheeks.

The first time I touched Cam like that, I was so tentative, daring to slide my fingers beneath his open jeans. Fucking terrified of doing the wrong thing. But he'd shuddered in my arms and breathlessly came on my stomach.

It was the hottest moment of my life.

"More control now," he rasps against my ear, telling me he's with me. Even when *with me* means four years ago.

"Yeah?"

Reaching behind him, he nods, blindly letting us in and then pressing me into the wall beside the door. "Yeah."

Our eyes meet, and I slide my hand over his fly, squeezing the steely length of him. "Whatever control you've found? I'm going to break it."

And then I spin him around so it's his back to the wall, and drop to my knees.

CAM

Trevor has no idea. My control broke the second I found him back in town.

That conversation at dinner, having him actually tell me how his life isn't in a place that leaves him available for a relationship just brought reality back into focus. It reminded me that self-preservation is a thing. That we have the chance to be smart. All well and good until I touched him again and realized that protecting my heart stopped mattering.

For years I regretted not taking the chance we had.

And while he isn't offering me the same thing now that he was then, I'll take it anyway.

I'll take what we can have, while we have it, and deal with the aftermath when it comes.

For now though?

He reverses our positions, and when I'm the one with the wall holding me up— and it has to be because my knees are fucking jelly —this man who's been the longest-starring member of my fantasies drops to his knees and starts on my belt.

"Oh Jesus... you don't ha—"

"Want to." He pushes my fly open and frees my hard-on with a sure, confident grip. Thumb brushing over the leaking tip, his eyes haze. "*Need* to."

I nod, pretty sure I stopped breathing but too transfixed by the visual of Trevor taking me into his mouth to care.

He grips my thighs, those big hands rubbing up and down as he pulls me in, takes more, and then draws back until my dick bobs free of his lips.

Ocean blue eyes meet mine.

"Lose the shirt, Captain." His always deep voice has turned gravelly rough. Sexy beyond belief. "Want to see you while I suck you off."

Holy shit.

My hands shakily work the buttons as he watches, jerking me with slow, firm strokes.

I shrug out of one arm and groan as Trevor rubs over his fly. Then, time sort of stutters. My shirt is on the floor and I'm watching his mouth drag over me again and again, each time giving me the wet stroke of his tongue and then the deep pull of suction that has the nerves tingling along my spine.

He wasn't lying about wanting to look at me, either. His hot eyes are practically burning over my chest and shoulders. We push into fast-forward, his motions coming quick, my lungs working at triple time. I catch a glimpse of him jacking himself, the purple head of his cock pumping through his fist… And I'm fucking done.

Lightning shoots through my body, wracking me with pleasure so intense it feels like it's burned through to my soul. Gasping, I watch as Trevor swallows me down, his eyes clamped shut as his own release strikes.

I'm signing up for pain. This is a heartbreak guaranteed to happen. But it doesn't stop me from urging Trevor to his feet and kissing him again. Threading my fingers through his hair to hold him close.

We need to clean up. We need to talk. But as we stand here

sharing breath, the only thing I can manage is to ask for the one thing I can't live without.

"Stay."

Dorsey's doesn't open until noon on Sundays, and I've never been so grateful to be able to sleep in.

Trevor is a snuggler. He's a big, muscle-bound beast of a man who crushes it on the ice and makes this almost purring sound when he pulls me into him while he's sleeping.

Yes. I watched him sleep.

I'm telling myself it wasn't the creepy kind of watching someone sleep, but the amazed and slightly disbelieving kind.

Seriously, how is this beautiful creature in my bed?

And we're back to the not-creepy sleep-watching, because the sight of his blond bedhead and bare chest against my navy plaid sheets is like a fucking revelation. And those eyelashes—

Oops. Are opening.

"You watching me?" he rasps, reaching for me and pulling me in again with another contented sound that's almost as good as the one from the middle of the night.

"Yep. Total creeper." Guess even if I'm not ready to be straight with myself, I am with him.

He chuckles gruffly, pressing the stubble of his hard-cut jaw against my shoulder and then opening his mouth to bite it.

Fuuck, I like that.

Almost as much as the fact that he didn't startle out of bed, going from zero to sixty excuses for why he needs to leave in two seconds flat.

"You want coffee?" I ask, teasing his foot with mine. "Made some not too long ago."

He hums appreciatively and drags himself up to sit, elbows

resting on the spread of his knees, hands scrubbing over the back of his head. "Give me a minute and I'll be in."

"Take your time. There's a new toothbrush on the side of the sink."

I've got the coffee poured and hand him a mug when he meets me in the kitchen wearing a pair of black boxer briefs and the same smile I've been admiring since he moved to town in the eighth grade.

My kitchen isn't huge, but its U-shaped layout is perfect for him to lean into one corner and me in the other, our feet just touching.

This is the kind of morning I could get used to all too easily.

Which means it's time for a reality check.

I take a swallow of coffee and hold the mug in my hands, watching as Trevor does the same. Time to man up. "Last night was incredible."

He visibly tenses, meeting me with wary eyes. "More than that, even."

"But in the light of day, I've got to ask if it's something you want more of. Because if you ask me, the answer is yes. But—"

"Yes." There's nothing halfway about it. He sets his coffee on the stretch of counter between us and steps closer. "If you do, I do. No question."

I can't help smiling and then smiling bigger when his matches mine. Christ, it feels good to be with this man.

"Good. You know I do. But"— I set my coffee mug next to his, trying not to get caught up in how nice they look together — "even with some of the complications stripped away, there are some we can't ignore."

"Like what does this look like for the next few weeks?"

I take an unsteady breath because the more this clarifies in my mind, the less I like it. But I think I need it. "I don't want to ask you to be my secret or to feel like we're hiding. But at the same time, I know how easily I could get carried away with you. And if this isn't going to last, I guess... I just don't want everyone who's been waiting for me to find a nice man and settle down thinking it's happened."

Those big blue eyes hold steady. He's taking this seriously and, damn, I appreciate it. "So what do you want them to think? That we're just friends?"

I give him a hard shake of my head but then soften, realizing I don't know. What might be right for me might not be right for him. "If that's what you want, then okay. Maybe it's the simplest solution we've got."

He reaches for my hand. "Or?"

"Or we don't hide what we're doing. But in public, and only in public, we tone down *this* part." I nod to where he's now holding my hand in both of his. "I don't care if they think we're hooking up. If it looks like we're having some kind of summer fling."

One heavy blond brow lifts.

"So, I can give you all the fuck-me eyes I want?"

I nod, feeling my heart speed up. "Oh yeah."

"Drag you out of parties before they're over..."

"Before they've even started."

"Buy lube in bulk..."

I cough out a laugh, pushing my dick down. Not that it does much good when he closes the distance between us, brushing my hand aside to replace it with his. "Not sure Dean's Pharmacy carries it in bulk."

"I'll order online."

I grab him by the back of the head with one hand and pull him in for a hard kiss, while the other slides into his boxers to stroke him.

God, I want him. Everything.

Just so long as it doesn't look like we're falling in love. Because when he's gone, it's going to be painful enough for me to deal with the fact that I already have.

CHAPTER 8

TREVOR

I was joking about the lube. Mostly.

We both had some on hand and, even though we haven't actually gone *there*, when we used it up this morning… I realized I really was going to have to make an emergency run to the pharmacy for more.

Not going to lie though, there is a thirty-two-ounce pump bottle sitting in my Prime cart, and over the past week I've come within a heartbeat of clicking the purchase button more than once. The only thing that's keeping me from doing it is that I don't want to be a pushy motherfucker. I don't want Cam thinking I need us to take that last step.

Because maybe it's the line we don't cross for a reason.

I mean, yeah, there's something about Cam that begs me to go all in. Even knowing we can't be anything more than temporary, every time I see this guy, my heart feels like it's trying to tear down my ribs to get to him.

Holding back is a challenge I wasn't expecting, but this one emotional discretion matters to him. So I fight the impulse to bring Cam a coffee every single morning and park myself on the couch in front of the bass-fishing show with all the geezers just so I can be close to him throughout the day. Watch as he stocks shelves and helps customers in his hot-as-hell Outfitters T-shirt. Ask him to show me how to hold my rod when he goes on break.

Ugh.

I've been good. All week. Which is why the second his truck pulled to a stop in front of my place last night? Yeah, the poor guy didn't even have a chance to turn the engine off before I had his door open and was hauling him out.

Demanding a reward for my restraint— and a *reward* is exactly what having him breathless above me, his fingers knotted in my hair as he comes deep in my throat, is.

So hot.

Not what I need to be thinking about standing in line behind my old lunch lady at Dean's.

"Gulls, thought that was you."

I turn, finding Neil beside me, eying my *not-fooling-anyone* bottle of Scope, bag of jerky, and generously sized but no thirty-two-ounce container of lube in my basket.

Not embarrassed. We're all adults here.

"Hey, Watson. Good to see you again." Neil was at the bar the other night when we met up with a bunch of the water polo players from Cam's team. Not that I had much of a chance to catch up with him, the way he and Judy were huddled together in a corner like they were the only ones left on the planet.

It was cute to see, especially after the way the guy used to moon after her in high school.

Now, there's something distinctly not cute about the look he's leveling me with. In fact, there's something downright menacing about it. Which is saying a lot, considering Neil has a Cosmo magazine and a box of tampons tucked under his arm.

"Everything okay?"

"Sure. Sure, it is." He smiles. Flatly. "You know Cam's my best friend. *Right?*"

My brows lift. *Well, damn.*

⁂

"I swear to God, Cam, he was giving me the talk," I say, handing him a beer and then dropping onto the opposite side of the couch and propping my feet beside his on the table. "Like *you-break-his-heart-I-break-your-face* style."

Cam's shaking his head, lips parted in one of those stunted laughs. "No."

"Yes." We clink our longnecks. "Hundred percent, yes. He *flexed* at me."

Damn, that laugh. This guy was always so reserved in high school. But now, he's always laughing, and I freaking love it.

"Now I know you're lying to me."

"I'm not." My head drops back against the cushions, and I sigh. "And it was *awesome.*"

He shifts so he's got one arm stretched across the top of the couch and he's facing me. "I talked to him. Told him not to get carried away about this."

"Ehh, he's your ride or die. Neil's probably excited for a chance to be the one looking out for you for a change, right?" I thread our fingers together. "Unless you think he's jealous and this decades-long business with Judy is all part of some long game to get with you... in which case, my *flex* is totes bigger than his *flex.*"

I demonstrate, popping some muscles for show and earning a hard eye roll.

"Baby, put those things away." And then after another sip of beer, he leans back, relaxed. "So, tell me about the call with your agent today. She got any good news for you?"

Not really. It was more of the same uncertainty, but damned if it isn't nice to be able to share it with him.

CAM

It's too easy imagining this man in my life beyond the two weeks we have left together. Two weeks. Every time I think about that ticking clock and what my life is going to look like after Trevor's gone, my chest gets that too-tight feeling of holding my breath at the bottom of the pool.

I don't like it, but I just keep diving back in regardless. Because this, the way things have been between us since he got back here, is *everything*.

We've been together every night. Sometimes at his place. Sometimes at mine. Always when we close our eyes and still when we pry them open in the morning.

It's so good, but it's just a fling.

I try to convince myself that's the magic of it— the whole no-expectations-beyond-the-end-of-the-month thing. That we're living outside of reality, and *that's* why it's so easy, so effortless.

Maybe I'd be able to believe my own bull if it wasn't for one little thing… we've been here before.

Back in high school, Trevor and I ran in different circles. He played hockey and I swam. Both winter sports, which meant that even in a community as small as Wildren, there was a divide. It wasn't hostile, but people had to choose how they spent their Friday nights. And those choices carried over into lunches and the time between the bells during the school days too.

So while we were *friendly*… we weren't really *friends*.

But somehow, any time we ended up in the same space— paired up for badminton in gym class, dissecting a cow eye in biology, or waiting in the hall to be called in for the vision test— something just clicked.

We laughed at the same jokes and got exactly what the other was saying, whether it was debating the merits of French fries over tater tots or falling into that one shockingly intimate conversation about me losing my mom and him losing his dad in grade school.

We clicked so well, it scared me. And at a time when I was still working so hard to keep my secret, there was this boy who made me feel like anyone walking by could see what I was thinking about him.

Worse, that *he* would.

There were times I avoided him for that alone. And then times when I got reckless and leaned into that easy connection just for a minute, just praying that no one would notice. That's what I was doing the night of Finch's party.

Following him out to the lake to make sure he was good was reckless, but I couldn't resist. Just like I can't resist now.

The risk isn't the same now. It's higher. Because every night we spend together with him telling me about the players he skates with and me sharing stories from my water polo season, every time he decides to try to teach me to cook something and then has to kick me out of the kitchen to save it... every time we fall into bed, tearing at each other's clothes with a desperation beyond my imagination makes me see how perfect this could be.... If only everything about our lives was different.

I know the hurt is coming. I know saying goodbye again is going to wreck me. But after all the years of living in fear, maybe my reserves of self-preservation are exhausted. Or maybe being able to go all in with this man and having this month without holding back is worth whatever heartbreak comes after.

TREVOR

For a guy on break, I'm managing to keep damn busy... which is critical to ignoring the fact that I'm about one week from ripping my heart out and leaving it here in Wildren.

Don't think about it.

In addition to catching up with old friends and the odd jobs I'm knocking out at Finch's place, I got permission to use the high school gym to work out and the rink to offer a few free hockey clinics in the afternoons. Coach tells me there's some real talent on the team this year, and it's cool to be able to share my knowledge and experience with kids who have the same love of the sport as me.

But what makes my damn year is when Cam shows up with his cousin's tiny five-year-old to the open skate for the mini-mites. She's pink from head to toe, outfit, cheeks, even the strawberry-blond curls... and already you can see this little firecracker likes to win. She skates like a demon and makes no bones about picking the puck up off her kindergarten friend's sticks. It's hilarious and a little scary, but not nearly so much as watching my semi-secret boyfriend... who I've never seen skate for a reason... fall on his taut, perfect ass.

"What were you doing today?" I laugh, walking into Cam's place a few hours later and finding him tossing back a couple ibuprofen.

"Probably fucking up my water polo match tomorrow night, but mostly looking for an excuse to see you."

"I both love and hate that answer." I take the bottle from him and put it back in the cabinet above the toaster.

"You're awesome with those kids," he says, sidling up to me and hooking a finger through my belt loop. "Betsy told her mom she was going to grow up and play on your hockey team. Which is bull-shit, by the way, since last week she was planning to play water polo with me."

Slipping my arms around his waist, I kiss the underside of his jaw. "Stings, huh?"

And that answering laugh rumbling against my chest is something else. It's the kind of thing someone could get used to, even if he knows he shouldn't.

"You really hurt?" I ask, hating that he might be.

He shakes his head and gives me a wink. "Nah. I'm tough." And when he sees my concern is real, he adds, "Seriously, it's nothing loosening up with a swim won't take care of."

"Practice tonight?" I didn't think he had one.

"Tomorrow. Thinking about hitting the lake before dinner though. You mind?"

"Not even a little. In fact, I've got ingredients for chicken piccata in the fridge. Maybe I'll head back and start it. Or"— I let my hands do a little shameless wandering over his ass, pressing into him in a tease I'll absolutely be regretting until I get him naked again— "maybe I'll meet you on our dock. Hang out a while, and we can save dinner for later?"

That groan is everything and, no surprise, we end up making out with my back to his fridge and him sucking on my tongue while we rock into each other. It's too good, but I don't want him swimming in the dark so I pull away, giving his hard-on a parting caress.

"See you in a few." I start for the door.

"Hold up. I got a couple bottles that'll go great with your dinner."

I have no idea what pairs with piccata, but I nod and wait. He rustles around in the kitchen for a minute before coming out with a loaded reusable grocery bag.

This time the kiss is just a sweet peck that leaves me humming as I back toward the truck. "Swim fast, Captain."

He hooks his hands on the frame above the door and leans out with a cocky grin. "State champ."

So. Hot.

I drive home wearing a stupid grin I feel through every cell in my body. I'll get the chicken out, grab my trunks, a couple towels. We could eat on the back terrace.

Talk.

Talk about whether this really needs to end when I leave. If maybe there's a way we can—

I frown as I pull into my drive and catch a glimpse of another car through the trees. Being this far outside of town, it's not a place people drop by unannounced. So who?

Realtors? Squatters? Burglars?

But then I clear the trees and—

No.

Hell, no.

I pull to a stop, dread pooling in my gut. I know exactly who this asshole unfolding from the front step is.

Leo. My ex.

CHAPTER 9

CAM

*J*f there were a touch pad sensor on the floating swim dock in front of Trevor's, I'm pretty confident today would be my personal best time yet. And even without the timer, the fact that I beat him says I was blazing.

Either that, or maybe he liked the look of the bottle I sent and started without me? Ever the optimist— at least since Trevor pulled back into town three and a half weeks ago —I swim to shore and then start up to the cabin.

Halfway there, I hear it— *"I love you, T."* —and I trip over my next step.

Suddenly, it feels like I swallowed a gallon of lake water. Like it's in my lungs, choking me. In my legs, weighing me down. In my gut, making me sick.

I climb faster.

"Leo... you love me?"

The sound of Trevor's stunned laugh filters around the house, muted to the point that I can't read the emotion in it. Joy or disgust,

I have no idea. All I know is that I need to be there. I need to see this motherfucker who broke my boyfriend's heart... and I need to see what Trevor looks like when he looks at him.

Because suddenly the only thing I can think about is Neil and Judy and Harvey. And I'm realizing that if Trevor goes back to this jerk, I'm going to usurp Neil as Captain of the SIMP squad and be everything I begged my buddy to stop being. The friend. The rebound. Anything I can get.

I hear the door from the truck slam and gravel crushing underfoot as Trevor's voice carries to me loud and clear. "I don't think you know what that word means."

Rounding the side of the house, I play like I'm not about to die inside. Like I don't have a single thing to worry about.

Raising a hand, I push my mouth into a slanted smile, barely sparing a glance at the built dickhead standing in front of my boyfriend with a look of confusion and heartbreak in his eyes.

"Hey, babe. That was some workout." I toss my goggles by the front stoop, striding into Trevor's space, dripping wet and acting like the possessive dickhead I've become in the last two minutes.

I lean down and kiss him on the mouth. Not jamming my tongue down his throat, but for a lingering beat... *like he's fucking mine.*

It ought to be enough. But in for a penny, in for a pound. So I add, "Almost as good as the one you gave me last night."

He coughs, blue eyes going wide as they search mine like they're wondering who the hell took over my body.

From behind me, I hear the ex mutter a curse. And then, "Jesus Christ, you're... the goddamn *swimmer?*"

Huh?

Surprise more than anything turns me around. The prick is staring at me, sizing me up. Whatever. Crossing my arms, I step in beside Trevor... who's also still watching me, the slightest hitch at the corner of his mouth.

Gonna take that as a good sign. I turn back to the ex. "Guess so. Cam Dorsey."

"Yeah. Leo." He shifts uncomfortably, but then gives it up. "Leo Rossi. I'm uhh... Trevor's roommate. We play for the same team."

And now I get why even when Trevor was telling me about this relationship, he was so careful with the details. Nothing to indicate who this man was. No dots to connect.

This dick has no idea the respect Trevor has given his privacy.

"Do you play for the Slayers too?"

He blinks, and a flash of jealousy drifts over his face before he wipes it away. "No, I'm down in Springfield. Hey, man, you want to give us a minute here?"

That would be a hard no. I really don't. But I turn to Trevor, and the corner of his mouth is hitched even higher. "Is that what you want?"

For him, I would. But Trevor shakes his head and threads our fingers together. "Nope. You belong here. If Leo's got something to say, he can say it in front of you. Or he can go. Either way, it isn't going to change anything."

I swallow past a surge of emotion, nodding with a smile I'll give him the words to match when we're alone.

Leo ducks his head. "Come on, T. You know it's not over. Not for this guy."

I raise a brow, but Leo just grinds his molars together and blows out a breath. "Fine. You want to get yours? Okay. I deserve it after how I hurt you. You've got another week. Screw everyone in the state if you like. Get it out of your system, and I'll see you at training camp." He bites his lip and flexes his chest. "Just like last year."

I feel Trevor's hand tense in mine, and my blood starts to boil. In twenty-two years I've never been in a fight. Never even thought about taking a swing at someone, but those careless, condescending words have me finally understanding the urge to do violence.

"There's nothing to figure out, Leo." Trevor shakes his head in disgust. "It's over. If you've worked your shit out, I'm happy for you. If you haven't... not my problem. But yeah, I'll see you at camp. I'll be the 'out' hockey player fighting for a spot on the Slayers' roster. And you'll be just another player on the ice."

Leo pales, hands coming up. "Hold on. *Out?* You can't do that to me, man. We were roommates. We *lived together.* What will people think?"

Trevor shrugs. "They'll think you had a roommate who dates men. And I guess it's up to you if you want to be someone who didn't care or someone who did. Or even someone who dated me but made mistakes, learned from them, and is in a better place now. Whatever you do, Leo, it's up to you and it's *on* you. And... honestly, I wish you the best. But I'm ready to make some chicken and spend the night with the guy I love, and I don't want to waste a single minute I have left with him."

I've been listening, offering my quiet support to this point, but now—

Did he just say—

I turn to him, pulling his hand close to my pounding heart. He loves me?

Trevor ducks to kiss my knuckles as Leo rounds his SUV in a huff and slams the door. Neither of us look as he drives away. Because what matters is this. Now.

"Love, huh?" I ask in a voice choked with emotion.

"From that first night, Cam. I loved you then, and I love you now. And even though I understand the kind of life I have to offer you can never compete with the life you have here, I just... I want you to know that if it could... I'd love you forever."

My heart cracks open right then and there. Pulling Trevor into my arms, I kiss him hard and deep and with everything I have. I kiss him like I love him because the truth of it is that simple. I do. And when I break away, it's just enough to whisper against his lips, "I never stopped. I love you too."

206

TREVOR

He loves me. I don't know if my heart can take what those words are doing to it.

Kissing, we stumble toward the house. Our hands are everywhere, his suit is soaking my shorts, and all I can think is...

Keep him.

I need to find a way. I'll do anything. But first, I need to show him how much I worship him.

We make it inside, and Cam whips my shirt over my head, growling as he pushes me toward the bedroom, his mouth on my neck, my shoulders, my chest.

"Love you," I pant, when I feel the bite of his teeth followed by the pull of deep suction at my shoulder.

"Love you," he rasps, maneuvering me down the hall to my bedroom. "So fucking much."

My legs meet the bed, but before I tumble back, I shift my weight, pulling him around so it's his body falling beneath mine. I lick through his navel and nibble the side of that sexy vee as I pry my fingers into the insanely snug jammers and peel them off.

"Christ, you're gorgeous." I can barely manage the words through everything I'm feeling. The love, the purpose, the need... and the knowledge that even with my soul so full of all of those things, it still might not be enough to keep him. If I gave up hockey, would he even want me to start a life with him here?

It's a question I need to think through, figure out how to finesse and present in a way that doesn't pressure or overwhelm him.

It's a question that's going to have to wait.

Cam jackknifes up to sit, his hands holding the sides of my head as he kisses me. Then he pulls back to meet my eyes. "I want you. I need you inside me."

I freeze, my body and mind on the brink of short-circuiting at the visuals bombarding my mind. We've used our mouths and our hands. Our fingers. But we've stopped just short of actual penetrative sex, neither one of us bringing it up as if we both knew it would take us to a connection too deep for the limits we were trying to preserve.

But now? "Are you saying—"

"I want us to be together."

I cover his mouth with mine, pulling our bodies as close as we can get with me still half dressed.

"Where's the bag?" he rasps against my lips.

I pull back. "The bag with the *wine?*"

He nods, wrapping his hand around his cock and giving it a torturously slow tug. Damn, that's hot.

So hot that it takes me a second to realize what he's asking for. Wine. Because he wants something to help him relax a little?

I nod, taking a step back from the bed, eyes still riveted to where his fingers have moved over his balls and... lower.

"Be right back."

I run for the front of the house, leaping off the stoop to grab the bag I left on the drive next to the truck. Then I'm tearing back in, sliding into the bedroom before I realize— "Shit! Glasses and an opener. One second."

"Wait!" Cam's sitting up, that hand that was having all the fun a second ago, now held up in a plea for me to stop. And he's laughing.

Which I *love* to see but don't understand. "What?"

He points to the bag I'm clutching in my arms like a baby. "Just, um... you want to take a look in there?"

No. I want to devour him with my mouth, tease him open with my fingers and tongue. I want to make him come so hard he forgets every man he's ever been with before me.

But yeah, I set the bag on the bed and realize there's more than just a bottle of wine inside. Curious, I peek in and choke on a laugh.

CHAPTER 10

TREVOR

*T*he wine comes out first. I set it on the floor. Close enough in case he actually wants some. But I'm getting the sense maybe it's what else he's got in here he's after.

Like the gigantic pump bottle of lube. "Sixty-four ounces? Think it'll be enough?"

Cam's got the sexiest, most adorable pink tint burning over his cheeks. "For tonight? Probably."

I nod, extracting the next item. A far more conservative box of thirty condoms.

"I love you." I can't say it enough, don't know if I'll ever be able to.

"Then show me." Cocking one knee, he teases me with a view that takes my breath away.

My shorts and underwear hit the floor point two seconds later, and then I'm kissing and biting my way up his long, sexy leg, rubbing my face against his inner thigh and nuzzling beneath his sac.

He pulls me higher, begging for my kiss and then begging for more. I fill my palm and his with the slippery liquid and rub it over his shaft and balls, getting impossibly harder when I add more and generously rub it over his needy hole before sliding a finger in.

I pump slowly, in and out. Warming him up with one finger before adding another.

We kiss and tease, sliding together as I work him open. I take my time, watching carefully. Neither of us are virgins, but this will be *our* first time together, and I want to make it good for him. I want him to feel how much I love him. To know that he is my world.

I press deep, stroking over his prostate and reveling in the way he starts to shake and gasp.

"Need... you to... oh God, baby... Need you to fuck me."

Shifting onto my knees between his legs, I roll on a condom and cover it with more lube before lining the tip up with where he's waiting for me. Then slowly, carefully, I push inside.

"Relax for me, Captain," I whisper, shifting my weight forward to lean over him as I give him more, push deeper. As he lets me make his precious, perfect body mine the way my whole damn heart is his.

Our eyes meet, and a ghost of a smile flickers over his parted lips.

And it's perfect.

It's love.

It's worth so much more than the career I thought was my whole life. More than the place where I live. More than all the million things that occupied my life before I found him again.

"Never letting you go," I grunt, something savage and primal taking over as I piston inside him, angling my hips to make sure I'm hitting that sweet spot with every thrust. "Never going to leave."

He's shaking beneath me, gasping my name as our sweat-slicked bodies move together, as each thrust comes harder.

"More," he begs.

I give him more, his pleasure fueling mine.

"Harder… *God, like that.*"

I'll give him anything, everything.

"Trevor!" He throbs around me, his release painting my stomach and his with ropes of come.

And that's it. I'm done. Lightning races up my spine and I shout, coming inside him like I'm coming home.

CAM

I can hear the waves rolling in against the shore as the sky beyond Trevor's bedroom windows dims. We're lying together beneath the sheet, his big, muscly arm over my shoulder as my head rests against his chest. It's perfect.

After we cleaned up, we climbed back into bed and maybe even dozed a while. But mostly, I think we just wanted to *be*.

Here.

Quiet.

Together.

But it's time.

Tracing the lines of his chest with my fingers, I peer up at him. "Think now that the heat of the moment has cooled a little, you want to talk?"

His chest stops moving. "That what it was? The heat of the moment?"

I shake my head, shifting so I'm more on top of him than not. "It *was* hot. And yeah, we were caught up some. But no, not entirely."

Trevor brushes my hair from my eyes. "I love you."

Direct and to the point. This is the man from four years ago. The one who knew what he wanted from the start and, afraid or not, went after it.

"I love you too. So we both meant what we said about that."

He swallows, those beautiful eyes searching mine. "I meant what I said about everything. I can't leave you again. I won't."

I blink. He's not saying what I think he's saying.

"Hockey?" I choke out through a tightening throat.

But he's already shaking his head. "I choose you."

My heart goes into free fall, and this time I can't even form words. But he's there, rubbing his hand over my shoulder and arm, touching me like he needs the contact as much as I do.

"Cam, if— if that's too fast or you don't feel comfortable yet—"

"No." Pushing up on my arms, I brace above him to take a kiss and breathe him in. "Not too fast." It's four years past the time I should have grabbed him with both arms and never let go. "It's just there are more options here than you giving up your career. The sport you love. *Your dream.* Because, yeah, I know that's what this is. I remember lying out in that field beneath the stars all those years ago and you telling me you'd been dreaming of playing hockey since you were old enough to put on skates."

"Yeah, and you told me the only thing you'd ever wanted was to run your dad's store with him. It's the reason we broke up. This town, this life is *your* dream and it's no less important than mine. Besides, dreams change. Mine is being with you."

And mine is spending the rest of my life working to be worthy of the kind of love this man is giving me.

"Trevor, listen—"

But he isn't ready. "Why would you come with me? I can't offer you stability. Hell, after training camp, I have no idea which city I'll even be living in. If it's like the end of last season, it could be both. It could be like that for a long time. And then there's the travel. You'd be left alone—"

"Trev, that stuff— hell, I don't know what that will be like, but we can figure it out as we go. That stuff isn't stability to me. *You are.* Having someone I love who loves me back. Someone who wants our life, whatever it looks like and wherever it takes us, to be... together."

His face twists like he's in pain. "I don't want to wreck your life."

"Then don't make me watch you sacrifice who you are and everything you've worked for because you think it's what I need."

"But you love it here. Your whole life is here."

Taking his hand in mine, I hold it to my heart. "I do love it here. And I expect we'll spend a lot of vacations here. We can have both. I'll find a team to swim on or play water polo with during your season. I'll watch your games and meet your friends. I'll— *we'll* build a life that we can love together."

I wait for his argument, ready to talk it through all night or however long it takes for him to see, to believe. But then the most magical, amazing fucking thing happens. A tentative smile breaks across his lips.

My heart starts to hammer, and I kiss him hard and quick, pulling back to see that smile stretch as he begins to nod with me. "So we're doing this? Really?"

"Yeah, Trevor." I laugh, and kiss him again. "We're really doing it."

And then he's laughing too, his eyes tearing up. "I don't know what to say."

"Why don't you tell me you love me again, because I don't think I'll ever get tired of hearing it."

"I love you. I'm so damn in love with you, I can barely see straight. And I'm totally bringing you coffee tomorrow and watching you ring up sales in that hot freaking shirt all day."

Him and that shirt. "The guys will be thrilled."

And they are.

ABOUT THE AUTHOR

Hard core romantic, stress baker, and housekeeper non-extraordinaire, Mira Lyn Kelly is a USA TODAY bestselling author with over a million readers worldwide. She writes sizzly love stories with hot, possessive heroes who know how to laugh, heroines who give as good as they get, friends as close as family, and happily ever afters up-against-the-wall style! Growing up in the Chicago area, she earned her degree in Fine Arts from Loyola University and met the love of her life while studying abroad in Rome, Italy... only to discover he'd been living right around the corner from her back home. Mira now lives in Minnesota with her husband, four amazing children and two ridiculous dogs. When she isn't reading, writing, or indulging her weakness for hard cut abs, she can be found running the kids around, watching the Chicago Blackhawks, and cooking with her family and friends. Want to know when Mira has a new book releasing? Sign up for her newsletter at: http://www.miralynkelly.com/newsletter

or get in on the fun by joining her reader group at: https://www.facebook.com/groups/MiraLynKellyPJParty/

ALWAYS LOVE ME

CLARE REBECCA MCCARTHY

CHAPTER 1

Of course, it shattered. That's what happens when fragile and in motion, meets solid and unyielding. Inevitable, really.

Glass shards skittered across the butcher block, coming to rest beside the flower vase and the magnetic knife holder. One jigsaw-shaped piece tiddly-winked into the blue ceramic fruit bowl, where it sat among the mandarins and spotty bananas.

Those were the fragments that tried to defy gravity. Not so lucky, the rest of the carafe. The bottom dropped like, well, like a glass coffee pot smacked on the corner of a maple butcher block. It hit the floor with a *pop*. What followed was a high-speed time-lapse film of continental drift. Glass continents and islands of various sizes settled amid seas of black decaf. Cabinets and shins were spattered.

Suddenly aware of her bare feet on the linoleum, she stood in place, holding the now useless black plastic handle. She set it down in the sink, bent, pivoted at the waist, and groped under the sink for a dustpan and brush.

She stood again and reached for the paper towels. Feet rooted in place, she gathered the largest bits by hand. That was when the tremors started. Her hands shook. Her forearms cramped as she tried to control the spasms.

Just a coffee pot, she thought. *You're here; this is now. Focus and clean it up. It has nothing to do with...*

Saying the name aloud was all it took to break her resolve. She sat against the cabinets, heedless of the glass under her coffee-soaked pajama bottoms, and willed her hands into submission.

"Transactional?" Michelle snorted. "Like prostitution?"

"Oh, please! Not even The Hulk wants to smash this." Gael waved her hands dismissively at her body.

"Smash? What are you, sixteen? And do I have to remind you that you promised to be kinder to yourself? There are plenty of people who would want to get with you. You're smart and funny and kind. You need to let someone in. So to speak."

Gael held her friend's gaze, nodded to acknowledge the kindness. Pre-transition, Gael had been so steeped in self-loathing that she couldn't even take a compliment. Michelle was training her not to deflect or reject.

"Maybe you're right," Gael said.

"Maybe?!"

"OK. You're right. But looking for someone means getting into the marketplace. That's a transaction. And shopping requires money. In romance, what's the currency? Wealth, prestige, youth, or beauty. Preferably a combination."

"OK," Michelle agreed.

"The first two are out of the question because we decided to be teachers."

Michelle rolled her eyes. "Yeah, what were we thinking?"

"I was drunk for most of the 90s," Gael shrugged. "I blame that. So, no money, no power, no youth."

"Speak for yourself."

"Objection sustained," Gael continued. "Anyway, that leaves beauty. And I'm not even close."

"Yes, you are. Look at you in your sundress, with the girls on display. And don't start listing off all the body parts you're unhappy with. We all feel that way; insecurity doesn't make you special. Nobody looks like the magazine covers, not even the cover models."

Gael nodded. "But you know how, when you create a LinkedIn profile, you're marketing yourself, right? You need to have something that grabs their attention within five seconds, or they move on to the next applicant. Dating's the same. Only, instead of selling yourself to potential employers, you're targeting. . ."

"Potential johns?"

"And we're back to prostitution," Gael smiled. "Seriously, though. The five-second takeaway on me is not compelling. And most people aren't gonna look any deeper than that. Which sucks, because I'm like a novel; I come with a time commitment. Besides, I'm not sure I have the skill set to be in a relationship. "

"I disagree. Your past doesn't count. You weren't really *you* when you were closeted. You're different now, body and soul. But I agree: online dating isn't for you. You need to get out and meet people. You can't spend the rest of your life making out with your cat."

"Nomi likes our Netflix & Chill time," said Gael. "And speaking of private time, I'm off to the ladies'. Wanna come?"

"I'm good."

"When Alex gets here, order me a sangria?"

The Twelfth Night (the owner was a reformed English major) was an oasis for Gael and Michelle. No matter how hectic life got, they never let more than two weeks pass without meeting at The Twelfth for a drink or two.

Gael stepped out of the July humidity and into the cool quiet of the bar proper. Adam was behind the bar.

"Surprised to see you on the day shift," Gael said. "Big plans for tonight?"

"My mom's 75th," Adam replied. "The family's taking her out to dinner."

"Tell her 'Happy Birthday' from me," said Gael.

Adam had been at the taps five years ago, the first time Gael and Michelle had stopped in. An unexpected snow storm had stretched a quick after-work drink into a three-hour stay. Had to wait 'til the plow came through. Safety first, after all.

That night Gael decided The Twelfth had been designed specifically for her. It was part pub, part restaurant, part used book store. Along the west wall, opposite the bar, were floor-to-ceiling bookcases. In addition to a half dozen small tables, The Twelfth had an area with overstuffed armchairs, where one could relax and read with their beverage of choice. The books (but not the drinks) were also for sale to-go, paperbacks for $2, hardcovers for $4.

The bookcases even had a ladder on an iron runner, like in Henry Higgins' study. The ladder was padlocked to an iron ring. Gael looked at it now with equal parts embarrassment and pride. Once, on a dare from Michelle, Gael had hopped onto the ladder, slid the length of the wall, and acted out the bookstore scene from *Beauty and the Beast*. The Twelfth's management chained the ladder the next day.

Banquet room was upstairs; restrooms were in the basement.

"Hey Gael," said Alex, who was closing out a check at the hostess station.

Gael smiled. "Michelle's gonna order when you get a chance. I'm off to powder my nose."

"If that's where your nose is, you should ask for a refund from your surgeon."

Gael shook her head in mock offense, striking a "Girl, please" pose.

Descending the narrow stairwell, Gael remembered a time when smiling was rarely genuine. Michelle had remarked how, pre-transition, Gael never seemed to smile with her whole face. *Lots to be grateful for these days*, Gael reminded herself.

The sangria and Michelle's prosecco (with fresh strawberries) were sweating on the table when Gael returned.

"How are things with Mari?" Gael asked tentatively.

"Better. We're talking more, so that's good."

"The librarian thing? Still?"

Michelle winced. "She doesn't bring it up, but I still feel guilty."

"You know you didn't do anything, right? It was harmless flirting. . ."

"That Mari and Bella walked in on. Shit, Gael. I don't know what I was thinking."

When Marisol and Michelle got engaged, they asked Gael for a wedding gift that wasn't on any registry. Gael's final act before HRT was a visit to a fertility clinic. And now Michelle and her wife had a stunningly beautiful five-year-old named Isabella.

About six months ago, Marisol was picking Bella up from daycare. They were meeting Michelle in the public library to pick up books for the week's bedtime stories. Michelle arrived first and was chatting with the children's librarian. She complimented the woman on her Tom Ford sandals. In Michelle's defense, people who wear thousand dollar sandals to re-shelve copies of *If You Give a Pig a Pancake* are looking for attention.

The librarian, whom Marisol later christened "that Dewey decimal *puta*," bent her leg to display the little gold lock on the sandal's strap. Michelle leaned in to look. And that's when Marisol and Bella walked in. Story time was a little tense that night and for several thereafter.

"I admire how you guys talk through your problems," Gael said. "Communication's never been my strong suit. You'd think, being a language teacher, I'd bring stronger skills to the table."

"Appetizers, ladies?" Alex appeared behind Gael. "How's that nose?"

"Thank you for asking," Gael said with exaggerated perkiness. "My surgeon says it's Hollywood caliber. I'm not really sure what that means, but I'm pretty sure it's a compliment."

Alex slapped her shoulder playfully. "How's Mari?" she asked Michelle. Alex and Mari had been a couple for a hot minute some years back.

"She's good. Busy, but good. Is that new art, Alex?" asked Michelle. "It looks great."

Alex extended her right arm to display her sleeve of tattoos. Gael hoped her tiny involuntary gasp would go unnoticed.

"I added the caged heart two months ago," she said, pointing to her bicep. "So now I had him extend the tendrils from the rose on my shoulder into the cage."

Gael's mental jukebox played a Dropkick Murphys song about expressing love and commitment in a rose tattoo.

"Can I get the mini-caprese kabobs?" she asked.

"Beet salad for me," said Michelle.

"And another round, ladies? Be right back."

Gael watched Alex take the order inside. Not for the first time, Gael gave silent thanks for The Twelfth's uniform: black jeans, black T-shirt. Long sleeves in the winter, short sleeves or tank in the summer. Alex went with the latter today, displaying the ink on her arms, shoulders and back.

Gael forced her attention back to her friend. "I love being properly gendered," she said. "It's such a small thing. But it makes me disproportionately happy."

"Well, aren't you easy to please," said Michelle, rolling her eyes.

The conversation took its inevitable detour into school talk. Michelle recounted the antics of Alan the Ass-Waffle, as she referred to her principal. She had taken an FMLA-approved twelve-week leave at the start of the 2021 school year. Bella was a toddler. Schools across the country were taking precautions against the pandemic, but teachers understood that *safer* wasn't even remotely *safe*. Michelle chose family over work. Alan now took every opportunity to remind her she was not a team player.

Eventually, the conversation circled back to intimacy. Michelle asked, "Do you think you're using COVID as an excuse? So you don't have to reach out to anyone?"

Gael sipped her drink thoughtfully. "At first, yeah. We work with kids, so you err on the side of caution. But masked and six feet apart is no way to meet someone. Now, thirty months down the road, I don't know. Yeah, I guess I'm probably avoiding things."

"When's the last time someone got past your defenses?"

Gael lied, "About eight years." It was more like ten, well before transition. "I'll flirt, but beyond that? I can't. It's part-inertia, part-fear. I've worked so hard to be healthier, to live in stillness and gratitude. I don't want to jeopardize that just because I want to be held."

"Well, let's game this out a little," said Michelle. "Pretend you meet somebody. You flirt a little, like you do with. . ."

"Alex," Gael started.

"Oooh, good one! I could definitely see you and Alex together."

"No," Gael hissed. "I mean, she's behind you. Hi, Alex."

Gael hastily gave her full attention to systematically removing the condensation from her glass. Alex set down the appetizers and drinks. Gael darted a quick glance. If Alex had heard the conversation, her expression betrayed nothing.

When they were alone, Michelle leaned in and said conspiratorially, "So, Alex?"

"I think she's. . .I just . . .It's not. . ." she stammered, shut her eyes, rocked a little in her seat. "Please don't. . ."

"You know I wouldn't. I get it; I do. That haircut is sharp enough to cut paper. And those forearms? She's hot alright. Marisol always did have excellent taste in women."

"I could happily spend an afternoon tracing her tattoos," Gael sighed.

"With your tongue?" teased Michelle. Gael squeaked involuntarily.

"Kinda robbing the cradle there, aren't you? How old do you think she is?

"I'm guessing 30-ish. That's not so young."

"Old enough to know better," Michelle teased. "What do you know about her?"

"Not much. That one time she had an after-shift coffee with us, she said she was holding down two jobs. Three shifts a week here at The Twelfth and then working the loading dock at— where was it? Wal-Mart, maybe?"

"Target," Michelle corrected.

Gael immediately fell into her trademarked process of talking herself out of something, barricading feelings with reason. "This is probably just Barista Syndrome. You flirt; you think, 'Was that real?' A rational person understands that the answer is always "Hell, no!" She's doing her job. It's a transaction. She gives me the illusion that I'm attractive enough. In return, she gets a loyal customer who tips well."

"You don't really think Alex is that mercenary, do you?" countered Michelle.

"No, I meant in general. Look, male or female, I don't want to be that obnoxious jerk who feels entitled to hit on the hot waitress."

"That's not what you're doing. Alex knows your sitch. Even if the answer is no, she'd put it in the right context. Maybe she'd even be flattered. Hold that thought; *voy al baño.*"

"Promise you won't say anything to Alex?"

Michelle squeezed her friend's hand reassuringly, then walked inside.

After transitioning, Gael had made herself a number of promises. Be kinder to yourself. Stop apologizing so much. And as to romance, be patient; wait for someone else to take the lead. If you change the dynamics, you might change the outcome. But, come on! Ten years and four months! Pretty soon you're gonna need an archaeologist to find your, uhm, nose.

"What if Alex isn't interested?" Gael fretted. "I'd be too ashamed to come back here. Being with Michelle at The Twelfth is part of what keeps me balanced. I can't lose that. Yeah, there are other places, but this is our spot. I don't want to ruin it.

"What if Alex *is* interested and I bollix it up. Again. Michelle's right; this would be my first time in the right body, but is that enough? I'm not good enough for someone that gorgeous.

"Maybe she's a smoker, or she's religious, or she wants kids. Oh my god! What if she likes reality TV shows? I'm screwed either way. If she turns me down, I'll spiral into depression. If she says yes, the anxiety will eat me alive. Goddammit, I thought I was healthier than this. Why do I. . .?

Michelle returned to find Gael scrunched up in the chair, knees against her chest, eyes screwed shut.

"Shh, it's OK. You're safe. Give me your hand and let's focus on the breathing. In — two, three, four. Release slowly — two, three, four, five, six. Keep your eyes closed, but let's put your legs back on the ground. Slowly, now. Good. Another breath in; hold it; out. Open your eyes."

"I'm sorry," Gael said. "I worried myself into a bad spot. I couldn't breathe. I'm sorry."

"Don't apologize. You're safe; I'm right here. Take a sip. You OK now?"

Gael nodded, wiping her eyes on the cocktail napkin.

"Fortunately for you, I solved your problem while I was in the bathroom. I know what you need."

"More Lexapro?"

"No. You need Narcissist Radio."

"What's that, a phone app?"

"No, it's a game. You get all tense, right? When you think about being with someone? Narcissist Radio is what you need."

Gael considered being offended. Was Michelle saying she was an egomaniac? *I frequently have my head up my butt, but narcissist?*

"Just listen," Michelle smiled. "I was sitting inside and Joe Cocker came on the playlist. So, I started in on something I do on my commute. I swap the 1st and 2nd person pronouns in love songs. So, I'm in there peeing away, and singing about how I'm everything someone hoped for and needed.

Together they crooned the chorus. And they laughed.

"See? That's the point. Self-doubt freezes you. But if you break the tension, you can move past that shit. Laugh and release. Narcissist Radio is so silly it pulls you outside yourself. Then you're grounded in perspective, not panic."

Gael considered the idea. "Like how a scare will cure hiccups,"

"I was thinking, more like how a toddler can be distracted out of their tantrum," teased Michelle.

"Shut up. Does make sense, though."

Michelle adopted a faux radio DJ voice. *"Narcissist Radio. W-E-G-O. All me, all the time.* You try one."

Gael thought for a moment, then, focusing on the exquisite image of the back of Alex's neck, she began. Applying the rules of the game to Prince's lyrics, she waived the requirements of wealth, cool, and astrological compatibility in favor of a. . . kiss.

As if summoned, Alex appeared and asked, "Karaoke night already?"

Caught mid-lyric, Gael looked up at Alex and blushed.

"Tell me you didn't hear that," she said. "Michelle, did I ever tell you about that time I was babysitting? Bella told me I was the worst singer she ever heard. 'In my entire life,' she said. She was three."

Alex chuckled. "From the lips of babes. One more round?"

"We're good," said Michelle.

"Right back with your check."

Gael watched her go. *To be honest, it is kinda hard to breathe around Alex. Those grey eyes, the raven hair, thin lips. Those silver labrys earrings: definitely a top.*

They paid the bill, left 50%, and sat quietly in the moment. Gael re-centered by being grateful. A dear friend, a safe place to be vulnerable, cold drinks on a hot afternoon. The friends gathered their things and hugged goodbye.

"I'm gonna check out the bookshelves before I go," Gael said.

"The bookshelves, huh? Right. Good luck." Michelle smiled, crossed her fingers, headed toward the parking lot.

Gael sat back down. The cost of being closeted was eternal vigilance. She'd hidden herself behind a defensive wall for thirty-five years before coming out. Over time, the inner voice had devolved from protective to critical to downright abusive. It spoke now in soothing tones.

You don't need to do this today if you're not ready. You don't need any more books. Let it wait. There'll be other Saturdays. You can work it into a conversation with Alex more casually. There's no shame in knowing your limits.

The voice was so very reasonable. This wasn't surrender, just a strategic retreat. Another time then.

"Change your mind?" asked Alex.

Gael started out of her reverie. She fumbled for a cover story. Maybe she should pretend to fiddle with her phone. Maybe she could pull off being light-headed in the sun. Or maybe she should, for once, just be honest about what she wanted.

Before Gael could speak, Aretha Franklin's voice wafted over the patio speakers. The Queen of Soul reminded her that even a lost soul can be reclaimed by something as simple as a kiss.

Gael looked at Alex and smiled. With her whole face.

CHAPTER 2

$\mathcal{M}$ateo surveyed the K-Cup selection in the basement of First Congo. He plunked a pod of Green Mountain Coffee's Nantucket Blend into the cockpit and punched the single serving button. The machine whispered, burbled, and sluiced caffeinated goodness into his paper cup.

The coffee maker was a donation from a former group member who'd since moved out of state. *One of the many effects of COVID,* Mateo thought. *Recovery's hard enough without worrying about whether someone coughed over an open coffee pot.*

He fit the plastic lid on his cup and took his usual seat in the circle of folding chairs.

Leonard called the meeting to order and explained the ground rules. These were affectionately known as Leonard's Laws. Leonard held up a laminated poster of these rules superimposed over an image of stone tablets. The Ten Commandments of Anger Management.

There were fewer than a dozen people in the circle tonight. Mateo knew three from previous meetings. Christy was a single mom with twin boys. Vic split his time between AA and this anger management group. And the Rachel Maddow looking one, whose name Mateo could never remember.

Leonard requested that the noobs introduce themselves, then asked for a volunteer to begin. Mateo's voice was low and thoughtful.

"I've been thinking a lot about what you said at the last meeting, Leonard. About trying to locate where in your body you feel the stress, or the anger, or whatever. How paying attention to that can help manage the feelings. Rule #7, right? Anger is an Emotion, Not a Strategy.

"I started thinking back to my second tour in Afghanistan. Our FFB was near Herat, not too far from the Iranian border. Up in the mountains, there isn't much the Taliban doesn't know about. Their recon is outstanding. Two tours there, one in Iraq, I never lost the feeling of being watched. Like a constant background hum. What's that saying? 'You're not paranoid if they really are watching you.'

"One day, a foot patrol found an IED near the Jebrael Library. The patrol contained it; nobody got hurt that day. But we were all on alert. Next day, I went out with a mounted patrol, five of us in an APC. Like I say, no stealth required. The Taliban knew we'd be coming. The APC is blasting Megadeth in all directions. Let 'em know, y'know? Don't fu. . .sorry, Leonard. Rule #4: No Cussin'. Don't *mess* with us.

"I was thinking about that day. My patrol and I stayed sharp, clear heads, deliberate actions at all times. No mistakes. But inside, I remember a sensation. Like I was leaning into the rubber band on a slingshot. A tightness sort of in my chest, but beneath the surface. Didn't mean anything in the moment; we had a job to do. But now that I was on the outside lookin' in, I remembered it.

"Anyway, that was then. Now, at work, there's this manager guy. He's an absolute. . . jerk."

Leonard nodded appreciatively. Christy gave Mateo a double thumbs-up.

"He's got that, whaddyacallit, Napoleon Complex. He's about

five feet four inches tall, all chest and bluster, you know? Got an answer for everything, even when he doesn't have a fu. . . a clue. Lazy and quick to blame someone else for his mistakes.

"So, I get home, and I realize I'm feeling that same tightness in my chest. That same kind of torque, right? And the light bulb goes *click*. I sit down and put myself into the memory of that patrol again. Me in the present convinces past me to relax that tension. And when I come back out of the memory, I feel fine.

"Long story short: I've been making a little ritual of it every night. Half an hour in a dark room with one candle for a focus point. I pay attention to each part of my body, toes to head, nice and slow. And I let my mind go wherever. If it makes a connection to a memory, I try to pay attention to that. Sounds silly when I say it, but it's working."

The group shared supportive comments. Leonard praised Mateo for his efforts. "Remember that, in the moment, when you feel a negative outcome coming," he addressed the group, "having a plan can save you. Have a safe place to go, whether in your mind or in the real world."

So far, so good. The phone rested silently on the arm of the couch. Michelle had agreed to be on call for Gael on the night of the date. In the event of an anxiety attack, she could either talk her down, or come get her.

Marisol, who worked as an engineer at a small gaming software company, remarked that Gael's date night prep routine was surprisingly similar to the process of debugging code. She and Michelle sat at either end of the couch, watching a group of track-suited Koreans play a lethal game of Red Light, Green Light.

Michelle paused the show as her wife said, "Does Gael really need to prepare for every contingency? I love her too, but sometimes I think *su corazon esta*. . .all lists and diagrams."

Michelle nodded. "I think of it like improv comedy. Gael only feels secure enough to improvise when she has an outline in her head. She lived way too much of her life closeted, fretting about being discovered. Some scars don't fade."

"I want what you want, *mi vida*. I want to see her happy. I'd just hate to see her miss a chance because it wasn't part of her emergency evacuation plan."

Michelle locked eyes with her wife. "You haven't called me that in a while, Mari. Not since. . ."

"It wasn't intentional," she said. "I was upset at first."

"Don't I know it. You slept on the couch that night."

"That was a mistake," Marisol said. "*Don't let the sun set on an argument*, my mother used to say. We should have talked right away. *Lo siento*."

"It's just as much my fault," said Michelle. "I could have come to you. I've been waiting for the right moment, but also sort of avoiding it too. I was telling Gael how I still feel guilty."

"You did nothing wrong. I overreacted. Between Bella and work, we've both let chances to talk slip by. *No mas*." Marisol mimed wiping her hands clean. "I'm good. Are you good?"

Michelle scootched closer. "I'm good," she said, kissing her wife's forehead, chin, and lips. Marisol's kiss was backed by fire and force. And forgiveness.

They paused for breath, forehead to forehead, "*Te amo*" whispered Marisol. "But know that if I ever see that *hija de puta* near you again, I will shush her permanently." Then she smiled and added, "No matter how nice her shoes are."

Gael chose The Blue Iris for dinner. Just upscale enough to be special, but not so high-end that she'd regret the expense if things went all pear-shaped. The Pan-Asian menu offered enough variety to sidestep any allergies or dislikes Alex might have. What's more, it was centrally located.

Oh, the pile of discarded outfits! For the third time, Gael tried on the burgundy satin blouse she'd already rejected twice.

"First button or second? Second. If I go down in flames it won't be from lack of trying. Which skirt makes my ass look irresistible? No, that's asking too much; I'll settle for least repugnant."

"Stop," she caught herself. "Don't do that. You look good in that tulip skirt with the ruffled edge. Let's finish up and go."

Sandals, teardrop earrings, silver anklet. No necklace. Why obstruct the view? Faintest touch of Whispers in the Library on each wrist and behind her right knee. Light makeup on the eyes. No lipstick = no smudges.

And then all the prep was behind her. She walked into the Blue Iris, glancing at herself in the mirror behind the bar for reassurance. She scanned the room and saw Alex at a back table. Her date (!) raised her glass as an invitation. Gael approached with all the confidence she could muster.

Alex stood, walked to meet her, and leaned in. Expecting a cheek-kiss, Gael turned her head. Instead, Alex held her lips millimeters from Gael's ear, whispered, "Fuckin' gorgeous," released her, and moved back to her seat against the wall.

Gael, who had closed her eyes at the approach of Alex's mouth, froze for six seconds. Tik. Tik. Anxiety drained away, replaced by a rush of something warm and nice. Tik. Tik. Best. Opening line. Ever. Tik Tik. Maybe you should open your eyes again.

A waiter appeared, took Gael's drink order, said he'd be right back with menus.

Gael smiled, laughed, and shook her head.

"What?" asked Alex.

"Nothing. It's silly. I. . . I practiced our conversation on the drive over," Gael blushed. "I imagined what we'd talk about, and tried to anticipate what I'd say."

"You mean, like Travis Bickle? 'You talkin' to *me?*'"

"Slightly less psychotic than that. I'm unarmed, by the way" Gael smiled and held her hands up in mock surrender. "But I was really nervous. It's been a long time."

"How are you feeling right now?"

They locked eyes.

"Calm. Safe. Like I'm where I'm supposed to be."

Alex nodded. "That's good, then."

The waiter took Gael's drink order and refilled Alex's water glass.

"Are you not drinking? Should I change my order?" asked Gael.

"You're fine," Alex assured her. "I don't drink, but no judgment. Mom had a problem; I learned it's not for me."

"Any brothers or sisters?" Gael asked.

"Only child. My father died when I was three. Not really a first date conversation."

The waiter returned and set a glass of cabernet on the table.

Gael said, "I chose this place because it's kind of magical. I'm Irish, so not much of a tolerance for the spicy. But this stuff feels much more like comfort food than, I don't know, mac & cheese. Or fries with gravy."

"Fries with gravy? Is that a thing?"

"Oh yeah. I don't believe in ketchup," Gael continued. "The Iris's specialty is this thing called Khao Soi. It's a curry noodle soup. Makes me happier than I'd ever imagined a soup could. I'm not ordering it tonight only because I sweat when I eat it."

"Can't have that," Alex said, hiding a grin behind her menu.

"Even on my darkest day, Khao Soi makes me smile."

"As long as it doesn't make you sing," Alex teased.

"I have a perfectly lovely, if somewhat baritone, voice. No matter what Bella thinks."

The waiter returned. Gael ordered the salt & pepper shrimp, Alex the stir fry string beans with chicken.

They charmed the interim with small talk. Alex spoke of her job in the Target warehouse, unloading tractor trailers, operating fork-lifts, running the pallet wrapper.

"That seems like it'd be a really testosterone-heavy atmosphere," Gael said. "That's not a problem?"

"I'm just one of the guys, you know? The older guys, they've seen it all and are basically cool. Once they saw I could handle the workload and do the job safely, they were on my side. Did have an incident once, but, you know."

"Can I ask?" Gael said.

"College boy, entitled little prick. Followed me into the bathroom. That was his first mistake. Wanted to prove his theory that a dyke could be cured by seeing 'a real man.' He started undoing his fly. I feinted at smashing his nose. While he got his hands up to protect his face, I planted my boot heel on his foot. Down he went, yelling and cursing. I hooked a finger in each nostril, dragged him out to Demetrios, the shift supervisor."

"Holy shit!" Gael said. "I hate that I have to ask this, but how did you not lose your job over that?"

"Almost did, but Demetrios stepped up for me with HR. I got an official reprimand, sort of a strike one notice. Had to complete an anger management course. Demetrios and the guys strongly hinted to the kid that he should find employment elsewhere. Hasn't been seen since."

Their meals arrived and they tucked in.

"Do you see yourself there for the long haul?" asked Gael.

"I have a five-year plan, but money's tight. It's starting to look like eight or ten years might be more realistic."

"What's the end goal?"

"Rather not say," Alex deflected.

Gael leaned across the table, a move that conveyed sympathy and, not coincidentally, revealed a strategic amount of cleavage. "You can tell me."

Alex held her gaze. She took a bite, chewed thoughtfully, and said, "I want to open a pet grooming place. With a mobile van for house calls."

Gael's face lit up. "That is so cool! I have two cats, you know. Would you do me for free?"

Alex sat, mouth agape, fork halfway to her mouth. "Phrasing?"

Gael blanched and avoided eye contact. "I'm so sorry. I didn't mean. . ."

"Don't apologize. You're cute when you're flustered."

Alex described how she'd written a business plan, was working toward her NGDAA certification, and was scouting for locations.

"All while working two jobs. You're Wonder Woman," Gael said. "When you open, promise you won't go with some cutesy pun name. No *Laundromutt* or *Bark Avenue*."

"Seriously? Is there anything about me that says cutesy?"

Gael took the opportunity to survey the woman sitting across from her. Angular features, slim frame, kohl-lined eyes suggestive of an Egyptian goddess. Alex wore a thrift store suit jacket, black with gold pinstripes, over her crisp white tee.

"No," whispered Gael. "Just hot."

Alex returned the stare.

"Let's get the check," she said. "It's time we were elsewhere."

CHAPTER 3

*T*hey sat together against the headboard.

"You're nervous," Alex said. It wasn't a question.

"Yeah," said Gael. "First time since transition. Have you been with a trans woman before?"

Alex shook her head. "You said at the restaurant you felt safe with me. You still feel that way?"

Gael nodded.

"Then here's what we're gonna do. We're gonna go slow. Tonight will be about learning."

Gael wore the crestfallen expression of a child told no cookies before dinner. "But kissing's my favorite part. Can there be kissing?"

"This isn't a game," Alex chided gently. "It can be a one-time thing, or we can look down the road. Time'll tell. But honesty and trust have to be at the center. Understand?"

"I do. Sorry."

"That's another ground rule: no apologizing. I mean it, Gael. I get the feeling *sorry* is your oxygen. I need you to be less fragile."

"OK," Gael promised.

"Tell you what," Alex conceded. "If you can go the next hour without apologizing, there'll be kissing later. For now, I'm gonna sit here. You're gonna stand over there."

Gael stood and moved and stood at the foot of the bed.

"There's a candle on the dresser. Light it, then shut off the overhead."

When Gael turned back, Alex stood, removed her jeans and top, then repositioned herself against the headboard. "You still OK?" she asked.

Gael nodded again, and did so truthfully.

"Good," said Alex. "Take your top off. Slowly, please."

Gael did, hung her blouse over the bedframe, and stood facing Alex. She thought about covering herself, but instead dropped her arms to her side.

"I'd like you to lift your breasts, please."

The significance of the request was lost on neither of them. Top surgery leaves scars. A physical reminder of a past better left unacknowledged. An admission of life in a queer body. Some people fetishize queer bodies. Others find them repellant. Dangerous ground, rendering vulnerable anyone who stood on it. Alex was asking for a show of trust. Gael looked into her heart, found only calm, and did as asked.

A long silence followed. Gael didn't flinch. Alex sat unmoving. Exhaling slowly, she said, "You. Are. Beautiful. Put your hands down, please. Now, I'd like you to take off your skirt and panties."

Gael marveled at the absence of anxiety, her oldest companion. *Where's the shortness of breath? Why aren't I deflecting my insecurity with jokes?* Unironically and without fear, she was stripping. Gael maintained eye contact with Alex as she hooked her thumbs into the waistband of her panties and wriggled them to the floor.

"Since bottom surgery, have you come?"

"By myself," said Gael.

"I'd like you to show me. That's all we're doing tonight. I want to see what makes you feel good. I want to hear it and feel it. I'd like you to sit here between my legs and get yourself off. I'll hold you, maybe I'll whisper some encouragement, but I won't interfere. Is that something you'd like?"

"Yes, please," whispered Gael.

Over the next hour, the rest of the world faded to silence, then vanished altogether. For perhaps the first time in her life, Gael was completely present. The heat of Alex's body at her back steadied her. Alex's breath on her neck heightened each sensation.

When Gael shuddered to a stop, Alex gently bit her earlobe and whispered, "Good girl. Thank you for trusting me. Tell me how your body feels right now."

Gael did, in fragments and sighs.

Alex said, "I want you to hold onto that. Whenever you feel not good enough, whenever you start beating up on yourself. Know that you deserve to feel this way."

There were tears. Then there were kisses. In time, there was sleep in the safety of loving arms.

"And you'll be a good girl for Tia Gael?" Michelle asked her daughter.

"Yes, Momma," Bella said, burying her face against Michelle's neck.

"You two are going to have so much fun. Tia Gael has everything planned out, don't you Tia?"

Gael held up her clipboarded list; Marisol shook her head in mock exasperation.

"I've put more fun into this list than any normal human could. Only Super Tia could bring this much fun!" Gael stuck out her chest, mimed a lightning bolt across it, and yelled "Zzbzzssh!"

Bella giggled, trying to imitate her aunt with a "Bzzz!" She wriggled from Michelle's hip and ran to Gael. "Show me! Show me!" she squealed.

"See right there? That says *alpacas*. Wanna go visit the alpacas at their farm tomorrow? And," Gael said, pulling out a tote bag from behind the couch, "since we have two nights of tubby time, I brought this!"

"Duck wars!" Bella grabbed the bag and dumped two dozen plastic duckies onto the floor.

"Duck wars," Gael agreed. "And you are *so* gonna lose this time."

"No, you're gonna lose!" Bella retorted. "Cuz I'm The Emp'ess of Duckland!"

"We'll see," said Gael. "You play with those for a bit, while I talk to Momma and Mami."

Marisol put her hands on Gael's cheeks. "You're so good with her. She's lucky she has you. So are we. And not just because you're giving us a getaway weekend."

Gael put her hand to her heart. "You're sure you're OK with Alex staying over tonight?"

"Many hands," said Marisol. "Besides, you've been together a month now. You're practically *esposas*."

"It's true," Gael said, turning to Bella and saying in an exaggerated stage whisper, "I *like her* like her."

"You two are to confine all activity to the guest room," Michelle scolded. "I put out clean sheets and towels in the guest bath."

"You will never know," Gael teased. "Laundry room? Carport? Butcher's block?"

"Shut up," Michelle countered.

"Momma, you're not a'sposed to say *shut up*," Bella corrected.

"Sorry, sweetie. Momma's just joking with Tia."

The three women unnecessarily ran through the details one last time. Bella belonged to her Tia as much as to her parents. And Gael had contingency plans for any events, up to and including a zombie apocalypse.

"Enjoy your B & B," Gael said, smirking. "Lots to do in the Berkshires, if you manage to get out of your room."

Bella hugged her mothers more than dutifully, but without tears. She was excited for her weekend with her Tia.

When the sound of her parents' car had receded, Gael said, "OK dinner's in an hour. I can either make Worm & Frog Casserole or we can order a pizza."

Bella deliberated solemnly while arranging the ducks into battle formation, then said, "Pizza, please."

With much splashing and laughing, Bella retained her title of Empress of Duckland. The victory meant she got to position all 24 ducks as she liked in her bedroom. Everyone knows that duckies in large quantities are a solid defense against bad dreams. Alex joined them after dinner, which meant that Bella got twice the bedtime stories and twice the goodnight kisses.

By 9:00, Gael was on the couch, curled into Alex's shoulder.

"Thanks for taking the night off," Gael said. "I know Friday's a good tip night."

"Bella's great," said Alex. "I mean, I'm glad it's a temporary gig. I couldn't do this 24-7."

"I know," laughed Gael. "When she's a teenager, I'm hoping I can be a refuge for her rather than one more adult messing up her life."

"Are Mari & 'Chelle planning to tell her about, you know, about you before?"

"We've talked about it. It depends on what Bella needs as she gets older. I'm cool with things as they are. Right now, I'd rather not complicate her relationship with the coolest aunt ever. But we'll see. We agreed that I'd pick up a quarter of her college costs, if she decides to go."

"What?" gasped Alex in mock alarm. "She's already five years old! You haven't already filled out the applications?"

"I'm not that bad," Gael said. "Wait, I'm not that bad, am I?"

"You're perfect," said Alex, leaning down for a quick kiss.

"Speaking of money," said Gael, "I wanted to talk to you about something. Promise you'll think about it before you answer?"

Alex nodded.

"I've been thinking that you could move faster on your five-year plan if you moved in with me. My house is big enough for us both, and renting is just throwing money away."

"You're not afraid of being a lesbian cliche? Moving in together after five weeks?"

"I'm trans; I spit in the face of stereotypes," said Gael. "We could split everything but the mortgage. That way, you're saving money every month. I'm saving on utilities and groceries. Plus, I get to wake up next to you every morning. Everybody wins."

Alex sat thinking. "That's a big step," she said, "but I can't argue about the finances. Thanks for offering. Let me think about it?"

"Of course. Want some tea?" Gael stood and headed into the kitchen. She stopped in the doorway and, looking back over her shoulder, asked, "Should I make a chores chart now or wait 'til you make up your mind?"

After Mateo, Christy began to describe her week. The twins had picked up a stomach bug at school. "Two exits, no waiting," was how she described the violent intestinal distress.

"Of course, I caught it next. The boys thought the sight of me rushing into the bathroom was hysterical. At one point they were standing outside the bathroom door, giggling.

'Mommy's pooping her guts out,' said Max.

"Yep," said Steven. "There goes her liver.'.

'Oooh, that was a spleen.'

'And that was her intestes,' said Steven.

'That's *intestines*, anus-face,' Max gasped between guffaws.

'Mom! Max said *anus*!'

"They chased each other into the kitchen, where Steven tripped over the pile of Legos I'd told them to put away earlier. Steven took a header. I heard the scream as his mouth bounced off a chair on the way down. I scrambled to clean off and pull up my pants. There was blood on the floor, on the table, on both boys; Max had tried to help stop the bleeding.

"I got them in the car, and to the ER. Had to stop twice to puke on the side of the road. He lost one tooth, and a second is loose. Fat lip, bruised chin, blood-stained T-shirt. Max said he thought having the four mutant turtles smeared with blood was pretty bad-ass. Steven gave a gap-toothed grin and agreed.

"'Do we have to wash it, mom?'"

"I got 'em home, put 'em to bed. And I just had nothing left, you know? I realized I hadn't slept more than two hours at a stretch for the better part of a week. And I was like, why am I all alone with this shit? Who's gonna take care of *me*?

"I'm back on the toilet, falling asleep, head full of dark thoughts, and I see my bathrobe hanging on the back of the door, right? Ugly green Goodwill thing faded to grey, patched in a few places. But the belt loops are still solid. I looked up at that flannel belt, and I. . . I. . . I was so angry and alone.

"It was just for a second." Now the tears started, hot and silent and ashamed. "I thought how easy it would be to loop that terry-cloth belt around my fists and. . . and." Her shoulders convulsed; she closed her eyes. "I saw myself do it. I wondered how long it would take. I thought, 'I'll go to jail, and then I'll go to hell, but at least this will end. This *not being good enough*? It'll end.

"And just like that, it was over. I was exhausted and scared and disgusted with myself. How could I be that angry? I would never hurt my boys, would I? I took the whole robe and jammed it into the trash. This wave of shame went through me.

"I just wanted to hide. I sat down in a corner of the hall closet, curled up in a ball, and sobbed. When I woke up in the morning, Steven had curled up with me. I don't remember him coming in, but there he was, asleep in my arms."

Respectful silence held everyone in place. Heads nodded in sympathy. After a few beats, Leonard asked the group for reactions. Rule #1: No Judgements. The group reviewed strategies to combat or forestall that loss-of-control moment. A first-timer asked if there were crisis hotlines to help with that. Mateo offered to give Christy his number after the meeting.

"Text anytime." he said. "I'll be there."

Christy listened to it all, but wasn't ready to make eye contact for a long time.

CHAPTER 4

*A*lex slipped out of bed silently so as to not wake Gael. Grabbing her shirt and a pair of Marisol's pajama bottoms, she slowly opened, then reclosed the bedroom door. Pausing to listen at Bella's door, Alex headed downstairs to the kitchen, where she made a pot of coffee.

Her Saturday shift at The Twelfth started at 10:30. A little quiet time in the backyard would give her a chance to think. She sat on the bottom stair, feet in the damp grass. Clippings from the recent mowing clung to her soles and ankles. The sun had yet to decide whether it wanted to clear the horizon, but a growing pink and orange light suggested it soon would.

She blew on the steam rising from her mug, watched it dance away and back, sipped tentatively.

What to do about Gael's offer? She couldn't argue that inflation was making her business plans feel less likely every month. With no equity, she had nothing to borrow against. And the reality was that sooner or later, something unexpected – car problems, health issues, rent hike – would devastate what little savings she'd managed.

The waking up together part was very appealing. There was no denying she and Gael had chemistry. Did they have what it took for the long haul? Only one way to find out, Alex thought.

Bella complicated things a little. The triangle of Gael, her daughter, and Bella's mothers seemed pretty well-balanced. Would adding another person throw it off kilter? Alex wasn't keen on kids in general. What was that line from the Hobbit movies? "Nasty disturbing uncomfortable things. Make you late for dinner!"

While Alex didn't want responsibility for a child, she had to admit she loved watching Gael at it. Joy radiated from Gael's face and voice around Bella. There was silliness and mentoring and comfort and, for lack of a better word, responsibility. Gael was most fully alive when she was with her daughter. And Alex loved seeing it.

Alex decided to have one more cup before slipping back into bed to wake Gael. She put her mug on the butcher's block, turned to the counter, and removed the carafe from the burner plate. Lost in thought, she turned too quickly, banging the carafe on the corner of the block.

Of course, it shattered. Inevitable, really. Glass shards everywhere. Like the break on a pool table, everything scattered at once. Alex's immediate thought was how to get everything cleaned up before Bella came downstairs. Dustpan, brush, paper towels. Gonna have to scour everywhere. Did I see one bounce into the fruit bowl?

As she picked up the largest pieces from the floor, Alex flashed back to an earlier time. Broken glass. Blood. Anger and shame. Fear in the eyes of someone she loved.

The crash had awoken Gael, who arrived in the kitchen to see Alex sitting on the floor amid the mess, head in hands.

"Alex, are you OK? What hap. . ."

"Go back upstairs, Gael," said Alex darkly.

"Let me get the vacuum cleaner. I'll help you. Are you cut?"

"Gael for fuck's sake!" Alex shouted. "Will you stop talking? Just go back upstairs, please. I'll fix this." She raised her head enough for Gael to see the rage in her eyes.

Gael took a breath, about to say something, then thought better of it and went upstairs. Alex heard her enter Bella's room. Great. The crash had awoken the girl as well. Gael slipped into her Tia voice, but it sounded more tentative, more performative.

Alex swept and mopped and searched all the nooks in the kitchen. Convinced she'd removed all the visible pieces, she ran the vacuum over the floor and counters. Sure enough, a few slivers jangled into the vacuum hose. *Sometimes the danger is hard to see*, she thought, and, if she were given to tears, she would have lost it then.

Instead, she grabbed her bag, walked out the back door, and drove home.

CHAPTER 5

*G*ael's phone pinged after midnight.

Can't talk yet. Sry. Meet me W 7 pm, 1st Cong Church?

Over the course of the day, Gael's mask had held. She told Bella that Alex had left to go to work. Not an outright lie. She'd held herself together in the morning at the playground, where she and Bella discussed the fast-approaching kindergarten year. She didn't cry on the bike path, where Bella said she wasn't ready to take off the training wheels yet. She remained stoic at the alpaca farm. And at night she laughed through yet another loss at Duck Wars.

But once her daughter was asleep, the facade broke. She turned on the television to cover her sobs. She had a glass of wine at 9:30. It failed to take the edge off, but she was unwilling to go for a second. She took a book to bed, tried to focus, but the scent of Alex was all around her. She held the pillow to her face, cried a little more, and fell asleep.

The text woke her and she spent the next two hours cycling through emotions. Relief. At least Alex had reached out. Disappointment. Couldn't they talk in person? Insecurity. What did I do to cause this?

Then she took a break to pee.

Back in bed, the carousel of moods. Indignation. Just delete the text. Let Alex stew for a while. Serves her right. Then, in rapid sequence, came guilt, apologies, and confusion.

At 2:13, she decided the adult reaction was to give Alex her space. She texted "K" and took her book down to the couch. It was after 3:00 when she fell back to sleep.

Alex sat on the front steps of the First Congregational Church watching as, on the sidewalk, a battalion of ants worked to remove a mantis corpse.

"Alex?" said Gael hesitantly as she rounded the corner and approached.

"Thanks for coming," said Alex. Her voice sounded relieved but her eyes held sorrow.

Gael nodded, waited for more.

"I told you about how, after that incident at the loading dock, I had to complete a course in anger management. Well, I stayed in the group. I don't go all the time, but I try to keep it regular. Maybe once a month. They're about to start inside now.

"I wanted to explain, but I needed to be in a safe place. This is where I'm safe. Not that I'm not safe with you, but. . . Will you come in and listen?"

Gael nodded, took Alex's hand, and walked in the side door and down to the basement meeting room.

Gael listened as Leonard ticked off the rules. She thought how brave Mateo was for trying to break old patterns and reach for something new. Her heart ached to hear Christy bare her heart.

Then it was Alex's turn.

"I'm Alex. Some of you have heard this story before, but I need to tell it again tonight. This is Gael. Last weekend, Gael asked me to move in with her. It was an easy decision, really." She looked Gael in the eyes. "I can't think of anything I want more.

"But then, Saturday morning, I accidentally smashed a glass coffee pot. I thought about Corinne, and it brought me to my knees. Gael deserves to hear the story, even if it means she changes her mind about me.

"My father died of a brain tumor when I was three. I don't remember him. Mom never recovered from the loss. She chased his memory to the bottom of a lot of bottles. I don't remember her drinking being a problem when I was little, but I do remember the smell of gin on her breath when she tucked me in at night.

"In high school, I sort of became her caretaker. Recovery was never in her plans, so I felt a lot of resentment. I was pouring all this effort and energy into a losing battle. I don't think she even noticed how out of control it was. If she'd sobered up, maybe she'd have thanked me.

"I'd try to get her to eat so there'd be something in her system to soak up the booze. Used to put out a plate of Ritz crackers with peanut butter because that's what I liked. I'd clean her up after she'd pissed herself. I started putting a towel down on the recliner so I could just wash that instead of scrubbing the cushion with stain remover twice a week.

"Came out when I was sixteen. Didn't go well. I wanted to wait until she wasn't half in the bag to tell her, but that was always a pretty short window of opportunity, you know? She slapped me, called me a slut, told me to get out of her house and not look back. I did. And I didn't.

"Just before the pandemic and the lockdown started, her landlord found her dead in her shitty little apartment. Alone. Renal failure: diabetes and hypertension. Bottle of Bombay Sapphire and a box of Ritz on the table beside her.

"Always thought we'd work it out down the road, you know? She'd sober up; we'd have a mother-daughter talk. Get some closure. Never happened. Never will.

"I decided to go back to Indiana for the funeral. A few of my relatives – not many, but enough – were on mom's side of the whole queer thing. But the closure would be worth the stress of them whispering and nudging each other, you know? I'd spent my adolescence being there for mom. Figured, one last time, I'd do what she couldn't.

"Corinne and I were in the bedroom, arguing about it. She didn't want me to go. Said it'd just upset me. Said old wounds should stay closed. Said I shouldn't put myself in a position where small-minded bigots would be judgmental. She got more passionate as she argued.

"When she said I didn't have to atone for the sins of a bitter old drunk, all the anger came out. Anger at her for not understanding. Anger at dad. If he'd lived, maybe mom never would have reached for a bottle. Anger at mom for being weak."

Alex paused, steeling herself to go on. In the silence, Mateo said, "I got you."

Alex shook her head slowly. Mateo nodded slowly and repeated, "I got you."

"I pushed Corinne. It was just instinctive, but it had anger behind it. She lost her footing, fell backwards. Her head went through the bedroom window.

"You know how, in the movies, there's a way glass shatters? That's because it's a prop. Real windows aren't like that. Her head's snaps back, and she's surrounded by jagged shards. It's like a giant mouth with all these sharp teeth still in the frame.

"We're in a fourth floor apartment, and she's practically hanging out the window. She cut the back of her neck, and there's a piece of glass sticking out of her shoulder. I acted on instinct, grabbed her by the belt and pulled her back in. I pulled her in, and her arm raked against one of those teeth. Opened a gash from her wrist to just above her elbow."

"She screams, and for a second, I don't know what to do. Corinne fell to the floor. I got her a towel, called 911. Ambulance took her to the hospital; cruiser took me to the station.

"I'd thought I'd be charged with assault or domestic abuse, but

Corinne wouldn't press charges. I don't know why. She refused to talk to me. A week later, I was served with a restraining order. That was two years ago.

"Except for work, therapy and this group, I've stayed to myself since. Haven't even been interested in being with anyone else. Nothing was worth the risk. Until you, Gael. I want to live with you. I want everything that goes with that.

"But when the glass hit the floor, I remembered: I don't deserve that. I'm one of the monsters. That first night? You said you trusted me. What if I hurt you? God, what if I hurt your daughter? I'm sorry, I can't. I don't deserve it."

Mateo held Alex's hand. Christy looked up from the floor and offered words of encouragement. Gael stood and walked out the room.

Alex had found no tears to mourn her mother's death. She'd felt deep remorse, but had not cried over Corinne. At the sight of Gael leaving, the levee broke and decades worth of tears came in a flood.

The meeting concluded, Alex found Gael sitting on the church steps. All traces of the mantis were gone.

"You're still here?" Alex said. "I thought. . . Doesn't matter. Can I sit?"

Gael nodded. They sat in silence as the last group members headed to their cars. They sat in silence as Leonard locked the door behind him. They sat in silence for a while thereafter.

"Thank you for coming," said Alex. "I knew losing you would be the cost, but I wanted you to hear it. You deserve the truth."

"That first night we were together," Gael began." You kept checking in. 'Are you feeling safe?' Why did you do that?"

Alex said, "I saw that you were pretty insecure about your body. I knew you'd need to feel safe to open up to someone else. I wanted it to be special for you, however things went between us."

"I know you know this," said Gael slowly, "but I'm going to say it anyway. My bottoming for you is a thing between us. It doesn't mean that I'm weak or indecisive outside the bedroom."

"I know that," said Alex.

Gael nodded thoughtfully. "The way you do that, how you make me more confident, it's made the last five weeks the best of my life. I don't want that to end. I need you to understand that I didn't hear anything in there tonight that changed how I feel about you or what I want."

"But," said Alex, "how can you feel safe, knowing what I am, what I did?"

"You said that meeting was your safe space. I left because I respect that. I didn't want to make it about us or about me. And I needed to think. Can you listen now?

"You're no monster. You have trauma. Sounds like more than one trauma point in your life. The trauma sometimes expresses itself in anger, little bursts that make you feel out of control, right?"

Alex nodded.

"Up until I came out, I believed I was damaged. Anyone who loved me was just deluded, because I knew I was unlovable. Being closeted was nonstop trauma. I hated myself for being different. I hated having to lie. I hated everyone and everything that convinced me I needed to lie to survive. When I'd see queer events, when I'd go to pride parades with Michelle and Marisol, I hated myself for being too afraid to be out.

"The difference between you and me is where we directed that anger. You have the occasional outburst. I turned all my rage inward. Everyone tonight was talking about the same thing: control, or lack of control. Well, I had to control everything I said, everything I did.

"Your tattoos? You control the narrative, you tell the story on your body. The rose is for Corinne. Sealed in blood. Every time you see it, you remind yourself of what happened. The caged heart? That's you. Tell me I'm wrong."

"All my art tells a story," said Alex. "This tendril is the track of her wound. At some point, I realized she'd probably had plastic surgery to cover the scar. I decided I'd wear it instead."

Gael continued, "Because you deserve to suffer, right? I kept it all in. And, over time, all that internalized rage morphed into self-loathing. Something bad happens? I deserve that. I'm alone or anxious or depressed? That's where I belong; I don't deserve anything more than that.

"You have a problem. So do I. You're aware of that problem. So am I. You're actively working to be healthier. Me too. So, I have to ask: are we more likely to succeed alone or together? Seems to me, the incentives are much stronger together."

Gael stood, walked down three stairs and knelt before Alex. "I understand what you said in there. Do you think I would do anything that would jeopardize my daughter's safety?"

"No," whispered Alex.

"Damn right. I would die for her. I would kill for her. I will do everything in between to protect her. And I'm asking you to be in her life. To whatever extent you're comfortable. But I want you there. In my house, in my bed, in my heart."

Gael leaned in towards Alex's lips, then swerved so that her mouth was millimeters from Alex's ear. "Plus," she cooed, "There'd be kisses. What do you think?"

Through a very different type of tears than she'd shed earlier, Alex said, "Yes. Please."

They stood and held each other, then walked arm-in-arm to the parking lot.

"Oh my god! Wait!" Gael shouted.

"What's wrong?" Alex asked.

"I know just what you need! Michelle taught me this strategy for when I start losing perspective. It's called Narcissist Radio!"

"Gael, this doesn't involve you singing, does it?"

"Shut up. It might. You pick a love song and change *I* to *you* and vice versa. It's silly and it forces me to say nice things to myself. I bet it'd work with temper too. Here: I'll show you an example."

"No, Gael. That's OK. You don't have to do that. I think I get the idea."

Gael started slowly, hoping for the sultry Whitney Houston purr.

"Please don't," said Alex

Gael showed no signs of stopping. In fact, she became more animated. She sang of "the way," both being in it and every step of it.

"This is punishment, isn't it? You're punishing me."

Gael took a deep breath as she headed into the chorus.

"The kid was right, Gael. You have the worst singing voice ever."

Undeterred, Gael extended her arms. She sang of love, of memory, of forever. She closed her eyes and pictured Whitney in the video. She hoped, in vain, that the image would inspire her to overcome tone deafness with passion. It didn't.

Alex covered Gael's mouth with her own. The kiss lasted either two minutes or two decades; it was hard to tell. When it ended, Alex whispered, "I love you."

Gael whispered, "You will always love me."

ABOUT THE AUTHOR

ESCAPE TO NEW ZEALAND

ROSALIND JAMES

AUTHOR'S NOTE

The Blues, Crusaders, Highlanders, All Blacks, Racing 92, and other teams mentioned in this story are actual rugby teams, and New Zealand is a genuinely beautiful place full of wonderful people. However, this is a work of fiction. Names, characters, places, and incidents are products of the author's imagination or are used fictitiously and are not to be construed as real. Any resemblance to actual events or persons, living or dead, is entirely coincidental.

ESCAPE TO NEW ZEALAND: PAST CHARACTERS APPEARING IN THIS BOOK

Marko Sendoa, Nyree Morgan. JUST SAY (HELL) NO (Bk 11). Marko is a blindside flanker (No. 6) for the Auckland Blues and the All Blacks; Nyree is a painter.

Rhys (Drago) Fletcher, Zora Fletcher. JUST COME OVER (Bk 12). Rhys is the coach of the Auckland Blues and a former All Black (flanker); Zora is a florist who was married to Rhys's late brother. She is also Hayden Allen's sister. Zora has one son, Isaiah Fletcher; Rhys has one daughter, Casey Fletcher.

Kane Armstrong, Victoria Gibson. JUST SAY CHRISTMAS (Bk 13). Kane is a lock for the Canterbury Crusaders (and Luke's brother); Victoria is a prosecutor in Auckland (and Nyree's closest friend).

Grant Armstrong, Miriama Armstrong. JUST SAY CHRISTMAS (Bk 13). Grant is the former coach of the Otago Highlanders and Luke and Kane's father; Miriama is Nyree's mother.

Carefully consider, what prevents you from living the way you want to live your life?

\- The Dalai Lama

NOWHERE TO RUN

*T*here's no elegant way to walk out on somebody with an enormous striped ginger cat in your arms. Unfortunately, Hayden Allen only realized that later.

He hadn't been able to wait for the lift. Instead, he walked fast up the stairs of the flash Wynward Quarter apartments and knocked at the door, feeling the excitement rise in him like bubbles in a glass of champagne. It wasn't tickets to Tahiti, but maybe it was even better, because it was personal. Anyway, it was too soon for anything like that. He knew it was too soon. Two and a half months—too soon.

He couldn't help it, though. He had a hopeful heart. Broken too many times, but he kept coming back for more. This time, though … this felt like it could be the real thing.

He stood in front of the apartment door and willed his heart to slow, shifting the cat in his arms, because the thing must weigh about ten kg and was carrying around another half its weight in fur. Maybe this was a stupid idea.

Harden up. It was a brilliant idea. You just have to execute. Get out of your comfort zone and take a leap. He rang the bell. And waited.

And waited.

Julian had said he'd be staying home tonight when Hayden had mentioned he'd be working late. The plan had seemed perfect.

Wait. Obviously, Julian wouldn't come to the door if he wasn't expecting anybody. But he didn't always lock the door, did he? Should he check?

Julian could be mercurial, especially lately. One day loving and affectionate, the next distant. Hayden had thought, *Give him space. It's a lot. It feels like a lot to you, too.* Now, he tried the handle. Unlocked. Still, he hesitated. Was that too much, walking in?

Not with a gift, surely.

He pushed the heavy door open. He'd been right, he realized with outsized relief. There was music coming from the speakers in the lounge, the sultry, bluesy stuff Julian favored when he was relaxed—or randy—and the smell of something delicious wafting in from the open ranch sliders.

It was going to be all right. It was going to be *better* than all right.

He kicked off his shoes with some difficulty—no hands—and headed out there, noticing the bottle of wine in the ice bucket on the kitchen bench along the way. Dinner and wine? That worked.

Julian was on the balcony, facing away from Hayden, dressed in shorts and T-shirt as usual, his lean body elegant even while tending to the oversized barbecue that was among his prize possessions, or, as he would say, "The one thing New Zealand does well, other than sheep, sailing, beaches, and a casual dress code." A pristine white yacht pulled out of its slip in Viaduct Harbour below, the sky was the serene blue of late spring, the drifting white clouds were reflected in the water that slapped against the quays, and the scent of grilling meat made Hayden's mouth water. As did the glass of white wine at Julian's elbow.

Julian had the best nose for wine Hayden had ever seen—and he used it. He could polish off a bottle by himself and only become sharper, his wit more cutting. Taste too sophisticated for Auckland, maybe, which made sense, because he was British. British, with a glamorous flat, a glamorous boat, a glamorous life, a way of looking down his aristocratic nose that thrilled Hayden ridiculously, a thorough knowledge of music, the ability to order the best food in three languages, a case full of classic books that he'd actually read, and the quickness of brain to converse wittily about all of it.

Jane Austen's version of an accomplished lady, in fact.

A plate of scallops breaded with dukkah waited on the metal benchtop, ready to be grilled at the last minute, but it was the paper packet with its white label that caught Hayden's eye. First Light wagyu beef tenderloin, and the sizzle of the filets on the steel was making his mouth water. That and the asparagus ready to go onto the barbecue with the scallops.

He was already tapping Julian on the shoulder when it registered. Scallops and First Light wagyu? To eat dinner at home? Alone?

Julian had excellent taste, though. Excellent, expensive taste.

Julian turned with a smile that lit up his electric-blue eyes, the chiseled cheekbones and the shine of his blonde hair, as always, making Hayden's heart beat faster. And then the smile left his face as if it had never existed. "Hayden. Dear boy. This is a surprise. Thought you were working late. Did you text me?"

"Wanted to surprise you." Hayden shifted the cat in his arms. The ginger tabby had been purring all along, and now, he decided to vocalize. The sound that had charmed Hayden at the shelter, full of chirps and varied tones. "With this," Hayden added. "Cat. For you. Like you wanted."

Julian stared at the animal, then said, "It's not the best time. I've got friends coming, as you said you were working. How about tomorrow instead?"

"Oh." Hayden was aware of the cat's weight, dragging at him. The thing was still talking, probably about scallops. Hayden hadn't had dinner yet—he hadn't even thought of it—and his stomach was telling him it was past seven-thirty. He was starved, in fact, and he didn't know when you fed cats. What if he was starving the cat, too? He had a bag of food in the car. Should he go get it? Clearly not.

He'd been right. It was too soon. Too much, and too soon. He'd been stupid.

"Babe?"

The sound came from behind them. From inside those ranch sliders.

It was one of those moments frozen in amber. Hayden turned, feeling like his head weighed twenty kilograms, and saw him. Tall, muscular, and fit as hell. Crisp dark hair, brown eyes, drop-dead handsome.

Hayden recognized him. First, because he was an actor on *Courtney Place,* New Zealand's favorite soap. Well, New Zealand's only soap, but who was counting. And second, because he was Julian's ex, whose photo Julian had shown him early on, telling him how he'd burnt the physical copy and broken the frame for good measure. "Burnt the deep-blue cashmere/merino/silk jumper he bought me, too, the one that matched my eyes, and sold the skis, which was all mad," he'd told Hayden. "But, heigh-ho, you know I have to have my drama, and I didn't want any reminders of the possible love of my life. Totally forgetting about the glory of that fabric blend, of course. The skis, now, I could live without. So much effort. He was such a materialistic boy, though, and to be brutally honest, there wasn't much happening under the looks. Whereas *you,* my darling, are all about what's real, aren't you? A wee bit earnest and boringly sincere, maybe, under *your* lovely looks, but then, you *are* a Kiwi."

"You didn't have to hang onto the reminders," Hayden had said, pulling him close and ignoring the brittleness. "I'm here now, and I'm real. *And* boringly sincere."

He was real, all right. Really stupid. All he could say was, "What? Oh. Are you—"

The bloke put an arm around Julian. "Mmm, lovely steaks. You *said* you had a surprise." He yawned and added, "Lovely nap, too," then asked Hayden, "I don't know you, do I? Trevor Makiri-Jones.

Julian's partner." He eyed the animal in Hayden's arms. "D'you always travel with a cat? Odd."

"But I'm—" Hayden started to say as the cold enveloped him.

Julian said, "I can explain."

Trevor said, "Explain what?"

Hayden said, through the buzzing in his head, "I don't know. That he's been cheating on me? What's the explanation for that?"

Julian didn't say the "explaining" thing again, or maybe he'd never said it to Hayden, because he told Trevor, "We were taking a break, or that's what you say now. What it *really* was, though, was breaking up. How did I know that you wouldn't be buggering off again this time? That *is* your pattern, do admit."

"Wait." There was ice where Hayden's blood should be, and more of that prickling buzz. In his arms. In his hands. He could still feel the cat, but that was the only thing anchoring him here. "You weren't cheating on me. You were cheating on *him*. We've been together two and a half months," he told Trevor. "It wasn't a fling."

I brought him a cat, he wanted to say, but that was stupid. Everybody could see the cat.

"So you see, I wasn't cheating on you," Julian told Trevor, still ignoring Hayden. "We were on a break. As noted."

"Not three weeks ago, we weren't," Trevor said. "That's not a bloody break, that's overlap. And I'm sorry, but what the hell is the story with the cat?" He sneezed into his shoulder, then did it again. "I'm allergic, and I'm on the call sheet for tomorrow. Can't be dashing and dangerous with a red nose, can I? Also, I clearly need to be breaking up, or at least having a fight, and whoever you are, toy boy, you're in the way. Two and a half months isn't a relationship. It's a fling. Sorry. You've been flung."

"No!" Julian said. "Don't go." Again, not to Hayden. "Give it a minute. Let's discuss. And then make up, because you know you'll want to make up. If it weren't for breaking up and making up, we'd have no relationship at all. That's our spice, and you know it."

Hayden wanted to make a statement. A declaration. A denouncement, possibly. His vision was blurring, though, and he was drowning. He could never get angry at the right time. Why couldn't he get angry? All he felt was humiliation. He said, forcing the words past the tightness in his throat, "Apparently I just got myself a cat. Either that, or it's back to the shelter with him, but he's an awesome cat. I'm pretty awesome, too. You're missing out on me."

"I'm sorry," Julian said, not sounding nearly sorry enough. "But I told you—Trevor's the love of my life. Look at him. Look at his *life,* then look at yours."

"I'm a lawyer," Hayden said, hearing how stupid it sounded.

"Looking at contracts for people with actual money? Really too dull for words, darling. And I meant an *elegant* cat, maybe a temperamental Siamese with some suggestion of pedigree, not some stripey ginger you got from the SPCA. You're so middle class. Such a striver. Which is lovely, of course, but not for me. Stay," he told Trevor. "I've made this fab dinner. Stay and eat it with me, and we'll talk it out. I was vulnerable. I was *hurting.* You know how I am."

No graceful exit, then, just a walk back down the stairs, because there was a couple at the lift—holding hands, then coming close for a kiss—and Hayden couldn't be around happy people tonight.

He got back to his car somehow, even though he couldn't even remember which floor of the garage he'd left it on and had to walk all the way around three floors searching for it, pressing the button on his key and trying not to panic. When he recognized it at last, he had to lean against it for a minute. His boring, middle-class, silver Mitsubishi sedan, which he'd bought used, because new-car prices in New Zealand were mad. He wasn't even a striver. He was just ...

Dull, apparently. He'd never thought he was dull. Was he hopelessly, pitifully mistaken?

No. You're not. You can't be. It's him, not you. Are you basing your self-esteem on the opinions of cheating Poms now? And their shallow soapstar boyfriends?

The pep talk wasn't working.

An older woman stopped and asked, "All right?"

"What?" He stood up again. "I—I'm fine. Sorry. Fine."

"You're white as a sheet, love," she said. "Sweating as well. Having any chest pain?"

Yes, he wanted to say. "No," he said. "Thanks." And opened the car door.

He didn't have a cat carrier, so he put the cat on the passenger seat. This morning, he'd had a partner and no cat. Now, he had a cat and no partner, and he was so hungry, he was lightheaded with it. Or maybe that was grief. He couldn't even tell what he was feeling.

He laid his head against the steering wheel and breathed. In and out. In and out. Hoping the woman had left, and that she wasn't ringing the ambos at this moment. *That* would be embarrassing. What would you say? "Sorry, not dying, just heartbroken again?" Half of him wanted to laugh at the idea.

Not like it hasn't happened before, he told himself. But where some men grew calluses, it felt like he lost a layer of skin every time, and now, every nerve was exposed and screaming.

He'd been so *stupid.* And he wasn't somebody anyone could love.

Stop it, he tried to tell himself. *It's a bump. That doesn't mean it's you. Maybe you should ring the ambos. Always one hot one, with ambos.*

It didn't feel like a bump, though. It felt like a hole ripped straight through his heart. Like he couldn't do this anymore.

He felt a soft tap on his face and turned his head. The cat was standing on the center console on his hind legs, one snow-white paw on Hayden's shoulder, the other tapping at his cheek.

"Reckon it's you and me, George," he told the cat. He didn't know where "George" had come from. It just had. "Two blokes with nowhere to go." His throat closed at the thought, but he kept talking. That was what he had. Talking, and being funny. He'd be funny again. He had to be. "Guess we're going there together."

Luke Armstrong woke up hurting.

Yes, it was Monday morning, and yes, he'd played a rugby match last night, and yes, he was a prop, which meant his job was as much about collisions as any demolition derby driver—or any demolition derby *car*—which meant he always hurt.

This hurt was different, though.

He rolled out of bed and stood up, forcing himself to feel his bare feet planted on the floor, to look out the window and take in the day. The rooftops of Paris were shrouded by drizzle this morning, the beads of moisture collecting on the glass, the swallows that swooped in acrobatic flight during the long summer evenings long departed for North Africa in search of warmth.

Luke knew how they felt. He wasn't relishing being out there himself today.

He made his way over the ancient floorboards to the bathroom with its black-and-white tile, ducking his head through the low doorway. Five minutes later, after sluicing his head with cold water and then doing it again when the first time didn't work, he was in the kitchen making coffee and cooking a pan of eggs to fuel him for the trek to the practice facility. The hardest journey of the week, when every cell of your body was screaming for rest.

He'd been playing rugby almost as long as he could remember, and he was used to hurting, used to going on when he didn't think he could. That was his world. That was his life. So that wasn't why he was still standing here, staring in the mirror at red-rimmed eyes. It was because ... he couldn't do this anymore.

Thirty minutes until he had to be out the door. He downed a couple of paracetamol, washed them down with two glasses of water, pulled on track pants, then opened the refrigerator, hauled out the seven bottles of strong, dark *Bière de Noël* that remained there, opened the tops one at a time, and poured them down the sink, watching the liquid gurgle away in a foaming chocolate river.

So he'd broken up, or, rather, been broken up with. It had been more than two months, and it was time to quit wallowing. Time to either choose to be alone, or start the whole cautious process of finding somebody again. Always careful. Always hiding.

He could be lonely, though. He could be in pain. He knew how to be both of those things. He'd had practice.

What he couldn't be was pathetic, and drinking alone was pathetic. Drinking was starting to feel pathetic, full stop.

Eggs. Toast. Coffee –too much of it. Trainers. Jacket. Checking his bag by rote for the mouthguards and gear that would be there, because they were always there, because he always cleaned and packed them the night before. Even when he'd been drinking ... much too much. Out the door and down the stairs, worn in the center by the passage of centuries of feet, and out into the courtyard, his legs like lead. He'd feel better once he'd got stuck in with the boys, and better than that once he went for some physio.

Or at least he'd know he hurt. Lately, he was beginning to go numb. He could play rugby hurt. He didn't know how to play it numb.

He was halfway to the practice facility when it hit him. He had to pull off into a side street, through the mad traffic, and sit, after a hasty check of his watch. He had eighteen minutes. Three minutes to work through this. Four at the outside.

His stepsister Nyree was getting married in less than three weeks, and he'd made no plans to be there, just gone along in this ... fog. She was marrying Marko Sendoa, though, which meant that Luke's father, Grant Armstrong, would be filthy. It was no secret that Grant loathed Marko, or that the feeling was mutual, despite Marko having played for him for years. Marko was playing for the Blues now, and that would've made Grant even filthier. Luke knew all about that. He'd left the Highlanders himself twelve years ago so he wouldn't have to play for his father anymore.

He couldn't leave Nyree to face Grant alone. Not at her wedding.

He couldn't go on like this.

He couldn't keep running. He'd run to Christchurch to play for the Crusaders. When that hadn't been far enough, he'd run to

Racing 92, all the way to Paris. Nearly ten years ago, and what was he doing? Still running.

Nowhere to run anymore. He'd run out of world, and he'd run out of excuses.

Time to turn and fight.

NOWHERE TO HIDE

*I*t's not every day you meet the man of your dreams while painting bunnies.

Hayden wasn't actually painting bunnies, of course. It just sounded funnier. He didn't have the skills for bunnies, according to Nyree Morgan, the artist who was transforming this formerly white-walled bedroom on Auckland's Scenic Drive into a little-girl version of a magical wonderland for the benefit of one Casey Fletcher, Hayden's newly-discovered niece-once-removed and the reason he'd taken the day off work to help.

It was all hands on deck, because Nyree was meant to be marrying Marko Sendoa on Sunday, which was exactly four days from now, and she'd gone overboard in her enthusiasm for this bloody mural, which Casey apparently absolutely needed for her first Christmas with her new family. Casey was about to be Hayden's step-niece, and his sister Zora's problem was Hayden's problem, because there was no other way his life worked.

Also, Nyree was pregnant, in addition to the imminent-bride thing, and her energy apparently didn't match her enthusiasm anymore. So he was helping.

He was a good brother, and a good uncle. He hoped. He'd been there for Zora and her son Isaiah at their hardest times, and Zora'd been there for his. Zora didn't need him that way anymore, though, because she had Casey's dad, Rhys. Zora had found a way to get loved back.

Hayden? Not so much, other than George the marmalade cat. But he was here for Zora anyway. Old habits died hard.

All he was really doing, of course, was painting the blades of grass *around* some bunnies. Blades that Nyree had helpfully pre-drawn onto the wall with colored pencils, so he'd know which shade. It was paint by numbers, was what it was. Artistically, Hayden was apparently eight years old.

He was thinking about all that, because you had to think about something when you were sitting on the floor painting blades of grass, and bunnies and little girls were a better spot than most. Besides, Nyree was concentrating too fiercely for conversation.

He wasn't the only one helping today. There was some New Zealand rugby talent around that, as always, made Hayden feel seri-ously undersized, not to mention desperately unfit, including Nyree's enormous stepbrother, Kane Armstrong. Kane played for the Crusaders, and Rhys Fletcher, the owner of this bedroom, was the coach of the Blues, but love conquered all, apparently. Especially as Nyree's own stepfather, and Kane's father, was the former coach of the Highlanders, which meant that three of the five New Zealand Super Rugby teams were more-or-less represented here today.

Of course, Grant Armstrong hated Nyree's fiancé, Marko Sendoa, and vice versa. On the other hand, Rhys Fletcher, the afore-mentioned homeowner, was Marko's coach now—and Hayden's soon-to-be-brother-in-law—so … here Nyree was. Here Hayden was. Here they all were.

It was all very incestuous and tortured, before you even got into the fact that Zora was *also* marrying her late husband's brother, who'd *also* been a rugby player. New Zealand was a small country, but not *this* small.

He was thinking that, and then he wasn't. Somebody else had

walked into the room, somebody big and stolid and unsmiling and *still*, and Nyree was talking.

"Everybody who doesn't know him—wait, the rugby boys will know him, obviously, so it's only Hayden—this is Luke. Armstrong. My brother. Well, stepbrother. Son of my stepdad, again obviously, but we can't hold Grant Armstrong against anybody, or I'd have to hate Marko, since he played for him for yonks. Also my mother."

"And you'd have to hate me," Kane said. "I played for him myself, *and* was raised by him. That's exposure. Hi, Luke. Sorry I didn't ring you yesterday. I was—"

"Yeh," Nyree said, a little absently, since she'd begun to paint what seemed to be a fairy riding a bird, sketching in a pointed chin, a wide forehead, with a few swift strokes. Nyree could make anything have a personality. "But you're both OK anyway despite the parentage. I'd give you a cuddle, Luke, but I'm too painty. Do my trees over there on the other wall, please, since you actually have talent."

"Oi," Kane said mildly, because Kane said most things mildly. Hulking as he was—Hayden didn't think he could count as high as Kane was tall, and at this moment, he was painting clouds onto the ceiling without a ladder—Kane didn't radiate much but good humor off the pitch.

Unlike Luke. Hayden couldn't get a read. He could get goose-flesh, though, and it was happening.

He wasn't attracted to rugby players, possibly because rugby players weren't attracted to him, and he refused to be that needy.

Normally.

No.

"Well, he does," Nyree said, painting in the suggestion of feathers on the bird's blue wings. "He's got fingers like sausages and knuckles like ping-pong balls, but he used to draw wicked cartoons of our weird family to make me laugh when I was an awkward teen, with the specs and the brace on my teeth and all. Oh—Luke, Hayden." She jerked her chin in Hayden's direction and kept painting her bird. "Zora's brother. Lawyer. Luke's a rugby player."

"You could say that," Kane said.

Hayden couldn't just sit here cross-legged and stare at the bloke like the dimmest lawyer ever to be admitted to the roll of barristers, could he? "Why could you say that?" he asked.

"Plays for Racing 92," Nyree said. "Paris. Tighthead prop. That's the front row. Also captain for England for the internationals. Here for the wedding, and missing two matches for it. That's loyalty, eh."

"Captain the last two seasons, that's all," Luke said, the first time he'd opened his mouth. "Doesn't mean I will be again."

"Right," Nyree said. "After you won the Six Nations last year? The European Championship," she told Hayden.

"Excuse me," he said. "That much rugby knowledge, I have. I'm Zora's brother, remember? I also know that a prop's in the front row, thank you very much. I *am* a Kiwi."

Luke wasn't looking at Hayden, and he seemed not even to have heard him. Had he been that obvious? Please, no. Luke was looking away, though, so probably yes. In fact, he picked up a brush and began studying the outline of trees that Nyree had sketched onto the end wall as if they fascinated him. One mangled, deeply cauli-flowered ear was glowing red, though, and the color was creeping up the back of his thick neck, too, all the way to the edge of his close-cropped dark hair.

Oh, bloody hell. He *had* noticed. Hayden wanted to laugh, it was so squirm-worthy. On the other hand, he was also pathetic, so maybe not so much on the laughing.

Luke was the size of a boulder. He was the size of a *tank*. His voice seemed to come all the way from his barrel of a chest, quiet and deep and powerful as the waters of the Waiau River, born in the harshness of the Southern Alps and flowing to join some of the coldest waters in the world.

At least that was how he seemed to Hayden, and he couldn't get his breath, even though, yes—pathetic. Luke's thighs were the size of tree trunks, his forearms corded with muscle and sinew. His nose had been broken much more than once, and he had a scar over one eye, another on his cheek, and, Hayden was sure, heaps more under his neatly-trimmed scruff of dark beard. Even his *hands* looked strong, and Hayden knew they would be. A prop's job was to hang onto his man in the front row of the scrum and push against the opposite line like a freight train. A prop didn't do any kicking, and he almost never carried the ball. All the guts and none of the glory, but when he tackled a man, that man went down.

Hayden kept painting grass, wishing that his usual cheerful line of chat hadn't deserted him, that his body wasn't tingling, that his very scalp wasn't prickling. He hoped nobody was watching. He hoped nobody could see.

"And I don't know whether I'm meant to say," Nyree went on, painting furiously but precisely on her bird, "but the secret's out to half the New Zealand rugby world since Luke turned up unexpectedly at our hen-and-stag night and spilled it, and anyway, secrets block my painting chi. Last chance to stop me, Luke. Three, two, one—everybody, Luke's gay. If you wanted to tell Kane privately, sorry and all that. But you're not here for long, and you never tell anybody anything, and he needs to know now, I reckon, so he has time to absorb before you leave again. Come to think of it, the gay thing is probably *why* you never tell anybody anything, and why you never stay long, either. How have you kept that secret? Why haven't you told us before?"

Everybody stopped painting. Everybody but Nyree, that is, who'd moved on to another bird, this one clutching a tiny envelope in its talon.

"I …" Luke said, then stopped. "I don't know what you want me to say. That I told my oldest mate the other night and it got so awkward that I had to leave his house, and he doesn't know how to be my mate anymore? That I know more of that's coming my way? I knew it wouldn't be easy. I knew not everybody would accept it. And I said it anyway, so here I am. Out."

Hayden couldn't be silent anymore. "You tell yourself," he said quietly, "that it's practice for the tough ones, but it turns out they're all tough ones. And if you're a rugby player …"

Luke didn't answer. He said, "Right. Trees. Painting." And then stood there and didn't, until he turned around again and looked. Not at Hayden, and not at Nyree, who wasn't painting anymore, either. He looked at Kane.

His brother.

Kane said, "I'm sorry, bro. I didn't know that was what you wanted to talk to me about. So you wouldn't have to say it in front of everybody."

"Yeh," Luke said, and that was all. The moment stretched out, and Nyree said something, but Hayden wasn't listening. He was watching Luke. And Luke was still watching Kane.

Hayden knew about your sibling who was there for you when your parents weren't. He knew how much it mattered. He held his breath and thought, *Please. Say the right thing. Nobody deserves to be hurt like this.*

"I don't know what to say here," Kane finally said. "What the … the protocol is." Which didn't sound good.

"There's no protocol," Hayden said, because somebody had to say it, and he was the one who knew how. "There's just telling the truth, and asking for the truth. It's what you don't say that puts up the barricades, and it's too hard to get over those barricades."

Kane said, "Then I guess … it's that I can't see you any differently. Still my brother, aren't you. Still the one who taught me how to be a man. Maybe a decent man. The only one who taught me that."

Luke's ears were redder than ever now, and he stared at his brother, mute, like he couldn't believe it. Like he couldn't hope for it.

Kane went on, still slowly, "That's why you never stick around. It's why you went to France, and why you stayed there. Why it felt like you didn't want to … to know me anymore. I thought it was like

Mum and Dad. That we weren't meant to share, or to say. That we were meant to be OK alone. Strong, like they said."

Luke said, "I didn't … I couldn't …" And stopped. He was still holding the paintbrush, but his hand was shaking. He looked at it as if he couldn't believe it, then put his hand out. For support, maybe, but his hand must have touched wet paint, because it jerked back, and he said, "Sorry, Nyree. I didn't …"

His legs were shaking now, too. He crouched down, dropping the brush, and put a hand over his eyes. His body turned away. Hiding.

Hayden knew about hiding.

Nyree was there, then, her movements quicksilver. Crouched beside him, her pregnant belly against his side, her arms around him. "You're my brother," she said. "And I love you. Nothing will ever change that. *Ever.*"

Luke's entire body was shaking now, and he must be crying, but he was still hiding his face, so Hayden couldn't see. Hayden would bet that he hadn't cried for years. For decades. Now, he couldn't help it, because when that dam broke, there was no holding back.

Kane was there now, too, though, on Luke's other side. Holding on. Saying, "Bro. It's OK. I love you. I always will."

Hayden had his own problems expressing emotion, possibly. Which was why he normally didn't.

He cried a little anyway.

Well, it was a touching moment.

COLD AS THE RIVER TYNE

*L*uke couldn't believe he was crying.

He didn't cry. He. Did. Not. Cry. He was crying anyway. In front of Nyree. In front of Kane. In front of … some young player named Tom, which wasn't as bad, because he didn't know him. But in front of somebody else, too. Zora's brother, Hayden, who was still sitting on the floor, painting blades of grass that were probably suitable for tiny mice to peek out from, by the look of things here. When Luke had come in and Hayden had turned to look at him, Luke had stopped breathing for a second.

His eyes were brown. *Bright* brown, if that was a thing. Amber, maybe, and full of life. His dark hair was cut high and tight, his jeans were cut close and stylish, and the sleeves of his blue-checked shirt were turned up two careful turns from his wrists, revealing some muscle. He looked like the kind of perfect that made Luke's tongue feel too big for his mouth and the rest of his body feel equally outsized, and made him completely aware that he wasn't good-looking and never would be.

He could almost hear René's voice, on that last terrible evening, in his restaurant kitchen, still wearing his white smock and checked trousers. Sitting, as always, over a late meal and yet another glass of wine, but with a sharpness hanging in the air and no ease at all. His final words were still easy to recall, because they may as well have been burned into Luke's heart. "You are like a bear. A big, scarred, *hairy* bear who can never be elegant, who cannot even converse. The so-entertaining *histoires* ... you cannot tell them. Even the boring small talk, you cannot do. And the hair that grows every-place but on your head. The ears, the nose, the *face* ... how can I look at them anymore? How can I *touch* you? With wine, yes, maybe, but it only gets worse. You aren't thirty-five yet, and I'm *forty*-five, and yet you look older. It is just too much."

"I—" Luke started to say. *I wax*, he wanted to say. *Every month. And you said you liked it that I was strong.* But you didn't explain, because you couldn't make somebody think well of you.

You couldn't make somebody love you.

"And it is even more than being ugly and hairy and battered," René said, taking another swallow of wine. "You are a coward. Yes, I said it. A coward. We can never go anywhere together, I can never tell anyone your name, not even my family, not even my friends, and why? Because you are afraid. Here I am, facing the world as I was made, while you, who are so tough, who are so brave and strong, are still hiding. You hide behind us, behind those like me. You let us face it for you, so you can keep your position, so the people cannot say, 'We don't want to watch a rugby player who is having sex with other men. Get him off this team. Get him away.' You hide, and you make me hide, too. You are a coward, and I cannot be with a coward anymore."

Maybe Luke wasn't a coward now. Except that he must be, because he was scared in a way he'd never been at school or out on the paddock in the toughest test match of his life. In a way he'd only ever felt when he was injured. He could handle any pain, any fatigue. Handle it, and rise above it. He couldn't handle being help-less, and he couldn't handle people seeing him that way.

He was pretty sure Hayden was gay, too. What he'd said ... he had to be gay, didn't he? And handsome and charming, with good hair, and he *could* tell the *histoires* and entertain the room. You only had to look at him to see it, but what did it matter? What did any of it matter, now?

Maybe he could never have made a good impression, but he could have done better than this, because he was still crying. It was summer in New Zealand, and the room was full of people and paint, but he was cold, and he was alone. Hot with embarrassment and tears, and cold anyway. As cold as the river Tyne. As cold as winter in the north of England.

As cold as his mother's house.

He didn't want to think about this. He wanted to think about anything else, but here it was, because he'd told his mother already, and she hadn't wanted to know. Now he was back in New Zealand and had told heaps more people. He was stripped bare, his secret out there for everyone to see. Out there for the rugby world to see. Out there for his *dad* to see. He'd torpedoed his life, and he was panicking.

He couldn't be tough anymore, and he couldn't remember a time when he hadn't known how to be tough. Not in primary school, where he'd learned to fight. Not at home, where he'd learned to shut up, and not at the boarding school he'd been dropped into at age nine, where he'd learned four things. One, that knowing how to fight was still a good thing, no matter how posh the school was, if you were nine and a New Boy, or if you just couldn't stand to watch other kids being tortured. Two, that being good at sport was even better than knowing how to fight, and Grant Armstrong's sons were always going to be big, strong, and good at sport. And as Grant was a rugby coach, what Luke was best at was rugby.

He'd tried to make that cricket instead, so he'd have his own thing that his dad couldn't touch, but the more he grew, the broader he got. He could go hard, and he could even go fast, but he couldn't go fast enough for cricket. Mostly, he could lift heavy things and get stronger, and he could stand solid and hit his man harder than anybody else, and he liked to. That wasn't cricket. That was rugby. Not the flash parts, sidestepping like a gazelle through the tacklers and across the chalk, being lifted by your mates and slapped on the back because you'd scored the try. The parts you did in the dark places, the parts that took nothing but grunt. He'd been a hooker, and then he'd been a prop, and a prop was what he'd stayed. A life in the front row, and the body and face to match.

Four things. Thing Three, that there was a name for what he was, and it was shameful. And Thing Four. That he was on his own.

Even in a rugby squad, that band of brothers, he was alone. He had a secret, and he couldn't let down his guard, or the one place he shone, his one spot of safety, would be gone.

And his dad would find out.

All of that, maybe, was why, on that first day of school, when his mum had stopped the car in front of the forbidding brick building, with its tower and arched windows that looked like the scariest kind of church, he hadn't thought about how his parents were getting divorced and his dad was going back to New Zealand. He hadn't thought that he was scared about that, and scared to be here. There was no point in it and nobody to care except Kane, and Kane couldn't know he was scared, or he'd feel even worse. So Luke had turned and said to his brother, who was only six and sitting there curled into himself, the tears running down his cheeks, "I'll see you at half term."

"Don't leave," Kane said, turning an anguished face to him. Kane hadn't learned yet that you couldn't say things like that. "Why can't you still go to school with me? Why can't you stay *home* with me?"

"I will go to school with you," Luke said. "Soon as you're nine. You'll come here and be with me."

"But that's *long*," Kane said.

"Stop blubbing," their mum said. "Nobody wants to see that. If you have to cry, cry in bed."

Luke wanted to do something, to say something, but he didn't know what to say. Kane was too soft sometimes, yeh, but that was

ESCAPE TO NEW ZEALAND

because he was kinder than any of them, and more loving, and wasn't that meant to be a good thing, even if it made you soft? Luke's Year Four teacher had said it was good to be kind and thoughtful, but his parents didn't care about that, and how would he know which was right? He didn't know what to do, so he just said again, "I'll see you at half term."

"Aren't you scared?" Kane asked.

"No," Luke lied. "This is where I have to go, so I'm going." And he did. He got out of the car and walked up the stairs, through the knots of other boys, the tearful mums, the proud dads, and didn't think anything at all.

He'd kept his promise, though, as long as he could. He'd looked after Kane once his brother had come to join him three years later. Kane hadn't had nearly as much coaching from their dad, other than a short visit to New Zealand every year at Christmas and a longer one in August, but he had more natural talent than Luke. At rugby, and at cricket, too. Luke still worried about how soft he was, but sport would help with that. Eventually.

Besides, Luke was there. He wasn't going to let anyone bully his brother, and every boy in school knew it. He might only be twelve, but he didn't care about pain. Most boys did care. When their nose got bloodied or they got hit in the ribs, they stopped. Luke didn't stop.

That was what he thought for a term, anyway. Until his mum collected the two of them for Christmas and told Luke in the car on the way home, "That's it for you, then. You're off to En Zed."

"What?" he asked.

"That was always the plan," she said. "You stay here until you're twelve, and then you go to your dad, so he can make a man of you."

Luke didn't say, *I'm not a man. I'm a boy.* No point. He said, "You didn't tell me that." His voice cracked, because the dread was hollowing out his belly, tightening his throat, but he kept his face as expressionless as he could, so she wouldn't see. You couldn't keep from feeling bad, but you could keep other people from knowing.

"Of course I did," she said. "It was always the plan."

"No," Kane said. Just one word, and this time, he didn't cry. He'd learned. But his face had gone pale, his hands gripping the seat.

Luke asked, "When?"

"After the New Year," his mum said. "The New Zealand term starts at the end of January, but Dad'll need some time to get you kitted out, and you'll need to be able to shift for yourself once his season starts and you're in school. You'll have to start the school year over again, of course, but that's good. Make you a bit older when it's time for First XV selection." The rugby squad that would compete for the national secondary schools championship. That was years and years away, and every boy who played rugby wanted to be on that squad and most would never get there, but it didn't matter. His dad believed in planning. He believed in discipline. He believed in structure. And he believed that all those things would make his sons elite rugby players, because they *were* his sons.

Luke had discipline, and he had structure. That didn't mean he had to like this. "Why am I going?" he asked. "Why should I? Why should Kane? Dad doesn't want us."

His mother glanced at him sharply, probably shocked. Luke didn't care. He knew he had to go, but why shouldn't he tell the truth first? Why shouldn't he *ask* for the truth?

"Of course he wants you," she said. "He wants to coach you, for one thing."

"He's got a coaching job," Luke said. "Let him coach them."

"You're his son," she said. "You've got his name."

"I'll still have his name whether I play rugby or not. What if I'm rubbish? Do I have to change my name?"

She stared at him once more, for long enough that he got a bit worried about her driving, but got herself under control again, of course. "Nonsense. You won't be rubbish. You'll do your best."

He wished he could say, *I won't, though.* But rugby was what he was good at, and anyway, you needed a place at school where you fit, especially when you didn't fit at all inside. He said, "So that's it, then?"

"Yes," she said. "That's it. You'll come here for Christmas every year, and you and Kane will spend the August holidays in New Zealand as always, as that's when Dad's season ends, and he'll make you an All Black."

"What if he doesn't want to be an All Black, though?" Kane asked.

"Of course he does," their mum said. "He's a Kiwi, isn't he?"

"Not really," Kane said. "We live here, not there. And you're English."

"In rugby," she said, "being a Kiwi is better. Why wouldn't you want your dad's coaching? You're lucky to have it."

Luke didn't know how to explain. He didn't know what to do. So when they got home, he did what he always did. He did his press-ups, he did his sit-ups, and most of all—he ran. Through the fog and the rain and the cold, past houses with their Christmas trees lit up even in the daytime against the gloom outside, the smoke curling from their chimneys. Luke tried to imagine the storybook families inside and couldn't quite do it. They'd play board games together, maybe, and drink hot cocoa in front of the fire, and maybe ... read books? Throw a ball for a dog? Do ... baking, possibly, and make special dinners? He wasn't sure. In his family, you were mostly either outside, training or being out of the way, or in your room, doing your schoolwork, or if you couldn't be either, shutting up. That was what he knew, and what Kane knew. Which may have been why Kane ran with him, doing his best to keep up, and why Luke slowed his pace for his brother. Running was what they did together, and this was the time they had left.

On the last day, the coldest yet, with the damp hanging in the air like streamers, he took Kane on the bus so they could run on the path beside the nearly-freezing river Tyne. He didn't quite know why. Maybe because it *was* the last day, and he felt like they had to do something.

Kane said, "If we kept running, would we get all the way to the North Sea?"

"Reckon we would," Luke said. "If we kept running."

"I think we should, then," Kane said. "We should get on a fishing boat and escape. We could be the crew."

"We don't know how to fish, though," Luke said. "And you're nine."

"You could look older," Kane said. "Because you have muscles. And I'm tall. I could look older, too. I could say I'm thirteen."

Luke wasn't sure what to say. After a minute, he said, "Thirteen wouldn't be old enough. And it'd be cold."

"Oh," Kane said. "Maybe it would be an adventure, though."

Luke had to smile. "Maybe."

Another few minutes with their breath coming out in puffs, their feet pounding against the tarmac, doing their best to outrun the cold. Finally, Kane said, "If you said you wouldn't go. If you refused to get on the plane. You could stand your ground. Dad's always saying to stand our ground."

Luke said, "It's not happening. We have to face it. It's not. We're kids, and that means you have to go where they tell you. In three years, though, you'll be in Dunedin with me. We'll be in school together again, for years this time, and when we're done with it, we'll be able to choose for ourselves. One thing I can tell you, though. When I'm grown, I'm not playing for Dad."

"How, though?" Kane asked. "If he says you have to?"

"Because," Luke said, "I'll be a man."

Now, he was a man, and he wasn't playing for his dad. He was back in New Zealand, though, and he wasn't sure what it meant.

How much would his dad care what he was or what he did, at this point? Luke hadn't even lived in the country for more than eight years, and he *had* been an All Black—for two seasons before he'd left the country—and Kane still was one. Kane wasn't playing for their dad, but he was here and doing the name proud, wasn't he?

Besides, it wasn't just the two of them anymore. They weren't their dad's last hope.

Well, they were the only sons, so probably they *were* the last hope, from Grant's point of view. But maybe it wouldn't matter as much now, especially since their dad wasn't coaching anymore.

You know it'll matter. Grant wasn't coaching because he'd been passed over once again for the All Blacks, and because the Highlanders hadn't renewed his contract this time. Luke didn't know what Grant thought about that, because he hadn't been home for yonks, but he could guess. "Bloody soft," Grant would say. "Drew Callahan? He knows how to be a skipper, he knows how to play the game, but as a coach? A 'player's coach.' What's that? Coddling them, is what. Understanding them. I don't need to understand them. They need to understand *me.* I have a system. It's been proven to work. All they have to do is commit and dig deep. If they won't, that's not my fault. Heaps more fish in the sea, boys willing to work hard, gagging for a chance at Super Rugby."

So, no, Grant wouldn't be taking any of it philosophically, even though he was sixty and rugby wasn't the only thing in his life anymore, because he had, astonishingly, remarried three or four years after Kane's arrival in En Zed, and that marriage had changed almost everything. Everything but Grant's nature.

Miriama Armstrong, Luke's stepmother, was a petite, pretty, gracious Maori lady with a core of steel. She'd made a warm, colorful home for all of them, and somehow, she'd wrapped Grant around her finger in a way Luke's practical, stoical mum, a better match in every way, had never managed to do.

They'd had a daughter, Kiri, who was a teenager now and all right. Shut down a bit, like Luke and Kane, around their dad, not to mention her mum, who could give Grant a run for his money when it came to pushing her children, but who wouldn't be?

Nyree, that was who.

Miriama's daughter, the fringe benefit or the forced addition—

Luke had a feeling Grant saw her more as the latter—had been awkward and a little clumsy back then, at thirteen, fourteen, fifteen. She'd had a brace on her teeth and specs perched on her nose, and had been plump, too, which Luke was sure had horrified his father. Nothing Grant had ever said had made Nyree disciplined, orderly, or good at sport or maths—or shut her up or changed her mind, either. She'd laughed and she'd cried, and she'd always, always talked back. She'd emoted all over the shop, in fact. Luke had been astonished, but he couldn't say he'd learned much, because he'd been nearly out of the house by then, and anyway, it was too late to change. He was who he was, and that was that. But he'd liked her. He still did. Somebody had to talk, he reckoned, or the world would be a pretty boring place.

He thought about Nyree, her outsized life force, and her own surprising upcoming marriage to Marko Sendoa, a hard man amongst hard men, while he painted trees, because he didn't want to think about any of the rest of it. About what had happened with his mate, Matt, especially, when Luke had tried to tell him. How appalled he'd been, and how quickly his mind had seemed to fly back to all that nakedness in the changing sheds, all that grabbing in the scrum. It hadn't gone well, and Luke had only just started telling. The fellas at Nyree's hen party had seemed OK, and so had Marko, but what would they think if they were asked to play with Luke now?

Was he being brave at last, or just stupid and self-destructive? Why had he come out with this now, when he had absolutely no idea what he was going to do if the worst happened and he was out of the game? Why hadn't he waited until he'd retired, at least? He'd never had many mates, but at least he'd had a team. At least he'd had parents, such as they were.

What would he be if he had none of it?

Stop it, he told himself, going on doggedly with the trees. You didn't stay at the top level in international rugby without some emotional equilibrium. He'd always had that, even as a kid. He'd done what he could to make his life work out, and he'd learned to live with the parts that didn't. His parents hadn't been much on loving kindness, but they'd cornered the market on stoicism, and it had rubbed off.

If he didn't have stoicism anymore, though. If the raw places hurt too much to hide … what would he have then?

He didn't know, so he painted trees and didn't talk.

Eventually, he'd find out. And then he'd deal with it. No choice.

.

OBVIOUSLY GAY

$\mathcal{I}$t had gone six, but Hayden was still painting blades of grass when Zora came in to announce, "Twenty minutes until pizza. Marko phoned and said he was collecting it on the way over. Seems unfair that the two of you have to do the painting *and* buy the pizza, but Marko insisted, and since pizza is Casey's favorite and it was Rhys's turn to cook anyway, events snowballed."

"I'll just do this next bit first," Nyree said, which Hayden could have predicted. Nyree was a woman on a mission, even if that mission was painting fairies. At the moment, she was painting a mouse peeking out of Hayden's grass, which had been inevitable.

"Marko said you'd say that," Zora said. "He says he'll take the brush out of your hand again, and carry you downstairs in front of everybody if he has to. He's getting you one with veggies and cheese, though. I'm supposed to tell you that."

Nyree laid down her brush. "Because I'm not allowed to eat cured meats. He'll also have them put pesto sauce on it, just so I *won't* be able to resist. And he absolutely *would* carry me downstairs, or make me think he was about to. Is it bad that I like that about him?"

"Not to me," Zora said.

Hayden gave an exaggerated sigh, because he needed to perk up here and be entertaining, not think about a rugby player who'd barely looked at him. Again—less pathetic yearning, more sparkle. "Not to me, either. One can only dream. Not about Marko," he told Nyree, "so no worries. I'm not attracted to people to whom I'm not attractive, and probably vice versa, if I could work out the implications amidst the paint fumes. I should print that first part on a T-shirt, though. It'd save *so* much explaining. I'm saying it out loud, since we're discussing the subject. Now hear this. I don't want your man—that's for you and Zora, Nyree—and if you *are* a man, I almost certainly don't want *you*. I'm more selective than that, thank you very much."

There. That should do it. He could be attracted. That didn't mean he was putting himself out there to be rejected again.

"What's wrong with cured meats?" Tom asked.

"Risk of listeria," Nyree said. "Ask Marko for the full list of things I'm meant to eat and not eat, and he'll tell you. He gets a bit boring about it, in fact. Folate, beta-carotene, Omega-3 fatty acids, protein grams, choline … I didn't know choline existed, much less that it was a thing."

"It's in eggs," Luke said.

"I know," she said. "How do *you* know?"

He shrugged. "I have to know. I have to stay big, but fit. It's my job."

"Oh," Nyree said. "Well, obviously. You do a good job at it, though. Staying big."

"Yes," Hayden said. "You do." Which he shouldn't have said, but—no. He was being insouciant. That was a French word. It meant, "Showing a casual lack of concern." Which was perfect in all ways.

Kane said, "I'll pass on pizza. I have a date."

Hayden waited to hear Luke say he was leaving, too, but he didn't, so he couldn't feel *too* uncomfortable, could he? Of course, he was here for Nyree, and she'd made it clear she wanted him, so that was good. And as there was nobody kinder than Zora, that was good, too. Coming out wasn't easy, and she knew it.

When they'd washed up and gone downstairs onto the deck, overlooking about a hectare of green fern trees and palms and the calm blue waters of Manukau Harbour far below, and were letting the warm breeze take away the stiffness and the smell of paint, Nyree said, "This is a very good house. Like you're out in the bush, but comfortable. A bit different from Paris, Luke. Feels so much more … remote."

"True," he said. "But you're right. Comfortable."

"Do you have a house in Paris?" Rhys's daughter Casey—the bunny-lover—asked. "Like in *Madeline*? Is it covered with vines?"

"It's a book," Rhys said when Luke looked confused.

"I have a flat in Paris, yeh," Luke said. "That's where I live. No vines, though."

"Because he plays for Racing 92," Zora's son Isaiah told his cousin. "I *told* you."

"You said France," she said. "Paris isn't France."

"Yes, it is. Paris is the capital of France." He sighed. "It's good that you're going to be in Year Three next year. You need to learn more things."

"Oh," she said. "I thought Paris was very fancy, though." She looked at Luke doubtfully, and he smiled.

Oh, no. He was every daddy fantasy Hayden had ever had, *and* he was kind? He should have said no to pizza. His waistline did not need pizza. He also didn't need to do any more yearning.

"It is," Nyree said. "Paris is magical, even in the rain. *Especially* in the rain. There's no place in the world that looks better in gray than Paris. The buildings are colored cream, the silvery light glistens off the river in a way that makes your heart heal, and the streets are made of stone."

"Well, some are," Luke said.

"Luke's flat doesn't look one bit like you might think, either," Nyree went on, ignoring him. "The front doors of the building are arched and painted blue, and the stone above them is arched, too. Luke's flat is at the very top, up five flights of very old stairs, and the wood of the banisters and the red stone tiles on the landings have been rubbed smooth by hundreds of hands and feet over hundreds of years. Imagine all those people with their secrets and their joys, going up and down those stairs, living their lives."

Casey had stopped eating and was staring at Nyree in awe. "Inside," Nyree went on, "there are huge, dark oak beams going across the ceiling all through the main room. Six of them, with nicks on them from where somebody shaped them a long time ago, and white plaster between them, and shiny wood floors that have been walked on and polished and loved, over and over again, that look like a craftsman did them who lived only to make beautiful floors, because he laid out the wood in the shape of fish bones. There's a kitchen with black-and-white tiles on the floor, set like diamonds instead of a draughts board, just because it's more beautiful, and a tiny black-iron-railed balcony off the dining room that you get to through a pair of French doors with curved tops and curving black metal handles. The glass between the panes is wavy and thick, because it's so old, and it makes everything outside look a bit wavy, too, like a painting. There's just enough room out there for a little round table and two chairs, and there's a perfect view across the tiled roofs of more cream-colored buildings where more people have lived for hundreds of years, and between them, you can see the branches of trees in a tiny park. In the summer, the swallows fly over the roofs. Their wings are a dark blue, bright as jewels, and pointed at the ends, and so are their tails, and they swoop and dive like ..."

"Like fairies?" Casey asked.

"Exactly like fairies," Nyree said, and Hayden could practically see the swallows getting painted onto that wall. She had, what, two days to finish this mural, and she was still adding things on?

Elite rugby players were some of the most disciplined people on the planet, and Nyree's stepfather was a rugby coach. She was marrying an elite rugby player, too. None of it seemed to have influenced her much.

"You've seen my flat once," Luke said. "When you tear a ligament in your knee, the stairs aren't quite as nice, the kitchen's pretty small and the bath is smaller, and you have to duck through a doorway to get to it or you hit your head. You have to stand in exactly the right place to see the park, and some people would say that it doesn't have storage space. But I like it all the same."

"Sounds good, though," Hayden said. "Are you secretly sophisticated, Luke?"

"No," he said. "I just like it." His face went wooden, so, again, he'd seen.

No more flirting, Hayden told himself. He told himself that heaps. It usually didn't work. He couldn't seem to turn it off. And if the fella was this hot? He *really* couldn't turn it off.

Never mind. He was insouciant.

"It sounds very fancy and very expensive," Casey said. "You can still make your apartment pretty, but you can only have a view if it's expensive, because views cost extra."

"That's probably because French rugby pays better," Isaiah said. "It *does,*" he said, when Zora looked at him. "New Zealand rugby only pays about five hundred thousand dollars a year even if you're an All Black for a long time, unless you're a very *top* All Black, and French rugby can pay two *million* dollars a year. That's four times as much."

"I don't get paid two million dollars a year," Luke said.

"But you're the captain for England, too," Isaiah pointed out. "When you play on an international side, you make even *more* money. If you win a championship, you get more than that. That's why Uncle Rhys is so much richer than my dad was, because my dad wasn't an All Black very much and Uncle Rhys was always one. Also, Uncle Rhys is a coach, and coaches get paid the most of all. Maybe you'll be a coach later, and then you'll *really* have a lot of money. Then you could have a bigger flat where you don't have to duck your head."

"We're not going to talk any more about what Luke gets paid," Rhys said. "As it's not very interesting. Beer. Hang on." He went inside for it.

"Oh, I don't know," Hayden said. "Of course, I'm a lawyer, so I have an excuse, but I find money pretty interesting. *Not* having it can get interesting, hey, Zora."

"It can," she said.

"Being poor isn't interesting," Casey said, "because you can't do as many fun things when you're poor. You can do fun things that don't cost money, though, so it can still be interesting that way. You're supposed to say 'broke,' though, not 'poor.' 'Broke' sounds better, like you might be richer later on, so you just need school lunch for now. That's what my mommy said when she was alive."

"True," Hayden said. "Though in New Zealand, you say 'skint.' Means you're waiting for payday. And, of course, you can be broke no matter how much money you make. All you have to do is spend more than you make, and hey presto, you're broke. Or skint. Or both. Also, Isaiah, you could consider this important detail. Rugby doesn't last that long. If you're a lawyer, your career can last until you're seventy. Longer, if you like, and you're getting more experience all the time, hence better compensated. That means 'paid more,' Casey. Whereas in rugby, you're done when you're thirty or possibly thirty-five, if you're very lucky. After that, you have to find something new to do. Coach, maybe, like Isaiah says. Buy a restaurant, hang your old jerseys behind glass on the wall, and probably go out of business. Very unstable industry, restaurants. Or you could talk about rugby on TV. That always seemed like a good job."

"Depends how well you talk," Luke said. "You could do it, I reckon." Hayden laughed in surprise, and then wondered if it was an insult. Luke's face had lost the wooden look, though. His eyes were warm, in fact, and fixed on Hayden, and he lost his breath again.

His hopeful heart, turning toward that warmth and strength like a sunflower turning toward the sun.

Or maybe Luke was amused because Hayden had just implied that he was bound to fail dismally as soon as he retired. Which could be soon, now that he'd come out, because had any active player ever come out?

No. Whoops. Not too tactful, but Luke still looked amused, so maybe he just thought Hayden was charmingly clueless. Hilariously rude. Something like that.

"A scientist is more like a lawyer," Casey said. "You can be a scientist until you're old, because scientists in movies always have white hair, and kind of crazy hair. That's good, Isaiah, since you want to be a scientist. You don't like to brush your hair, either. Except that I don't think scientists make very much money, and you want to make lots of money. That's the bad part."

"You have to be a scientist and also invest," Isaiah said. "I think buying houses would be the best for investing, because people need houses to rent, and Auckland doesn't have enough. You should probably invest," he told Luke. "If you have extra money from playing rugby in France."

Luke actually smiled. "Thanks. I'll keep that in mind."

"Do you speak French?" Isaiah asked. "Because it's *France*," he told Casey. "And they speak French, not English."

"I do," Luke said. "My French is pretty good after eight years, actually."

"You don't talk very much," Casey said. "So maybe you don't need to know too many words." And Luke smiled some more.

Definitely hot, strong, and kind. Hayden was going to be lost here pretty soon.

Get it together, he told himself. *Have a drink or something.*

"Fair point," Luke said, just as Rhys came out again with the beer and held a bottle up to him. "No, thanks," Luke said. "I'm good with water." And Hayden thought, *Wait, what?*

"Keeping up your fitness, eh," Rhys said, sitting down and

offering one each to Marko, Tom, and Hayden. Hayden found himself waving it off, which annoyed him, but he couldn't help it. He was a mirrorer. It was science. You had mirror neurons in your brain that responded the same way whether you did a thing, or watched somebody else do a thing. He had empathy. Why was that bad?

Or he was just an impossible people-pleaser, which *was* bad. He was going with the mirror neurons.

"Maybe you'd like to mention your giving up to some of the boys at the wedding," Rhys said. "My players, anyway, though we'll give Marko a pass as he's getting married."

"Cheers," Marko said. Almost the first time he'd said anything. He'd mostly just sat there looking dark and amused. Well, he was a flanker, like Rhys had been, and flankers tended more toward action than words. Bashing the other fella and poaching the ball, seemed to be the idea. Fierce, you could call flankers. Or hard men.

Luke was different. Strong and solid and deliciously brooding, yeh, but without as much of that … edge. Of course, what did Hayden know? Nothing, that was what.

"I'm not drinking much these days," Luke said.

Hayden assessed him. "No?" He wouldn't have said it if he hadn't wanted to talk about it, would he? He didn't go around spilling his guts, it was clear.

"No," Luke said.

"Why not?" Casey asked.

"Because I'd been drinking too much," he said.

"Oh," Isaiah said. "Because you're an alcoholic."

"Isaiah." Rhys's voice was quiet, but it was firm. "No."

"Your family's here, though," Casey said, "because Nyree is your family. She can do a nintervention, if you're an alcoholic. I saw it on TV."

"*Casey Moana.*" That was Rhys, and Casey looked startled. She probably didn't hear that voice much, or see that face. Hayden had only seen it on TV himself, and he'd never heard the voice. "Both of you," Rhys said. "Luke doesn't need an intervention. Even if he did, that would be his business, and maybe his family's business, but definitely not ours. And you don't tell somebody that he's an alcoholic," he told Isaiah.

"But he *said* ..." Casey began.

"It's OK," Luke said. "Good to hear, maybe, for kids. I'm not an alcoholic, because I can still have a beer without wanting more. I just don't want one. I decided to see what it felt like to be sober all the time, and I found out I liked it better."

"Rugby players always drink beer after games, though," Isaiah said. "My dad used to drink heaps after games, I think."

"That wasn't really my problem," Luke said. "I was careful after games."

Ah. So as not to lose his head under the influence and say or do something he shouldn't, Hayden would bet. Other blokes could be wild and stupid and get themselves into trouble, and nobody would think much of it. Using the wrong pronoun, though ... much too easy, and catastrophic.

"Drinking too much can happen in all sorts of ways, though," Luke went on, which Hayden wouldn't have expected. "Like if your partner's a chef. Chefs work long hours and tend to drink wine— sometimes heaps of wine—to wind down at the end of the night, and you might be keeping them company. Wine's not really the best way to wind down, but I only found that out once I stopped trying to do it that way."

And there was Hayden's heart, dropping straight down again. *That* was why Luke had come out. Not because he was opening his heart, or whatever stupid thing Hayden had thought. Because he had somebody he couldn't bear to hide anymore. Which was good.

"A chef is a cook," Casey told Isaiah. "But in a fancy restaurant, with a tall hat, like in *Ratatouille*."

"I know," Isaiah said.

"Does she have a hat?" Casey asked. "The chef?"

"He's a man," Luke said, and his ears went red again. "Yeh. The restaurant had a Michelin star. That's a big deal. Means it's in the guidebook, and he had a hat and the checked trousers and white smock and all. Got to look the part, eh."

"Oh," Isaiah said. "Your partner was a man? Does that mean you're gay? You don't look like a gay person. Not like Uncle Hayden."

Now, both Rhys *and* Zora said, *"Isaiah,"* in stereo, and Hayden laid his forehead against the table and groaned.

"Gay means …" Isaiah was telling Casey even as Rhys and Zora said it, and Casey said, "I *know*. We had it in school. It means boys go out with boys, and girls go out with girls, and it's OK. Except you're supposed to say LGTBQ, and some other letters."

"LGBTQ plus," Isaiah said. "You got the letters backwards."

"There isn't one way people are gay," Tom said, absolutely unexpectedly. He'd spoken up even less than Marko, but then, what was he, twenty-one? At his coach's dinner table, and sitting with England's captain? "Not one way they look. You may think there is, because you see some people who you're sure are gay—LGBTQ—and you assume they're . . ."

"Representative of all gay individuals," Hayden said. "Like me. *Obviously* gay. What an entertaining day this is proving to be."

"But Tom's right," Zora said. "You don't know about all the people who *aren't* obvious, since you don't go around asking everybody their sexual orientation. Because you're more polite than that."

"Well, if you're Isaiah and Casey, you do, apparently," Hayden said. "Anybody else want to come out? Anybody who isn't obvious, that is? No? Good. I'm oddly exhausted. And I have a meeting at eight o'clock tomorrow, so …" He stood up. Enough fruitless yearning and weirdly desolate heartbreak, and definitely enough pretending to be insouciant. "Cheers for the pizza, Marko, and for the company, everybody. Hope you get it done tomorrow, Nyree."

"What?" She sat up and blinked. She'd fallen asleep on Marko's shoulder, apparently. "Oh. I'll come back in the morning and finish up. I've had so much help today, I can do it. Kane said he'd come back." She looked the question at Luke, and he nodded. "Good," she said. "Two's all I can keep busy, Tom, so I'll just bother my brothers. Thanks for all your help. After that, I'll sleep all day Friday, and I'll still have Saturday morning to pack for the wedding. Heaps of time. Casey's room has turned into a bit of a group project, that's all, and group projects can be brilliant."

"Yes, they can," Hayden said, "and I painted the blades of grass. Remember that when you see it, Casey. And ... I'm off."

Definitely time to go.

STRONG AS OAK

*A*s usually happens, Hayden's exit sparked a general exodus, and five minutes later, he was standing in the driveway with Luke and Tom as Marko and Nyree climbed into Marko's car, at the back of the queue, and reversed out of the driveway. Luke's car was next, but he hesitated a moment, and Hayden thought …

He wasn't sure what he thought.

Now, though, Luke said, "Well … I'm off myself," and put a hand on the door.

Hayden thought, *Good. Only answer.* And instead of saying, "Well, goodbye!" he said, "We could go have a drink if you like, toast your big day. Nonalcoholically, of course, which makes it an even more blameless idea. I don't feel like going home yet anyway. It's still light out, and barely seven-thirty. Whenever I'm with Zora and Rhys, I feel like I've aged thirty years, like I'd better run out and buy a spectacularly unsuitable convertible in a desperate attempt to hold onto my vanishing youth. Why is that?"

Tom was looking between the two of them, and Luke looked frozen, like he had no idea how to answer that. Hayden thought, *At least I was insouciant,* tried not to feel rejected, and said, "Or not, of course. Whichever."

"No," Luke said, the color rising into his cheeks again, and Hayden thought, *Clearly not insouciant enough.* Luke added, though, "I mean—sure. That would be good."

To celebrate coming out, obviously, or at least to come to terms with it. To talk things over, maybe, except that Luke didn't seem like the chatty type.

Oh, well. You had to look out for each other, didn't you? Not like the rest of the world would do it. Hayden said, "There's a place near Britomart that's surprisingly quiet. That could work. It's called Caretaker, and I've heard they do nonalcoholic as well. Not a gay bar or whatever you're imagining," he added hastily, "so no worries, no more coming out required."

"Sounds good," Luke said. "I'm staying at a hotel in Viaduct Harbour. I'll park and walk over, meet you there."

Viaduct Harbour again. No escape, it seemed.

Just because he's staying there, Hayden thought, *doesn't mean he's anything like Julian.* And tried to believe it. But when he'd sat in the deep murk of the basement bar for fifteen minutes, then twenty, he started losing faith. He didn't even have Luke's number, and Luke didn't have his. If he stood Hayden up, that didn't mean he was rejecting him. It just meant it was too much right now.

Or that he was rejecting him.

He wanted to put his head down on the table again. He clearly *was* too fragile to be going out, however casually. He was fit company for George the cat, and possibly a movie.

Or, of course, wine.

No. Luke had been right about the wine. Drinking alone and sad —no. It should be George and the movie, or even better, the gym. If he went home now, packed his kit, and went to the gym, he could be home by ten. The gym was definitely better. He'd go right now. He'd just—

The dim doorway of the place darkened even more, and then somebody approximately the size of a tree was wending his way among close-packed tables and chairs with surprising grace, his eyes fixed on Hayden's.

The forehead-on-table thing was probably a bad idea right now. Also hyperventilating.

"Hi," Luke said when he'd pulled out a chair and sat. And smiled.

"Hi," Hayden said, and, because he wanted to babble on, something about being glad Luke had come, or possibly about the cat, he told Luke instead, "So you know—they don't do regular drinks so much here. You say what you enjoy—sour, sweet, bitter, and so forth—and they make you something special. An adventure, is the idea."

"Ah," Luke said. "An adventure." And looked at Hayden again.

OK. Not so good for the hyperventilation issue. Hayden held it together, though, and when they'd given their orders to a server who vanished into the gloom again the same way he'd swum into view, went on, "You've been living in Paris, so the darkness and cramped quarters will be a feature, not a bug. Or not. I don't really know, other than films. I've been to Paris once in my life, on my gap year. Got bedbugs in a hostel and itched for days, and saw the Eiffel Tower and the Mona Lisa. I'm one step removed from reading *Madeline* for my knowledge. Never read *Remembrance of Things Past*, much less remembering the title in French. I read *The Three Musketeers* as a kid, though. Does that count?"

"Probably," Luke said. "I never read the Proust one myself. Started it once, and got about a hundred pages in before I gave up. Seven volumes of tormented introspection. No, thanks."

"Tormented introspection," Hayden said. "Good one. Did you read it in French?"

"Yeh," Luke said. "Maybe I'm not as dumb as I look, eh. Though, like I said—only a hundred pages." And smiled.

This was too hard.

Hayden looked at his water glass, picked it up, and set it down without taking a drink. "I need to say something."

Luke's smile vanished. "No worries. I know."

Hayden looked up, startled. "What?"

"That it's just a drink," Luke said. "No worries."

Hayden shook his head. "Wait. Start again. This is awkward." He tried to laugh, but for once, he couldn't. He also couldn't think how to be insouciant. "What do you think I'm saying?"

"That you …" Luke stopped, then went on. "That you don't want me to think this is more than a drink. Never mind. You don't need to say it. I look at my face in the mirror every day."

Their drinks came, and the second the server had left, Hayden said, "Wait. You think I'm not attracted to you? You can't even tell? Geez, this is rough." He blew out a breath. "Why are the things I want always so rough?"

Luke looked at him, then down at his hands, which he'd laid flat on the tiny table as if he were about to push off and sprint for the exit. Those were scarred, they were enormous, and Nyree was right about his knuckles. Hayden thought about that, because he didn't want to think about what he'd just said. "I know why it's tough for me," Luke said. "I'm not going to say 'rough.' I'm not rough. If that's what you're after, it's not me. I know how I look, but I'm not that guy. I'm never going to be that guy."

"Oh." Hayden had no idea how to react. No idea what to do. He'd been flooded with dread, and now, he was flooded with something else. "That's good," he managed, "if we're going there. Going to say that, I mean." He took a sip of his drink, tried once again to laugh, and said, "Right. I'm going to say what I need to say, and then we can finish our drinks and you can walk out, and I'll know that at least I told the truth, instead of going along with … whatever. That I wasn't desperate."

Luke's hand came out to cover his, and Hayden stared at it some more and tried not to feel the warmth and the safety of it. You weren't safe because a man touched your hand, and he knew it. "It's

OK," Luke said. "We don't have to see each other after tonight. Whatever it is, you can say it."

The cold was rushing in again, drowning Hayden. "Got it," he managed to say. "No, thanks. That's a no."

"Wait," Luke said, pulling his hand away. "What?"

"What I wanted to say," Hayden said, "was that I can't tell whether you've got somebody already. The chef with the wine. That I couldn't tell if he was the present, or the past. I wanted to ask Nyree, but I didn't want to be that guy, scared to ask the truth, scared to *tell* the truth, so I thought I'd ask you instead. I'm telling you that I don't want to be your ... your prize for coming out, some fella you'll never have to see again. I'm not going to be cheated on again, and I'm not going to be cheated *with*. If it doesn't matter, I don't want it. I know I don't look ...." He hauled in an unsteady breath. "Serious. I know I don't *seem* serious. That doesn't mean I'm a toy. That doesn't make me anybody's temporary entertainment."

"Hayden." Luke had his hand over Hayden's again. "I'm not with somebody. I'm fairly spectacularly *not* with somebody, in fact. The chef is in the past. I'm not pretty, and I know it. I'm not quick or clever, and there's nothing flash about me except my flat and my pay packet. I'm strong as oak, though, and I'm steady as hell. And I don't cheat. I don't hurt, I don't lie, and I don't cheat."

Hayden tried to say something, and he couldn't. "So come on," Luke said. "Let's go somewhere quieter, where I can see you and you can see me, and we're not shouting out our deepest secrets. Because I want to kiss you."

Hayden had an elbow on the table, his hand in his hair. "It's not this easy," he managed to say. "It's never this easy."

"Yes," Luke said, and that voice was deep, it was strong, and it was sure. "It can be. It is."

Hayden pulled into a parking garage in the Wynward Quarter, using a passcard to do it, and Luke wondered why and decided not to ask. If Hayden had brought Luke home with him …

No. Don't go there. Hayden hadn't made any conversation, beyond, "This is me," when they'd come to the car. Nervous, Luke thought, and the tenderness that had welled up in him when Hayden had put his hand in his hair back in the bar was right here again.

Hayden needed somebody strong. Somebody kind. Strong was the one thing Luke knew how to be. Kind, he wasn't so sure about. He reckoned he'd do his best.

Hayden found a carpark, turned the car off, and sat there like he didn't know what to do next. Luke thought, *He wants to know he's not a toy. What do I do about that? Not jump him, that's sure.* "Maybe we could sit a bit, eh," he decided to say. "Maybe turn on the radio."

"Oh." Hayden turned the key, switched on the sound system, and fiddled with the dial.

His hand was shaking.

"Here." Luke put his hand over his. "I can do it, if you like."

"You can't know the stations. You don't even live here."

"But I can still find music," Luke said, and he did. An alternative station, it had to be, maybe the university's, playing something reggae-inspired, with that upbeat, relaxed vibe. He asked, "OK?"

Hayden said, "Sure. I like that you asked. Shows patience, consideration, and so forth. All admirable qualities." Making conversation, obviously, because he was so clearly nervous.

What now? They both had their seatbelts off, but Hayden wasn't moving. Luke finally said, "We don't have to do anything tonight, you know."

A long pause, and Hayden said, "You know, your gentleness is pretty devastating."

Luke said, "When your job is being a hard man, you lose your taste for it as recreation, maybe."

"Hopefully not completely," Hayden said.

Luke smiled. Hayden would always bounce back, he was guessing. "Never mind. I think I know what you like. And if I don't … you can tell me."

Hayden put his face against the steering wheel. "OK. I give up. This is too bloody much. I may *be* in Paris. If you get any better, they're going to put you in a film. Please. Come on. Kiss me."

Luke said, "If you'll peel your face away from that steering wheel, I will." Feeling sure again. Feeling strong.

Hayden sat up. Not fast. Slowly, like he didn't dare to breathe. Luke knew how he felt. He put his hand against Hayden's cheek, pulled him closer, and kissed him. Gently at first. Carefully, exactly because he didn't want to be careful. He held back, and holding back was a buzzing thrill. Hayden's mouth under his, and then Luke's other hand around his head, too, to hold him better.

Heat. Power. Desire.

Hayden's hand, finally, on Luke's shoulder, and then his other one, and he was moving into Luke, starting to breathe hard, and Luke couldn't be quite as gentle now. He kissed Hayden harder, felt the edges of that perfectly-cut hair under his hand, felt Hayden's mouth opening under his, and burned.

Five minutes went by, because the song changed. Then it changed again, and Luke saw the steam on the windows out of the corner of his eye and got a jolt of fear. You didn't call attention to yourself. You didn't court discovery.

Wait. He'd already been discovered.

He couldn't shake the unease, though. Which meant, maybe, that it was time to go. He pulled back and said, "Give me your number, and I'll text you tomorrow. We could have dinner, see where we get. No pressure. Sound OK to you?"

"Yeh," Hayden said on a breath.

Luke should have gone, but he kissed him once more, because he couldn't help it, then said, "I'll text you," and got out of the car.

His legs were steady. His mind wasn't. His mind was thinking, *Bloody hell.* And, *Tomorrow.* And, *Be careful with him.*

It was standing in the tunnel, bouncing on your toes, rolling your shoulders, preparing to run out onto the field, centering yourself so the hammering of your heart, the pulsing of the blood in your veins didn't overwhelm you. It was knowing that you'd be hurting, and you'd be sweating, and by the end of eighty minutes, your legs would have that tremble in them, all the way down deep in the muscle, because you'd given it all you had, and you'd left everything out on the paddock.

It was being ready to play the game full-tilt, flat to the boards. Win or lose.

It was living.

STAKEOUT IN THE PARKING GARAGE

*H*ayden didn't drive away at once. He couldn't manage it. He sat there, his hands on the steering wheel, and stared at the concrete wall ahead.

Wow.

Maybe he should get out of the car and walk around a while. He could text Luke and ...

No. What was he, seventeen years old?

A tap on the window made him jump, and then it made his heart pound.

When he turned his head, he didn't see somebody almost as broad as he was tall, with biceps that looked like he was smuggling snakes under there, coming back to say that he couldn't possibly wait until tomorrow.

He saw, in fact, Julian.

He rolled the window down. He could do that, because the car was still on, the radio still playing soft and low. "Hi," he said, and couldn't think of anything else to say.

Julian had crouched down to look into the car, which meant his head was centimeters from Hayden's. He didn't say hello. He said, "Come out."

Hayden thought, *Why?* He actually had his hand on the door handle, that was how used he was to thinking Julian was fabulous and that he was lucky to be with him, but he took it away and asked, "Why?"

Julian sighed. "Because I want to talk to you, obviously."

"Maybe I need to get home to my cat." Hayden's head was still seriously turned around, and he wanted to let it stay there. He wanted to think back over every minute of tonight, not marinate in disasters past. Possibly go to the gym after all, if this leaping energy didn't settle soon.

Tomorrow, he thought, and got a kick of mingled lust, anticipation, and, possibly, fear. The kind of adrenaline rush that said there was no choice.

Julian said again, "I need to talk to you. Get out of the car."

Hayden got out, because Julian wasn't going anywhere, and he couldn't exactly back out and run over his foot, could he? Or sit in the car while Julian tapped on the window, because that would be a ridiculous scene, and he wasn't much for drama anyway.

"Right," he said, when Julian had backed up out of the space to make room and Hayden had slammed the car door. "I can't wait. Groveling apology? Cutting remarks about my life that you failed to think up the first time around? Let's have it."

"Why are you parking in my garage?" Julian asked.

Hayden laughed. He couldn't help it. "Did your family buy it, then?" He could have said, *Because I'm a thrifty Kiwi, and I bought a bloody expensive monthly pass to visit you that still has two days to run,* but why should he?

Julian looked down his aristocratic nose. He wasn't far off two meters tall, another fact that had once made Hayden swoon. Now, Hayden was noticing that he was possibly a bit ... weedy. Julian didn't do much working out, because, he'd said, "Horses, racing shells, and possibly a bit of boxing at school, dear boy. Those are the only necessary pursuits of an English gentleman. At least one who inherited the Lumley physique, don't you think? I'm not sweating like a navvy just to fit in with the latest trend. They're the ones who want to look like *me*, but you know— *L'habit ne fait pas le moine.* The habit doesn't make the monk," he'd translated for Hayden's benefit. "The monk is made of what lies within." He'd laughed as he'd said it, though, and added, still laughing, "Which is bloody pompous, of course, but there you are, I *am* bloody pompous. Or confident. We'll call it that, shall we?"

At the moment, though, Julian wasn't saying that. He was saying, "You know what I'm talking about."

"No," Hayden said, "I find I can't imagine. Other than the groveling apology. I can just about imagine that."

"You're stalking me."

"I am?"

"You know you are." Julian sighed again. "Look, dear boy. It was awkward, we'll both admit, but you need to face facts now. I'm with somebody else, and you need to move on. It was terribly nice, but it's over."

"Uh-huh." Hayden had leaned against the car now and folded his arms. He should be trembling at the confrontation, but somehow, he couldn't. "How's that going, then? Still blissful? Everything you've ever dreamed of? Did he replace the cashmere jumper yet?"

"We're going to Fiji in the new year, actually," Julian said. "Since you ask. Trevor wants to sail there, as he's got a break from work. Lovely adventure, don't you think?"

Hayden had to laugh. "In that boat? It's over a thousand nautical miles to Fiji. Ten-day sail at the best of times, with nowhere to stop, and we're still in the midst of cyclone season. You'll either drown or get blown off course and die of thirst."

"I can sail." Now, Julian's voice was stiff. "And Trevor's learning. And we'd buy a bigger boat, obviously."

"You can sail in Waitemata Harbour," Hayden said. "Maybe up the coast a bit."

"And you'd know better?" Julian asked.

"Well, yeh, I would. Enough to know I'm not sailing to Fiji, anyway. Also enough to know that I'd go stark raving mad after ten days on a boat that size, and likely cannibalize my partner if things went pear-shaped and the stores ran out. And when Trevor says 'we,' he means ..."

"He has money," Julian said.

"Boat money? Really? Saved up, then, has he? Or is he spending it as fast as he's earning it? While he's on a 'break from work'? I know a little something about fellas who get into a lucrative line of work and piss it all away. I wouldn't count on his half." Hayden was doing exactly what Isaiah had been rude for doing—talking about how much money people made. He also didn't need to be having this conversation, but he found he didn't much fancy scuttling away, either, as if Julian had wounded him.

"At least he's not dull," Julian said. "At least those 'fellas' he knows aren't rugby players, with all their brains in their hands and feet."

Now, Hayden was the one sighing. Also regretting that he'd engaged. "It's been lovely catching up, of course, but honestly, a *tiny* bit dull. I need to go home to my cat. George gets lonely. Also peck-ish. Past his teatime."

"I'm sorry if your life isn't exciting without me," Julian said. "I'm sorry you haven't found anyone. That doesn't mean you can come here and lurk in the shadows like this. If Trevor finds out, it'll scare him."

The hilarity was rising in Hayden's throat. "Which would be the point of stalking, if I were stalking. And I thought he was so strong and fit and exciting. I'm sure I've seen him having a stoush with somebody on TV. That all for show, then? He can't throw a punch? Can't even take on a lawyer?"

"I'll ring the police," Julian said.

"Do that," Hayden said. "Please. Ring them now, so they can explain the nature of my offense to me."

"You're a *contracts* lawyer," Julian said. "Not a criminal one. You don't know."

"You're right," Hayden said. "Not about the law, because I do know that, but that I fail to understand your predicament or the threat I pose, other than poking holes in your sailing dream. Dim, I reckon. But, fun as this has been …" He opened the car door, rested his hand on the top of it, and turned for a last word. "I really do need to go feed my cat."

FINE FOR PENGUINS AND BONOBOS

*L*uke didn't sleep well that night, either. For a different reason than the desolation of the night before, when he'd realized that even his best mates might not want to be his mates anymore.

No, it was Hayden.

He was a man who compartmentalized. There was no other way to live his life and play his game. He didn't fall head over heels. He didn't walk around in a fog. He couldn't afford to.

Hayden was bursting through all his compartments. *Because you're not playing,* he tried to tell himself, and knew it was a lie. *Because you have to see Dad this weekend.* Maybe, but at two in the morning, with his body about to levitate off the bed from sexual tension?

No.

The next day, he filled in the details on a rocky cliff while Nyree painted in swooping blue swallows, then, the second the cliff was dry, added gnomes digging for gemstones. While he painted, he thought about tonight.

Someplace flash. Someplace absolutely high-end. The kind of place he'd never been with a partner, because it would look romantic. The thought made his breath catch and his stomach seize up, but he knew he'd be doing it anyway. In fact, he went outside during a break in the action, found the right place, and made a booking.

That was that. Time to put this out of his mind and paint.

He managed it for an hour or so, until Rhys knocked at the bedroom door.

Nyree said, "Go see who it is, will you, Luke? But do *not* let those kids in. There's no peeking." She was painting like fury now, a smear of blue on one cheek, that deadline approaching fast. Not looking much like a woman getting married in … three days.

Luke opened the door. Rhys. That was good. He wasn't going to have to tackle Casey, anyway. Nyree called out behind him, "Whoever it is—you're not allowed to see."

Rhys smiled, and Luke stepped out and closed the door behind him.

Rhys said, "How's she going?"

"Oh, you know," Luke said. "Says she'll be done in an hour."

"Will it be today, you reckon?" Rhys asked, which showed that he understood Nyree's flawed sense of time.

"Yeh," Luke said. "Because I don't see Marko putting off the wedding for this wall. But not in an hour."

Rhys said, "Casey wants to have an unveiling party tonight, for her bedroom and Isaiah's. Nyree painted his ceiling."

"Oh." Luke wasn't sure what else to say.

"And she wants to invite everybody," Rhys said. "You and Kane, for two, and a few more. Zora's parents, and Hayden, of course. Finn Douglas, too, and his family."

"Oh," Luke said again, but he could feel the flush creeping up his neck. Zora's parents would be Hayden's parents, too. He'd never met parents. Not in his life experience. But they wouldn't have to know, right? Not like he and Hayden had to announce anything. Not that there was anything to announce anyway. He'd be Nyree's brother, that was all.

That was when the second half of Rhys's announcement hit him.

Finn Douglas, currently coaching at the Blues with Rhys. Luke had only played with him on the All Blacks, but he knew one thing for sure. Playing with him, like playing with Rhys, was heaps more comfortable than playing against him. Finn was a South Islander, like Luke himself, born to a farming family, a bit rough around the edges, and as hard a taskmaster in the gym as Luke. Not exactly the type to embrace different forms of sexuality.

And his family. "What family?" he asked Rhys. Stalling, he knew.

"Wife," Rhys said. "And four kids, with the fifth coming any day. Anyway—this is meant to be an invitation, one you can pass along to Kane as well—and tell Nyree, obviously. I warn you, Zora's working like mad on Nyree's wedding flowers, so the kids and I are in charge of this party. Sausage rolls are likely to feature heavily."

"Oh." Luke hesitated, and Rhys asked, "What?"

Nothing to do but say it. "I was going out with Hayden tonight. After this." Luke stared straight ahead and didn't think. Not about Finn Douglas, especially. Finn had been what Luke himself had aspired to be, back in those early days. A hard man. A disciplined man. A team man.

A *straight* man.

Harden up. A mantra that normally never failed, but was getting more difficult all the time. He could make his body do almost anything. His mind, though ... his mind didn't want to go there.

"Ah." Rhys scratched his nose. "OK if I invite you both anyway? Can you go out after? If not, say so. The kids will want Hayden to be there, but you could leave straightaway, if you like, and avoid the sausage rolls."

Luke smiled just a bit. "Nah. If it won't be fraught, with the parents and all." *And Finn,* he didn't say.

"Mate." Rhys put a hand on Luke's shoulder, and Luke felt the weight of that hand. That Rhys wasn't afraid to touch him the way he'd have done before, after a match. "It's my house," he told Luke. "Mine and Zora's. We invite who we like, and if anybody doesn't like it, they can bugger off."

Luke had to smile a bit more now. "Even her parents?"

"Especially her parents." Rhys grinned, a pirate's smile. "You have no idea. But you'll find out."

He did.

Not right away, not with all the excitement over the rooms. Isaiah's, first, which was painted like the night sky. The colors glowed nearly purple in some places, and for some reason, Nyree's friend Victoria, who was dating Luke's brother Kane, was playing the cello for this, something soaring, poignant, and powerful. Russian, Luke would bet that was. It sounded Russian, like every pleasure came with the promise of pain. Like life was beautiful, and it hurt.

Luke listened to the aching melody, looked at the swirling purple clouds and the dots of silver stars above, and thought of the first time he'd seen the Aurora Australis. On a school trip, that had been. There'd been a boy named Quentin Furman on that trip, and Luke had longed for Quentin, a skinny, brainy, quick-witted kid with a flashing smile, with every hopeless fiber of his fifteen-year-old being.

Quentin would never feature on any rugby squad. He'd never even feature on any *soccer* squad, because, he said, sport was boring. He was brilliant at maths, though, and Luke, who wasn't too bad at maths himself, could only watch in fascinated wonder as Quentin grasped the concepts and found the solutions almost without need of a calculator.

The way he'd smiled, too, when the teacher, Mr. Hereford, had asked him to show his work.

"I can't show my work," Quentin had shot back, bold as brass. "My work's in my head."

"Step by step," Mr. Hereford said. "That's how we do it. Shows that you understand the concepts."

"I don't even *know* step by step," Quentin tried to explain.

"Then find a way to know it," Mr. Hereford said.

Luke never talked in class if he could help it, but somehow, he was saying, "If his hand knows what to put down, isn't that the same way your feet know what to do in rugby?" Because Mr. Hereford was also his rugby coach. "They know what to do because you've trained them, but you can't break it down and say how you know. You just know."

"Was I speaking to you, Armstrong?" Mr. Hereford asked.

"No, sir," Luke said. "But—"

"Then why does this concern you?"

"Because he's right," Quentin said. "Do you stop him out on the paddock and tell him to diagram his moves? Ask him how many kgs per square meter of force he's exerting in the scrum?"

"That's enough from both of you," Mr. Hereford said. "Let's move on."

Luke had felt himself flushing, but Quentin had looked back at him and grinned, his floppy hair hanging over his forehead, his eyes dancing, and Luke had been so confused.

On that weekend, outside their hut on that school trip to the rugged coastline of the Catlins, where they were meant to be recording their sightings of sea lions and yellow-eyed penguins, the cold Southland night had swirled with light. A vivid neon green near the dark horizon, shading to hot pink, to purple, and then the colors fading to the deepest blue, the pinpricks of stars showing through in the thin air down here at the bottom of the world. The boys laughed and joked around him, and beside Luke, somebody said, "We should walk down a bit farther, get a better look without these arseholes. Take it in, maybe."

Luke didn't have to look to know it was Quentin. His heart was beating so fast, he thought it must be visible even in the dark. "Sure," he managed to say.

The dark. The cold. Sitting on a rock, feeling Quentin's warmth beside him, even though they weren't touching. Not wanting to breathe, not wanting to move, for fear he'd break the spell and it would be over. Staring at those glowing, pulsing lights and wishing for courage.

Finally, Quentin spoke. Not in his usual quick, sure fashion, his voice moving up and down the register, lively as a bird's, in a way Luke never managed. In a voice Luke hadn't heard before. "Thanks for coming to my rescue the way you did."

"Uh … when?" Now, Luke was sure Quentin could tell. Panic. Desire. Confusion.

"In maths class." Luke felt Quentin shift, saw his arm move, heard the *plink* of a small stone hitting a bigger one. "Nobody's done anything like that for me before. Not a rugby player, especially."

"Oh." Luke wasn't sure what to say. "It wasn't fair," he finally decided on. "You can't help being brilliant, I reckon."

"Neither can you."

"I'm not brilliant. Last thing from it."

"You're good at everything," Quentin said. "Sport, and maths, and history. Probably the rest as well, but I don't know. I haven't seen."

"I just work hard." Luke knew it was lame. He didn't have anything else, though. "I don't have … talent. Not the fizzing kind. Not like you."

"Luke." Luke jumped at hearing his name. "You do have that. What, you think it's all quick feet, quick talking? That's what the world thinks is brilliant. What if they're wrong?"

Luke didn't say anything. He couldn't.

"What if people like you," Quentin went on, "are just as important? Doesn't there have to be a … a foundation for things?"

Luke could see him out of the corner of his eye. Staring straight ahead, the same way Luke was. "Reckon that's what I am," he said. "A foundation."

"Also," Quentin said, "I think you want to kiss me. Of course, I could be horribly wrong, and you could beat me blind for saying it. I'm going to stand up now, ready to run. I'll deny I said it, too."

"I don't—" Luke managed to get out over the sound of the blood in his ears. "I can't— Don't go. Please. Don't go."

Quentin had moved away before the next school year. Luke hadn't cried. It was just another way life changed, he'd told himself, lying in bed dry-eyed, staring into the darkness, seeing those Southern Lights dancing across the sky despite himself. Another thing you had to move on from, because you were made wrong.

He hadn't kissed anybody else for more than four years, and even then, only when he was on tour, in some big foreign city where nobody knew his name and nobody cared about rugby. And still, every single time he'd done it, he'd expected the walls to come crashing down on him.

Now, he looked around him as the music played. Zora and Rhys, standing together, Rhys's big arm slung over Casey's shoulders, his other hand holding Zora's. Kane, watching Victoria play her cello as if he'd found what he'd always been looking for. Zora and Hayden's parents, their dad, Craig, a tight-lipped, stiff-backed sort of fella, and their mum, Tania, deliberately gracious. A bit like Grant and Miriama, in fact. Not as extreme, maybe, but Luke recognized the species. And then there was Finn Douglas, his arm around his pregnant wife, his toddler son held in one big arm, his older daughter too cool for this, his younger one all in.

All these families. And three people standing a little apart, standing with nobody. Isaiah, who would always stand apart, who would never be sure where he fit, because, like Quentin, his mind didn't work like everybody else's. It worked faster and more logically, and it took leaps. And Hayden, his cheerful side in full display tonight, with a brittleness to him that hurt Luke's heart. And, of course, him.

After that came more of all of it. Casey's room, and the buzzing fairies, the upside-down winged horses flying onto the ceiling, the mining dwarves and bunnies and mice and trees and witches. Casey climbing up on her bed and bouncing there, unable to contain her joy.

It was all pretty good, even if Luke had only painted the trees. A successful Christmas present, he reckoned, for a little girl whose mum had died, a Maori girl who hadn't known what that meant, who'd come across the world to a dad and a family she'd never met and a life she'd never imagined.

Who needed to know that somebody still loved her.

Rhys and Zora had given her that, and that was something, wasn't it? That was kindness. More important than brilliance, possibly. Luke didn't know much about parenting other than what he'd seen up close, but this way seemed better to him.

He hadn't had a chance to talk to Hayden. He'd barely had a chance to say hello to him, and he still hadn't when they went upstairs. Rhys was pulling sausage rolls from the oven, Finn's wife Jenna was taking a quiche and salads from the fridge, and there was talking and busyness and moving tables and chairs out on the deck, and dishes and cutlery and glasses and things to drink. And Hayden, taking a seat across from his parents, while Luke hesitated until Hayden looked up at him and said, "Come sit by me."

It was Quentin on the rocks again. It was the hopelessly exciting, impossible wonder of that first, awkward kiss, those first tentative touches, and the Aurora Australis in the night sky.

"OK," Luke said, and did. And still, Hayden practically vibrated with tension. Rhys was looking at the two of them speculatively, and Luke tried to tell himself, *He already knows. He's said it's OK with him,* but he couldn't quite get there, because something was off. Something was wrong.

Finally, when everybody was tucking into their dinner, Rhys told Hayden, "You've sacrificed a fair bit of your time to us this week, mate. I remember when you'd have had something to say about our general dullness. What happened to that?"

"Uncle Hayden doesn't think we're boring," Casey objected, her hand wrapped around another sausage roll. The sausage rolls had been her idea, no surprise. "He helped paint my room, so he wanted to come and see."

"Of course he doesn't think you're boring, darling," Tania said.

"Or maybe," Hayden said, still with that tension in his body but the usual smile on his face, "it's all good, because for once, I brought a date. Well, I met my date here. Close enough."

Luke went still, but he could see Kane looking up, the alert expression on his face.

"Oh?" Hayden's mum's smile looked pasted on, and his father wasn't smiling at all.

"Luke and I are going out after this," Hayden said. "Which is, yes, a fair bit of public announcement for *very* early days, and yet here I am announcing anyway. I'm going out with Luke. He is my date tonight. That noise you hear is the closet door banging behind him. Also behind me, possibly, in a way. Huh. Who knew? I've never brought a date around my parents, much less a boyfriend, and I'm over thirty. Isn't that odd?"

"You know we love you, darling," Tania said, her social smile still firmly in place. "But you don't need to tell us about it, surely."

"Not the time or the place," Craig said. "I'm amazed you don't know that. Social skills, the teachers always told us you had. Verbal skills. Girls' things, because you were rubbish at science and worse at sport, but here you are, not using any of them."

"And yet," Hayden said, "I find, astonishingly, that I choose this time and place. You'll have to get used to it, I suppose."

"Bloody wonderful." Craig muttered it to Tania, but Luke heard him perfectly. "Not just one rugby player in the family, or even two rugby players. We're all the way to three now. Jesus Christ. Next we'll have *his* brother."

The last sentence fell into one of those sudden lulls you got in a gathering. Finn's head went up, all the way at the other end of the table, as if he'd sensed it, and Kane's face darkened.

Zora said, "I heard that, Dad." Her voice was tight. "You can't say that."

"No," Rhys said. "You can't. Not in our house, and not just

because I was a rugby player myself. Tough to tell them that, was it?" he asked Hayden.

"Well, yeh," Hayden said, "since you ask. Also, I'm drinking lemonade in order to be supportive. Very little liquid courage in lemonade."

"You aren't supposed to talk about people, Grandad," Casey said. "And being gay, or LBTG … LBG …"

"LGBTQ Plus," Isaiah said. "It's normal."

"Well, not quite *normal,* darling," Tania said. "But that's all right, because we all love Uncle Hayden, don't we? Anyway!" She clapped her hands. "Who wants dessert? I think I saw some yummy cookies in there."

"Yes, it is, Nana," Isaiah said. "For example, there are two male penguins in New York City who are mates. Once they even tried to hatch a rock like it was an egg."

"Which would be," Craig said, "unproductive, reproductively speaking. Unsustainable. And occurring as an exception. Abnormal by definition."

Finn's older son Harry, who was probably twelve or so, was frowning and pushing up his specs like a professor about to impart important knowledge. "Heaps of bonobos have bisexual behavior, though. There was a study that said seventy-five percent, which makes it *not* the exception."

"Which would be more significant if we were bonobos," Craig said. Arguing with a twelve-year-old. Not his best look.

"Bonobos are the most related to humans of any animal, though," Harry said, absolutely unfazed. "We share 98.7 percent of our DNA with them, so it's *very* significant. Also, there are male giraffes who do homosexual behavior sometimes. And female—a kind of antelope. An African antelope. And sheep right here in New Zealand, because some rams would rather mate with other rams than with ewes, even when there are ewes around. There are heaps of other examples, too, but those are the main ones I remember. If you like, I can look all of them up and email you the results." Veering danger-ously close to disrespecting your elders, but Finn wasn't objecting.

"*Harry,*" his sister Sophie said. "How do you even *know* all that?"

"Because he knows things," Isaiah said. "Especially about animals. Knowing things is good. It makes you more logical."

"The main thing," Harry said, "is that it's true. It's data. It's *evidence,* and besides—what happens in science is what's supposed to happen, not what you thought would happen. That's the whole idea of science. You can't pretend not to notice things just because they aren't what you wanted to find."

Zora said quietly to Luke, "A bit more than you were expecting tonight?" With a smile that said she got it.

"Yeh," he said, starting to smile himself. "But good."

Hayden put his arm around Luke's waist like a declaration and said, "Yes. Good. Sorry, Dad, but I came out a long time ago, and it's time for me to finally *be* out. I'm tired of hiding, especially from you, and I can't do it anymore. Zora loving Rhys isn't shameful. Look at her. Look at *them,* and the kids and all. How can you think there's anything wrong with them being together, just because she was married to Dylan first? Dylan is dead. Sorry, Isaiah," he added.

"That's OK," the boy said. "I know he's dead."

"And there's nothing shameful about my life, either," Hayden went on. "I may not have won a Nobel prize or whatever you imag-ined for your son, and I may have girl qualities—thanks for the misogyny, but I'd call them lawyer qualities—but I haven't done so badly, have I? Here I am, supporting myself, got my flat and my car and my job and all, and I haven't developed a drugs problem or been ignominiously sacked for my embezzlement issue yet. I haven't loved the person you'd have wanted me to, and neither has Zora. Does that make us defective?"

"You don't want me to answer that," Craig said.

"Well, yes," Hayden said. "I find I do want that. I think it's time."

CAVUTO NERO, SIXTEEN DOLLARS

*B*y the time he walked out with Luke fifteen minutes later, Hayden's legs were practically shaking.

Not that much else had happened. His dad had said again, "Not the time or place." Victoria had jumped in with a question for his mum about clothes for the wedding, and nobody else had said anything about it.

Other than Rhys and Zora, who'd got up to see Luke and Hayden out. Zora had given Hayden a cuddle and said, "I know what kind of brother I have, and it's exactly the kind I want. I'm lucky to have him, too."

Hayden had choked up a bit at that, but Rhys was shaking his hand, then Luke's, and saying, "Well, for once it wasn't me putting their backs up. Cheers for that," and giving his pirate's grin again. "Also, I hope you're going out someplace brilliant. I'd say glass of wine, but …"

"Yeh." Luke was looking so stolid, it was as if he were carved from wood. "Sober's still better."

"Speak for yourself," Hayden said, and tried to laugh.

"You can go on and have a glass of wine," Luke said when Hayden had parked in the Wynward Quarter garage again and Luke had parked beside him. "Or two. Won't bother me. Like I said—not an alcoholic, just making a choice. At least I hope so. Giving up hasn't been too hard, though, so I don't think I can be."

"Is anything too hard for you, though?" Hayden asked, trying to shake off the jitters. "Doesn't seem like it to me."

"Heaps of things feel too hard," Luke said, starting to walk with that absolutely upright posture Hayden had almost never seen on anybody else. Like he didn't have to slouch along, to be cool. Like he was sufficient unto himself. "They don't turn out to be too hard, though, long as I keep moving."

"Admirably mentally healthy," Hayden said, keeping pace with him. Out onto the pavement now, where Luke turned right, not left. Which was good, because Julian's flat was about fifty meters to the left, and Hayden didn't need another angsty confrontation tonight. "Admirably optimistic."

"Which you are as well," Luke said.

"Well, I pretend to be," Hayden said. "Fake it till you make it. Where are we going, exactly, if I can make so bold as to ask?"

"Oh." Luke stopped dead. "Should I have consulted? Sorry. I went ahead and booked. Esther, in the QT Hotel. Sound OK?"

"More than OK," Hayden said, "but …"

"If it's about the money," Luke said, starting to walk again, "I asked you. Means I'm paying. First time I've ever done that, actually, because it makes it look like a date."

"But then," Hayden said, "it *is* a date. Out in the open and all." He wouldn't have called himself "steady," still. In fact, he was fizzing. "But you don't have to pay for me. Crass to mention it, I know, but I *am* a lawyer. I don't make international rugby money, but I do all right. Which doesn't mean anybody's taken me to Esther's. Well, a client for lunch once, but we won't count that. We'll pretend it's my first time."

Luke shot a look at him, but all he said was, "Good," then, after a moment, "So if it's not the money, what was that about?"

"What was what about?" Hayden couldn't remember.

"The way you were just then," Luke said. "Like there was something wrong with this. About the place, or me asking you, or whatever. I wanted it to feel ..." He hesitated. "Romantic. I don't normally get to be romantic. I've never given somebody, uh, romance."

So what have you given them? Hayden wanted to ask it, and he didn't. He wanted to *know* it. "That I was wondering," he said, "if that was where you were staying."

"No," Luke said. "Thought that could be pressure. I'm staying back there near the garage, at the Sofitel."

"Also pretty flash," Hayden said.

Luke shrugged one big shoulder. "They had a room. I wanted to find someplace fast."

"So French rugby really *does* pay better." Hayden was getting his sparkle back, somehow. "And here I thought you were just impossibly hot. Didn't realize I could do some gold-digging as well."

This time, Luke smiled, but when Hayden went on to say, "And you got a room there when your mate turfed you out," the smile left his face.

"Yeh," he said. "I did." He stopped in front of enormous glass doors. "This is it." Holding the door for Hayden. Romantic again, or something.

They didn't talk while they walked across to the restaurant, or while they were being seated, either. The place was Kiwi-flash, which meant that the kitchen was open, a wood-fired pizza oven was glowing hot, the banquettes were sleek and modern, the hanging lights were some kind of trendy thing that looked like lobster buoys, and the floor-to-ceiling windows took in the view of the Viaduct. Hayden picked up the menu and, whatever Luke had said, gulped a bit. He'd thought at first, *Oh, lovely. Scallops with black pudding and pumpkin? Chargrilled*

Mangonui snapper filet with taramasalata and salmon caviar? Yes, please, and then had realized that those two dishes alone added up to about seventy-five dollars, and then there were the vegetables, which could easily add another thirty. And who knew what they'd charge for water?

Help.

He said, "I'm not all that hungry, actually. The linguine looks good." And only twenty-nine dollars. You couldn't tell him that Luke was normally a big-spending sort of fella. He looked more like a meat pie and, yes, a beer.

Luke looked up in surprise. "What, after working all day?"

"I sit to work. And I *did* have a sausage roll. Also lemonade."

Luke set the menu down and studied Hayden comprehensively enough to make him want to squirm. "You think I'm gobsmacked by the prices, regretting asking you. I live in Paris. Also, I was with a chef for over two years. Got half my dinners out for free, if you want to look at it like that, so I came out ahead there. And I don't like bad food. But here's the real question. Why can't you believe that I wanted this to be special?"

"Uh ..." Hayden wanted to run his hand over his hair. Instead, he sat still.

"Because nobody's ever treated you like that, maybe," Luke went on slowly. "Nobody's ever treated me like that, either. We could try treating each other better. It's a thought."

"Oh," Hayden said. "All right, then. But I do want to hear about you coming to stay at the hotel."

Luke didn't smile, but Hayden thought he might be trying not to. "That the pound of flesh, then?"

"Well, yeh," Hayden said, "or it's a way to make me feel slightly less raw when you ask me why my dad was such a dickhead."

Now, Luke's smile was real. "Order first, you reckon?"

When the air left Hayden's body, he realized how tense it had been. "Yes," he said. "Order first. And if it's really all right with you to pay much too much for all this—what's cavuto nero when it's at home? Or do I blindly order it and hope for the best?"

"It's kale," Luke said. "The dark kind."

"Well, they could just say that," Hayden said, "but then they probably couldn't charge sixteen dollars for it."

No wine, but he didn't need wine, not tonight. He was floating, suspended in a bubble of deliciousness that started with the just-caught, tender bites of scallop cooked with chile and lime, and drinking fizzy water, but not too much, so it wouldn't wash the taste away. Looking at Luke opposite him, his face relaxed for once, as he ate Cloudy Bay clams with sherry and peas. Not requiring Hayden to sparkle, not asking him to dance for his supper. All right with just being here, while patrons came and went around them, the bar got a little louder, and the laughter rose and wafted out through the open windows.

"You wanted to know about my mate, the other night," Luke finally said.

"Yes," Hayden said, "if you want to tell me. When I came out … but we're not talking about me. We're talking about you."

Luke shrugged again. "I'm probably happier if we talk about you, but all right. Met him at the Crusaders when we were twenty-two or so, young blokes without much of a clue, making more money than we'd dreamed we could, hoping it would all last."

"But your dad was your coach before that," Hayden said. "You must have known you'd make it."

"Doesn't mean what you'd think. Not that you'll be good enough, it doesn't. I was in the First XV at school, yeh, but so were hundreds of other fellas. And I only wanted to do it if I …"

"What?" Hayden asked.

"If I kept loving it. I couldn't stand to do it because it was what my dad wanted, and at the same time, it was what I'd worked for since I was a kid."

"For your chance to shine," Hayden said.

"No," Luke said. "For my chance to get away and live my own life. Which I did, which is why the Crusaders."

"And the fact that you were gay …"

"Yeh. Well." Luke pushed a clam around, then seemed to make a decision and stabbed it. "I didn't share that. With anybody. Reckon I hid it a bit too well, with how shocked Matt was the other day. I tried to tell him it wasn't like that. That naked bodies don't mean the same thing to you in the changing sheds, that grabbing his jersey in the scrum and having him grab mine was just rugby, not foreplay. Maybe I should've told him that I never fancied him. I have a thing for—" He stopped again.

"A thing for what?" Hayden asked. "Mashed potato? Small feet? What?"

Luke smiled. "For blokes like you, I guess. Clever. Good-looking. Talkers. And I guess … thinner. Matt was a prop, too. No beauty contestants in the front row, and I don't much fancy kissing somebody's ear if it's as mangled as mine. And mostly, that there has to be spark coming back, or nothing catches fire. I can look at a fella and think, 'Yeh, he's fit,' but if there's nothing coming back, it doesn't … catch."

"But he didn't believe you," Hayden said.

"Maybe he would've if he'd listened a bit longer. Made some awkward jokes, laughed a fair bit, and then I went off to bed and so did he. I could hear some talking from in there, though. Him telling his wife, and her being shocked. So in the morning, I got up before they did, left a note, and found a room."

"You don't think …" Hayden began slowly.

"What? I know what I heard from him. I know what I *saw* from him."

"That he may just have needed some time," Hayden said. "If it's been that long—surely he knows you better than that."

"Dunno," Luke said, "and I wasn't keen on waiting around to find out. He hasn't sent me so much as a text since, though."

"And you're wondering whether you can keep playing," Hayden said, "once people know."

"Well, yeh." Luke finished his clams, and the waiter came by and whisked the plates away. "Time will tell, I guess."

"Right," Hayden said. "Well, I've got nothing that juicy. Just, you know, garden-variety parental angst and so forth. As you saw."

"When did you come out?" Luke asked.

"Do you really want to do this?" Hayden asked. "Tell these stories?"

"Well, no," Luke said. "Not right now. I want to … hear about your sister, maybe. Hear about the kids. Be entertained, possibly."

"With tales of fairies and bunnies," Hayden said. "And of Casey Moana and Isaiah."

Now, Luke was smiling for real. "Worse things to talk about than fairies and bunnies. Tell me about them. About Casey and Isaiah, and why Casey's got an American accent. They're funny kids, eh. Expressive, you could say. Tell me about Zora. I know about Drago—Rhys. No need to tell me about him. One of those players who tells you who he is by what he does out on the paddock. Rugby's a bit like golf, I reckon. You can tell heaps about a man by how he plays golf. Whether he cheats when he thinks nobody's watching. Whether he gets narky when he has a bad round, if he blames the caddy or the wind or nothing at all. I haven't played golf with Drago, but I've played rugby with him."

"With him, or against him?" Hayden asked.

"Both. One of them's easier. So go on. Tell."

Hayden did. The restaurant turned down the lights and changed the music, because it was late enough for that now. The snapper melted on his tongue, and eventually, so did the burnt Basque cheesecake with marmalade and chocolate sorbet—eighteen dollars. He'd suggested sharing, and Luke had said, "Nah. I'm having apple tart. Eat what you like and leave the rest." So Hayden talked and somehow managed not to eat every bite of that impossibly rich, creamy cheesecake, and Luke listened and laughed a bit sometimes and looked thoughtful other times, and Hayden felt …

Heard. Seen.

Known.

No wine at all, and he was melting, buzzing, by the time they walked out. Luke hadn't touched him, hadn't said anything remotely romantic, and Hayden was more aware of the bulk of him, the heat coming off his body, the size of his hands and the scars on his face, than he'd been since he was a kid. He was having some trouble breathing again, in fact, because that was the Sofitel ahead of them, and the parking garage beyond it.

The deciding moment. He didn't know Luke, not really, so why did it feel like he did? Why did he know that whatever choice he made tonight, it would be OK? And what *did* he want to choose? He couldn't even say.

Outside the doors of the Sofitel now, and Luke saying, "Want to take a bit of a walk?"

Hayden let out his breath. "You cannot imagine how much I want to do that."

Luke smiled. "Let me run up for a hoodie, then. Bring you one as well? It'll be cooling off a bit, down by the water."

"Yes," Hayden said. "Please."

"Five minutes," Luke promised, went inside, and strode toward the lifts.

Hayden wouldn't go in, he decided. More consistent messaging. *If you want to be special to somebody,* feel *like you're special.* Act *like you're special.*

Of course, Luke was only here until Christmas, and then he was leaving. For *France.* Where he lived. What was that, twenty thousand kilometers? The only rational choice was to grab this good thing right here, right now, to soothe his aches and try to soothe Luke's. If he was so breakable that he couldn't even manage short-term anymore, if he was going to weep and play Sam Smith songs on repeat when Luke left, he really *was* going to end up alone with George.

But it felt wrong. That was all. It felt wrong, and he didn't want to rush. He wanted to savor. He wanted to be desired, not as a distraction for tonight, but for himself. He wanted to want it so much that he felt like he couldn't wait, and he wanted to wait anyway.

So he waited amongst the late-evening strollers. Hands in the pockets of his dress trousers, scuffing absently at a rough edge of the red-brick footpath with his shoe, trying not to anticipate, and failing.

"Oh, bloody hell." The voice came from behind him, and Hayden stiffened. Not Julian's voice this time. Trevor's.

Hayden didn't want to turn. He turned anyway. It was the two of them, each with two heavy carrier bags. Coming back from doing a shop at Countdown, obviously. Cozy. Domestic.

He thought about saying, "Hi," but he didn't. He just stood there. For once, he wasn't going to try to deescalate. He was just going to wait and see what developed.

He did take his hands out of his pockets, though, in case something happened. They looked like something was going to happen.

Not that he'd be much chop at fighting, whatever he'd told Julian. He'd be rubbish at fighting, he was fairly sure. He'd never even tried. He was pretty good at running away, but he didn't feel like exercising that talent tonight, so it might be fighting anyway. Kicking, he reckoned. Grabbing the other fella and pulling him close so he couldn't land a hard blow. And, when necessary, curling up on the ground with his hands over his head. That, he definitely knew how to do.

Julian said, "That's it. I'm calling the police." And then just stood there, because his hands were full of grocery bags. Finally, he set them down, upon which they promptly fell over and spilled out mandarins and potatoes and avocadoes, a bunch of bananas sliding out with them. The rounder fruit and veg rolled all over, and Hayden wanted to laugh, and also considered whether you could do any damage by hitting somebody with a potato. Alas, probably not.

Julian ignored the rolling veg, clearly going for an "I meant to do that" vibe, and, yes, he was pulling his phone from his pocket.

A fella walked by, looking at his own phone, and stepped on the avocado. He stumbled, swore, scraped his shoe, covered with green goo, against the bricks, and said, "You may want to pick those up."

Everybody ignored him.

Trevor said, "We shouldn't call the cops. We should kick his arse instead."

"Oh?" Hayden asked. "Have you learnt to do that, then? I heard I scared you. And as I'd hardly scare a twelve-year-old girl ..."

Yes, Trevor was advancing, his fists balled up, and Hayden thought, *Right. Kicking's going to have to do it, because I have no idea how to punch.* Meanwhile, Julian was talking urgently into the phone. Something about a stalker, and a threat.

Which was when Luke came out of the double doors.

RUINING THE CASHMERE JUMPER

A few things happened after that.

Trevor took a swing at Hayden, aiming straight at his nose, and Hayden somehow managed to twist away so the blow landed on the side of his head. Which *hurt.* He staggered, and then did what he'd thought of before, which was still the only thing he could think of. He stepped into Trevor and grabbed him by the shoulder. Or, actually, by the jumper. *Cashmere,* he thought. *So soft,* even as his head rang and pulsed with pain. Trevor pushed back and tried to wrench away, then slapped Hayden across the face, which hurt *more,* while Hayden hung on for dear life, because it was, yes, still all he could think to do.

They staggered around together like that, and Julian said, "What the hell. Do stop, Trevor. The police are coming. Let them handle it."

Trevor didn't answer. That was because he was levitating backward. *That* was because Luke had grabbed him by the back of the jumper and was literally holding him up off his feet. Trevor's legs were kicking, and he was yelling. Something like, "Get the fuck off me!"

Which was when Julian dashed in, grabbed the *front* of Trevor's

347

jumper, and then stepped on a potato. Agrias, they were, unfortunately extremely oval. Julian's leg went out from under him, he yelped, and Luke let go of Trevor's jumper and stepped back.

It was like a ballet, if the dancers were extremely clumsy and the choreographer was rubbish. Julian's arm flailed, he let go of Trevor's jumper, his *other* arm flailed, and he stepped on the bunch of bananas with the leg that wasn't already in the air. The bananas squished, his foot slipped, his entire body twisted, Trevor grabbed for him, and the two of them went down together, bang-crash, straight onto the pavement in a pile of assorted fruit and veg.

Hayden said, "Pity you never … thought of another reason I'd be lurking. And that the reason can beat both of you at once." And laughed. Possibly hysterically. Also held his head and thought, *I was in a fight. I fought.*

Well, he'd held on, anyway. He hadn't run, and he hadn't dropped and cowered. He was counting it.

Luke asked, "Are you all right? Let me feel the head."

Hayden said, "I'm not sure if I'm excited or sick. Or sick and excited." Then he decided, because he turned, staggered, and vomited into the gutter.

Brilliant, he thought dazedly. *This is attractive. Also, all that lovely food.*

Luke had a hand on his back, fortunately or unfortunately. By the time Hayden managed to stand again and was wiping his mouth with his hand, wishing Luke weren't standing quite so close, Luke had his mobile out and was talking.

"I don't care that it's been phoned in," he was saying. "Or about the police. I need an ambulance. Got a TBI here. Hard blow to the side of the head, over the ear. Dizziness. Vomiting. Ambulance."

Hayden said, "You're terribly … capable." And tried to laugh.

"Don't talk," Luke said. "Sit down."

Hayden would have, but Luke had turned and was running faster than Hayden would have credited from a man his size. He was grabbing Trevor again as he legged it for Julian's place, and once more,

Luke had the back of Trevor's jumper. This time, he practically dragged him over to the others.

That's cashmere, you know, Hayden would have said if he weren't still in "gasping" mode. He still, somehow, wanted to laugh. *Probably silk as well. Probably cost six hundred dollars. He's going to hate that.*

Julian had been picking up the fruit and veg—more of it now, since both he and Trevor had dropped their bags. There was also a carton of eggs leaking yellow goo onto the bricks. Now, he whirled and said, "Take your hands off him, you barbarian," like Prince William objecting to a scene unbecoming to royalty. "We're leaving," he decided to add, as the two-toned wail of a police siren approached.

"No," Luke said. "You're not." He grabbed Julian as well, not seeming to care that Julian topped him by half a head. Julian swung an arm, and Luke swung him around. The blow landed on Luke's shoulder, and he said, "You'll have to do better than that, mate, to bring me down." Sounding ... almost amused.

The police car had stopped, and two officers got out, a woman and a man. Hayden could see that, because he'd staggered over to lean against the hotel window, his hands on his knees, feeling sick again. A couple at a table inside were staring at him, he noticed. He wanted to wave at them in an insouciant sort of way, but he didn't have the energy.

The older cop, a woman, asked sharply, "What's going on here?"

"This one punched my mate here," Luke said, jerking his chin at Hayden.

"*Which* one?" the cop asked.

"This one," Luke said. He lifted Trevor again and shoved him toward the cop. "All yours."

"Excuse me," Julian drawled. "Would you lot kindly ask this fellow to unhand me?" Sounding like a nineteenth-century novel, and Hayden thought, *What if he's actually an imposter? Is this really how the upper crust talks, or is he an international con artist? I have no idea. No, not possible. What, in Auckland? Not exactly the second home of the jet set. He'd be in New York City, or maybe Palm Beach. Pity.*

"And who are you, sir?" the woman cop asked Julian. The male cop had hold of Trevor, was snapping cuffs on him. Good.

"I am an innocent bystander," Julian said. Luke had let go of him, and he straightened his clothes and attempted to assume his usual superior air. "Or, rather, the victim of a stalking. My friend and I came upon this person, the one against the wall, whose name is Hayden Allen. He's been stalking me recently, and here he was, doing it again. It's honestly been rather frightening, and my friend, who is possibly a bit rash at times but whose intentions are, obviously, excellent, attempted to ... to push him out of the way."

"With his fist," Luke said. "In the side of the head."

"I'm not a ... stalker," Hayden managed to say. He was still feeling sick, and now, Luke was there, lowering him to the pavement, where he wanted to put his head between his knees but didn't. "I was just ... waiting for my own friend."

"Twice?" Julian said. "I don't think so."

"As I'm staying here, at the Sofitel," Luke said, "I *do* think so." He went over to the double doors, picked something up from the ground, and brought it over. "I was just collecting a couple of hoodies, as it's getting colder. Put this on," he told Hayden, then, when Hayden didn't move fast enough, helped him do it.

"Luke Armstrong, aren't you?" the male cop asked. "There can't be two men with that face, not to mention the rest of it, but you're in the wrong country. Missing a match, I'm thinking."

"Well, yeh," Luke said. "I am. Back in En Zed for my sister's wedding. My mate here was waiting for me, like I said, not stalking anybody. The tall one has delusions of grandeur, I reckon."

"Excuse me," Julian said. "I live about a hundred meters away, and I've caught Hayden hanging around here twice now."

"Last night," Hayden told Luke. "In the parking garage." His head really did hurt, and all he wanted was to lie down. He was never going to be a rugby player.

"Ah. When I'd just left him," Luke told the cops. "Again, not stalking."

"Who are you, exactly?" the female cop asked. "Luke who?"

"Armstrong. Captain for England," the male cop said. "Plays in France as well, though he's a Kiwi. Grant Armstrong's son, but not quite a traitor, I guess." Which was a joke, apparently. "There was only ever going to be one winner here."

"Rugby?" she asked. "Or ..." She looked at Luke speculatively. "Well, yeh. That's got to be rugby."

More two-toned wailing, and now, the ambulance was pulling up, two ambos jumping out.

"Over here," Luke told them.

Hayden said, "Honestly, I don't need the fuss. I just need to go home and lie down."

Luke ignored him. "TBI, I think," he told the ambos. "Got hit in the side of the head, right here." He pointed to the spot. "Vomiting, dizziness, weakness."

One of the ambos probed gently with his fingers, and Hayden let out a gasp. "Let's get you to hospital, then, mate," the other man said. "Looks like you've been hit here on the cheekbone as well."

"Wait," the female cop said. "We'll need a statement."

"Get it at the hospital," Luke said. "From both of us. He's not going anywhere for a while, and I'll be with him."

"You can't just let him walk away!" Julian said, losing some of his aristocratic cool. "He *attacked* us!"

"Which one did?" the female cop asked. "The one your friend hit? Or the one who was holding both of you up at once by the jumper while you hit *him?*"

"Yeah, nah," the male cop said. "You're not on the pavement, and you don't need the ambulance. That's not attacked. If Luke Armstrong attacks a man, reckon he stays attacked."

NOT HOW WE DO A FIRST DATE

"This is possibly," Hayden told Luke, "the most embarrassing episode of my life. It's got competition, but still."

Where was he while making this confession? On a gurney in a wailing ambulance, that was where, with an ambo beside him and Luke sitting on a bench opposite.

"Why?" Luke asked.

"Why? *Why?* Let's see. Because I stink of vomit, just to get that one out of the way. Because I've just been bashed again, but this time with extra drama and humiliation. Because you ruined your evening coming to my rescue, and now you're going to be spending it in hospital. Oh, and possibly because you got hit yourself, and it was my fault."

"First," Luke said, "I've stunk of vomit more times than I care to think about, and even when I didn't, somebody else always did. Second, you didn't ruin my evening, and I've spent heaps of time in hospital. Heaps of time visiting mates in hospital, for that matter. And hit? You call that hit?" He laughed. "Nah, mate, that wasn't 'hit.' Who was that bloke?"

Hayden glanced at the ambos. "Tell you later."

"What, because we're gay?" Luke had a spot of color high up on each cheekbone, but he was sitting solid, hands on his knees. The way, Hayden imagined, he'd sit on the bench waiting to go into the game, if he ever did sit on the bench. Hayden was guessing it didn't happen often. "I came out. People are going to know I'm gay."

"That's right. You … you did." Hayden was getting another wave of prickly sweat, and with it, another wave of nausea. "Going to be … sick again," he managed to get out, and the ambo held an expandable blue plastic tubular thing for him to retch into while Hayden thought, *Good thing I don't fancy you, mate, or I'd be even more humiliated than I already feel.*

The ambulance was still turning corners and wailing, so they weren't there yet. Hayden wondered dimly where they were going, hoped it wasn't his dad's hospital, and decided he didn't care. He just wanted to lie down on a bed that didn't move.

It was the hospital, then. Yes, his dad's, Hayden saw as he was wheeled into it with Luke following behind, but orthopedic surgeons didn't tend to work all hours, so his dad was likely to be at home and to stay there, nursing his grievances at the sad preponderance of rugby players in his kids' lives and possibly wondering where he'd gone wrong. Or, more likely, wondering where Hayden's mum had gone wrong.

After that, there was a CT scan, a bit more retching, some more cold, prickly, clammy skin and the feeling of the ground dropping away from under your stomach, and Luke sitting by the narrow bed in the ED, wiping Hayden's forehead and mouth one more time with a facecloth, then handing him a plastic cup with ice chips.

Hayden said, "You can go home. Honestly. This is too dull for words. Also, I wasted all that fabulous dinner."

Luke said, "Shut up. And give me your hand."

"What?" Hayden would have sat up and stared at him, but he didn't feel like it.

"Your hand," Luke repeated. "Give it to me."

Hayden did it, possibly because Luke was one of those

commanding fellas. Which, all right, was possibly attractive. Luke took it, laid his fingers and then his thumb across the inside of his wrist, then began to rub the thumb in a circle.

"Uh …" Hayden said, "I'm not feeling all that sexy at the moment. Can't believe you're finding me attractive, either, no matter how much rugby you've played."

Luke smiled a little. "Acupressure. For the nausea."

"Oh." Maybe it was helping, or maybe it just felt nice. Soothing, possibly. "I'm trying to remember the last time anybody held my hand."

"Hasn't happened much to me, either," Luke said. "Never in public."

"Other than your mum," Hayden said. "Which was a long time ago, in my case. I'm over thirty, despite my youthful physique. Don't look too closely around the eyes."

"Not my mum," Luke said. "Not that I recall."

"Oh." Hayden considered that. "Pretty bleak, then, your childhood."

"Yeh. Pretty much. So who was that? Both of them."

"The tall one was my ex. Who was cheating on me with the other one."

"Ah. The reason you're a bit touchy on the subject."

"And it's even worse than that," Hayden said, because why not? "I wasn't even the main attraction. I was the side piece, as it turned out. What's that thing they say? Everybody should get to be the star in their own life? Not so much that time."

"Never mind," Luke said. "You can be the star in my show. I'm not much for shining."

"Oh, I don't know," Hayden said. "I thought you did pretty well back there. Holding up both of them at once … that was good. I'd have swooned, except, you know, I was already swooning."

"Fella's a wanker," Luke said, and Hayden had to laugh.

"The other one's on TV," Hayden said. "The one who hit me. Soap star."

"Ah," Luke said. "Fancies himself."

Which was when the two police came in, which meant Hayden had to make his statement. Which was fine, until they got to the part about why.

"The tall one was a partner," he said reluctantly. "An ex."

The cop stayed stoical and wrote it down. Well, he'd probably figured it out. Hayden wasn't exactly butch, and Julian had practically written the book on "effete." The cop said, "You may want to apply for a protection order, then."

"He wasn't the one who hit me," Hayden said. "That was the new partner. Anyway, I'm a man. As you see."

"Doesn't matter," the female cop said. "It's called intimate partner violence, not violence against women. Hurts just as much for a man to be bashed. No sex-linked gene for pain."

"Oh," Hayden said. "Well, no, thanks. I doubt they'll bother me again."

"The one who hit you has been charged anyway," she said, "as there was damage, and we have witnesses."

"Did you recognize him?" Hayden asked. "Or did he tell you who he was? I'll bet he told you who he was."

"No," she said. "He wasn't keen on telling us who he was."

"Courtney Place," Hayden said.

"Oh." She digested that. "I don't watch the soaps. Probably be good for his image."

"As long as they don't mention the 'gay' bit," Hayden said. "As we're being open here."

"The other one told us who *he* was," the male cop said. "Related to Lord Somebody, he says."

"Wanker," Luke said.

The female cop didn't smile, but the male one did, a bit. "He continues to say you were stalking him."

"Yeh, well, I wasn't," Hayden said. "I was waiting for a mate, like I said. Him." He'd have jerked his chin at Luke, but his head still hurt, so he jerked a thumb instead. "I know him through my sister," he added. No reason the "gay" part had to come into this where Luke was concerned. There was coming out, and then there was being sucked into the midst of a gay love triangle. In public. In New Zealand, the smallest, most curious place in the world. Worse, in New Zealand *rugby,* the ultimate home of manly men.

"Better to wait for the police," the woman said, "than take matters into your own hands. Sir."

"Which was why," Luke said, "I didn't hit either of them. I held onto them instead and waited for the police."

"Better to let them go," the woman said, "and tell us later. As they were known to the victim."

"Yeh, nah," Luke said. "I'm not much for letting things go."

"Noticed that," the male cop said. "All the same," he added hastily at a look from the other one, "good that you left it to us." He finished writing on his clipboard. "Well, that's about it. If you'll just read these over and sign."

Luke read over his and signed his name. Hayden tried, but his eyes didn't want to focus. Luke must have noticed, because he said, "I'll read it to you."

The female cop said, "We'll ask that he read it himself. Procedure."

Luke said, "Not with concussion. I'll read it." And did.

Hayden lay back against that rubbish flat ED pillow when the cops had gone, looking white and exhausted. "They're going to wonder whether you're gay," he told Luke, apparently thinking that he still had to be witty and charming. "I wasn't sure how to create a diversionary smokescreen. Possibly beyond my capabilities at the moment."

"I noticed you trying," Luke said. "When you said the thing about knowing me through your sister."

"Well, yeh," Hayden said. "Best I could do. D'you think the

doctor's coming back soon? And this is so not the way to do a first date. Fairly uncomfortably vulnerable, in fact."

The doctor walked in just then and said, "No brain bleed visible now, but you'll want to keep an eye on your symptoms. If they don't improve within the next couple of days, and definitely if they get any worse, ring your GP to arrange more tests. If it's bad, come back here. A bleed can develop over time." He handed over a paper. "Things to watch for. Do you have somebody to stay with you tonight? It would be better."

"Oh." Hayden didn't glance at Luke. He extremely pointedly didn't glance at him, in fact. "I can ask my sister."

"I'll stay with him," Luke said. "I've had a fair few TBIs, know what to watch for."

"I can—" Hayden said, and stopped.

"Good," the doctor said. "You can go home, then, but take it easy for a few days."

"No worries," Hayden said. "I'm a lawyer. I just sit and type."

"Maybe not tomorrow," the doctor said.

"But I—" Hayden began.

"Not tomorrow," Luke said. "Eat. Drink. Rest. Monday's soon enough."

"You sound like you know," the doctor said.

"I should," Luke said. "And I do."

THE DADDY OF YOUR DREAMS

*T*hey took an Uber to Hayden's place. It was in a modern apartment block off The Strand, with what Luke guessed an estate agent would call a "sea view": shipping cranes, stacked containers under security lights, and a behemoth of a car carrier unloading its endless stream of cheap, used compacts, which were rolling, rattle-*clunk*, rattle-*clunk*, rattle-*clunk*, down the ramp. He guessed it still counted, though, because the dark void behind the ship was surely Waitemata Harbour, and beyond it would be Rangi-toto, Auckland's iconic volcanic-cone backdrop.

The apartment also had a marmalade cat in it, who came running up the second the door was open, talking and meowing for all he was worth. The cat began rubbing himself against Hayden's ankles, then started walking toward the kitchen alcove, looking back all the way and talking some more.

"George," Hayden said, with what Luke was guessing was about the last of his energy. "And it is not pathetic that I have a cat. I like him. Just now, he wants his tea. He has dry food, but he likes the canned kind best. High maintenance, possibly. A cat of refined tastes."

"He can wait a few minutes," Luke said.

"He's—" Hayden said.

"Where's the bedroom?" Luke asked.

"Flattering," Hayden said, "but possibly overly optimistic."

Luke said, "Never mind. Got to be over there," and walked that way, hoping that Hayden would follow him. Fortunately, he did.

"The view reminds me a bit of Newcastle," he told Hayden, once Hayden was finally sitting on the neatly made bed in the minuscule bedroom, which had no view at all, or even any windows, but did have an enormous framed poster of *Rent* hanging over the bed like a defiant two fingers up the bum of New Zealand masculinity.

"You're meant to think it's flash," Hayden said, not lying back in the way Luke could tell he wanted to, the way Luke wished he would. "I'm thinking that comparison may be insulting. It has a sea view and a lovely deck." The marmalade cat jumped into his lap, and Hayden's hands closed on it. The cat butted his head up under Hayden's chin, and Hayden took a deep breath and may have blinked back a few tears.

"I noticed," Luke said, wishing Hayden would start getting undressed. "Nice kitchen as well. And excellent lobby."

Hayden sighed. "I know. Not much character, possibly. I've got pictures hung and all, though, d'you notice? I've decorated in stylish black and white and all that. Also, it has a pool and a little gym. And a carpark. And I can walk to work. I've kept thinking I should try to buy a place, but—" He trailed off, and Luke thought he knew why. *Because I thought I'd be with somebody, and we'd choose it together.* Hayden was hopeful, apparently. Luke had always assumed he was on his own.

"Speaking of that," Luke decided to say, "I'm going to get you settled here and feed the cat, and then I'll go back for your car. No need to pay that overnight bill."

Hayden closed his eyes and swore. "I have a monthly parking pass, but … what time is it?"

Luke looked at his watch. "Eleven-fifteen."

"Oh, bloody hell." Hayden looked exhausted at the thought. "I *had* a monthly pass. Runs out at midnight. I thought—good, because I wouldn't be tempted to spend the night."

"Ah. The pass was because of the wanker." Luke didn't touch the other part, but he filed it away. *Vulnerable, like you thought. Possibly like you.*

"Yeh," Hayden said. "That's his garage. OK, that'd be good, if you're sure you don't mind. Otherwise, who knows, Trevor may decide to key my car. Or burn it. It would be beneath Julian's dignity, but Trevor? He could very well set it on fire and do a dance around it. Have you noticed that this is all my fault? Odd, but there you are. You go on, if you don't mind, and I'll feed George, then take a shower and climb into bed. I have a couch, if you like, but really— you don't need to stay, *or* to get the car. I'm fine. Just tired, and my head hurts. You got me home, so—thanks."

That was heaps of talking for somebody in Hayden's shape. Luke considered. "On second thought, we could just leave it there for now, and I'll get it in the morning."

"And pay the bill," Hayden said. "I told you—I'm not a toy. I pay my own way."

"You're bloody stubborn," Luke said.

"Don't sound so surprised." Hayden was still sitting up. "I need to brush my teeth. Take a shower. Burn these clothes. Get over my humiliation. We could have breakfast, if you like."

Luke smiled. "I've definitely changed my mind. Car can wait. He won't key it. He knows that if he does, I'll find him and do him over, and I won't care. I live in France, and they're not going to extradite me over a spot of easily healed revenge. Let's get you out of these clothes and into the shower."

"I can—" Hayden began.

"Nah, mate," Luke said. "You can't. I'm going to unbutton your shirt now. Don't get excited, because I'm not."

"Geez, thanks," Hayden muttered, but he let Luke do it. When Luke started on the trousers, though, Hayden put his hand over Luke's. "I'll do it. And I'll get into the shower, too. By myself. If you'll feed George—" He blinked. "Well ... I'll be grateful."

Luke wanted to say, *Who made you think that nobody would want to help you?* He didn't say it, because he was pretty sure he knew the answer. His parents. Men. Life. Hayden was nothing like him, and he was everything like him.

He went back to the kitchen and found the cans of cat food in a cupboard. The shower began to run, but the cat must have heard the can opener anyway, because he came running in so fast, he practically skidded to a stop in front of his dish, where he sat like a dog ready for his dinner and let out a few impatient meows as if to say, "I'm waiting here, mate." Luke put the dish down, and the cat put his paw on its edge and looked up at him.

"You can eat it," Luke told him. "I don't want it." The cat eyed him suspiciously, then bent his head and took a nibble before jerking bolt upright again and checking for an attack from the rear.

"Seriously," Luke said, "your horrible food is safe from me." Upon which the cat meowed and resumed his dinner, and Luke looked out a carton of eggs, finally ran a loaf of bread to earth in the freezer, made two cups of tea, and fixed a plate. The shower had stopped. Good. He took the plate and one of the mugs of tea into the bedroom with the cat padding behind, still talking up a storm as if he had Things To Say.

Hayden looked up, startled. He was standing in the middle of the room, hair wet, in a pair of sleep pants, holding a T-shirt. Luke was being nurturing—he hoped—but still ... Hayden looked *good.* Slim and strong. He may have made Luke's mouth water a bit when he pulled on that shirt.

Abs. He had abs himself, but they were a bit ... buried. By necessity, but still. Didn't mean he didn't appreciate the hell out of them on somebody else.

Nurturing, he reminded himself. "Brought you something to eat," he told Hayden. "Easy on the wonky stomach."

Hayden eyed the plate. "I don't eat bread. And, yes, it was in my freezer, and I may also have had pizza last night. We're glossing over that unfortunate episode. A moment of weakness."

Luke set the plate down on the bedside table. "It's Vogel's soy and linseed, not a French pastry. Six grams of protein, heaps of fiber, the good kind of carbs, and no added sugar or preservatives. I'd eat it every day and twice on Sunday if I could get it, and I'm about as careful of my diet as it's possible to be. Also, you didn't get much out of that dinner."

"Sausage roll, though," Hayden said, but Luke could tell he was weakening.

"Doubt the sausage roll stuck, either," Luke said. "I saw how much came out."

Hayden groaned and sat on the bed again. "Thanks for reminding me. I needed that." The cat jumped into his lap again, and he clutched it and kept on looking white and exhausted.

"Get in there," Luke said.

Hayden tried to glare at him. It didn't work. "If I'd wanted somebody to boss me around, I'd have invited Rhys over."

"Yeh, well, you didn't," Luke said. "You invited me."

"Not exactly," Hayden said. "As I recall, you invited yourself."

Luke sighed. "Get in bed. Eat your eggs. Turf me out in the morning, if you like, once you tell somebody else that you've had a TBI, so I don't have to worry about you dying alone."

Hayden got himself under the duvet, but of course, he had one more parting shot. "Who knew that the hot rugby player of my dreams would be so bloody maternal?" He picked up his mug of tea, which was at least a start, and the cat crawled onto his stomach, curled up, and got stuck into purring like he was motorized.

"That's not maternal," Luke said. "That's the daddy of your dreams."

"Fine," Hayden muttered. "Be irresistible. If I ask you to sleep with me, can it be because I find you sexually enticing, not because I want somebody policing how much of my eggs and toast I eat?"

Luke smiled. One of the weirdest days of his life, and it kept taking yet another odd turn. All the same, it was better than most any day he'd had for months. "You need a cuddle?"

"Yes," Hayden said. "All right? Bloody *yes.*"

"Then that," Luke said, "is what you'll get."

HE TOA TAUMATA RAO

*S*o it hadn't been exactly the way Hayden had imagined his first few days would go with a man too good to be true. It had been better.

Weirdly.

He hadn't done any more vomiting, for one thing. Always a plus. He'd fallen asleep surprisingly fast despite his headache, with the aid of a few Panadol. And, it must be confessed, with the aid of a bulky man in bed beside him, dressed in boxer briefs and T-shirt, whose body radiated more warmth than any beach.

First, though, Luke had given him the Panadol and told him to drink a glass of water. Hayden had objected, but only because he'd felt it was required. He'd been dozing even while Luke was in the shower, and once he'd come out, all thick thighs, chest, and biceps, and crawled in beside Hayden?

Yes, he'd fallen asleep. A waste of their first night, or the best first night ever. Hard to decide.

When he woke, Luke wasn't in bed, and neither was George. On the other hand, there was a lovely smell of bacon frying. Hayden thought, *I should get up. It's probably late. Also, I don't have bacon. How can I be smelling it?* But then he fell asleep again.

He woke to the pressure of somebody else on the bed. George, who'd jumped onto his chest and butted his head up under his chin, but somebody else, too. Luke, sitting on the edge of the bed, dressed in rugby shorts and a different T-shirt—a navy-blue one with the Adidas logo, exactly the same sort of thing Rhys wore, probably because he'd got it for free—saying, "Want to get up, or have breakfast in bed?"

"Now that," Hayden said, "is what you'd call a hard question. I want to get up, or I should. What time is it?"

"Nine, about there," Luke said.

"Nine?" Hayden sat up too fast and had to hold his head. "I need to phone the office."

"Go on and do it, then," Luke said. "And then have breakfast."

"How are you dressed differently?" Hayden asked. "How do we have bacon?"

"Went to the hotel and changed. And bought bacon. At Countdown, in the Wynward Quarter. Know who I saw there?"

Hayden forgot about his head, and about the office, too. "You're joking."

"Nah. Well, they lost their eggs and half their fruit and veg last night, didn't they."

"What did they do?"

Luke smiled. "Scuttled out like they were the rats and I was the cat. Very nice. You going to do that restraining order?"

Hayden felt, somehow, better than he had for months. "I think I already have one."

They went for a walk to the Wintergarden at the Domain after breakfast, strolling along the track beneath pohutukawa trees decked out for Christmas in their brilliant red candles of blossom, then looking at orchids and banana trees in the hothouse and a riot of pink and purple lupine in the seasonal greenhouse. After that, they had a coffee at the café, sitting in the shade of an umbrella amidst the cabbage trees, palms, and beds of yellow iris bright as the sun, and watching a mother duck followed by seven fuzzy babies swimming after her, the last duckling in line straggling a bit until the mum quacked her hurry-up order. All of it lazy and slightly guilty, like bunking off school, only better.

"I'm meant to be drafting a contract for Fonterra," Hayden said, not wanting to drink his latte, because the barista had done a swan on it in foam and it was too pretty to destroy.

Luke raised his eyebrows and took a bite of date scone, upon which he'd slathered a truly astonishing amount of butter. "Thirty percent of the world's dairy exports, and the biggest company in En Zed. Your firm does their work, eh."

"I know why *I* know that," Hayden said. "How do *you* know that?"

"I'm a South Islander."

"Not now, you're not."

"Close enough. So your firm does their work, and you do their contracts."

"Well, this one, anyway. Not the senior partner, of course. Just assigned to draft it up." Hayden felt a little shy. Nobody ever thought his work was interesting. Well, they had a point—it *was* mostly commercial contracts. He couldn't help it, though. He liked the precision of contracts, the way you had to use all your skill to get them exactly right. Possibly like accountancy, and very few people thought accountants were sexy. You never heard of accountant fetish wear, for example.

"Mm," Luke said. "Sounds to me like you're somebody there all the same. But then, I knew that." He ate another bite of scone, and Hayden watched abstractedly as the yellow butter—New Zealand butter, churned from the milk of cows that grazed all year round in lush pastures—he knew that because of the Fonterra contract, but it would be hard to miss if you had eyes and looked around you— melted and pooled over the flakes of rich pastry, studded with hefty chunks of date.

Why were the things you wanted most always so bad for you?

Luke must have seen him looking, because he held it out and said, "Have a bite."

"Oh. No. Thanks."

"Why not?" Luke asked.

"Uh …" Hayden couldn't catch hold of his thoughts. They would be there, nearly in his grasp, and then they'd skitter away again. It was extremely disconcerting. He had focus. He had analytical skills. That was nearly *all* he had. He clutched the edge of the wooden table, felt its solid warmth under his hands, and fought down the sudden panic.

"What?" Luke asked, his eyes sharpening.

"Nothing. I'm fine." Hayden took a sip of coffee, then remembered the swan and got a painful wrench. Because of his *coffee.*

There was Luke's hand, over his again. "What?"

"My brain's not working too well." Hayden tried to laugh, and found himself letting go of the edge of the table. Somehow, his hand turned, and now, Luke was holding it. In public. In Auckland. The courage of that moment … something tore loose inside Hayden's heart. He felt the tears welling up, and couldn't stop them.

"It's all right." Luke's voice was deep as the sea, strong as the tide. "It's a TBI. That's what they do. That's why you're giving that clever brain of yours a rest."

"Does it …" Hayden had to take a breath. "Come back?"

Luke smiled, just a little. "Well, so far. Least I don't seem too stupid yet. Course, I'm not a brilliant contracts lawyer, just doing some pushing and shoving in the front row."

"And captaining England." Hayden had control of himself again. "As a prop. Are props captains? Isn't your head usually …"

Luke smiled some more. "Up somebody's bum? Nah. You're thinking of the third row. Dunno why, but I am. Have a bite of scone, or tell me why you won't."

"If my brain is Swiss cheese," Hayden said, trying to make a joke of it, "all I've got is my lithe body and pretty face."

"Ah. You think that's why I like you."

"Well, yes. It generally is. Could this conversation be a little more squirm-worthy? Expose my unaccustomed vulnerability a little more? This is our third day, or possibly our fourth, depending how you count. We're meant to be in a fog of lust, not talking about me getting fat and stupid."

This time, Luke actually laughed, which was something, at least. Of course, he was laughing at Hayden, so ... "Nah," he said, the white scars around his eyes crinkling with the skin as he kept smiling. "I'm in a fog of lust, no worries. How about you?"

"Well, yes," Hayden said. "I can't think, of course, and I can't move my head very fast, which makes me unsuitable for recreational pursuits, but what's left of my brain is definitely—"

He broke off, because a kid was standing at the table. Nine or ten, about Isaiah's age, with an expression on his face like Casey's habitual one. Determination, you'd call that. He had an extremely round head. "Hello," Hayden said, and Luke slipped his hand out of his and half-turned to the kid.

Who wasn't looking at Hayden. He was looking at Luke. Fixedly. "My mum says you can't really be Luke Armstrong," he said, "even though we *live* in England, and I've watched you heaps, and I said you were. She says maybe you're some other rugby player, but probably not, because you're eating scones, but *I* said—"

"Well, yeh," Luke said, "I am. Scones and all. You've got a discerning eye, eh."

The boy blinked pale-blue eyes. "A what?"

"You're a good spotter," Luke said. "Your mum doesn't know I'm a Kiwi, maybe."

"But you're not really," the kid said. "You were born in England. In Newcastle, which is still England, even though it's not London. I'm from London. But your mum is English even if it's Newcastle, which is why you can play for England, even though you're usually in France. Why do you play in France if you're English?"

"I like France," Luke said. "But my dad's a Kiwi. If you know all that, you must've heard."

"He is a *bit*," the kid said. "Not for ages, not when you were born. Why didn't *he* stay in England? Lots of rugby players from New Zealand play in England. Some do from South Africa, too. Some do from Australia, even, though my dad says they're not usually as good as the ones from New Zealand and South Africa. But not you."

"No," Luke said solemnly. "I don't. It happens, eh. I'm guessing you play as well, as much as you know about it. What's your position?"

"Loosehead prop," the kid said. "Because I'm a bit fat."

Luke nodded and didn't smile, though Hayden thought he wanted to. "Good choice. Working on your running and your strength, too?"

"Yeh," the kid said. "But *I* think I should just work on my eating, so I can get bigger and push people over better."

"Got to run, too, even if you're a prop," Luke said. "And you can push people even better if you add some muscle."

"OK," the kid said dubiously, as if this might be some trick designed to keep him from rugby glory. "But *you're* a bit fat, too, and I saw you pushing a lorry tire down a field. Turning it over, like, which the man said meant you had 'incredible strength and fitness.' That's what he said, even though you're—"

"A bit fat. And eating scones," Luke agreed. "On a bit of a holiday, is why."

"But it's the middle of the *season*," the kid said, looking scandalized.

"Well, that's the beauty of being a prop," Luke said. "You've got room for a scone or two. Now, if you were a halfback, had to sprint around the paddock the whole game barking like a terrier, scones would be out of the question."

The kid nodded. "That's why I'm glad I'm a prop. Cake is my favorite."

"Want a photo," Luke asked, "before you go back to your mum?"

"Yes, please," the boy said. "Because otherwise, my dad will say it wasn't really you, and I must have imagined it. He's always saying that. I don't know why, because I'm not good at imagining."

This time, Luke *did* smile, and said, "Go get your mum's phone, then, and we'll do one. And then I need to get back to my scone. Otherwise, my mate here will scoff it all."

When he'd dispatched the kid, whose name was Roger—a prop name if he'd ever heard one—Luke turned back to Hayden and said, "You never did tell me why you wouldn't eat a bite of my scone."

Hayden said, "Well, obviously, because I long to be a terrier sprinting around the paddock like a madman and barking orders at everyone, and Roger says they can't have scones." Making it light again, as if the vulnerable moment hadn't happened.

"Think he'll like me as much when he finds out I'm gay?" Luke asked. He tried to make it light, too, but it wasn't easy.

"I don't know," Hayden said. "Why did you decide to do it? Why didn't you wait, at least until you retired?"

Luke looked down at the remains of his coffee, swirled them in the porcelain cup. "Dunno, really. I just couldn't hold it in anymore. I couldn't lie anymore. It was making me numb. Separating me from myself, I guess." He tried to smile, and couldn't. "Makes me sound like I've got some kind of mental illness. I'm pretty sure that's what my dad will say."

"Ah." Hayden was the one eyeing him much too closely now. Luke much preferred that the vulnerability stay on the other side of the table. If he could have sex with Hayden, it would be easier. He'd be in control then. Gentle, because he tried hard to be gentle, but in control. As it was …

Hayden went on, "Day after tomorrow. On the other hand, it's going to be a big wedding, and your brother will be there. Zora and Rhys, too. And Nyree, of course, though she'll be a bit busy. How was Marko about it when he found out?"

Luke shrugged. "Hard to tell what Marko's thinking. If he had a real problem, though, he'd say so. Not a very devious fella, Marko."

"What's he like to play against?" Hayden asked. Possibly steering the conversation away from the shoals. Hayden wasn't devious, but he was ... tactful, Luke guessed. Socially skilled. Something like that. Something he wasn't.

"Like you'd imagine," Luke said. "Battering ram. Heaps of mongrel in his game. Tackles like a bloody locomotive, and is none too gentle about it."

"So he and Nyree are ..."

"Well suited," Luke said. Yes, definitely a better topic.

At that moment, Hayden's phone rang. He was pulling it out of his pocket when *Luke's* phone rang. Luke looked at it.

Marko. Speaking of the battering ram.

He couldn't help it. He got a lurch of the stomach, like it was flipping over, and not in a good way. Marko didn't want him there. Afraid it would spoil the day if his dad got wind of the gay thing. Which was fair. More than fair. It was Nyree's day.

And if it was Marko who had the problem?

Luke would do what was best for Nyree, he guessed. He'd make an excuse. He'd go back to Paris. His life wasn't here, and his family was ... a bit fractured. That was all right. He was used to it, and everyone lived in the world alone, as far as he could see. They just pretended they didn't.

Harden up. Be a man. Hayden was talking to somebody, being bright and cheerful and funny again, like he wasn't concussed and hadn't been bashed. Luke was willing to bet nobody but him would ever know.

More than one way to be strong, he guessed.

There was a Maori thing his stepmother Miriama had used to say. "He toa taumata rao."

Courage has many resting places.

He answered the phone.

372

CHANGE OF PLAN

*M*arko said, "Change of wedding plans, mate," and Luke thought, *Here we go,* and tried not to care.

It was his *sister.*

That's why you have to take it.

Oh. Marko was saying, "My grandmother's pretty crook. Down in Tekapo. That's—"

"I'm from Otago," Luke reminded him. Tekapo. Barely a dot on the map in southern Canterbury, but a wilder, more scenic place it was hard to find. The Mackenzie Country. The high country, in the shadow of Aoraki Mount Cook, beside a glacial lake of an astonishing cloudy turquoise. Barren, some would say, but a place where your soul could find peace if you were a quiet man. An Otago man, and somehow, his dad notwithstanding, Paris notwithstanding, he was still that.

He thought about that, because he wasn't sure what was coming next.

"Oh. Right." Marko laughed. "Sorry. Of course you are. Things are a bit fraught at the moment. Anyway—the flash wedding in Northland's out, and we're doing it at my parents' instead, so my grandmother can be there. Much smaller group, obviously, mostly family, and whatever we can cobble together for the rest of it. Hoping you can still come, because it'd mean a lot to Nyree. It'll mean last-minute bookings, of course, and we don't know yet where everybody will sleep. Not going to be much accommodation available just before Christmas, so it's likely to be a tent. Fair warning. Sheep farm, also, though you won't have to sleep with them."

"OK," Luke said. He was standing at the edge of the patio, looking at the ducks on the pond. A mum, followed by her babies. Calm on the surface, and paddling like mad underneath. A bit like him.

"Good," Marko said.

"What can I do to help?" Luke asked.

Marko exhaled. "Round up the drink, maybe. My mum will have the food sorted, she says. She'll borrow chairs from every neighbor around, and my family do music, so we're good there. I haven't rung Kane yet, but Nyree's probably talked to Victoria, as she's the maid of honor. Not sure, honestly."

"I'll ring him," Luke said. "We'll bring the drink. Just tell me what time the thing starts, and how many people. Beer, wine, champagne, fizzy stuff, water. About like that?"

"Yeh. Thanks," Marko said.

"Your grandmother OK?"

Marko exhaled. "Not sure. Pneumonia, and she's old. I didn't know what to do, tell you the truth. Nyree said, though …" He stopped, and Luke thought his voice might not be entirely steady when he went on. "That what matters is that we get married with the people we care about around us. That the rest of it was just a party."

"Nyree's all right," Luke said.

"That's why I'm marrying her," Marko said, which made sense.

Luke hesitated, then said it. "Only thing—I was thinking I might come with Hayden, as you gave me a plus-one. If you don't have room, though—"

"Long as you don't mind sharing that tent," Marko said. "But I assume that's OK." Not sounding fussed about it.

Harden up and say it. "My dad could hear about me, one way or another, and I don't want to spoil your day. Koti James knows, and he's your best man, I hear. Kane, too, obviously, though he's not going to talk. But if it's small, there'll be no avoiding Grant, and who knows what Nyree will decide it's good to say."

Marko actually laughed. "You're not wrong. Never mind. He can choose which one of us to hate more, that's all. Spoilt for choice, eh. Also, Kane *will* be there, and Rhys and Zora are still coming. Zora's doing the flowers. Again, smaller scale, but Nyree wants flowers."

"Yeh," Luke said. "She's a colorful person."

"Too right. So that's reinforcements, possibly, as Rhys Fletcher may be the only man who can shut Grant up. He shut Hayden's dad down pretty well the other night, and he's an arrogant bastard."

"Grant doesn't much care if there's an audience," Luke said. "Or that it's an occasion."

"Mate," Marko said. "I played for him for almost ten years. He can't be worse than I've already seen. Anyway, who bloody cares? It's my wedding day. Nothing he does is going to spoil that."

When Hayden rang off, Luke was still on the phone, his back turned. Hayden couldn't read that back, and when Luke rang off and walked toward him, he couldn't read his face, either.

"Interesting news," Hayden said, as soon as Luke sat down again. "Seems I'm going to be a wedding celebrant. Fortunately, I know how."

Luke stared at him. "What?"

"Nyree and Marko," Hayden said. "Oh—wedding's changed. It's going to be in Tekapo."

"I know," Luke said. "Just got off the phone with Marko. But you're—"

"Yeh," Hayden said. "A celebrant. Hopefully I can remember my lines by then. Or even read. Otherwise, you'll have to hiss my cues at me like a prompter in a bad grammar-school play." He felt a bit giddy. That could just be concussion, of course.

"Why are you a wedding celebrant?" Luke asked.

"Because when the law changed, not everybody would marry the queer folk. I realize I'm not exactly an advert for wedded bliss, but I *am* a lawyer, and I do have some friends, so I decided I could marry them. Well, not *marry* them, but officiate. I'm not a polygamist, no worries."

He was babbling. That was because Luke was looking ... some way he couldn't tell. "And I realize it's your sister," Hayden went on, "and that you care that somebody does it right. But I'm pretty good at marrying people. I think I believe in it, though I don't know why I should. Astonishing, really. Anyway, Nyree told Zora they didn't have anyone to do it when she rang to ask her about bringing flowers down there, and it's in two days. And just because I seem frivolous—"

"Hayden." It was a bit abrupt, and Hayden's head jerked up, which hurt. He put a hand to it as Luke went on. "No. It's just ... I was hoping you'd come, I guess. I'm surprised, that's all."

"Taking a date to a wedding is normally a big step," Hayden said. "We'll excuse ourselves from that. No expectations here. I've married heaps of people. Hasn't made me take the plunge yet."

Luke smiled. "Nah. But you're going to be sleeping in a tent this time. That may be new."

Luke and Hayden didn't have head-banging sex that night, either. Hayden still looked bloody fragile, and by three o'clock that afternoon, Luke sent him off to take a nap.

Half of him thought, *What do you think you're doing here, mate? It's about a week until Christmas, and that's when you're leaving—for the place you actually live. And if you want a discreet fling, you're in the wrong place.* But his heart wasn't listening. He'd never been good at being anyplace but where he was, and where he was just now was ... here. So he turned some music on low—Paris jazz, the smoothest thing you could possibly listen to, and the most romantic, too, for his money—read his book some more, and eventually, as Hayden slept on, pulled out some more of the groceries he'd bought that morning in a completely unaccustomed and unreasonable moment of foolish hope, and set to work. Because, for one thing, every time he came back to New Zealand, he remembered the things he liked about it, and one of them was food.

Why should he be comfortable here? He'd lived his life in thirds: first England, then New Zealand, then France, and most of his time in New Zealand had been with his dad. And all the same, there was something about it he liked. The mountains, maybe. The humor. The fact that you could wear shorts to a restaurant.

He gave up thinking about it, because thinking about feelings wasn't his best thing. Instead, he made a protein and fruit smoothie to tide him over, and then he caramelized onions, cubed and roasted four different colors of kumara—New Zealand had the best veg in the world—had to do with the soil, he guessed—and, when the cubes had been through their own caramelization in the oven, whisked together tahini, wholegrain mustard, olive oil, maple syrup, sea salt, and a bit of juiced orange into a dressing.

Hayden came out of the bedroom at last, still looking tired in that way you did when you were recovering from a head injury, and Luke said, "Ten minutes till dinner. You could find us a movie, maybe." While Hayden did it, looking like that was about the limits of his powers, Luke coated his four salmon filets—one for Hayden and three for him—in a mix of spices and seared them in a pan while he tossed the cooled kumara and caramelized onions with the dressing and two bags of tender, tiny-leaved rocket with just enough kick to it. He toasted and buttered a few slices of that Vogel's bread, because his calorie counts had been pretty low today, arranged two plates and one mixing bowl—his salad wouldn't fit on the plate—and brought it all over to the coffee table.

"Shocking to the French," he told Hayden, "eating in front of the TV, but I may be an uncultured fella. You ate fish last night, so I thought you might like this."

Hayden put a fork through the blackened crust of the salmon, uncovered the tender pink flakes beneath, and sighed. "I may've died after all last night. You'd better be bad in bed, because otherwise, you're too good to be true."

Luke smiled. "You may find out. Although there's a tent in our future."

"Yes," Hayden said. "The tent. You could kiss me tonight, though. I could even touch you at last. We could be gentle, I guess. Go slow. What d'you think?"

"I think," Luke said, "that it'd be good to go slow."

They went, in fact, *very* slow. That was because Hayden fell asleep before the movie was over. Which meant another night with Luke's arm over Hayden's chest and Hayden pulled up close against him.

Hayden went to sleep right away. Luke lay awake and ached, and tried not to think about Sunday.

A BAD IDEA ALL AROUND

*H*ayden woke early. At least there was that, he thought as he sat up in bed and his head didn't actually swim. It didn't feel *good*, but he could form a somewhat coherent thought. Which was, *Where'd he go?*

No smell of bacon this morning, and no sign of a living soul in the apartment except George, who was, at the moment, *not* draped over Hayden's head like a hat. That was because Hayden had dislodged him when he'd sat up, which George had protested loudly just before he'd jumped off the bed and trotted off. After a minute, he came back, meowing like he had a knot in his tail.

"You can wait five minutes," Hayden told him. "You're about one kG away from qualifying as a sumo wrestler." Upon which George let out a series of grumbles that clearly translated to, *I am a starving wraith of a cat, and I'm calling the SPCA.*

"I hate to tell you, but you're going to be alone for nearly two days starting tomorrow," Hayden said. "Nothing but water and kibble. I'm expecting a picket line of cats out on the pavement." He did, though, go into the kitchen and open a can of food. He was possibly a sucker. Also, he was trying not to wonder where Luke was. *Letting you sleep, that's where. Off living his life, which he has every right to do. If you get needy and clingy, you know he'll be gone. Insouciant, that's you.* He could be insouciant now that his head was better.

He hoped.

George was already scoffing the disgusting mixture—trout, the smelliest and his favorite— when Hayden saw the note.

Meeting Kane to work out. Back around 11. I fed the cat.

Luke was feeling better. More settled. Not because he'd had a chat with his brother, because he hadn't, but because they'd done what they always did instead, which was go for a run up every hill around, including three times fast up and down the steps to Mount Eden, feet flying. Agility was important.

Unfortunately, now that he wasn't nine, Kane was faster. Either that, or Luke had got unfit as hell in a few days. Afterward, though, they ran back to Les Mills in Britomart and started stacking weights on barbells, and the Earth was back on its axis again.

This was more like it. Three sets of kettlebell jumps, power cleans, clap push-ups, and much more, followed by minutes of side and front planks, and this time, it was Luke setting the pace. Always his preference. After that, it was on to pullups with a weight chained to the belt around your waist, and then the bench press. When Luke had added the last weight to the bar, locked it down, and was lying on his back, Kane asked, "How long have you been benching a hundred ninety kGs?"

"A while," Luke answered. "Ready?"

"If you are," Kane said, which was what passed for banter between them, and spotted him.

Luke was on his third set, pushing hard through the final reps, when Kane asked, "You meeting Hayden here?"

Luke focused. Three more. Up fast, down slow, with Kane's big hands hovering just under the bar, but no worries. If your arms weren't shaking, it wasn't hard enough, that was all. When he'd finished and Kane had slotted the bar again, Luke sat up, wiped his head with a towel, and asked, "What?"

"Because he just went past," Kane said. "Shove off. I need to do mine."

Luke stood up, but said, "He can't have done."

"Why not?" Kane asked. "Looked fit enough to me. Vic goes here, too. She doesn't like it, but she goes. Does some sort of weird class that's ballet, but not, and uses the elliptical machine and maybe the recumbent bike. Very slowly. Heaps of people work out even though they hate it. Odd, but there you are, people can be odd. Odd that they don't like it, or odd that they do it anyway, whichever. Now, Nyree … I don't think she's ever met a barbell. Seems to suit Marko OK, though, and he's a pretty fit fella."

Luke wasn't listening. He was at the door, looking down the passage. A couple of women in spandex, holding water bottles, but no Hayden.

Of course it wouldn't be Hayden. He had concussion. He went back into the weight room, full of the clank of iron and the grunts of men who thought making noise meant everybody would be impressed.

Kane asked, "You spotting me, bro?"

"In a minute," Luke said. "Why did you think it was him?"

"Because it *was* him."

"You've seen him twice."

"Yeh, so I know what he looks like. Why, isn't he meant to be here?"

"No," Luke said. "He's not."

Kane had sat up on the bench, finally, because Luke wasn't coming back. A fella who'd been grunting loudly nearby for no discernible reason hovered as if to say, "You planning on getting on with it anytime soon, mate?" Possibly he didn't like the thought of asking that of the two of them, though, because he went over to the squat rack instead.

"Bro," Kane said, ignoring him, "I'm not saying I'm good at relationships, because I'm rubbish, but I'm pretty sure you're not supposed to be jealous. Controlling is a thing. A *bad* thing, especially if you're that much bigger and stronger. You could ask Vic. She has opinions about the subject. Prosecutor, you know."

"I'm not—" Luke stopped, because Hayden hadn't shared with anyone about the TBI, which meant he wouldn't want Luke to. "Never mind. Right. I'll spot you for this, and then I'm going to wrap it up."

It was all he could do to do it, and then to spend the time to rack the heavy weights again. Kane said, "Want to go for a coffee?"

"What? No." Luke was nearly out the door.

"Oh. OK." Kane hesitated, then said, "You're being odd. I'm saying that, because we're trying to share, or something. Be brothers, I guess."

"Right, then," Luke said. "Come with me. I'll probably be going for a coffee with you after all, because that can't have been Hayden."

Except that it was. Luke found him in one of the brightly lit, mirrored rooms where they did classes. Classes always seemed odd to him, full as they were of happy shouting, bright chat that would take your focus away from the matter at hand, and people dressed to impress for an activity that was only about getting fit, but they were always full anyway. No surprise that the world wasn't run by his rules.

This particular class was led by a slim bloke in tiny shorts—that was a look—and a singlet, who was standing up on a riser, a little microphone at his mouth to allow him to be heard over the pumping music. He had a barbell over his shoulders and was doing lunges while making jokes, which was fine. The thirty or so people in the class—half of them men, but let's say mostly men more like Hayden than Luke—were following along, laughing at the jokes and making their own. Also fine, except that one of them *was* Hayden.

"Oh, bloody hell," Luke said.

"What?" Kane asked.

Luke was already opening the door. Kane came in with him, but Luke barely noticed.

The instructor said, without missing a beat on his lunges, "Grab a spot at the back, boys."

Luke ignored him, too, and walked between the rows of lungers. No point trying to be inconspicuous, because Hayden was in the front row, and anyway, neither Luke nor Kane was built for subtlety. Luke got there and said, "Stop. You're done." Forcefully, maybe, because the music was loud. These people might be getting strong, though he was dubious, with those rubbish weights, but they were also risking hearing damage.

Kane was still with him, for some reason, which probably made too much of both of them for this space. Bit cramped anyway, with everybody lunging forward and back holding those bars. Unsafe, really.

Hayden stopped lunging, at least, and said, "What?"

"Contraindicated," Luke said. "After concussion. Also stupid." He shouldn't have said that part, he realized instantly. He needed to dial it back, but he'd practically had to carry Hayden to bed last night, and that ambulance ride hadn't been the most relaxed time of his life, either.

The instructor was ignoring them and going on to squats now. "Pump it up!" he was urging. "Let's get those bootys *toned!*" Not something you heard in a rugby training session very often. Neither was the "Whoo-hoo!" from the class that followed it. Very little "whoo-hooing" in Luke's everyday existence.

Hayden was starting to do squats now, the bar over his shoulders. No hope for it. Luke reached out, plucked it off, and set it on the floor.

Now, the instructor *did* say something. What he said was, *"Excuse me,"* in perhaps the gayest tone ever.

The man next to Hayden said, "Butch boyfriend, honey," and kept squatting.

Hayden said, "This is not all right. I'm working out. I read an—"

"Yeh, no," Luke said, then added, "Come outside, and I'll tell you why not." You were meant to talk things over. Right. He'd do that.

Another man was edging in from the other side. "I'm not saying I could take you," he told Luke, "but I'll have a go. If we all piled in … Come on, you lot." He looked around and bellowed it into the sudden silence, because the instructor had switched off the music. A little knot of men, sporting the kind of grooming that told you they were probably not the straightest arrows in the quiver, crowded around, and somebody pushed Luke in the back, or tried to. He felt it, he just didn't move.

Kane said, "Oi." Mildly, but he also put a hand out and was probably pushing back, and since Kane had a hand the size of a rugby ball, that would be some push.

The instructor hopped off the platform and hustled out. Calling for security, Luke guessed. This was even more stupid than the stoush amongst the fruit and veg, because this time, he was the one starting it. He also had the feeling the cops would be here soon. Again.

He ignored everybody else and told Hayden, "You're hurting yourself."

"I read a thing," Hayden said.

"A thing?" Luke asked. "What thing?"

"I read a thing, too," the man who'd objected first said. "About abusive partners."

Kane said, "Luke? Abusive?"

"Honey," the man told him, "take several steps back."

"Hang on," Kane said. "I'm sure we can—"

Luke was still ignoring him. "What thing?" he asked Hayden.

Hayden was turning red now. "It *said* that exercise was good for … you know. What happened. After a couple of days of recovery."

"After *what* happened?" the objecting man asked. "The mind doesn't exactly boggle, because we can all see, but—you know, sweetie," he told Hayden, "you can say no. Yes, he *looks* lovely and fierce, but is he, really? If he hurts you? And the other one, too? I know they say there's no correlation of size with, well, *size,* and everybody *thinks* they want it, but when you come down to brass tacks ..."

Luke was sure he was so red by now, his head was about to burst into flames. Kane looked gobsmacked. Getting an education, Luke guessed.

"He has concussion!" Luke said, because there was no other way out of this.

"Oh, sweetie," the objecting man said. "No. Not if he hits you in the *head.*"

"I did not," Luke said through his teeth, "hit him in the head. Somebody else did."

"The article said," Hayden told him, "that moderate exercise after two days of rest was helpful in regaining cognitive function. It's been almost two days, and the wedding is tomorrow! I can't be stupid for it!"

"You're never *marrying* him," the objecting man said. "Gurl, it's intervention time."

"No," Hayden said. "I'm marrying two other people. I mean, I'm not *marrying* them, but I'm—"

Luke said, "The article probably said that an individualized, progressive sub-symptom-threshold aerobic exercise program was helpful in regaining cognitive function and returning to play. That means a treadmill. A *monitored* treadmill. I'd have been happy to help you with that. All you had to do was ask."

"I'm doing an aerobic exercise program!" Hayden said. "All right, also some strength training, but it *is* an individualized, progressive program, because it's my program that I've worked up to. I'm not an idiot."

"A treadmill," Luke repeated, "or a stationary bike. This is too much. Is your head hurting?"

"Well, yes," Hayden said, "a bit. But—"

"Was it hurting when you started?" Luke asked.

"Well, no," Hayden said. "Not as much. But I've been pushing it a bit, so—"

Security was here. Brilliant. Luke could tell, because it was a man in a black T-shirt with "Security" printed on it in white, in case you'd missed the overdeveloped upper body. He'd skipped a fair few leg days, Luke noticed, which meant he'd go over like a ninepin the moment you gave him a push. Power came from the lower body.

"We're just going," Luke told him. "He's been overdoing it, that's all, after his injury, and as I'm his, uh …"

"Trainer," Kane said. "We're his trainers. Saw him in here and had to pull him out. Contraindicated. With his injury."

"You can *not* disrupt my class," the instructor said from behind the security bloke. "I don't care *who* you are." His shorts really were short. Also red. He added, "People pay for this. People *plan* for this. *I* plan for this."

"Right," Luke said. "Apologies. We'll just put this bar back and go."

"I think you'd better leave, mate," the security guard said. A bit late, but Luke reckoned he had to earn his money. He wasn't trying to grab Luke, but then, that would've been a bad idea.

"Yeh," Luke said. "I agree. Cheers. Talk to you about it at home?" he asked Hayden.

"Fine," Hayden said. "I'm searching for a witty comeback, but I don't have one, so … fine. Let's go. But I will note that I'm desperately embarrassed, so cheers for that."

"Yeh, sorry," Luke said. "I should've thought, probably."

"You think?" Hayden asked.

"You too, mate," the security bloke told Kane.

"Yeh," he said. "I've had my workout anyway. Sorry," he told the room. "Carry on. Looks like, uh, heaps of fun. The music, and the, uh, shouting and all. Great class. We're just going."

"Aren't you—" the security guard started to say. Not to Luke. To Kane.

"No," Kane said. "Never met the fella. I get that a lot, though." And fled.

A HARD BARGAIN

"*A*ll right," Hayden said, when they were out on the pavement again. Time to assert himself. "Why? That's my regular Saturday morning class, for your information. My support group, you could say. The crème de la crème of queer Auckland, we like to think, and are they ever going to have questions. Also, I think you just outed yourself," he told Kane.

Kane looked startled. "No, I didn't. I said we were your trainers."

"Excuse me," Hayden said. "Nobody is going to believe that."

"Oh." Kane digested that for a moment. "Good thing I don't live in Auckland, then."

Hayden wanted to tell him that Christchurch wasn't exactly halfway around the globe and that Kane wasn't exactly anonymous, given that he was probably pushing six foot eight, had biceps like young trees, and wore black-rimmed specs, but he didn't. He was still embarrassed as hell, he was narky, and he was confused. When Luke had snatched that barbell away … he didn't know what he'd felt.

They hadn't even slept together!

Kane said, "Well, I'll be shoving off. See you at the airport tomorrow."

Hayden didn't say goodbye. Neither did Luke. He was still looking like a baffled and enraged bull. Possibly mostly baffled, but how could you tell? Luke said, when Kane was gone, "Your place, or my hotel. Choose."

"No," Hayden said.

"No?" Definitely a baffled bull.

"You can't just haul me out of there and expect me to go with you! Where'd you go to relationship school? *No.*"

"Oh." Luke seemed to consider that. "OK. What do we do, then?"

Hayden sighed. "My place. I need home turf."

"OK." Luke set off, then, seeming to realize Hayden wasn't with him, turned back. "Not good to walk?"

Hayden put both hands to his head. Not because it hurt, though it did, a bit. Because he wanted to laugh, and he also wanted to scream. "You are not in charge here," he informed Luke.

"Oh." Luke considered that. "Reckon I'm used to being in charge."

"I noticed."

"Right," Luke said. "I wait for you to start walking, or what?"

"Well," Hayden said, "that would be one idea."

Luke did it. You had to give him credit. He didn't talk, though. Not all the way up Beach Road, not through the lobby, not up in the lift, not down the passage to the apartment door. By the time Hayden was putting his key in the lock, he was so wound up, he was shaking.

They went inside, George came pelting up, meowing as if he'd been alone for days, and Hayden dropped his workout bag and said, "*Say* something."

Luke said, "I thought I was meant to not be in charge."

Hayden was sweaty. He was hot, because it had been sunny out there, and the class had felt extra hard. He was also nervous. Luke had sweated, too, because the back of his T-shirt was soaked, and his biceps and thighs were pumped like he'd blown them up. He was giving off pheromones and testosterone like he'd cornered the market, and he didn't look nervous at all.

Hayden gave it up, stepped into him, pulled down his head, and kissed him.

Luke stood stock-still a second, and then his bag hit the floor. Half a second after that, both arms were around Hayden, his tongue was in Hayden's mouth, and he was backing him up against the wall.

Oh, yeh, Hayden thought with what was left of his brain. *Do me like that.* And then he stopped thinking, because Luke's mouth was at his ear, then his neck, and Hayden's hand was under Luke's shirt, feeling the valley of his spine, the muscle that rose on either side. If he hadn't been against the wall, he'd have been on the floor, because his knees were shaking.

Luke's hands were on Hayden's shirt, he realized dimly, and then his shirt was over his head. Luke was kicking off his shoes, and Hayden thought, *Oh,* and started to do the same, but he couldn't, because Luke was backing him through the flat, kissing him all the way.

Oh. Bloody. *Hell.*

Be gentle, part of Luke's brain was trying to tell him, but his body wasn't getting the message, because he had Hayden on the bed, was pulling off his shoes and socks, his shorts, then yanking off his own clothes. Something may have ripped in there, because there was a sound like fabric giving under his hands. He'd been sweating like a bull, and he couldn't care, because he was over Hayden, hands and mouth greedy, and Hayden was holding on, gasping, and then, when Luke found a brown nipple, rising into him and calling out.

He was restless. He was selfish. His hands wanted to be everywhere at once, and his mouth and tongue had a mind of their own. He was grabbing, stroking, kissing, and he needed more. He needed this body, and he was taking it.

Trying to slow down, trying to be careful, and failing. His mouth around Hayden, and Hayden's hands in his hair, clutching. The sounds he made, and the way his body tightened under Luke, and all it was doing was pushing Luke higher, ripping away more of his self-control.

He'd meant it to be slow. He'd meant it to be careful. Loving. Caring. Tender. All those good things. Unfortunately, Hayden's skin was soft as silk on the insides of his biceps, his thighs were lean and lithe, he had those abs, he smelled like vanilla, and by the time Luke turned him over and found that his back was even better and he had an arse like a peach ... all he wanted to do was to touch and kiss all of that while Hayden writhed and moaned under him.

And then to fuck his brains out.

So that's what he did. He barely managed to get the condom on.

Holy *shit.*

Hayden wasn't sure he could breathe. He could be dying, in fact, because his legs were shaking, his heart was pounding, and he felt like he'd just been hit by a truck.

"Holy shit," he finally managed to get out. Luke was still over him, pressing him into the mattress, and he was being crushed in the most delicious way.

"Yeh." Luke rolled off him, then pulled him into his arms. "All right? Your head?"

Hayden tried to laugh. It wasn't easy. His *stomach* muscles were shaking. It was like the aftermath of the most intense fitness class ever, the kind where you felt like you'd have to crawl home. "I'm not even sure I'm still alive."

"Bloody hell." Luke's hand was on Hayden's head, stroking his hair back with a hand that was surely shaking, wasn't it? Was that possible? He was kissing Hayden again, wrapping himself around him, and it was like being surrounded by all the power and all the comfort in the world. "What did I do?"

"I'm fairly sure," Hayden said, that laughter still flooding him, "that you did just about everything."

"Sorry. I snapped. Not an excuse, I know. I just—I'm sorry."

Hayden was flooded, somehow, with tenderness, and now, he was the one holding Luke's battered head in his two hands, kissing his hard mouth. "Did you notice me telling you to stop?"

Luke's whole body went rigid. "You did?"

"No. That's the *point*. I didn't. Are you saying this was outside your normal pattern? That I shouldn't expect this every time?"

"Yes. Of course not. I mean ... bloody hell. Yes, you shouldn't expect that, and no, that's not me. I was rough, when I meant to be gentle. I'm careful. I know I'm strong, and I ... I don't even know why that happened. *How* it happened."

"Well, I like to think it's because I'm irresistible," Hayden said, "and if you don't stop apologizing, I'm going to lose my lovely buzz. That would be a pity, because I think you just rocked my world."

Now, Luke went still for a different reason. "It was all right?"

"Well, I may have lost the use of my legs," Hayden said, the bubble of hilarity rising, "but what a way to go."

"I didn't even take a shower," Luke said.

"No. You didn't. And neither did I."

"Yeh," Luke said, "but you smell good."

Hayden laughed out loud. "So do you. You can stop worrying now. And if you *can't* stop worrying ..." He kissed Luke right on his battered ear. "You could take a shower with me."

They did, and that was good, too. Kissing and touching and stroking, languid now, and so satisfied. When they were under the duvet, the blood running through Hayden's veins like warm, thick honey, his body wanting nothing but to fall asleep, he forced himself to say, "We didn't talk about your attitude in there. At the gym." Communication was fundamental, after all.

"Oh." Luke went still again, which Hayden had decided was

Luke's way of saying, "I am having powerful feelings." He was pretty sure he was right, because that was *all* Luke said.

Hayden said, "I'm thinking that was concern."

"Well, yeh. It was. I couldn't believe it. I saw you in there, and I … I couldn't believe it. But maybe I shouldn't have done it like that."

"Well, no," Hayden still wanted to laugh, but he was oddly touched, too. "I'd say that wasn't the best approach."

"OK. What should I have done instead?"

That brought Hayden up short. "That's your response? No defensiveness? No explanation of why your way was the only reasonable solution?"

"I'm a sportsman," Luke said. "Can't afford to ignore coaching, not if I want to get better."

Hayden had to kiss him again then, didn't he? And to run his hand down his arm, because, hello, *muscles.* "All right. I'm trying to think what a better way would be. I know there was one, because I was in the middle of a class. A class you interrupted pretty comprehensively, and I may never be allowed back. You could've waited for it to be over, of course, and told me later. There's that option."

Luke considered. Hayden could *feel* him considering. "I could've, but I did think you were hurting yourself. Didn't feel safe."

"And I could ask you why you're qualified to judge for me, but, of course, you *are* qualified to judge. So inconvenient."

Luke laughed, the first time Hayden had heard it all day. "Sorry, but you're right. I am. That was dangerous, and I felt like I had to stop it. Also, because you brought it up—I didn't go to relationship school anywhere. Pretty obvious, I'd have thought. Rough as guts, in fact."

Hayden thought it over. "How about this, then? And by the way, this is the most bizarrely adult fight I've ever had with a lover. You could have come in—possibly *without* your brother, because that was over the top, though my friends are thrilled to bits, I'm sure, by the testosterone excess and the general levels of drama—touched me on the shoulder, and asked if you could talk to me outside."

"Thought that was what I did."

"I think it was more like, 'Let's go. You're out of here.'"

"Oh. Well, maybe. Right. Got it. Polite request next time."

"Yes. No commanding."

"None?" Luke could be smiling, and Hayden had to smile back, didn't he?

"Well, all right, in bed," Hayden said. "But that's all."

Luke sighed. "It's a hard bargain. But I reckon, on consideration … I'll take it."

EVERYBODY FRONTS UP

*L*uke couldn't remember an afternoon as relaxed as that one. The most productive thing they'd done, beyond his making coconut, lime, and sambal grilled chicken with coconut rice for dinner, watching another movie with Hayden, and *not* having sex again, because Hayden had concussion and Luke had already done too much—which he reminded himself about pretty sternly during that movie, when Hayden was in his arms and he was touching that soft skin again—was to take the short walk to Sephora.

Yes, the makeup store, which Luke didn't even recognize for what it was until they were standing in front of it. He'd assumed from the name that it was a flash clothing store, or possibly someplace you'd buy a wedding present. Makeup wasn't something he'd been much aware of in his life. He looked at the window display, made up of enormous photos of bottles of scent and women wearing astonishing amounts of cosmetics, and said, "Uh ... this is new for me." While telling himself, *You can broaden your horizons,* and hoping he actually could.

If he can want a rugby player, and not the pretty kind, you can want somebody who wears ... whatever this is going to be.

Hayden said, "Yeh, well … concealer. I need expert advice. No thanks on the questions tomorrow." Proving what Luke had suspected—that he wouldn't want anybody to know about the bashing he'd got.

Weakness. Vulnerability. Shame. Nothing you wanted to share.

"I realize it's awkward for you," Hayden went on, "unless there's something you *really* haven't told me. No possible good explanation for why you'd be buying makeup with a man, especially a man as fabulous as me. You can wait outside instead and look butch."

Luke smiled. "Nah. New experiences are good. I'm coming in."

"All right," Hayden said. "Then I'm going to be queenly here. Watch my smoke." And went through the glass doors, head held high, fully here and, yes, fully fabulous.

He toa taumata rao.

Courage has many resting places.

The next day, he put the coming encounter with his dad out of his mind as much as he could and focused on researching what was good value in wine and beer and champagne before buying out half the stock of the Christchurch Liquorland. He and Kane made more than a few trips to wrestle all the boxes into the rental SUV, and then Luke got behind the wheel and drove them through the flat, uninteresting expanse of the Canterbury plain, two lanes of tarmac as straight as a die, then took the turn. Straight and flat some more, and then a rise to the land at last, and the line of snow-capped mountains in the distance coming closer. The Southern Alps, and Luke couldn't have described the state of his heart.

A bend in the road, and they were there. The cloudy blue-green of the enormous lake, seeming as always lit from below, backed by line after line of jagged peaks, the wisps of clouds trailing across their snow-clad summits, the sky above a cerulean blue. The tiny stone Church of the Good Shepherd on the shore, built like a hope and a promise by the people who'd first settled this inhospitable place. And the lupins, glorious in their height, their pinks and purples and oranges, bursting out along the shores in a riot of color. After the dullness of the journey, the pale dun tussocks of the Mackenzie highlands broken by nothing but the occasional flock of grazing merino, the Easter-basket extravagance of it was nearly too much to take in.

"A good day for it," Kane said. "A good place, too. Better for Marko, maybe."

Nyree and her mum were from Northland, originally, lush and green and surrounded by the sea, edged by kilometer after kilometer of golden beach. That was where this wedding had been meant to happen, about as far from this place as it was possible to get, but that was all right. Nyree was the lupins and the lake, that was all, and if you were marrying somebody, maybe that happiness, and *their* happiness, were enough.

Luke thought about that, and then he thought about unloading boxes of drink and bags of ice and setting up a beverage station on one of the folding tables covered with mismatched, cheerful tablecloths, all set around the edge of a cleared space in front of a big, rambling house overlooking the lake and backdropped by the Alps. Meanwhile, Zora and Rhys fastened flowers to a homemade arbor, Hayden went over to help, and Luke's father, who'd barely acknowledged his sons so far, directed people in setting up more tables and rows of chairs, barking orders like the rugby coach he still wished he was. Luke opened wine bottles, carried glasses, and poured drinks with Kane, working against the clock until, barely an hour later, they went into the house and he took his turn in an old-fashioned bathroom, changing out of T-shirt and rugby shorts and into dress trousers and a collared shirt before giving himself a last careful shave around his beard.

It wasn't much of an improvement, but it was the best he could do.

It was a wedding, then. Everybody sitting in those rows of

mismatched chairs, borrowed from every farm around, and Marko standing in front of the arbor with his best man, frowning ferociously, staring at the kitchen door, and looking, as usual, barely tamed. Hayden standing in the center, impossibly slim and handsome, the bruise not visible under the careful makeup, looking serious and maybe nervous. A stillness to the moment despite the breeze, like the day was holding its breath, and Victoria playing the cello. More of that sadness, possibly, along with the joy, because that was the way cellos sounded, and because Marko's grandmother was lying on a deck chair in the front row, looking like the wind could blow her away.

Everything passed, and so did everybody, the good and the bad together. Made it more important to live your life the way you wanted, maybe, because now was all you had, and if you weren't yourself, who were you? If nobody knew you, and you couldn't even know yourself ... how could you live an entire life like that? Why *should* you live an entire life like that?

He was so tired of hiding.

Nyree, then, coming out at last on her grandmother's arm in an ivory gown that clung to her pregnant curves, and Marko's face changing in a way that almost hurt to see. And Luke thought, *That's all right, then.*

She got there, Hayden began to talk, and it was even better, because he'd been right. Hayden was good at this.

"These rings," Hayden finally said, "in their infinite circle, represent your marriage, and the love that's greater than the sum of you. They symbolize the bond you share and the trust and faith you give each other, world without end. When you look at these rings on your hands, be reminded of this moment, and the infinity of your love."

Marko's voice, repeating after Hayden, and then Nyree's, as they slipped the rings onto each other's hands, Nyree having a bit of trouble sliding the thing over Marko's rugby-battered knuckle and Marko having to help her, which gave everybody a much-needed laugh. "I give you this ring as a symbol of my love," they told each other, "with this promise, offered freely and unreservedly: to love you today, tomorrow, always, and forever."

Hayden again. "You've made your promises today in front of all those who love you best, and have sealed your vows with the exchange of rings. Therefore, by the power vested in me as a wedding officiant of Aotearoa New Zealand, I now pronounce you husband and wife."

Looking like he meant every word of it.

Looking like the triumph of hope.

Luke wished he could kiss Hayden, afterward, and tell him he was proud. He wasn't good with words, but he could have managed that. Not the time or the place, though, for revelations, whatever Marko had said.

He was just thinking it when his father and stepmother approached. "Lovely wedding," Miriama said, practically glowing, petite and pretty and gracious as always, reaching out to give Luke a cuddle.

Luke gave her a kiss on the cheek. "Yeh, it was good. They're well suited, I think."

"Huh," Grant said. He glanced at the water glass in Luke's hand. "And you don't have a beer."

"No." Luke felt himself going stolid, going inside himself, the way he always had. "Seemed best. I'm all good."

Grant frowned, or maybe you'd say that his bushy gray eyebrows drew even closer together than they normally were. They slanted down his face in a perpetual V-shape, putting the exclamation point on his habitual expression. "You're staying here tonight, surely. No need to cut off the drink for that. I got the tents sorted around the back. Enough for everybody. Who are you bunking in with?"

Luke wished he did have a beer, and was glad he didn't. This was a test, he guessed. Another first to get through without alcohol. He said, "Hayden Allen. The celebrant."

Kane had materialized from somewhere to stand beside him, and so had Rhys, though he was keeping back. Drago had always looked like he was watching from the coaching box even when he was playing. Judging, you could call it, or measuring, bringing his calm and his focus with him. He looked that way now.

Had the two of them been keeping an eye on him all along, waiting for this? Luke hoped not. This day was meant to be Nyree's.

He caught sight of Hayden, then, talking to Marko and Nyree, saying something that made Nyree laugh out loud. He glanced up, caught Luke's eye, and stood hesitating. Questioning. Luke jerked his chin at him. *Come on.*

Just in case this was it.

He'd been an All Black. Briefly. He'd stood on the field and done the haka, laying down the challenge to his opponents, affirming his bond to his brothers. For nearly a decade more, he'd played for England and had faced that challenge. Everybody had a different approach to the most fearsome intro in rugby. Some smiled, a dickhead move that tended to backfire. Some glared. Luke, though, had stood with his arms over the shoulders of his teammates and let the challenge sink into him. Outwardly impassive, but absorbing his opponent's energy, letting it fuel his own rush of adrenaline, ready to turn it back on him once the whistle blew.

Hayden headed over, approaching from behind Grant even as Luke's dad said, "Not a good idea. Fella's a …" He glanced at Miriama. "He's queer as a three-dollar note."

"True," Hayden said with his disarming smile, slipping around Grant's back, plucking Luke's water glass from his hand, and taking a long drink. "Probably why I'm such a good dresser." He handed the glass back to Luke. "Thanks. I was parched. Good job on the ceremony, didn't you think?"

Bravado, you could call it. Luke called it what it was. Courage, or something more than that. Mana. He said, "Yeh. It was. I was proud."

And told his dad, "I'm bunking in with him because I'm queer as a three-dollar note myself. Although not as good a dresser."

He couldn't help it. It just came out.

The whistle had blown.

A few seconds passed. Miriama stood there, looking shocked and probably horrified, her eyes darting to Grant. Grant just stood there, and Kane had edged that much closer.

Grant said, finally, when Luke didn't—what? Laugh and say he was only joking?— "Pardon?"

"I'm gay, Dad," Luke said.

"But you're so ... *tall*," his stepmother said. "And so ..."

"Ugly," Luke said. "Yeh, I've heard that one."

"You're not ugly," she said. "Of course not. You're just ..."

"Strong," Hayden said quietly. "Yeh, he is. That's why I love him." Luke looked at him, startled, and Hayden shrugged and said, "Seems I can be brave, too. Too soon? Oh, well."

"No," Luke said. "Not too soon. Me too." He cleared his throat, took a breath, and said it again. "Me too." Feeling like that fella who'd been pushing the boulder uphill forever, but had finally been allowed to let it go. Feeling like he could fly.

"Yes," Miriama said, ignoring that. "Strong. That's what I meant." Grant, on the other hand, looked like he *had* heard it, and like he still couldn't believe it.

"Well, my goodness," Miriama said next, and gave a little laugh. "I need some time to let that sink in. Maybe, darling, we should go sit a minute and do that," she suggested to Grant, which was about as likely as that Grant would let the skipper give the pre-match talk in the sheds.

"If you are—that," Grant said as if he hadn't even heard his wife, "why tell everybody about it? Why spoil Nyree's wedding with it?"

"He's not spoiling it." That was Kane. "That would be you. Still time to back off, though." His big frame was nearly shaking with tension, but he had a hand on Luke's shoulder, his fingers gripping hard, and Luke felt him the way you felt your mate's solid body beside you in the scrum and knew he was right there with you. That he'd front up today, and next game, and every game after that. That he'd never quit.

"You knew." Grant's hard gaze landed on Kane. "And you did nothing."

"No," Kane said. "I did something. I told him I loved him. He's my brother. He's a good one. Why wouldn't I want him to be happy? Why wouldn't I want the same thing for him that I've got? To be able to bring the person he's fallen in love with to Nyree's wedding?"

"When did I ever tell you life was about being happy?" Grant asked.

"You didn't," Kane said. "That's why I said it."

Grant's voice was rising. "You aren't saying this to anyone outside the family," he told Luke. "You aren't sharing it with anybody in rugby. You'd never hold up your head again."

"Too late," Luke said. "I already did."

"He shared it with me," Rhys said, "for one." He was beside Kane now.

"And you're telling me you wouldn't show him the door pretty smartly, if he was one of yours," Grant said.

"That's what I'm telling you," Rhys said. "New Zealand Rugby's committed to diversity. I got a memo about it. You probably did too."

Grant's face had gone brick-red, and the eyebrows were practically standing up on their own. "And is France? Is England? Who's going to be willing to strip down in the sheds with him? Who's going to be packing down with him in the scrum? Would you?"

Rhys shot a measuring look at Luke, and Luke stared back at him and tried to breathe. Rhys asked, "Grabbed anybody's bum in the showers so far, mate?"

A gasp from Miriama, and a bark of a laugh from Kane. Luke's jaw relaxed a fraction, and he said, "Not yet."

"They're pretty safe, you reckon?" Rhys asked.

"I reckon so."

Grant said, "PC crap. You know what this is as well as I do." His finger was out now, nearly stabbing into Rhys's chest. "It's signing his death warrant in rugby."

"If it is," Rhys said, "I'd say that's his risk to take. Whatever you think, whatever you feel, don't you think he's felt it and thought it already?" He asked Luke, "How long have you known you were gay, would you say?"

"Since I was five or six," Luke said.

Miriama gave a little moan, and Grant said, "Not possible."

"Yeh, Dad," Luke said. "Possible."

Another voice. Nyree's. Marko was with her, and their half-sister Kiri, too. "Luke?" she asked. "Mum? What's going on?"

Miriama opened and closed her mouth, then said, "Luke is, ah … having a word, darling. It's a bit fraught at the moment. No need to worry. Five minutes."

"Five minutes?" Grant said. "Five *minutes?* Five minutes before you leave, is what it is," he told Luke. "Spoiling your sister's wedding, spouting this rubbish."

"No," Nyree said. "Luke's not leaving. I don't want you to leave, either, or Mum, and if you have to, I'll be sorry."

"Darling," her mother moaned. "No. Your beautiful day."

"My day's still beautiful," Nyree said. "My day's *more* beautiful. Everybody in it is telling the truth. That's beautiful."

"The truth isn't beautiful," Grant said.

"Depends how you look at it," Nyree said. "My truth is, and here it is. Luke is gay. Kane's in love with Victoria. I'm married to Marko bloody Sendoa, forever and ever. Maybe none of that is what you'd choose for us, but you're not the one who gets to choose." She told Kane, "Though you're probably doing all right so far, even though you're not a Highlander. Still in the South Island, so that's something."

"Cheers," he said. "But I may make a move to the Blues, because … there's Victoria. Could want a chat," he told Rhys.

"Oh, bloody hell," Grant said.

"Yeh," Nyree said. "That's three of us, then. Who knows? Maybe Kiri won't disappoint you. What do you think?" she asked her sister.

Kiri said, "I don't know. But I don't want Luke to leave." Brave of her.

Nyree told Grant, "Maybe I know how you feel, a bit. I've got all sorts of dreams for this baby in my belly. I feel like I know who she is. The truth is, though—I don't really know her at all. She'll show herself to me, and to Marko, bit by bit, and I'll only have two jobs. To teach her, and to love her."

"Easy to say," Grant said. "When you don't know anything about it."

"Not easy at all." That was Rhys again. "I do know something about it, and I can say. Not easy at all, and the only choice there is. What are you going to do otherwise? Throw your son away?"

"Throw both of your sons away," Kane said. "We're a package deal."

"I did my best for you," Grant said. "All I ever did was my best."

"You did, Dad," Luke said. "And so have I."

A long moment, stretching out forever, and Nyree said, "And then you paid for me to go to Uni, even though I never studied anything worth learning, so who knows, hey. Change is possible."

"That's true," Miriama said. "And Nyree's grateful, darling. So am I."

"Anyway," Nyree said, her cheerfulness possibly forced and possibly not at all, "if you want somebody to do what you say, I reckon you should get a dog. Words to put on top of the wedding cake. Or, in this case, the pavlova."

SEEING STARS

*H*ayden danced with Luke. He could tell it was Luke's first time ever from the stiffness in his body and the hesitation in his normally sure movements, and something in Hayden melted a little more at that. Marko's family were playing the tango, though, guitar and violin and flute and more, and Marko and Nyree were teaching the rest of the group the dance. Anyway, at this point, *everybody* knew they were gay, so—no time like the present. Seize the day, and all that.

There was coming out, though, and then there was dancing the tango with your male lover in front of his rugby-coach dad, while said dad drank yet another beer and looked like his head would explode, and also like he was wondering whether it was still called infanticide if the kid was in his thirties.

Luke didn't talk much afterward, just helped clear up the detritus of the day, rinsing out the astonishing number of bottles and carrying them to the bin, hauling tables and chairs, then getting into Marko's dad Ander's ute with Marko's little sister to return the many borrowed items to the neighbors. When Ander said, "No worries, I'll do it tomorrow," Luke said, "Nah. I may as well. You'll have the sheep to take out, and I haven't had any drink."

Marko's dad looked at him, long and slow, and Luke didn't flinch, though Hayden thought he might want to. Finally, Ander said, "I'll say thanks, then."

Luke said, "Nyree's my sister. Least I can do." Which was practically a declaration from Luke, and was probably masking what he was really feeling—a strong desire to be out of here.

By the time Luke got back, the hills and the few scraps of cloud overhead had turned a brilliant orange and the lake was glowing like a sapphire. Luke found Hayden sitting on the patio, sat down beside him with yet another bottle of fizzy water, and said, "Nice out here. Sunsets are always better in the mountains, not sure why. Nearly nine-thirty, too. Close to the longest day of the year."

"Yeh." Hayden stretched out his legs and took in the view some more. He'd found a jumper, because there was a bit of nip to the air now, but Luke was still in his shirtsleeves, seeming unbothered by cold. "The sunsets are more brilliant up high because the air's thinner, which means more colors of the spectrum can make it through. Also no air pollution."

"You know some things," Luke said.

"No. Isaiah knows some things, and he tells me. He texted me while you were gone and told me that the Mackenzie Basin is a Dark Sky Reserve, so I should make sure to look at the stars, especially since it's a new moon and not going to be cloudy. He also says we're having a geomagnetic storm, which means solar winds and a greater chance to view the Aurora Australis, except that it's summer, so, alas, probably not. I shouldn't try to take photos of the stars, he says, just observe, because observing is better anyway."

Luke said, "I agree about that one. I was just thinking that today, that living is better."

"Than dying?" Hayden asked. "Well, yeh."

Luke smiled. "Than not paying attention, I meant. Living in the, uh ..."

"The moment," Hayden said. "I wonder how much I do that."

"I do it in rugby," Luke said. "No choice. Not always otherwise."

"Well," Hayden said, "maybe we should try to do it tonight." Feeling a little shy again. He'd told Luke he *loved* him. He'd always calibrated that, before. Six months was the absolute minimum, and it had been more like six *days*. This whole thing was like careening downhill on your bike without brakes, and Hayden wasn't much of one for careening.

"We should," Luke said. "Upside of being in a tent, maybe. You can stick your head out and see the stars."

"I'll go get ready for bed, then," Hayden said, choosing his words carefully and feeling his tongue go thick, as if he'd been drinking instead of relentlessly sober all day, "since there may be a bathroom open now. There was a general exodus a while ago. I get the feeling there may be some sex happening in there, though it's tactless of me to say it. The tango *is* a bit sexy."

"Very sexy," Luke said, "and my first time." He looked straight at Hayden. "Glad it was with you."

It was nearly too dark to navigate by the time Hayden came around to the back of the house. That was how quickly night had fallen. Luke was, fortunately, standing outside the tent, which meant Hayden wasn't blundering around knocking into things, especially since he couldn't hear more than a murmur of voices from a couple of the tents, so most people were probably asleep and wouldn't have appreciated his waking them. Their tent was small, one of those two-man deals in which you could just about sit up and that was all.

"How long has it been since I've been in a sleeping bag?" Hayden asked, when they'd crawled in. "I am an urban animal."

"It's been a wee while for me, too," Luke said. "Here. Let's unzip one and put it on the bottom, then put the other one on top. Cozier, eh."

"Right," Hayden said. "OK." Getting that tongue-too-big feeling again. But when he was lying on his back with Luke's big body pressed up close and warm beside his, and they both had, yes, their heads stuck out of the end of the tent and were watching the night sky transform, he forgot it.

At first, it was only a few stars. As they watched, though, the sky darkened and more and more appeared. Not just pinpricks of light, but whole … whole *waves* of them, or clouds of them, some bright and some dim, blazing in the night like a million candles, turning the sky as much purple and blue as black. "The Magellanic Clouds," Hayden told Luke, who'd said precisely nothing so far, "there, around the Milky Way. Not actually clouds, but whole other galaxies, very far away. Again, Isaiah."

"Mm," Luke said. "I don't know the stars that well, especially in the Southern Hemisphere. I like them, though."

"Want me to tell you?" Hayden asked. "The constellations and all?"

"Yeh," Luke said. "That'd be good."

"Jupiter and Saturn," Hayden said, pointing. "There in the southwest, that very bright spot. They look like they've merged, but of course they haven't, it's just their position right now. The Great Conjunction, they call it. Rare, so we're lucky. And Mars. You can see that it's a bit red. And Orion in the north."

"The Hunter," Luke said.

"Betelgeuse, the red supergiant, in there, and Rigel, that one's a bit blue. You can actually see the colors down here, at least I'm pretending you can. The Southern Cross, helping you find your way south and back home again. And the constellation Carina, there. That's meant to be the keel of a ship, and the bright star is Canopus, the helmsman, steering the ship. Sailing through the night sky."

"That's nice," Luke said. "A nice thought."

"I'm never sure, though," Hayden said, "if it's better to look for the patterns you know are up there, or just to … to look at all of it for yourself."

"Something to be said for that," Luke said.

Hayden shivered, and Luke said, "We can scoot back inside and zip the tent up. Warmer, eh."

"Yeh," Hayden said, feeling ridiculously shy again, but comforted, too. Luke was possibly the most noticing person he'd ever met, and definitely the most solicitous. Well, other than the other day, but he'd take that, too.

When the stars were zipped away, they fell silent, only their breath audible in the silence around them. Hayden finally said, "I was proud today. Of you. Proud of you."

"Same," Luke said. "Of you."

"Me? What did I do?"

"The wedding. That was nice. Did you write that?"

"Some of it." Shy again. "The part about the rings—I wrote that."

"It was nice. And it sounded like you believed it."

"Well, good," Hayden said. "That was the idea."

Luke found his hand under the sleeping bag, and laced his fingers through Hayden's. And Hayden took a breath.

Get out of your comfort zone. You want your life to be different? Make *it different.*

"Could we try something new?" he asked.

"Well, yeh," Luke said. "Probably. But—tent."

"What, in case I scream?" Hayden tried to laugh. It wasn't easy. "I want to ... I want to touch you. And hold you, and kiss you, and do some other things. Basically, do the things I want, the way I never do. Though—consent, of course. It's hard to ask, but dancing, today ... how I feel ... how I feel about you ... I want to."

And held his breath.

Right, Luke thought. *Right.* He said, "Uh ..."

"Or not," Hayden said, "if you're not comfortable."

"Could be hard for me to keep quiet," Luke said, trying to make a joke. His heart was, suddenly, beating like it was the eightieth minute and you were making that last, desperate defensive stand. Ka-*boom*. Ka-*boom*. Ka-*boom*.

"Oh," Hayden said. "OK, then." And shifted, infinitesimally, away.

"But," Luke said, "I've got some self-discipline, control over my reactions and so forth. Maybe good to put them to the test."

At first, it felt weird. And wrong. Hayden lying over him, kissing him—that was OK. Hayden's tongue in his mouth, though, his hands in Luke's hair. Hayden's mouth traveling slowly over his cheek, to his ear, his hand stroking Luke's face. Then he was kissing his ear as if he didn't know how mangled and unappealing it was. Luke felt it, because the tissue was sensitive despite its appearance, and it felt good, but Hayden couldn't *want* to …

He said, "I can get those fixed once I stop playing. I know they're not—"

"Shh," Hayden said into his ear, his voice nothing but a warm breath. "You're meant to be disciplined. And I love that you're strong and a bit … battered."

You do? Luke wanted to say, but Hayden was kissing his neck now, there below the edge of beard, and that felt *good*. Hayden kissed like he had all day and all night, his mouth seeking out new spots, testing for a reaction, and Luke shifted under him and breathed harder. His hand was under Hayden's T-shirt, running over his skin, and he wanted …

"Not your turn." It was another of those breaths again, and Hayden had hold of Luke's shirt now, was shoving it slowly up as he moved his body down. Kissing every centimeter he uncovered, even though Luke was too big and his skin was nothing like soft. Hayden's hand stroking over his side, up his ribs, Hayden's mouth on every one of those ribs, moving up to his chest. Pulling the T-shirt over Luke's head, then going back to his neck. His chest. His ribs. His belly. All of it too slow, and Luke needed to get there. He needed to get there *now*.

Shifting again, his hand around Hayden's head, and Hayden taking that as an invitation to touch him more. Hands on his forearms, his biceps, his triceps, as if he were memorizing him, as if he wanted to know. A mouth on that softer skin at the side of his bicep, a tongue licking along his upper arm.

Luke *couldn't* be feeling this much, not with the way people normally touched his body—beating on it—but he was anyway. He was hauling in deep breaths, trying hard not to make a sound, nothing but the metallic, pulsing melody of crickets around them, but so many people asleep.

Or awake.

Hayden's hands, finally, on the waistband of his sleep pants, pulling them down. Slowly again, until they were all the way off. Luke had his hands on Hayden's waist, gripping hard, and Hayden asked him, his voice thrillingly low in the dark, "Want me to take my clothes off?"

"Yeh," Luke said. It was just about all he could manage.

"Then I will," Hayden said. "Because I want to please you tonight."

It was that, and it was also torture. Luke couldn't decide which. When Hayden was naked over him, though, his hands stroking down Luke's huge, tree-trunk thighs like he loved them, which wasn't possible—that was pleasure. And when he whispered, "Turn over," that was a thrill that ran down his body like vinegar hitting your stomach, making the buzz run through every nerve pathway and straight to the cramp, releasing the knot, making you gasp.

He turned over.

More touching, then. More kissing. Hayden's hands on his back, his mouth in the hollow of his spine, moving down. Luke wasn't beautiful, last thing from it, but Hayden touched him like he was, lingering at the base of his spine, just under the tailbone, that exquisitely sensitive spot you never got used to. His hand between Luke's legs, feather-light touches on his inner thighs, so close and nowhere close enough.

Oh, God. He couldn't. He *couldn't.*

Up on his elbows, then, because he had to feel that hand. The sensation that was somebody behind you, pressed up close, not knowing where their hand or their mouth was going next, and Luke was gasping.

He could control his voice. He couldn't control his breath. And when Hayden whispered, "OK for me to do this?" and he felt the first slippery touch of lube …

It wasn't that he'd never done it, but he'd never done it like this. Never with so much vulnerability, and knowing he'd agreed to it. He managed to say, "Yeh," and that was all.

It wasn't anything like the way he'd done it. It was so much better. Slow and easy, and with Hayden touching him, holding him. Hayden's hand sliding down his side, and Luke's own hands fisting in the fabric of the sleeping bag, pulling hard, holding on. Completely unable to control his breath anymore, lost in the sensation.

Hayden's movements faster now, more urgent, and Luke's hands were gripping harder, the tension winding up, then winding higher until it was too much, and it was too late. He was spinning, tumbling, burying his face in his fists to keep the groans inside.

Rising higher, then higher still. Going into the darkness, and seeing stars.

Lost. Shattered. Broken.

Gone.

Something woke Hayden, and at first, he couldn't figure out what. He was lying with Luke, arms and legs tangled together, and had come slowly up from fathoms-deep sleep to … something.

Oh. Morning, he thought, because there was some light. It didn't *feel* like morning, though. He disentangled himself carefully from Luke, trying not to wake him, fumbled for the zips at the bottom of the tent, slowly undid them, and stuck his head out into the chill on hands and knees.

At first, he couldn't sort out what he was looking at. Dawn, but it didn't look like dawn. It looked like …

Luke's voice, then, coming out of the quiet dark. "What is it?"

"Come see," Hayden said.

Luke beside him, head and shoulders emerging from the tent. "Oh," he said.

"It's the Aurora," Hayden said, "isn't it?"

"Yeh," Luke said. "I've seen it once before." His head disappeared into the tent, and Hayden thought, *That's all?* and tried not to be disappointed. He hadn't been going for sweet and sensitive, even though Luke was, surprisingly, some of both, and those things called to him as hard as the strength did. He'd been going for butch, though, clearly, and that was what he'd got.

Be careful what you wish for.

Just as he was thinking it, Luke appeared again with the pillows in one hand, hauling up the sleeping bag with the other. "Here," he said. "Let's watch."

They were quiet, then, looking at the flickering light overhead. A band of bright pink on the lower part of the horizon, with a strip of neon yellow at the bottom and a fade to blue-violet at the top. And more. Vertical lines coming down through the color like those solar winds were touching the earth. It was like nothing he'd ever seen before. It was magic.

Luke said, "Only other time I saw this was on the first night I kissed a boy."

Hayden went still. "Oh?" he said, and hoped that was just prodding enough.

"Yeh," Luke said. "I was fifteen. It was terrifying."

"Yeh," Hayden said. "I get that."

"I know you do. That's why I told you." And after a minute, "Thanks for that, earlier. I've never done anything like that. I mean, I've *done* that, but I've never been …"

"Vulnerable," Hayden said. Right now, Luke felt nothing like that.

His arm was around Hayden, and Hayden's head was on his shoulder. He felt strong as oak. Strong as *rock*.

"Yeh," Luke said. "Reckon you know more about this than I do, though. Could be I've been a bit … limited in my, uh, expression."

"You can need somebody," Hayden said, "and still be a man."

He couldn't see Luke's face, but he could feel his sigh, all the way from his considerable depths. "Yeh," he said. "That. Thanks."

SPLINTERS

*I*t was the day before Christmas Eve, and they were having dinner with *Hayden's* parents this time. That was the problem with the holidays. It was so hard to get out of things. How did you nurture the tender shoots of your new love in this kind of rocky territory?

When his mum had invited him and said, "Zora and the kids are coming, too, of course. Just a lovely, casual family meal before Christmas," Hayden had asked, "How about Rhys?"

"Oh, he's coming, too," she said. "Six-thirty Friday. I know I don't have to tell *you*, darling—you always dress so beautifully—but a teeny hint to your sister …"

"Yeh," Hayden said, "probably not happening. And actually, I have Luke with me."

"Oh." There was a little silence. "Still?"

Breathe. "Well, yeh. He's my partner. Did I not mention that?"

"Of course you should bring him, then," she said. Not the most heartfelt invite he'd ever received. He wanted to say no, that they were going to … Waiheke, maybe, for the evening, because it was an island and you couldn't get back until the ferry ran—or possibly that he'd heard he might be kidnapped that day—but when he suggested it to Zora, she said, "Please, no. And leave me there all alone?"

"Well, not *all* alone," Hayden said. "You'll have, oh, three other people with you. Including Rhys bloody Fletcher, with mana up to the eyeballs."

"Without you, though," she said. "You can always think up something light and funny to say that makes everybody laugh, just when I'm about to lose my temper. Please come. Maybe it's better anyway. Mum and Dad *should* be inviting your partner, and if they're finally doing it, isn't that good?"

"Right," Hayden said glumly. "I'll be there." When he invited Luke, Luke just looked at him measuringly, then said, "OK," and went on folding laundry on the bed, lifting George off the pile and not commenting on the orange cat hair he'd be wearing on his T-shirt tomorrow. He'd given up his hotel room, because he hadn't used it once, and that had felt ... well, it had felt fine. Hayden had gone to work every day, Luke had gone to the gym and done whatever other heroic activities it took to maintain all that strength—flipping truck tires down a field was entirely possible—and cooked dinner, and then they went to bed, and, well ...

He could go weak in the knees from Luke looking at him from across a room, or from Luke's thigh pressed against his at a dinner table. As was happening right now, inconveniently.

Intensity. It was a thing. Urgency. Desire.

He'd fallen so hard.

It was better than noticing that his dad wasn't looking at either of them. Hayden and Luke could probably hold a least-popular-child competition. It would be a battle. Meanwhile, he'd just sit here, look at Luke's biceps, and have sexual fantasies. Much better plan.

His mum asked, "Would you pass the beetroot salad, please, Hayden?" He did. There was heaps left. His mum was what you'd call a rigorous dieter.

"So, kids," Hayden said, rousing himself, because conversation wasn't exactly sparkling here, "decorating is tomorrow? With cocoa, maybe?"

"Yes," Casey said. "We have to decorate, because the next day is Christmas, and Nana and Grandad and you are coming to our house for Christmas tea."

"And we cleaned the house today," Isaiah said, "so Nana can't say that the guest toilet is dirty. I vacuumed." Zora choked a little, and Rhys did some almost-smiling at that one.

"Dad is taking Isaiah and me fishing tomorrow morning, too," Casey said, "so we can catch fish for our barbecue on Christmas. If we don't catch any, we're going to have hamburgers and sausages instead. Hamburgers aren't very Christmasy, and fish isn't very Christmasy either, except you eat different things in New Zealand. Decorating makes it more like a party, though, even if you have hamburgers. It makes it so you can wear pretty clothes and give each other presents and be all happy."

"Including Luke, I hope," Zora said. "Please, Luke. Please come, if you'll be here."

"Your own parents want you to come to them, surely," Craig said. Ah, yes. The welcome committee was out in force tonight.

Luke looked like he didn't know how to answer that, so Hayden did. "Luke's volunteered to spend his Christmas with me, so we'll take that invitation. Catch another fish for him, will you, Isaiah? Keeps me from going through yet another Christmas tea as the lonely-but-making-the-best-of-it single uncle."

"But you *are* the single uncle," Isaiah said. "That just means you aren't married, and you're not married."

"It means you're not in a relationship that you're talking about," Hayden said. "I'm in a relationship now, and I *am* talking about it. Luke and I are flying to Paris on Christmas evening, in fact. Announcement. *More* announcement. That's *my* Christmas present. Isn't it a good one?"

"That's wonderful," Zora said. "That's amazing. Make it an early Christmas tea, then? Call it noon?"

"Well, yeh," Hayden said, "if you don't mind." He could tell he was too tense, was smiling too hard. "This year, I find I'd quite like to come. Astonishing what love will do, hey, Zora."

"And then Paris," she said, smiling at him and looking a bit misty-eyed.

"Yes," Hayden said. "And then Paris." He sighed. "I love how that sounds. Like a book title. *And Then Paris.* It won't be quite Christmas *in* Paris, but close enough. Spontaneous. Romantic. Of course, I'll be the only one on holiday, as Luke will go straight in to work again, but never mind. I think I can manage to entertain myself. In Paris."

"I'll make time for you," Luke said. "After training, I'm all yours." He smiled at Hayden, and Hayden took his hand under the table, because that was some declaration, especially in this crowd.

"It'd be close enough for me, too," Zora said. "Boxing Day in Paris works."

"Probably be raining," Craig said. "Why on earth would you miss out on summer?"

"Because," Hayden said, "I'm tired of being single, so is Luke, we've found each other and it's pretty special so far, so why not make the most of it? Because I want to go to museums and look at shop-window displays in the Rue Saint-Honoré and eat in fabulous restaurants. Because I want to walk beside the Seine after dinner, being in love and holding Luke's hand. And, possibly, to know that nobody's going to think that's an invitation to bash us."

"They can think it," Luke said. "They're welcome to try it, too."

"I don't think they'll try it, mate." That was Rhys, of course.

"Why would somebody bash you?" Isaiah asked.

"Because they'd be holding hands," Craig said.

"Ah," Hayden said. "Asking for it, you mean." He was, suddenly, furious, but still trying for Funny Hayden. It probably wouldn't be wise to alienate *both* sets of parents in the same week.

"If there are people out there who'll bash you if you give them a reason," his father said, "you'd be wise not to give them one."

"Would I, though?" Hayden asked. "Would I really? I'm not sure. I find myself eager to see."

"Do people hit you for being gay, you mean?" Isaiah asked. "Why?"

"Yes," Hayden said. "They do. I don't know why. Jealous of my fabulousness, maybe. I've had a tooth out. Been knocked down and kicked while I'm on the ground, too. *That* hurt."

"That isn't fair," Casey said. "You can't help it if you're gay."

"I didn't know that," Zora said. "Why didn't you tell me?"

"Because I was embarrassed," Hayden said. "Why do you think? I was humiliated. That's the point. Also," he went on, shaking it off, because he was *not* telling them about that ambulance ride—there was gay-bashing, and then there was bashing by gays, and he wasn't sure which was worse—"Luke is playing again almost as soon as we're back, and the next week, too, and I want to watch."

"I'll be on the bench," Luke said. "For the first game, anyway, as my match fitness will be questionable, just off the plane. You may get to see me play thirty minutes, though."

"That's all right," Hayden said. "I'll watch you on the bench. I just realized—I'm a rugby WAG. Who knew? They're going to have to come up with a new word for me."

"What's a WAG?" Casey asked.

"Wives and girlfriends," Isaiah said. "Like Mum was. Uncle Hayden will be a wife and boyfriend, he means. Wait, a husband and boyfriend. A HAB." He laughed.

"Can't wait," Hayden said. "Paris Racing scarf, d'you reckon, Rhys? Pale-blue and white stripes? Fetching."

"Very fetching," Rhys agreed, that smile lurking again. "Good on ya," he told Luke. "Good to have somebody in the stands. Is that a first?"

"Yeh," Luke said, the color creeping into his ears and cheeks.

"And after that," Hayden said, "in more announcing, in July, when Luke's season is over, I'm going back for two wonderful weeks. July in Paris? *That's* a time anybody would want to be there, and then, Luke *won't* be playing. Music festivals. Roses and roller coasters in the Parc Bagatelle. The palace gardens at Versailles, and the Cabaret at midnight. I'm going to make him be a tourist with me, because I want to see absolutely everything."

"You could go to the top of the Eiffel Tower," Isaiah said.

"We could," Hayden said. "We definitely could."

"Getting a bit ahead of yourself, surely," Craig said.

"Am I?" Hayden glanced at Luke, feeling his spark dimming. His dad had that effect. "Maybe."

"No," Luke said. "Or maybe—why not get ahead of ourselves? In rugby, at least, you plan to win. You don't plan for what you'll do if you lose. Reckon that's not a bad outlook. You could even learn a bit of French, Hayden. You've got seven months until July."

"Not always much stability in these relationships, from what I know," Craig said. "To say the least. I wouldn't buy your ticket if I were you."

Luke's ears were going red again. "He can buy his ticket."

"Dad," Zora said. "No."

"Could be we'll have to prove you wrong," Hayden said. "What will you say, I wonder, if Luke comes back here once he retires? Will you still be telling me we're bound to break up, maybe cite some study you read about it? I'm curious. Is it that we'll get bored with each other? I'm not going to get bored, and I'm not boring, either."

"No," Luke said, smiling a little now, and otherwise looking like a very large and extremely well-grounded boulder. "Safe to say you're not boring."

"Give the ones you love wings to fly, roots to come back, and reasons to stay," Hayden said. "That's the Dalai Lama. That's what I want. That's what I think I've got. Finally. Luke's got wings to fly already, and I'm going to do my best to make those wings beautiful. I'm going to do my best to give him a reason to stay, too."

"I don't know about the Dalai Lama," Luke said, "but I know that I'm coming back to New Zealand at some point. Decided that this week."

Hayden felt his knees going weak again, for a different reason this time. "You are?" They hadn't talked about the future, not beyond July, for obvious reasons. That it was too soon. Much too soon. Far too soon.

"Yeh," Luke said. "I am. I like it here. I fit here."

"Well, not entirely," Craig said.

Luke turned his head and stared at him, and Hayden wouldn't have wanted to be at the other end of that stare. "How don't I fit?"

"Well, obviously," Craig said.

"Obviously what?" Luke asked. "Because I'm half English and we beat the All Blacks last meeting? Yeh, that could give them pause, but if the boys could have a beer with us afterward anyway, reckon the rest of the country may forgive me, too."

"He means because you're gay," Isaiah said. "New Zealand isn't just for straight people, Grandad. It's for everybody. If you'd learned the anthem in Maori, you'd know, because that's what it says, but I guess you're probably too old."

"How come?" Casey asked. "Dad's old, and he knows it in Maori."

Rhys smiled, and Isaiah said, "Uncle Rhys isn't *old* old, though, not like Grandad. He's only about forty or fifty or something. Plus, he's Maori, like us, so of course he knows how to sing it in Maori."

"Forty-one, actually," Rhys said, the smile fully in evidence now. "Cheers for the 'fifty' idea. Of course, I did find a gray hair the other day, so decrepitude could be just around the corner."

Tania shot Craig a meaningful look down the table, and he didn't go on to defend his age-spotted, memory-losing self. Luke did go on, to Hayden's surprise. "I'm keeping my apartment, though. An apartment in Paris is never a bad thing. I could want to walk with you by the Seine, too," he told Hayden. "In winter. In summer. Anytime." And Hayden thought, *Thanks. In front of my dad, too. And you've got mana to burn, mate. If your dad can't see that, if my dad can't see that, I can, and I do. I want you so much, I don't know how I'm going to say goodbye to you.*

"So if it's not that," Hayden decided to ask his father, because this was rubbish and he was, suddenly, so tired of it, "What? Is it me that's bound to cheat, or Luke? And why, exactly? Because all men cheat if they can, unless women are keeping them from having their fun, so how would *two* men be able to resist? I can resist. Let me tell you, I can resist. Maybe some men can't. I can."

Maybe not perfect on the "light and cheerful" thing. Casey and Isaiah were sitting still now, their eyes going between Hayden and Craig as if they were watching a tennis match.

Craig said, "If things are so much better in Paris, maybe you'd rather stay there."

A frozen moment that seemed to stretch out forever, and then a crash that reverberated through the room and made everybody jump.

"Oh, no," his mum said, her hands over her mouth. "Oh, *no*. My Royal Copenhagen Full Lace serving bowl! How could I have knocked it off like that? How could I have *been* that careless? Don't get up," she told the kids. "Porcelain splinters, and you aren't wearing shoes. Craig, could you help? I'm sorry, everyone, but … I may be going to cry. My beautiful, beautiful bowl. It was a wedding present. Can you just …"

"I'll get it," Rhys said. He was on his feet already.

"I'm sorry," Tania said. "But please, just … go on home, all of you. I need a bit of time." She tried to laugh. "Never mind. I'll be all good by Christmas, and Casey and Isaiah—we have something very special for each of you. Just wait and see. Go do your decorating, and *don't* send me photos. I want to come in and be surprised. We are going to have the very *best* Christmas, all together. And please, Luke—do come. It wouldn't be Christmas without Hayden, and we want you, too. Of course we do."

"I'm sorry, Nana Tania," Casey said, her big eyes troubled. "I'm sorry you broke your bowl, and that you're so sad. It's extra sad to be sad at Christmas time."

"Oh, my darling," Tania said, "thank you. And never mind." She dabbed at her eyes with her festive holly-and-ivy cloth serviette, took a breath, and let it out again. "A bowl is just a thing, and things don't matter, not really. We'll have our Christmas together, and it will be lovely. I'll have a wee cry for my bowl tonight, and then I'll let it go and be happy I'm with my family. *All* my family. Aren't I lucky?"

NOT QUITE HALLMARK

*T*hree days after Christmas, and Hayden was in the stands in a domed stadium that was still managing Arctic levels of cold, or maybe that was just his pampered summer-in-New-Zealand body. He hunched into the folds of his pale-blue-and-white-striped Racing 92 scarf and wondered whether he was indeed in the WAG section. Yes, everybody around him was good-looking and extremely chic, but as most people in Paris were extremely chic and most of them were good-looking, that didn't tell you much.

The reason he wasn't sure whether he was in the right place was that he hadn't met anybody, because Luke had so far not come out here. Not that he actually *knew* Luke hadn't told people, but he hadn't said anything about it to Hayden and there hadn't been a fuss, so he probably hadn't. Of course, they'd only been here a few days, and Hayden couldn't read French to know whether there'd been a fuss he didn't know about, but he was assuming.

Had it been worth it to come? Absolutely, despite how cold he was right now, and despite the fact that he wasn't getting to see much of Luke. Luke left the apartment at some ungodly hour of the morning when Hayden was just coming out of his twelve-hour-time-difference jet-lag coma. Luke brought him a flat white first, though, from the kind of espresso machine full of stainless steel and dials, which was, hello? Pretty bloody wonderful—and came home again at close to six in the evening seeming about the same as always, not like somebody who'd abused his body all day. After that, Hayden produced whatever non-French meal he'd managed to come up with in his visits to the neighborhood shops, and they ... well, hung out and ate dinner and watched a cookery show, or an architecture one, which Hayden pretended to follow, and Hayden always fell asleep, exhausted from his day of exploring and the aforementioned jet lag, and possibly that bloody concussion, plus the attempt to understand a language he definitely did not know. Then they went to bed, which was thrilling as can be, every time.

That strength. That *body*.

So far, there hadn't been anything you'd call "nightlife." Luke had said, when Hayden had asked, "I don't really do nightlife. Not suited for it, I guess, and there's training, and ..."

"You might say the wrong thing," Hayden finished for him. "Or look at some cute boy too long."

"Yeh." Luke had been packing his kit for the game at the time, as calm and focused as a hunter in a duck blind—yes, New Zealand reference, but that was what Hayden had. "I'll be with the boys for a bit after the game tonight, too. Home around eleven, twelve, like that. I have my day off on Wednesday, though, if you'd like to do some tourist things. Good time for museums, midweek in January. The Impressionist one in the Musée d'Orsay is nice, and just across the Seine, so we could take a walk through the Jardin des Tuileries first. The Musée des Arts Décoratifs is meant to be good, too, in the Louvre complex. Art Deco, Art Nouveau, like that. You'd probably like it."

"Sounds extremely gay," Hayden said.

Luke smiled. "Probably. I've never been. We could go to a bistro afterward, if you like."

"Suits me," Hayden said, wanting to say instead, "When you come out, you won't have to worry about saying the wrong thing," but biting his tongue. This wasn't up to him, and if Luke was willing to go to a decorative-arts museum with him, that was a step, right? "And I get to watch you play."

So far, he was getting to watch everybody else play, because Luke was still on the bench. It was Racing 92 against Pau, whoever they were, and Racing had six points on two penalty kicks, while Pau had 15 on two tries, two missed conversions, and a penalty. Both the tries had been scored in the first half, though, and it was now Minute 54. Twenty-six minutes to go, and play was back and forth, back and forth. Men running with the ball, passing the ball, getting tackled hard, until somebody spilled the thing or kicked it away and possession changed, or until the referee blew the whistle and there was a scrum, for some unknown reason. After that, there was a scrum reset, because the structure kept collapsing, the referee pawing with his foot on the grass and having a stern French word as the big screens replayed the reset, as if you cared. Meanwhile, Luke was sitting on the bench in an oversized jacket, hands on his knees, watching like there'd be a quiz later. Occasionally, the substitutes would take a wee jog around the edges of the field to stay warm, but that was the limit of the Boyfriend Activity thus far.

Hayden's mind may have drifted. First to the impossible beauty of Luke's apartment, which was more like Nyree's description than Luke's, no surprise. The herringbone wood flooring. The high ceilings with their dark beams. The huge, multipaned, arched windows, and the marble fireplaces in lounge and bedroom. The balcony with its wrought-iron railing, and the modern-but-cozy kitchen and bath done in white and cobalt blue, all of it somehow harmonizing with the ancient diamond-patterned black-and-white floors and plaster walls. And the view over the rooftops to the park. It was the best apartment in the world, no question.

And then, of course, there was Paris. His feet hurt, that was how much he'd walked. It had rained today, and he hadn't even cared, had just gone to the Picasso Museum, which was close to Luke's place, because that was the kind of ancient-but-flash neighborhood Luke lived in—Le Marais, it was called, and it was fabulous—looked at pictures of people with their eyes in odd places, then decided that was enough culture and refreshed himself by exploring the five floors of the men's store at BHV Marais, the incredible department store housed in another of those old domed mansions. Being a good little bougie gay boy in Paris.

Fendi, Moncler, Givenchy, Gucci, and Valentino, all under one roof. Imagine that. He'd bought Luke a Fendi wool scarf with an elegant geometric pattern in beige and chocolate brown. It had cost so much, he'd had to shut his eyes to pay for it, but it was masculine, warm, and gorgeous, and Luke deserved to have somebody do something special for him. Hayden was willing to bet it hadn't happened often.

He could have gone to Notre Dame after that. It was just across the river. He could *see* it. He'd gone up to the fifth floor for a coffee and croissant instead. That had been a pain au chocolat, and it had been buttery, flaky, decadent, and incredible. He'd eaten it slowly, looking out over those historic slate rooftops and white-stone buildings some more, and thought, *Early dinner tonight, by myself, because Luke will be getting ready to play. Fish and veg and that is* all. *And no chocolate croissants tomorrow!* A very cute fella had brought his own coffee over and slid into a chair opposite him at the long table, too, which had been flattering and definitely wouldn't have happened at Notre Dame, so there you were.

They hadn't been able to communicate that well, but Hayden didn't really want to communicate. He felt off the market in a way he never had. It was very odd.

It hadn't even been three *weeks.*

Oh. Game. He checked. Still nothing happening.

So what had happened on Christmas? Not the fireworks he might have been expecting. Fireworks of an entirely different kind.

He'd been startled, despite Casey's promises about decorations and dressing up, when he'd seen Zora. She was normally more the shorts and T-shirt type, to their mother's dismay, which meant that just about the second Hayden walked through the door, he was taking her by the upper arms and standing back for a good look. "I think I know who's been a good girl," he said, "because Santa *so* clearly loves her."

Zora was laughing as Casey said, "That wasn't Santa. It was my dad. He gave her the earrings for Christmas, and he gave her the pearl necklace before. The earrings are real pearls and real diamonds. They're *really* fancy. Even though Auntie Zora usually isn't fancy, she likes being fancy sometimes."

"And she already had the dress, of course," Hayden said. "A wee bit sleeveless, a wee bit ruby-colored, and a wee bit form-fitting. Very nice."

"Because red is for Christmas," Casey said happily.

The doorbell rang, and Hayden couldn't help stiffening. He'd had to think long and hard about coming today. Why should he sign up for this, and more to the point—why should Luke? Neither of them needed any more of it.

Rhys said, calm as ever, "Ah. That'll be your parents, Zora. Come on, kids. Time for everybody to practice their 'Merry Christmas.'"

The three of them headed for the stairs, and Zora blew out a breath. Hayden said, trying for casual and funny, since he *had* come and couldn't exactly rush for the exit now, bowling over his parents along the way, "I can't decide on my bet."

"What bet?" Zora asked.

"Whether she says something first about the unsuitability of diamonds for daytime, or Dad goes straight for Luke. Tell me we're not having hamburgers, at least. I don't think I can take this day on hamburgers."

"We are having," she said, "fresh-caught kahawai with baby spinach, Thai curry sauce, and lime, on a bed of forbidden rice. Thanks to Rhys."

Hayden opened his eyes wide. "*Very* elegant. Oh, wait. I'm not just hearing 'Mum's horribly healthy salads arriving' down there.

I'm hearing excitement. Christmas is for children," he told Luke. "I'm reminding myself of that."

"You know," Zora said, "if they say anything, that won't be all right. Not with me, and not with Rhys. It's not happening again in our house."

"You could hold my hand," Luke said.

"Yeh, right," Hayden said.

"No," Luke said. "I mean you could hold my hand."

"Oh." Hayden thought that one over a minute. "Maybe I could. Statement, eh."

"Stand your ground," Luke said.

Movement on the stairs, and their parents were there. Their mum looked … different. Dressed as beautifully as always, and her hair as perfect as always, so that wasn't it. Like she'd been crying, or had been emotional, either of which was hard to imagine. She came into the room fast and said, "Hayden. Darling. Merry Christmas," kissed his cheek, then turned to Luke, kept the smile on her face, and asked, "May I kiss you as well?"

His face worked, and he didn't say anything for a minute. Finally, though, he said, "Yes." And smiled. And when Tania kissed his cheek, patted the other one, and said, "Merry Christmas," Hayden thought, *Well done, Mum.* And hoped.

His foolish heart.

His dad was there too, then, giving Zora a kiss and Rhys a shake of the hand, then offering Hayden a brief cuddle and pat on the back and putting his hand out to Luke. Luke hesitated for a bare second, then shook it. Craig cleared his throat and said, "Merry Christmas. I think I may not have been … entirely hospitable the other night."

"You think?" Hayden asked. He wasn't making a joke about this. He was done making jokes.

"Also," Craig went on, the words clearly pulled out of him, "I may have sounded … disappointed. I've done some, ah, thinking. And I'm proud of you, of course, Hayden."

He ran down, then glanced at Tania, who said, "I think what

your dad's trying to say, darling, is that we're both very proud of you. In your work, and in the person you've turned out to be. And that what we want most is for you to be happy."

"Yes," Craig said. "Of course."

"Thanks, Mum. And Dad. Uh … Merry Christmas, I guess." It wasn't exactly a Hallmark Christmas movie, but it probably passed for "heartfelt emotion" in his family.

His mum must have said something to his dad. Could she actually have enough emotional intelligence to know that Hayden had been a heartbeat away from walking out and not coming back? Not possible, but *something* had happened. Cautious optimism was the order of the day, he decided, and leave the Hallmark movie scripts for somebody else's family.

"What happened?" Casey asked. "Is somebody mad?"

"No," Hayden said. "Nobody's mad."

Christmas presents, then. Christmas tea, and pulling crackers and plum pudding out on Rhys and Zora's gorgeous deck. And finally, absolutely unexpectedly, Zora asking him, "D'you think you could do the wedding celebrant thing one more time before you go?"

"What?" Hayden asked. Luke's head came up, too.

"Rhys told me that a wedding is the only thing he wants for Christmas. And he *did* give me diamond and pearl earrings, so …" She was laughing, but maybe a little teary, too.

"It's what I wished!" Casey said, bouncing in her chair, her eyes round. "I got the wishbone in the Christmas pudding, and I wished and *wished!*"

Hayden said, "Of course I can. You know me, always ready to oblige. You'd need a license to make it official, though."

"I have a license," Rhys said. "I put the house as the alternative venue, as I've been wishing for quite a while myself."

"You're really terrifyingly competent," Hayden told him, and Rhys smiled.

"You're supposed to get married in a church, though," Casey said. "And send fancy invitations first with special handwriting."

"No, you're not," Isaiah said. "There aren't any rules like that. People get married in all sorts of places. The beach, and a hot-air balloon, and on the top of a mountain on the snow and ice, after they've climbed up it with ropes and crampons and everything."

"No, they don't," Casey said. "You have to have lots of people at a wedding, and they sit in chairs with ribbons on them and are very dressed up. And the bride has to have a white dress and fancy flowers, and Auntie Zora has on a *red* dress. I don't think they let you get married if it's not a white dress."

Isaiah sighed. "You don't need the chairs *or* the people. Or a white dress. Gay people can get married now, and men don't wear a white dress, so how could you have to have it?"

"Oh," she said. "But don't you *want* a white dress?" she asked Zora.

"When you get married for the second time," she said, "sometimes you don't wear a white dress, or do it with a big crowd. It's better if it's just the people you love most, and here we all are, so it's perfect."

"Plus she's getting married to my dad's brother," Isaiah said. "Which is all right, because it's not *her* brother, so it's OK for them to have sex even though he's my uncle. But heaps of people think it's not all right, and Uncle Rhys is very famous and very rich, so it might be in the newspaper again if they did a big wedding with a white dress, and people might not be nice."

"Oh." Casey considered that. "OK. And we did decorating and we're all wearing pretty clothes, so maybe it's all right. Except you're not very fancy," she told Luke.

"No," he said. "I'll stay out of view if there are any photos, how's that?"

"Nah, mate," Rhys said, and he was laughing. "We're not planning any photos, and we don't care how anybody looks. This is a Kiwi wedding."

It had been, too. And there'd been that time before it, when Zora had asked to see Hayden in the bedroom where she'd been getting ready, and he'd sat beside her on the bed and asked, "Is this about the service? If you'd told me ahead of time, I could've—"

"Yes," she said. "Partly. But I wanted to tell you that you're not some last-minute choice. The wedding idea was last-minute, but you're the only choice I could have made. When Dylan was dying and I was so tired that I could barely put one foot in front of the other, when the money was gone and I was so worried, you were always there. When you came over to cut my grass every week and take Isaiah to Kelly Tarlton to see the sea turtles, or to the planetarium ... you're the best brother ever, and the best uncle, and I need to tell you that today. Also, cheers for being as unacceptable as me, of course. We're in this together, hey. The two of us." The tears were sparkling on her lashes, and she gave a little laugh and pressed her fingers to her eyes.

"Oi." Hayden put up his hand, fist out. She bumped it with hers, and then they took hold of little fingers and shook. Their secret handshake, which they hadn't done since they were about ten. Hayden was getting a little choked up himself, to tell the truth.

"Geez. You're crying now?" he asked her, grabbing a tissue from the bedside table and doing some careful dabbing at her eyes. "You're wrecking your makeup. And same here. Who's had my back at every hideous family dinner?"

"Don't let Dad get to you," Zora said. "Though I think Mum must have said something."

"I think so, too. Only possible explanation. Think she broke her bowl on purpose? It looked that way to me."

"Hard to imagine," she said, "but if she did—" She tried to laugh. "That's love, eh."

"The Royal Copenhagen Full Lace serving bowl?" Hayden said. "Yeh, I'd say so. And—service? Ideas?"

"Yes." She reached over to grab a piece of paper. "This is what we want to say."

Hayden sat, now, in the chill and the noise and the smell of bad beer—rugby stadiums were all the same, even in France—and remembered the look on his sister's face when he'd prompted Rhys with the words, when the moment was so pure that it hurt your heart.

"With this ring I thee wed," Rhys had pronounced with the conviction of a man who knew exactly what he'd found and that it was forever, as he slid that ring home. "With my body I thee worship, and with all my worldly goods I thee endow."

Better than anything Hayden could've written, even if it was five hundred years old. Well, once they'd taken out the "obey" part, anyway.

It had taken Rhys more than forty years to get it right, even though he *was* terrifyingly competent, so maybe there was hope. Maybe you didn't always end up alone with your cat. Who was being looked after by Rhys and Zora this week, and hopefully not eating Casey's bunnies.

Wait. Minute 66, and still nothing happening, but a big, bulky man in blue and white stripes was trotting off, and somebody else was trotting on. And the crowd was clapping, because it was Luke, and he was a star. An unlikely, battered, locked-down star who'd never look for the spotlight, who only wanted to do his job.

There *was* an Aussie on the team, and a South African, and even an American. There was also a Kiwi. Hayden stood up, not caring how it looked, raised his hands over his head, and applauded.

That's my man, he said in his head to nobody. *And he's everything.*

THE MAN

*L*uke hated the bench. Whenever he was riding the pine, he was like a sheepdog in the back of the ute, panting hard, tail wagging like mad, every fiber of his being longing to get out there amongst it.

Fifteen to six didn't matter. Fourteen minutes left didn't matter. What mattered was this moment right now, when he was taking his place in the scrum, getting his body centered and low, so he could drive up into his opposite number. The scrums up to now had been rubbish, and he needed to fix that.

"Come on, boys," he told the others. "Let's get it right." The scrum was all about cohesion.

Crouch. Bind. Set. His mantra since the age of eight. All the angles of force in the scrum came through the tighthead prop. He was the cornerstone of the whole structure, and that was the way Luke liked it.

He didn't have to look to know when the ball came in. He felt the moment, and he drove up under the loosehead with all his might and felt him giving way, clearing space for Racing's hooker to get the ball with his foot and send it back. And just like that, they had what they'd needed most: time and space for the Number Eight to get the ball away to the halfback, for the backs to get into position, for the game to open up.

After that, it was all his jobs, which amounted to two words: domination and intimidation. The one place he didn't feel too big, because being the biggest was the point. Hitting the ruck to help out his teammate, smashing his opponent and driving him off the ball, moving fast, keeping his legs going, driving forward.

Power comes from the lower body.

Lifting in the lineout, hoisting the tallest man on the team high into the air to catch the ball, then setting him carefully down again, the reason you pushed all that tin in the gym. And finally, when the first-five kicked out a long penalty in the seventy-second minute that crossed the touchline inside Pau's 22 …

The maul. Henri Jaconde had the ball, was turned backward to the opposition, his legs driving, moving. Luke was beside him, bringing the power on one side while the loosehead drove on the other, and the rest of the forwards piled in behind even as Pau drove back at them with all their strength.

It was like pushing a concrete wall, but you pushed anyway, because that was your job, and this was your team. His ear being jammed painfully into his head, his entire body straining, and his legs moving. Moving. One step. Two. Five. A locomotive on the track, driving on.

Power comes from the lower body.

Behind him, he could hear the shouts from the halfback, a little Aussie who was running both his legs and his mouth, as halfbacks did. As Aussies did. Luke didn't need encouragement. He just needed to push, so he did.

Again, when the ball went back, hand over hand, to the halfback, he felt it and disengaged, running in support so he'd get to the breakdown fast, his legs still fresh, his chest heaving. The backs ranged out now, running their lines eight meters from the tryline. Trying it on in the middle, and the halfback yipping again.

A chance at the left, and they were taking it. Smooth, now, that they were free to play their game. A bullet shot from the halfback's hands, in and out of the winger's, the one Pau would have counted on to take it in. Off to the Number Eight instead, the big man running the tramlines just inside the field of play, putting his head down and his arm out. In and out of one man's grasp, the other bouncing off from the force of that fend. Over the line, diving, sliding, and Luke could feel the grin on the man's face behind the mouthguard, the joy of it. He was thumping him on the back himself, then trotting back to get set for the conversion.

A tricky kick from the corner. The first-five, a South African with the funniest technique you'd ever seen, clasping his hands together, wriggling his hips, looking up at the posts, down at the ball, then at the posts again, until you wanted to scream at him to get on with it.

But when he kicked the ball, it went through. The flags went up, and it was 13 to 15 with two minutes to play, and Racing would get the ball again on the kickoff.

One more chance.

Now or never.

Hayden wasn't thinking about Christmas anymore. He wasn't thinking about chocolate croissants or shopping or Picasso paintings with weird eyeballs.

He was just watching. Hands clenched together, breath coming hard.

His brother-in-law had been an elite rugby player, and his new brother-in-law was an elite rugby coach. It wasn't that he'd never watched the game. It was just that he'd only watched the exciting parts: the lithe, nimble backs, passing and kicking and running, shifting direction on a dime, looking so athletic.

The forwards were a different story, and Luke was a whole

different *book.* Impossibly strong, because they were doing a scrum again, on defense this time, and Racing was pushing Pau backward, then driving them off the ball. One person as the fulcrum of that lever. The one who'd taken two weeks off, had flown for twenty-four hours a couple of days ago, and had sat on the bench tonight for almost seventy minutes.

The backs must have picked up that new resolve, too, because after a game of dropped passes and missed opportunities, they were firing. Passing and catching and running, being tackled and getting up to pass and catch and run again. Meter by meter, down to the 10. To the 22. And getting nowhere.

None of that passing and catching now. Too risky, as the hooter sounded for 80 minutes. As soon as Racing lost possession, that would be the game. Instead, the forwards held on. One of them carrying the ball, getting tackled, and another picking it up and trying his hand, probing the line for a break that wasn't there.

One minute. Two minutes. Three. Still nearly ten meters out, still doggedly trying. The crowd on its feet, roaring, and Hayden's clasped hands at his mouth.

Yet another Racing forward running with the ball now, straight at the opposition, trying to run them over. Two of them grasping him, shoving him back.

Held up. That was the word. Held up. Any second now, it would be over.

Wait. Luke, his hands clutching the jersey of the ball carrier, shoving, reversing the opposition's momentum. Two more Racing players joining him, bodies bent nearly double. Another maul, and Luke leading the charge.

It was flipping the truck tire down the field. It was raw power.

Shoving. Shoving. Shoving. Bodies straining, muscles standing out on forearms and thighs and calves. You could see it. You could *feel* it.

Five meters out. Four. Three. Two.

Over the line.

Hayden only knew he was crying when he tasted the tears. Stupid. Ridiculously emotional, over a rugby game, but it wasn't the game. It wasn't even the win.

It was the man.

EASY COME, EASY GO

*L*uke had thought it would have happened already. He'd been back from New Zealand for ten weeks, and he'd told about half of the All Blacks while he was down there. Some of those boys were playing in France now, going for the money at the end of their careers, so why hadn't they talked?

He knew why. Mateship. Loyalty. He appreciated it, but if it wasn't going to come out naturally, so he could confirm it and take the heat ... what was he meant to do here? Hold a press conference? Talking at a press conference was his least favorite thing. He had to do it as England's skipper, but he was rubbish at it. The thought of using it to say he was gay ...

Yeh. No.

He could have told his team, but he wasn't playing for Racing at the moment. He was in the midst of the Six Nations international competition, which meant he *was* playing for England. He was the captain, he was responsible, and this would be nothing but a distraction. A huge one, when they least needed it.

All this rationalization. He felt like a coward, and he'd never been a coward. What was the right thing? Only one more test match to play after this week's match in Rome, and it was against Scotland.

Not England's toughest competition, you'd think, based on the record, but the rivalry was there all the same, fierce and deep. They'd be playing for the Calcutta Cup, the oldest trophy in rugby, and Scotland lifted for it every time. The score would be low, the battles brutal, and there would be a fight or two afterward. Not amongst the players. Amongst the supporters.

This time, they were playing the match in Edinburgh. How much more of a fight would there be if he'd come out by then? If his coming out meant England lost? He could take anything for himself, or he hoped he could. He couldn't put that on his team.

Do it after the end of the Racing season, he told himself. It was only three more months.

He sat on an anonymous bed in a Rome Marriott, which looked exactly like all the other hotel beds and all the other hotels in his life, focused on the exercise book in his hands, ran through his points for tomorrow's Captain's Run, and tried not to feel lonely.

He didn't get lonely. He was used to being alone. He'd been alone ever since he could remember, or at least since he'd been sent away to school. Ever since Hayden had gone home two months ago, though, there'd been an emptiness in his flat, in his life, that he hadn't known since that first day at school. Nine years old, walking away from his brother and into the cold.

The tears on Kane's face, not understanding.

Hayden's face at the airport, saying goodbye. Hayden trying to be funny and clever, smiling and smiling and smiling. Not touching and not kissing, because Luke couldn't. It was too public. He'd just stood there, arms at his sides, until Hayden had walked away. He'd kept standing there until Hayden was lost from view in the security queue.

Hayden hadn't looked back.

Wait. In this situation, Hayden was Luke. Wasn't he? Standing tall and walking away, because there was no choice. Because this was where he had to go right now, and this was what he had to do.

Leave. And be alone.

He closed his exercise book. He should go for a walk. He was in Rome, after all, and the evening would just be getting started out there. He should put on his jacket and Hayden's scarf, the most elegant piece of clothing he'd ever owned, and take in the city. Or he should ring Hayden, if he was lonely and missing him. Eight at night here meant eight in the morning there.

What would he say, though? Ask for comfort, when he was being a coward and Hayden knew it? Lately, there'd been pauses between them. Silences. Too much distance, and Luke couldn't tell what was on the other end of the line, but he suspected it was disappointment. Maybe disillusion. Hayden never asked him if he'd come out yet, why he was faffing about like this, but Luke could feel him wanting to, and he didn't know how to answer.

It was only a few months until July, when Luke would be done playing for the season and Hayden would come visit again, but it felt like he was standing in a long, cold, dark tunnel, unable to see the light. Unable to see the end.

He'd take a walk.

"How come you never bring a date to dinner anymore, Uncle Hayden?"

That was Casey, who was working hard on twirling spag bol around her fork. They were out on the deck again for this Friday-night dinner, because the day was glorious. Blue sky, blue sea, warm sun. Hayden put a smile on his face and said, "Luke's in France, remember? Well, actually, he's in Rome at the moment, preparing for heroics with England."

Casey stuffed a round ball of spaghetti the size of a clementine into her mouth, then chewed on it determinedly like a squirrel deciding to eat all the nuts at once. When she gulped down the mouthful at last, she asked, "How come?"

"How come what?" Hayden asked.

Rhys said, "Napkin, Casey."

"Why?" she asked.

"Because you have Bolognese sauce all around your mouth and chin," Rhys said. "Which is from Italy, by the way."

"Because Rome is in Italy," Isaiah said. "It's very historical there. And they speak Italian."

"I *know*," Casey said.

"You probably didn't," Isaiah said. "But that's OK. People don't like to admit they don't know something. You'd think they'd speak Latin, because that was what they spoke when they started Rome, but they don't. That's kind of weird. It's the same people, but they changed the language."

"You could look it up," Rhys said, and when Isaiah stood up, added, "After dinner. And tell us the answer. Got to be a reason, eh."

"Why do you always have to *know* things?" Casey asked.

"I don't know," Isaiah said. "I just do. It's good to know things. It's information."

"OK," Casey said. "Then how come Luke doesn't come visit you, Uncle Hayden? Dad goes away for rugby, but he always comes home."

"You have to go where you live, in rugby," Isaiah said. "You can't just go to another *country* when your team's training."

"But Dad goes to other countries all the time," Casey said.

"Because the team's playing there," Isaiah said. "You don't get to choose where you go. Unless your partner's having a baby or something, you have to stay with the team all season long. If you're an All Black, or playing for England like Luke, you have to stay for the test matches, too. It's almost all the time."

"Oh." Casey considered that while she twirled more spaghetti and Rhys said, "Start with a tiny bit, maybe, so you look a bit less like a snake eating a goat."

"Spaghetti is hard," she said.

"Yeh," Rhys said. "But tasty, eh."

"OK," Casey said. "Then Uncle Hayden could go visit Luke,

because he's not a rugby player. He could fly on a plane. You can lie down like on a bed," she told Hayden. "It has scary toilets that make a very loud sound, but you can't get sucked into the hole, so it's OK to go in them. And they give you cookies, too, and when Dad and I went, they let me see the front of it where the drivers sit."

"The pilots," Isaiah said. "In the cockpit."

Casey ignored him. "So why can't you go?" she asked Hayden.

Zora wasn't saying anything, but she was looking at him with too much compassion, like she knew. She couldn't, because he hadn't told anyone. He couldn't stand to. That Luke didn't call enough, and when Hayden called him, it was awkward.

He'd been so *sure.*

He said, "Well, I'm working, for one thing. Those contracts aren't going to draft themselves."

Isaiah said, "People take holidays, though."

"Yes," Hayden said "And I'm taking one. In July. More than two weeks."

"Oh." Casey considered that. "When Dad's gone, though, I'm very sad, and I miss him very much. But when he calls me and reads me a book, I feel better. Maybe you could call Luke and read him a book, if he's sad. I think he might be sad. Dad always says he misses me and Isaiah and Auntie Zora when he's gone, because rugby can be kind of lonely, so Luke might miss you, too."

Wait. If Luke was sad? *Luke?*

"You can need somebody," Hayden had told Luke that night in Tekapo when they'd been watching the lights of the Aurora dancing in the dark sky, "and still be a man."

What had Luke said? Something like, "Yeh. That. Thanks." Which wasn't much, but he'd meant it. Hadn't he?

He roused himself and asked, "What book would you recommend?"

Casey considered. *"The Kissing Hand,"* she decided. "That's the best book for missing somebody. It's kind of a baby book, but it's nice. I'm seven, so I don't need baby books now, but I still like it, even though it's about raccoons and I'm not a raccoon. So I think a grown-up might like it, too, if they were sad."

"Rugby players don't read books called *The Kissing Hand*," Isaiah said. "Ew."

Rhys smiled. "Oh, I don't know. Rugby players need kisses, too."

"Not on their *hands*," Isaiah said.

Rhys took Zora's hand and kissed her palm, then closed her fingers around it. "There. That's how I feel leaving. Like I want your mum to feel that kiss, just like the raccoon kid does."

"But you're not the one getting the kiss," Isaiah said, "so it doesn't count."

Zora's hand was still in Rhys's. Now, she lifted his and kissed his palm. "No," she said. "Rugby players need love, too. And so do men. When I say goodbye, I want Uncle Rhys to think that he can press his hand to his cheek and know that somebody loves him more than life." She laughed and dabbed her eyes with her napkin. "Sorry, Hayden. We're a bit goopy, possibly. He's got another road trip coming up, and it's a long one, and Casey's right. I miss him, every time."

How much does he care, Hayden wanted to ask, *if he won't even come out? How much can he possibly miss me if I'm still a secret, and he's OK with keeping me that way?*

Rhys and Zora had kept it secret, though, hadn't they? Rhys had done that for Zora, Hayden was sure, because he'd known what people would say, and he hadn't wanted her to face that.

But what if that's not it? What if that's not why?

Then you need to know. Harden up and find out.

He looked at his watch. Six-thirty.

This is madness. You don't have to be desperate. Insouciant, that's you. Easy come, easy go. It doesn't mean you'll never find love. Just another one that didn't work out.

He couldn't manage it.

ANESTHETIZE MY HEART

*H*ayden had never been so tired.

Pro tip, he told himself as he sat in the hotel lobby, nursed his fourth coffee, and tried not to (A) fall asleep, and (B) bounce off the walls from all the caffeine he'd consumed over the past ... however long it had been, because his brain couldn't compute the numbers. *Don't take a thirty-hour night flight to Rome on the spur of the moment—with a three-hour layover in Dubai, and not in the kind of seat that makes into a bed—after a very bad night's sleep, a full day of work, and a general sense of impending doom, and if you do, have somebody there to shepherd you in your daze of fatigue and incomprehension.* He'd been able to find out via Rhys where the team was staying —through some sort of international rugby fraternity, apparently, because the information had taken his brother-in-law about five minutes to gather—and had taken a taxi there. So here he was. In Rome, at Luke's hotel.

Except.

It was after five by the time he got through customs, through the mad Roman traffic—his first time here, but he was at once too blurry-eyed and too caffeinated to appreciate it—and arrived at the hotel, and when he got there, they wouldn't tell him which was

Luke's room. Well, of course not. He should have foreseen that. The bloke at the desk was looking distinctly shirty, in fact, and Hayden had to book a room to keep him from turfing him out. There weren't any regular ones left, so it was a suite. By the time he'd done that, the game was about to start, and he ... well, he was here, and he needed to watch Luke play.

This was ridiculous, he told himself more than once on the taxi ride to the stadium. He could have just *called*. But it didn't feel like it. It felt urgent. Or wildly extravagant to the point where New Zealand would be rescinding his passport for insufficient Kiwi thriftiness. Or both.

He found the ticket booth after some searching. He'd learned a bit of French—his over-hopeful heart again—but he definitely didn't know Italian. He'd missed most of the first half of the game, but he watched the second. The score at the end was 33 to 6, and England had the 33, but Hayden didn't care about that. Instead, he watched Luke, was thrilled by his strength and his skill and his heart, and so incredibly proud, too, and wondered yet again, *Is this the stupidest romantic move in a lifetime of stupid romantic moves?*

He remembered Rhys saying to Luke, though, "Good to have somebody in the stands. Is that a first?" And the way Luke's ears had gone red, answering.

Didn't everybody need somebody to care? Was it so wrong to want to be that for a man?

After the game, he went back to the hotel. He ended up walking, because there were no taxis, and he wasn't able to sort out how else to get there. The walk took an hour, but he thought, *He'll be with the team for a couple of hours anyway.* He knew the drill by now. Besides, he needed to move to stay awake.

By the time he made it back, it was eleven. He ate dinner in the bar, facing the lobby, and then got a coffee.

Any time now.

After an hour and another coffee, he moved into the lobby,

because he was falling asleep where he sat, so he needed to be where Luke couldn't miss him.

He stayed awake until one, scrolling mindlessly on his phone, his heart beating hard every time a group came through the doors. It was a Marriott, and a big one, so there were heaps of groups. At one-thirty, he got another coffee. Fortunately, Italians seemed never to go to bed.

He started wondering, though. He couldn't help it. Luke had said, sometime in there, that he'd found his partners overseas, times when the team was playing in some country where soccer was everything. Places where he could be anonymous.

He's out with the team. He's gay as can be, and he's straight as a die. He can't lie if he tries. That's why you fell in love with him.

I'm strong as oak, Luke had said, that first night in the car, *and I'm steady as hell. And I don't cheat. I don't hurt, I don't lie, and I don't cheat.*

It's one-thirty in the morning, and you've seen English rugby players come in for a couple of hours now. It was hard to mistake them, and none of them was Luke.

And Luke had been distant on the phone lately. Face it. Hayden was hopeful, but he wasn't *that* stupid, was he? Luke wouldn't have to be cheating. He could just be …

Done.

His eyelids were like sandpaper now, his limbs heavy and aching. He shifted in the chair, then shifted again. The last thing he remembered thinking was, *If you don't matter to him enough after all, if he can stand to lose you, if we're looking at goodbye here … you need to know. Not in July. Now.*

How did you anesthetize your heart?

They'd won the game, which was no surprise, but it hadn't been easy. It never was, whatever the scoreboard said or what the public thought. Luke had gone out with the boys afterward, had watched some of them get stupid and some of them hook up, and was working now on getting the worst of them back to the hotel. Business as usual, but for some reason, his body was dragging.

He was fit. He'd prepared well, same as always. He knew how to lift to meet the moment, no matter what was happening in his life, so why did his entire body feel pummeled tonight?

Get over it, he told himself. He'd be on the plane in the morning and headed straight to Scotland, and it would all start again. That was his job, and that was his life. He'd signed up for it with his eyes open almost fifteen years ago, and he still loved it. He'd get some sleep here and some on the plane, and he'd be fit to go again.

So he was lonely and felt like nobody knew the man he was. He ought to be used to that.

George Conley, the blazingly fast young winger who'd earned his first cap on this tour and had scored his first international try tonight, stumbled getting out of the taxi, and Luke caught him by the arm and hauled him upright.

"Check out the talent," George said, the moment they went through the hotel's revolving door. Luke looked. Four or five young women with shiny hair, short skirts, and high heels, heading into the bar. "Another beer," George decided, attempting to veer off that way. A few of the other boys were in the bar, Luke noticed. Well, he couldn't round up everybody. He wasn't actually a sheepdog.

"You're legless, mate," Freddie Pritzker, the centre, told George. "You try to talk to them, you're likely to piss yourself. They'll laugh, is what they'll do."

"I'm no worse than you," George slurred, which was very nearly true. "A bloke gets to celebrate."

"We're on the bus at seven," Luke said, "and it's past two already. You miss that bus, and there'll be no next game for you." New caps were all the same. "There'll be girls in Edinburgh," he decided to add.

"Faw," George said. "Scottish girls. They don't have hair like that. Don't have—"

"Nah, mate," Freddie said. "You listen to the Skip. Boring, but he's right. You can't miss the bus. I've had one or two too many myself."

More like five or six too many, but Luke wasn't saying it. He'd get them to their rooms, and if they went out again after that and made arses of themselves, well, he'd have done his—

He stopped. George kept going, tripped over his size 14 feet, tried to turn around with middling success, and asked, "What?"

Luke hadn't had a drink tonight. Nothing but fizzy water with lime. But he felt legless himself, like his head and body weren't working together.

Hayden was asleep in one of the big chairs in the lobby. Not looking perfect for once. His shirt was rumpled, and so was his hair.

Luke couldn't process it. He couldn't work it out. He'd texted with him … when? Thirty-six hours ago? He told Freddie, "Get George up to his room."

"Not sure I can, mate," Freddie said. "Not sure I remember which is *my* room."

"Five twenty-four," Luke said. "George is 513. Here." He grabbed a pen from his jacket pocket and wrote the numbers on the back of Freddie's hand.

Freddie blinked at them. "I don't— You can't—"

Freddie was twenty-three, George wasn't even that old, and Luke was the skipper. This was his responsibility.

He didn't care. He pushed the button for the lift, shoved George inside, pressed the button for 5, and stepped out again, telling Freddie, "Between the two of you, you should be able to read a room number."

The doors closed on Freddie's astonished face.

STAND YOUR GROUND

*W*hy was Hayden's bedroom so noisy? And so bright? He needed to get up, turn out the lights, and turn off the telly, but he couldn't open his eyes. He'd just …

"Hayden." Oh. There was somebody here. Also, he was cold. He grabbed for the duvet to pull it up, but couldn't find it.

"Hayden."

His eyelids struggled to open and finally made it. When they did, he blinked. This didn't make sense. It was bright, and loud, and somebody's impossibly broad body was in front of him, blocking the view.

Somebody wearing an elegant beige-and-brown wool scarf with a geometric pattern. A Fendi scarf.

He woke up.

Luke had been so tired, his legs had felt encased in concrete. Now, he couldn't feel them at all. He knew he was smiling, even though he couldn't feel his face either, and he was reaching down for Hayden, pulling him to his feet.

He was aware that a few of the boys were straggling out of the bar. The part of his brain that had been in charge for thirty-three years tried to say, *Let go of him fast. Why are you touching him? You're saying hello to a mate, that's all. Stand back.*

His body wasn't listening, because Hayden was blinking, then saying, "I realize this is unexpected. Should have asked if you wanted me here, probably. Oh, well, I didn't. Apparently, I'm impulsive. Or desperate, though I'm trying not to go with that. I just—"

Luke kissed him. His arms around Hayden like they'd never let go, and Hayden's around him like this was what he'd hoped for and hadn't dared to think was possible.

Or maybe that was Luke.

The voice came from behind him. English, and slightly drunk. "Oh, shit." And another one. "That's never the Skip. What the hell?"

He didn't pay any attention, because he couldn't care. He was laughing, then kissing Hayden again, because he was everything he'd wanted to see for two months now. He was the morning light coming through the window and the swallows returning in the spring. He was hope, he was joy, and he was holding Luke like he needed him just as much.

"Let's go," Luke said. "My room."

"I have a … suite," Hayden said, still blinking, still so good-looking, he made Luke's hands feel clumsy. "I had to get a suite. They wouldn't let me sit here otherwise."

"I have to be on the bus at seven," Luke said. "My room."

Three of the boys were waiting for the lift. Luke was holding Hayden's hand, and he didn't drop it. He said, "My partner. Hayden Allen. Came over to surprise me." No choice anymore, and still, the huge black moth that was his secret flapped its leathery wings in alarm.

"Oh," Trevor Martin said, then glanced at Henry Osandu. Henry, the explosive blindside flanker and enforcer, had been playing with Luke for six seasons now. The third bloke, Oscar Findley, didn't say anything, just stared.

Henry pressed the button for 5, and the lift doors closed. "Hi," he said to Hayden. "Henry." And put out his hand.

Hayden dropped Luke's hand to shake Henry's and said, his voice a little unsteady, a little giddy, "This probably comes as a surprise."

"Well, yeah," Henry said, and grinned. "A bit. He's so bloody ugly, I just figured he couldn't get a girl. Didn't realize he wasn't looking for one."

The lift stopped and the doors opened. Henry put out a big hand to hold them open and asked Luke, "Do we keep this on the DL? Or what?"

Luke took a breath. *Still time to back away,* the black moth hissed in his ear, its claws clutching at his skin. *Don't be stupid.*

"Not a secret," Luke said. "I'll tell the boys myself, on the bus."

Henry said, "Right, then." He turned to walk down the hall with the others, then turned and came back. The others came with him, because Henry had some mana. "Far as I'm concerned, it doesn't change anything. You've been a follow-me skipper from the start, because nobody picked you for your speeches, and I don't see why I should stop following you now. No business of mine who you sleep with."

"But—" Oscar said.

"But what?" Henry asked, fixing Oscar with his don't-fuck-with-me stare.

"Well," Oscar said, and faltered. "Well," he said again, "in the sheds and all, like."

"What, that he'll see you naked?" Henry said. "I think that ship has sailed, mate. And I imagine he's been averting his eyes pretty smartly, because if he's an ugly bastard, you're worse. Props."

"Still," Oscar said. "It's a lot to overlook." He glanced at Trevor, who nodded slightly, gulped, and looked uncomfortable.

"Mate," Henry said. "Look at his partner. Anybody like that on our squad? Anybody close?"

"Well, uh," Trevor said, "Dan Foster's pretty good-looking." The first-five. They were always good-looking. Something about that "running the boys around the paddock" thing. Cool, calm, and good-looking. Luke was thinking that, because he was sweating, and he didn't know what was coming next.

A door opened, and somebody said, "Oi, you lot. Shut up. Trying to sleep here."

"Skip's telling us he's gay, though," Oscar said, possibly because he had more than a few under his belt himself.

"He's what?" the man asked. Alex Stewart, that was, and now his roommate, Max Matthews, was crowding out behind him, wearing only a pair of rugby shorts, saying, "What's going on?"

Oscar explaining, and more doors opening. Two-thirty in the bloody morning, and all Luke wanted was to take Hayden back to his room and do what most rugby players wanted to do after the match, but possibly even more so. And say all the right things and hear all the right things, too, but mostly—

Well, yeh. It had been a long two months.

It was also the worst nightmare of his life, coming true. Like dreaming you were naked in class, then waking up and realizing it was happening.

Hayden said, "You could hold my hand."

"Yeh, right," Luke said.

"I mean," Hayden said, "you could hold my hand." When Luke looked at him, Hayden grinned a little crookedly and said, "Stand your ground."

"Oh. Right." Luke did it. It felt … bizarre. He was standing in a hotel corridor amidst most of his teammates, in the middle of the night, holding a man's hand.

Definitely his nightmare. And also the right thing, because it was Hayden's hand, and his hand was solid ground, the only thing anchoring Luke here. But he had no control, not even his super-power of shutting up and walking away. There was nowhere to hide anymore.

A buzz of talk. More and more men standing around barefoot in shorts and singlets, the newest arrivals being filled in by the others, and Luke in the middle of it, silent. What did you say?

Finally, Henry put two fingers in his mouth and whistled, long and loud, and everybody shut up. He said, "Right. What did you think, when he never had a girlfriend?"

Everybody looked at each other, and Henry asked, "Has he ever made a move on any of us?"

"Well, no," Oscar said, "but how do we know he won't?"

"I won't," Luke said. "Sorry, but I'm not exactly tempted by you lot."

Some laughter at that, and Henry said, "He's our skipper. He makes the right calls, and nobody empties the tank more out on the field. Not the chattiest bloke, but that doesn't bother me."

"Yeh," somebody said from the back of the group, "but do you want to take a shower with him?"

Henry waited a moment, and Luke thought, *This is it, then.* When Henry went on, though, he said, "You know my little sister, right? Aisha? Plays Sevens?" They nodded, and he said, "She's a lesbian. Married to a woman. You don't know that, even though it's no secret, because her teammates aren't bloody idiots, and they aren't worried that she'll grab them in the showers because she can't resist their fat, hairy arses. So they go out and play the game instead of spending their time obsessing about what kind of sex she has. I don't want to think about what kind of sex any of you have, so I don't do it. None of my business."

"But you're Nigerian," Oscar said.

"I'm English," Henry said, with the kind of flat stare that would make most men take a step back.

"Well, but your parents," Oscar persisted, possibly because of the drink.

"What, they should've tossed her out?" Henry asked. "Because they're from Nigeria? I don't think they're the ones with the problem here. If anybody has anything to say about my sister," he went on, folding his arms and giving them all the benefit of his hardest look, "they can say it to me. And if you want to say anything about the Skip, too. Here's your chance. Come on. Say it to me."

Some muttering, some shifting of feet. And somebody else stepping forward. Dan Foster, the first-five, who actually *was* good-looking and charismatic and all of that, saying, "This is a load of bollocks." Luke's heart sank, and he felt sick. Then Dan went on. "Luke's our skipper, full stop. Who thinks he's not a good one?" He looked around. Nobody spoke up. "Then what's the problem?" Dan asked. "Last I looked, it was 2023. And I'd like to get to bed. I ran about ten kilometers tonight, because the Italians can't tackle for shit, but they run like bloody greyhounds. I've got a new baby and a two-year-old at home, and this is my one chance to get some sleep."

Time to stop standing here like a poleaxed bull. Luke was the captain, at least for now. Time to act like it. "Right," he said, raising his voice so everybody could hear it. "That's enough for tonight. Break it up. Go to bed, and I'll see you on the bus."

He tried not to hold his breath, waiting to see if they'd do it.

They did. All but Henry, who waited until they were gone, then asked Luke, "All right?"

"Yeh," Luke said. "Thanks." He tried to think what else to say, and couldn't.

Henry nodded. "When are you telling Coach?"

"At the airport, I reckon," Luke said. "When I can have a quiet word. And if that's it, if it's over …" He put out a hand and tried to keep the emotion from showing. It had never been harder. "It's been an honor."

Henry took it and gripped hard. "Nah, mate," he said. "The honor's mine."

Hayden said, when Luke had stalked in his absolutely upright way to his room, betraying nothing, "And I thought it was hard for *me* to come out."

He was feeling a little shaken, honestly. That had been *intense*.

Luke let the door shut behind them and said, "We could talk about that. We could talk about you flying here and why you did it. Or I could kiss you."

Hayden said, "Uh, well, uh … let's do that." Heart pounding, breath catching. It was the look on Luke's face.

Luke stepped into him and did it.

It wasn't their first time, but that was how it felt. Lips and tongues and breath coming hard. Clumsy hands unfastening buttons, and shirts pulled up by eager hands. Luke's jacket dropping to the floor, Hayden's shirt, and still, Luke kissing him, his mouth avid and hard.

Hayden could hardly stand up.

He was naked, then, and Luke was still wearing his trousers. His trousers, and Hayden's scarf. Hayden said, as best he could with Luke's hands on his chest, his back, his sides, Luke's mouth at his neck, "You wore the … scarf."

Luke stopped kissing his neck, stepped back, and looked at him, and Hayden forgot to breathe. Then Luke took the scarf off, put it over Hayden's head, and pulled him in by it.

Bloody *hell.*

He'd never been touched with so much possessiveness. He'd never lain on a big white bed, had a man's mouth all over him, and been flooded by so much desire, all he could do was put his hands up over his head and surrender to it.

Heat. Passion. Desire. He couldn't … he couldn't …

He was making too much noise. He knew it, and he couldn't stop himself. When it got to be more than he could bear, he stuffed his fist into his mouth and bit down on it to try to quiet himself.

Luke stopped. His hand at the back of Hayden's neck, gentle now. "All right?" he asked, not sounding like himself, either. Sounding gruff, nearly strangled, and Hayden realized, somewhere in the dim recesses of his mind, that this meant as much to Luke as it did to him.

"Y-yeh," he managed to say. "Just … I love you." He was crying a little now. He couldn't help it. The emotion … it was too much. "And I'm … being loud."

Luke wasn't just touching the back of his neck now. He was kissing it, his hand stroking down Hayden's arm. "Nah," he said. "Not too loud. Want me to slow down?"

"No," Hayden said. "No. Please. *Please.*"

"All right," Luke said. "Then hang on."

Hayden did.

It took Luke a surprisingly long time to get his heart rate back to normal. That was love, maybe, because it bloody well wasn't fitness. When Hayden was in his arms and they were lying, spent, amidst twisted sheets, he managed to say, "I have to be on the bus in about three hours." And laughed, because that was how this felt.

He'd never been giddy in his life, but he was giddy now. The black moth that had held him down for so long loosed its clutching claws, flapped its leathery wings, hissed one last time in his ear, and vanished. Right or wrong, whatever happened next, he was free.

He was here. He was himself. And he was free.

He said, "I love you. It's not enough to say, and I'm not good with words anyway. But I love you. I didn't know if you …" He stopped, then forced himself to go on. "I felt like a coward. I didn't know if you'd want a coward."

Hayden stirred and turned, and now, his hand was on Luke's face. "I came because I had to know how you felt. What you wanted. I had to know if you felt the way I did. And you could never be a coward. Never."

"I didn't come out," Luke said.

"Well, yeh, mate," Hayden said, and he was laughing. "I think you did. How does it feel?"

Luke didn't know what was going to happen. It could all be over.

There'd be press, and the hell that was social media. He wouldn't read it, but he'd know it was out there. There was his Racing team, too, and the whole thing to go through again. And there was no other answer.

"Awesome," he said. "It feels awesome."

THE AULD ENEMY

*L*uke didn't want to wake Hayden, as tired as he'd looked and as little sleep as they'd got, but what option did he have? It was past six-thirty, and he needed to be downstairs in twenty minutes. He couldn't just sneak out without talking to him.

He settled for sitting on the edge of the bed and kissing Hayden's forehead. A gentle awakening, he hoped.

Unfortunately, Hayden shot up like a cork, and his forehead banged hard into Luke's nose. Hayden exclaimed and held his head, and Luke didn't exclaim and held his nose. Bleeding a bit. That was awkward. He grabbed a couple of tissues, leaned forward, and pinched his nostrils shut, and Hayden said, "I broke your *nose*. Sorry. Sorry. What … ice. I should get you some ice." He jumped out of bed and grabbed the ice bucket, which was interesting, as he was naked.

Luke said, still holding his nose, "You didn't break it. A bit of blood, that's all. You'll make life exciting for me if you go out there like that, though. Imagine the chat on the bus." He wanted to laugh, but it was hard to laugh with a bloody nose, so instead, he smiled. "You could tempt a few of them, too, because, bloody hell, but you're good-looking."

"Yeh, right," Hayden said distractedly. "Where are my clothes? You're bleeding so *much*."

Luke put out the non-pinching hand and pulled Hayden down to sit on the bed beside him. "I'm used to it. How's the head?"

"Oh." Hayden felt it. "A bruise, maybe, that's all."

"This relationship has been pretty hard on you," Luke said. "Physically." And smiled some more.

"Ha," Hayden said, but he'd lost the frantic look, at least. "Physically's the least of it. You're dressed already. How long do you have?"

"Fifteen minutes or so. I wanted to ask, though—" Luke hesitated, not wanting to put it out there, not wanting to ask for anything. This was already better than anything he'd ever had. What was he thinking, demanding more?

"What?" Hayden asked. Still naked. Still so bloody beautiful, and his heart …

"Not sure what your plans were," Luke said cautiously. "When you came."

"I think 'plan' may be generous," Hayden said. "I just came." He yawned. "Sorry, but if we're going to have a deep and meaningful conversation, I need coffee."

"Oh." Luke got up and went into the bath and came out with a cup. "It's not too bad."

"Thanks." Hayden took a long swallow. "So. What were we saying? Oh. Wait." He got up, then came back with a wet facecloth and gently sponged Luke's upper lip and chin. "How does it feel now?"

There was a lump in Luke's throat. He cleared it as best he could. "If you were planning on being over here for a bit, we could get you a room in Edinburgh. No partners allowed in mine before the match, and I'll be working, of course, but …"

Hayden said, "Oh. I'm … it's Monday morning in New Zealand. At least I think it is. I need to go back anyway, because I didn't clear this with anybody. I need to ring up soon, in fact. It was possibly impulsive. Or call it what it was. Mad."

"Oh. Right. OK, then." Luke glanced at his watch and tried not to feel disappointed. Or desolated.

"It would be harder if I were here anyway," Hayden said, "because I'm thinking you may get some press."

"Yeh," Luke said. "I think that's fair to say." *When did you get so soft?* he asked himself. *When did you start caring what strangers thought of you?*

"But," Hayden said, then stopped.

"What?" Luke asked.

"I'm trying to be brave," Hayden said. "Braver, anyway."

"I think you were that," Luke said.

"So I'm going to say," Hayden went on, as if he hadn't heard him, "that if you're asking that because you *want* me to come with you … if it would help, maybe, support and all that. Or, you know, love. Then … I can ring my senior partner and explain. Not sure *how* I'd explain, but I'll think of something."

Luke had forgotten about his nose. Mistake, because two big globs of blood fell onto his white button-down, team-required travel shirt. He pinched it shut again and said, "If there's a money issue, I could make that up."

"Luke."

"Oh," Luke said. "Sorry. You're not a toy and all that. Got it."

"No." Hayden's hand was on Luke's chest now. "I'll go out on a limb for you. You just did it for me, didn't you?" He was trying to smile, to be bright and funny, but it wasn't quite working. "I'm good at my job, and I'm tired of dancing around my life, trying desperately to be … to be acceptable, sure that if I take one false step anywhere, I'm out. Out of my family, out of my relationship, out of my job. If we want this, if it's worth it—let's go for broke. Let's stop protecting ourselves and do it. Flat to the boards. What do you say?"

"I say," Luke said, and decided, to hell with the shirt. He put his arm around Hayden and kissed him, blood and all. "I say—I'm in." He laughed. He had to leave, but this time, leaving didn't have to hurt. "I say—if you want that?" He kissed Hayden again and promised it. "I'm your man."

Another Saturday night for Hayden. Another stadium, not even domed this time. The stands were covered, but the wind was whistling. He didn't care. He *was* in the WAG section this time, because he'd actually met them.

"You're welcome," Madelyn Osandu, Henry's wife, had told him yesterday, when he'd met a few of them at Harvey Nichols to go shopping, which you tended to have to do if you flew across the world without so much as a change of clothes, and then been in the papers over and over again, possibly not looking as fabulous as you'd like as the first-ever rugby HAB. You had to represent, after all. Madelyn had gone on, "Though you're better dressed than most of us. You're the one getting the press this time, so that's something, instead of me copping it for not losing the baby weight yet."

Since they were being followed by about eight photographers at the time, she was right. Hayden hadn't done any interviews, and neither had Luke, but that hadn't stopped anybody from commenting, or the photos from appearing, either. The ones from Wednesday, Luke's day off, when they'd gone to Edinburgh Castle and walked down the Royal Mile—Hayden couldn't help it that he'd never been much of anywhere and wanted to be a tourist—and held hands, had been especially popular. Or disgusting, repellent, and "against nature."

Oh, well. Not like it was news that heaps of people in the world shared Hayden's dad's view of things.

"I can't say I think much of this scarf," Hayden told Madelyn now, wrapping the thing an extra time around his throat as they watched the teams finish their extremely enticing groin stretches and other manly displays and trot off the field. "Red and black. Basic as. English rugby needs a new designer."

She laughed. "Never mind. This is the last match, then it's back to French chic."

"Nah," Hayden said. "I have to fly home tomorrow. Back to work, eh." If he still had a job. His senior partner hadn't been best pleased with his sudden absence. The firm was stuffy. Law firms tended that way, but big commercial firms *especially* tended that way. Bad enough to be gay. Worse to be ...

Well, notorious.

They'd thought it was Luke's career that would suffer. Ironic if it turned out to be Hayden's.

"Oh, what a pity," Madelyn said. "I would've come over to Paris to shop with you. Sacrifice, but there you are." She laughed again, then sobered and said, "My son Duncan asked me about you yesterday. Well, about Luke, mainly."

"Oh?" Hayden asked cautiously.

"Yeh," she said. "He's seven. He wanted to know if gay people can play rugby, and I could say, 'Well, of course they can. There's our skipper doing it. That's why you're asking, isn't it?' And he said, 'I guess so.' That's going to means a lot to kids. Especially teenagers."

"I see that," Hayden said. "Not sure Luke ever wanted to be a poster boy for anything, though. He hasn't been enjoying this."

"Somebody had to be first, I guess," Madelyn said. "Sorry if it's been dread. It'll be worse tonight, fair warning."

"What do you mean?" Hayden asked.

"Watch," she said, "and you'll see. Never mind. He's tough, and they're all used to copping it over something, especially when Scotland plays the Auld Enemy. He can take it."

Easy for you to say, Hayden thought and didn't say. *We're tired of taking it. And why should we have to?*

Luke had run out of a thousand tunnels in his career. He'd run out at the head of his team dozens of times, too. He knew about hostile crowds and hostile stadiums.

It had never been like this.

They ran out to a rousing hail of boos, as full-throated as 67,000 voices could manage. Which wasn't unheard-of, but this was worse. He could hear, somehow, some individual words in the midst of that yelling, or he thought he could. He did his best to ignore all of it and lined up facing the stands for the anthem. At the end of the row, because he was the skipper, with Henry's arm around his shoulders and his arm around Henry's waist, since Henry was the next-most-senior player on the squad. If Henry wasn't comfortable with it, he didn't say anything.

The crowd did. "God Save the King" began to play, and the boos increased, drowning out the music. And then came the hail of drink cups. Murrayfield was a dry stadium, so beer wasn't the reason. It was Luke.

All you had at the end of the day, though, was your refusal to be cowed. If he hadn't backed down when he was nine and some twelve-year-old was beating him in the toilets, when his nose was bloody and he'd been kicked in the head, he wasn't backing down now. He didn't think, *I'm putting the team under the pump*, because there was no point. The anthems ended, and he jogged to his spot and braced for the kickoff. England were receiving, and that was all that mattered right now.

The ball was in the air, spinning high under the lights. Trevor Martin, the lock, who hadn't looked Luke in the eye all week, was backpedaling, then backpedaling some more, and Luke was running with him, behind him.

The ball was coming down. Too high, still, even as Trevor ran backward to get it. Misjudged. Luke saw his moment, reached for Trevor's waist, and lifted him overhead.

He felt Trevor overbalancing, reaching too far, then going arse-over-teakettle, headfirst and backward toward the ground, and Luke stiffened every muscle and held on.

It barely took a second, and he felt every fraction of it. When Trevor's feet were in the air, and when Luke started pulling him in the other direction. When Luke's arms came back to vertical and he could see Trevor's feet again. When he was planting his feet and bringing the big lock's 105 kG down slowly. Slowly. Not letting him fall.

Trevor's feet on the ground, the ball in his arms. Trevor hitting the line, and Luke right behind him, adding his weight. The crowd singing *Flower of Scotland,* willing their team on. Trying to get under Luke's skin, but he didn't need to let them.

The earth had shifted on its axis, and he was in the right place again. Doing his role. Anchoring his team. Pressing on.

No moment but this one. No purpose but domination.

He was here, and he was strong. That was enough.

Hayden was having a hard time breathing. They weren't even three minutes into the game, and England was driving, the backs with the ball now, handing it off. Down the field, playing like men possessed. Like it wasn't the beginning, but the end. Like they had something to prove.

The big screen overhead was showing it, of course. And then switching off to show that lift. How Luke had, somehow, held somebody up whose entire body weight was pulling him backward, and then lifted him overhead again and set him down.

How?

How?

Beside him, Madelyn was saying, "How did he do that? How ever did he do that?"

Hayden finally came up with the answer. "Because he had to."

Around him, the noise swelled. The crowd was on its feet, the

Scots singing and the English singing back. *Swing Low, Sweet Chariot* being drowned out, then rising again.

Scotland finally getting it together, stiffening their line. Repelling the backs, and then repelling them again, until it was the forwards taking their turn, the same way he'd seen it happen before, bashing into the opposition like the most brutal game of Red Rover ever.

Hayden had been rubbish at Red Rover. On purpose. In his opinion, if other kids wanted to brutalize him, he wasn't going to line up for the chance, and he wasn't going to dislocate his arms trying to stop them, either.

He had not been popular on the playground.

This was different. He was on his feet along with everybody else, watching Luke drive his team on. As if he was prepared to leave it all out there, and he'd do anything it took.

One player after another taking the ball. The singing louder now, the Scots emptying their lungs. The Scottish line holding. Holding.

Luke didn't carry the ball much. Hayden knew that. He didn't expect it. Luke was that fella just behind the ball carrier, helping him on, securing possession for the next attempt.

Two, three, four more attempts, and then a break in the line. The tall fella, the one Luke had lifted earlier, who'd been on the lift in Rome with them and hadn't said anything, just looked horrified, smashed his way through and drove on with Luke behind him.

Eight meters out. He was going to score. He was going to …

Players closing in fast from both sides.

He passed the ball to Luke.

A player driving hard at Luke, going for his upper body, and Luke plowing straight through him. Another one grabbing at his jersey, and Luke's legs never stopped.

Three meters. Two. A player coming so fast, he looked like he was flying, diving from behind for Luke's ankles, grabbing hold, hanging on.

It was like watching a totara fall in the forest, its roots holding as long as they could, and then the long, slow, inexorable crash to earth. Luke was falling. He was going to come up short. He was going to …

Luke strained. Stretched. Took another step even as he was being pulled down by the ankles.

I'm strong as oak, and I'm steady as hell.

The field nearly shook as he went down.

Over the line.

Men surrounded him. Henry, pulling him to his feet. Trevor, grabbing him around the waist and lifting him. Hands slapping him on the back even as Luke tossed the ball away and attempted to get back into position for the conversion.

"Settle down, lads," he shouted. "Get back. Let's move."

"Mate," Henry said, jogging beside him. "Take the moment."

"What moment?" Luke said. "We've barely started."

"Nah, mate," Henry said. "We're going to win it. Thanks to you."

A MURMURATION OF SWALLOWS

*I*t was well after eight in the evening on a late-July day, and the sun was slanting low over the varied, centuries-old rooftops of Montmartre to the west, the bulk of the Louvre to the south, the black iron tracery of the Eiffel Tower beyond. Hayden was leaning against a balustrade in the dome of the basilica of Sacré-Cœur, looking out through an arched window at a smaller dome below, fashioned by a master out of nearly white, fine-grained travertine limestone, with Paris spread out below him like a feast.

Luke didn't tell him what he was looking at. Not like Hayden on that night with the Aurora Australis. Not needing to explain, to put this experience into a box. Content to let it soak in.

They'd gone to Assemblages for dinner, near Luke's flat, had sat against a white-filmed wall of ancient brick while waiters came and went on wood floors nearly as old as the ones in Luke's flat. Hayden had eaten duck and Luke had eaten everything but the menu, the lights had been low and the atmosphere relaxed and, yes, romantic. In fact, the only problem was …

Well, yeh. The only problem was that Hayden flew home tomorrow. All evening long, as he was chatting and laughing and Luke was giving him that barely-there smile, he'd thought, *I can't do this. I can't.* Which meant that when they'd finished at last and Luke had asked, "Want to walk up to Sacré-Cœur and get the view? It'll take a while to get there, but it's nice," he'd answered, "Yes." And couldn't think of what else to say.

Hand in hand, then, on cobblestone pavements flanking impossibly narrow streets, past mortared stone buildings of gray and cream, past sidewalk cafes and motor scooters parked together like a school of fish. Luke getting stopped, then stopped again, by young people with startling hair, girls and boys both, and asked for photos. He told Hayden, after the third time, "I never wanted to be famous."

"Odd, isn't it," Hayden said, "that you didn't get there by being a rugby captain, or not exactly."

"Yeh," Luke said. "For my sex life. There's a startling development." And grinned.

It took an hour to walk to the basilica, and then there were the three hundred steps up a winding spiral staircase to the dome. Luke went first, but turned back and checked on Hayden so many times that Hayden got a bit narky about it.

"If you ask me how I'm going one more time," he said, trying and failing not to make the words come out in gasps, "I'm going to tell you to go up there alone."

Luke smiled. "Right, then. I won't ask. But if it's too much …"

"Yeh," Hayden said, thinking, *What is this? Thirty floors? There isn't enough aerobic conditioning in the world.* "What will you do? Carry me?"

"I could," Luke said, and he was grinning now.

Hayden forced his feet on. "I know you could. Stop telling me so. I'm feeling desperately unfit."

"Nah," Luke said. "I can't write a contract, so there's that."

"Ha," Hayden said, and wondered a little wildly, *Has anybody ever had a heart attack trying this? They must've done. Especially if they're trying to keep up with an international rugby forward.*

When they got to the top, though, it was worth it. Only a few people up here, braving the admission fees and the climb. The breeze blowing through the open arches, ruffling Hayden's hair. The swallows swooping over the roofs with their narrow, pointed wings and long, pointed tails, exactly the way Nyree had painted them.

Hayden said idly, "There's a rain cloud out there. We could get wet, walking home." That was a surprise, as clear as the day had been, only a few faint wisps of cloud showing even now in the evening sky.

"That's not a cloud," Luke said. "That's a murmuration."

"Is it locusts?" Hayden asked, trying to make out what he was seeing. "Or what?"

"It's swallows," Luke said. "Symbol of love and marriage, here in France. The Chinese say they're born of the tears of the gods. I should've told Nyree that. She'd have liked it."

A dark wave against the deep-blue sky, changing shape as if it were made of liquid, flowing like sand through an hourglass. An oval, then a funnel, growing larger and larger, and Hayden couldn't breathe.

"How many are there?" he asked quietly.

"There can be a hundred thousand or more," Luke said. "We got lucky."

"How do they know what to do?" Hayden asked. "How do they choreograph that?" It was a ballet, if a ballet were made up of tens of thousands of pieces flowing like a single entity. Like a hundred thousand birds in one body.

"Dunno," Luke said. "Reckon they fly with their neighbor. Sometimes, teamwork's better."

Hayden hummed, and they watched in silence as the birds formed and re-formed, as they flew upward in a column, then rushed down again and spread into a thin oval. Finally, Luke said, "You're going home tomorrow."

Hayden's hands tightened on the stone balustrade. "Yeh." He tried to think of something funny to say, and couldn't. It was another black wave, of desolation this time.

"I'm turning thirty-four," Luke said.

"I know," Hayden said. "Wish I could be here for your birthday."

"There's a time," Luke said, his eyes still on the swallows, "when you have to hang up the boots and find something else to do. I've hung on a year too long, maybe. Thinking this was all I have, that it's all I am." He turned, finally, and looked at Hayden, and there was so much in his eyes. Sorrow, and weariness, and something else.

Caution. And, maybe ... hope.

Hayden couldn't slow his heart. He couldn't catch his breath. "It's not all you are," he said. "You're a beautiful soul." He tried to laugh, but couldn't. "Sounds odd, but you are. I don't think you know half of what you are. Half of what you can be."

"Maybe I don't," Luke said. "But I'd like to find out."

"So ..." *Harden up*, Hayden tried to tell himself, and couldn't. "What are you saying?"

"I've been thinking," Luke said, "about what's next. I want to take some time, then decide. Isaiah wasn't right about the two million dollars a year, but he wasn't too far off. I'm thinking, maybe ... build some luxury houses. Something like that. Something I can do with my hands, as my hands are the part of me that works the best. Them and my back, anyway. I know what looks good, too. What makes people happy, I think."

"Oh?" Hayden wanted to hear the rest, and he didn't.

"And the other thing I know is ..." Luke had that flush mounting on his cheeks, his ears, and Hayden realized he was nervous. A wave of tenderness flooded him, and he thought, *He's like me. He's so much like me.*

"I know," Luke went on doggedly, "that I want to ... I need to see what we have together. If we're in the same place. If we're willing to give it all we've got, and if that's enough."

"I can ..." Hayden had to stop and take a breath. "I'd like that. In fact ..." He tried to laugh. "It's all I want."

Luke's smile started slowly, then grew. "Yeh?"

"Yeh," Hayden said.

"The question is," Luke said deliberately, "where."

476

"Oh. Where." Hayden thought, *You have to tell the truth. You have to be yourself.* "I can't work in France," he forced himself to say. "Or in the UK. Law's very … region-specific. That's all law is, in fact. I want to be with you, too, but I like what I do. I know it's not exactly glamorous, but it suits me, I've trained hard for it, and I like it."

Luke was smiling again. "Well, you see, that's why I'd be moving there. To En Zed."

"Oh." Hayden sagged against the balustrade and tried to catch his breath. "OK, then."

"But no worries," Luke said, "I'm going to ask you something hard anyway. Does it have to be Auckland, or …"

"It's not a big country," Hayden said. "And I don't think I'm that picky." He felt like he was climbing those stairs again, because his heart was galloping. "But I'm a *bit* picky. I don't want to live in … Gore. Invercargill. Hamilton, for that matter. Bulls, where you have to name your business some awful pun, or you don't fit in. What would I call my law practice? 'Feas-i-bull?' 'In-del-i-bull?'"

Babbling again.

Why was it so hard to believe?

Why was it so hard to hope?

Luke shouldn't be laughing, but he was anyway, even though he was also more nervous than he could ever remember being in his life. "Cheers for the list of duds. I was thinking, more … could we travel around a wee bit, maybe? See what appeals to us? D'you think you could …" He looked down at his hands. *Fingers like sausages,* Nyree had said, *and knuckles like ping-pong balls.* It was true. He was no prize, in so many ways.

"I probably can," Hayden said, "if you ask me. I'm flexible. There's my sign, for when we move to Bulls. 'Flex-i-bull.' Course, it makes me sound like I'm running a yoga studio."

He was joking, but he probably wasn't, inside. Luke knew that brittle look. He took Hayden's hand and asked. "D'you think you'd want to quit, too? You've said that they're a bit hidebound there, at your work. Pretty buttoned-down. Maybe we could try something more ... casual. Have a life. Or a lifestyle, maybe."

"The gay lifestyle," Hayden said, still trying to joke. "I'm still trying to figure out what that is."

"I think," Luke said, "that it's being together. Being happy. Being ourselves. Living somewhere beautiful and relaxed, and maybe with more than farmers around, so they may not be quite so shocked by us. Someplace where you can still wear shorts in a restaurant, though." He smiled, and wished it were steadier. "Want to toss everything else aside with me and try to find it?"

Hayden took a breath, and then he smiled as, behind him, the swallows soared. "Yes," he said. "What's life, after all, if it's not an adventure? And what could be better than taking that adventure together?"

EPILOGUE

*L*uke had never imagined he'd have a wedding day, much less a flash one.

He and Hayden—and George, the marmalade cat—had settled on living in Wanaka, in the end. In his opinion, the most beautiful place in the world, in his home soil of Otago, pretty cosmopolitan for New Zealand, and with a healthy population of rich people needing both luxury homes and contracts. All good, and living with somebody who loved you—*really* loved you—was even better.

And still, on the early-autumn day when he'd got down on one knee on the shores of Lake Wanaka at sunset with the Southern Alps ranged in the background, he'd asked the question with his heart in his throat and nothing in him believing he could be this lucky.

But Hayden had said yes.

Luke had suggested, when they'd got around to discussing the actual "wedding" part, which took some time, because he'd had to be giddy for a while first, "Keep it small and simple, probably, so there's no fuss."

Hayden had looked at him searchingly. At least Luke thought

that was what it was, though Hayden could just have been enjoying his crème brûlée with passionfruit pulp and mango and coconut gelato. They were in Bistro Gentil at the time. Modern French cuisine with New Zealand meat and produce—what could be better? Especially if you didn't have to pretend it wasn't romantic.

"Is that really what you want," Hayden asked, "or what you think your parents would want?"

So—searchingly, not just excellent crème brûlée.

"I don't know," Luke admitted.

"You don't want to invite your rugby teammates?" Hayden asked. "Our friends here? Have a party, with dancing and all, now that we know how to do the tango? Admit that you were created just for me?"

"Well, yeh," Luke said. "But …"

"How about if we embrace it?" Hayden asked. "Go on and be, you know, out and proud. Ask some of the big queer mags if they'd be interested in sponsoring it, maybe. First major international rugby player to come out while he was still playing, getting married with his teammates from three countries cheering him on? That's a story. Also much cheaper."

Luke had to smile. "I know I'm marrying a Kiwi now, anyway."

"Family's the people who want you," Hayden said. "Not the ones who don't. If your parents think our big, glam gay wedding is disgusting and rubbing people's nose in our fabulous gayness and they'll never be able to show their faces again, or if my dad thinks so, isn't that their loss? You know Nyree and Kane and Zora will be there. So your dad won't drive a few hours from Dunedin. So we never spend Christmas with your family again, or with my parents, either, though my mum's going to put her foot down about that, it's pretty clear, and drag my dad along whatever he says. Don't we want to have Christmas, and our wedding, too, with the people who actually love us? Loving somebody isn't accepting them only if they live the way you want. If we …"

"If we what?" Luke asked. He wouldn't say he was comfortable, exactly, but he was riveted. Hayden had that effect on him. It was like his world had opened up. Like you'd got specs for the first time and could see all the colors and the leaves on the trees.

Now, Hayden was the one who wasn't looking comfortable. "Well, I want to say it, so I'm going to say it. What are we, if we're not honest?"

Luke covered Hayden's hand with his. "Some people have said, since I came out, that I've got mana. I don't have half the mana you do. Go on and say it."

"If we ever want to have kids," Hayden said. "Adopt, use a surrogate, whatever. Isn't that what we want to show them? Would we only love them, accept them, if they turned out to be queer?"

Luke sat stock-still. "No," he said.

"No?" Hayden rocked back a bit, then rallied. "OK, then. Just an idea."

"I don't mean—I don't mean *no*," Luke said. "Not that I don't want to do that. Maybe I'd want to, if I knew how. If I thought I could love a kid right, and have a … a happy home. I mean, no, of course I wouldn't only love them if they played rugby, or loved the right person, or were as clever and beautiful as you, or whatever you're thinking. Though I think that if we go for surrogacy, we should use your sperm." He tried to smile. It wasn't easy. "They'd be prettier, anyway."

"But if they had yours," Hayden said, "they'd be strong. Never mind, we don't have to decide now. OK, then. Back to this glamorous wedding that's going to set the world alight." Trying to be brisk, to be funny, as if he'd opened his heart too fully.

Luke loved him so much, it actually hurt. He remembered that cold, rainy Christmas, when he'd run through Newcastle with Kane, day after day, unable to visualize life in New Zealand with only his dad for company, the bleakness in his heart matching the weather. He'd tried to imagine what happy families did at home, how they spent their time, and failed. Now, he knew. "I want to do what makes you happy," he said. "If that's a big wedding, that's what I want. And I'd like to dance with you." He could see it, suddenly. He could see the photos, and the emails from teenagers, the ones that said, "Thanks for letting me know it's OK." The ones that told him those kids didn't feel so alone anymore, because there was a rugby star who was like them.

Now, he stood beside Hayden in front of the lake and the mountains on a warm December afternoon, two years to the day after they'd met, under a floral arbor that Zora and Rhys and the kids had spent the morning decorating, all crimson, white, and gold. Everything about them saying, "We're here, we're doing this, and we aren't one bit ashamed to tell you so." Wearing charcoal trousers and a white dress shirt so fine, you could pass it through his wedding ring, looking at Hayden wearing the same thing, and not worrying about how many rugby players were watching him do this, or that his parents weren't happy, even though they'd come. Just grateful that the people he cared about most had decided they wanted to be here.

He was getting married to the love of his life.

Pretty awesome, really.

Sometimes, you couldn't be insouciant.

The celebrant started to talk. Hayden knew what he was going to say, because he'd written the service, with help from Luke. They'd written their own vows, too, so he knew his already, though he didn't know what Luke had done. Something simple, probably. He knew what their rings looked like, brushed platinum from Tiffany, each boasting a discreet, inset baguette diamond, and he knew what the inscription inside his said.

To H from L. Love you forever.

And still, his cold hand shook in Luke's.

The day was warm, the sun glorious, the lake sparkling blue beneath the mountains, the videographer recording for posterity and somebody else paying for the whole thing, and still, his hands were cold.

Luke looked at him, and Hayden wondered how he'd ever thought Luke was guarded, because there was honesty in that look that made his knees tremble. Luke told the celebrant, "One sec."

Wait, Hayden thought in a sort of daze. *What?*

Luke said, low enough that the crowd of two hundred-plus couldn't hear him, "We've got this. I just need you to hold my hand, and we'll do it together. OK?"

"Yeh," Hayden managed to say. "OK." And was grounded again.

The celebrant's words, going by in a kind of dream, Hayden's vows, which he somehow dredged up from memory, and then Luke's.

"I promise to love you," the big, bearded man opposite him said, the flush rising all the way to his cauliflower ears. "To hold you when you need me, and to let you hold me when I'm the one who needs it. I promise to walk with you until the end. I promise to care more about you than I do about myself, and to give you everything I have until the day I die."

Hayden thought, *Oh, my God. I cannot believe this is happening. I can't believe you're mine.* And then Luke went on, a twist of a smile around his mouth, his hand around Hayden's like he'd never let go. "I told you this once before, and I'm going to say it again. It seemed to work pretty well the first time, and you know I only have so many words, so here it is. I'm not quick or clever, and there's nothing flash about me and never will be. I'm strong as oak, though, and I'm steady as hell. I don't hurt, I don't lie, and I don't cheat. I stand solid, and where I stand, I stay. That's a promise."

You could call that a vow.

Hayden had always had a hopeful heart. Finally, the hope was justified.

Finally, the hope was here.

EXPLORE MORE

- Luke's kumara salad with caramelized onions and citrus dressing (Kumara are sweet potatoes/yams)
- The Fendi scarf Hayden gives Luke
- The Royal Copenhagen Full Lace Serving Bowl!
- *The Kissing Hand*
- "Beast" Mtawarira lifting his man over his head, Sharks rugby
- Highlights of Italy v. Ireland in Rome, 2023. (No rugby game is ever easy, no matter the teams' records.)
- Paris viewed from the top of Sacre-Coeur
- A murmuration
- Bistro Gentil, Wanaka
- Rippon Hall wedding venue, Wanaka
- Hayden & Luke's wedding rings

ABOUT THE AUTHOR

I met my husband Rick at UC Berkeley when I was 21, so I really do believe in True Love and Happily Ever After—which helps a lot in writing about them! We renewed our vows a few years ago with the help of our two grown sons. Our home base when we're not having our own adventures is in Berkeley, California, where the summers are foggy and the food shopping is the greatest.

WHY NEW ZEALAND: My husband's job as an engineer, and mine as a marketing consultant, have given us the opportunity to live in many different wonderful places in the U.S., Australia, and New Zealand. During the latest stint, 15 months living and working in Auckland, I fell in love with New Zealand: the beauty and diversity of the landscape (not to mention the seascapes), the Maori culture and its integration into the country's life, and, perhaps more than anything, the people: modest, good-humored, unfailingly polite and hospitable, and so very funny. I wanted to share what I loved so much about the country with everyone I knew—and didn't know!

THE BOOKS: We had traveled to Wellington to watch the final of the Rugby World Cup in a pub as the start of a North Island holiday. I was absolutely overwhelmed by the intensity of All Black fever that gripped the entire nation during the World Cup, and the stature of the players themselves at all times. I had never seen anything remotely like it. I started wondering what it would be like to be so intensely admired and instantly recognizable in a country that has zero tolerance for bad behavior—and how hard it would be to find the right partner in that kind of spotlight. And that is where

JUST THIS ONCE was born—walking through the rhododendron gardens of Mt. Taranaki, two days after the World Cup final. Writing that first page was terrifying, but within weeks, I knew that I'd finally figured out what I wanted to be when I grew up.

Sign up for my newsletter, get all the inside scoop, and never miss a release! www.rosalindjames.com/newsletter

LOVE WINS

CYNTHIA ST. AUBIN

AUTHOR'S NOTE

In deciding which of my existing characters I wanted to invite to be part of this anthology, the answer came to me almost immediately: Katherine Abernathy, trouble-causing younger sister of art-loving werewolf Mark Abernathy from the Tails from the Alpha Art Gallery Series. As readers of the series know, Kat makes a bit of mischief for Hanna and the crew in the first book of series but retreats to plot behind the scenes for the next several stories. She'll be making her grand re-entry into the narrative soon, along with a character you'll meet in the following pages, and I thought, what better way to introduce them both than a twisted retelling of sibling-centric Hansel & Gretel? Against the backdrop of a fairy tale classic—with a few other familiar favorites peppered in—Kat finally gets her say, and her perfect match. I hope you enjoy!

   -Cynthia

CHAPTER 1

SOMEWHERE SCOTTISH, 1691

ove at first sight.
Much like *happily ever after*, it's a concept I've always hated.

In my opinion, they're about the laziest ways to begin or end a story.

Completely unrealistic as well.

Because the first sight is never the one that matters. The one that matters is three years down the road when the bloke who once made you blush starts leaving his toenail cuttings all over the privy and tossing his trews on the floor. Or worse, ceases wearing trews *at all* when he's at home.

Show me a lass who hasn't wanted to kick her man's hairy coin purse when he's bent over the woodstove, and I'll show you a liar.

But my brother *was* a man—at least sometimes—so he didn't understand this.

Unlike me, Mark Andrew Abernathy, the great bloody doofus, still believed in love at first sight *and* happily ever afters.

This fact was annoyingly, disgustingly obvious as I sat across the sticky pub table from him, enduring the pathetic, puppyish look of longing in his eyes.

Across the noisy hovel, the object of his affection flounced up to a table of weary travelers, boring them with a soliloquy that lasted at least a fortnight on the various cheese offerings of the Drunken Goat Inn.

I could tell by the glazed look in their weary eyes that they've tuned her out, but their rapt attention is still fixed on the tits that her corset has squeezed up to the base of her neck. They're not half bad if I'm honest.

The tits, not the travelers.

The wench they belong to was tall as well, but not what you'd call delicate. Particularly not the hips, which were round enough to balance a full tray brimming with ale glasses.

A fact not lost on the louts drooling down their dirty doublets.

"I'd wager there's more wood beneath that table than beneath their arses," I said, attempting to wrest my brother's gaze from the basic bar floozy.

Mark gave me a half-hearted grunt of acknowledgment, not even pretending to listen.

I shoved a half-empty stew bowl directly at his chest, feeling a pulse of satisfaction when it caught him hard in the sternum.

"Gonnae no dae that, Kat," my giant, dumb lug of a sibling growled, batting the bowl aside.

My hand flashed out to catch it before it could sail off the table's edge and burst to bits on the inn's muck and straw-covered floor, drawing attention to our presence.

"You might as well save the heavy artillery, Mark. *She cannae hear ye*," I mocked, doing a decent job of approximating a Scots brogue thicker than the spring mud stuck to everyone's boots.

It was easier to slip into than I was altogether comfortable with.

Like my brother, I was born in the Highlands, but we've lived abroad long enough to have lost the burr when we talk to each other.

Which we did less and less these days.

"It's not her," I said, picking up my glass of what passed for

Scotch in a place like this. For the first time in as long as I could remember, I thought longingly of Caisteal Abernathy, where there were bottles older than Christ's nappies in our father's wine cellar.

"You don't know that." Mark's normally warm and resonant voice was flat and cold.

"Just because she's working in a shifter-friendly pub doesn't mean she's one of us," I pointed out.

His jaw flexed, and his eyes narrowed as one of the men at her table made a lewd gesture behind her oblivious back. "Not yet, maybe."

I heaved a disgusted sigh and sagged back in the uncomfortable chair. "How many times have we been through this now? Twenty? Fifty?"

"Five." He managed to pack the short syllable with a significant amount of pain. Eighty years ago, it might have been able to reach me. Now, it just intensified my already simmering irritation.

Still, I knew my brother. He was as bloody-minded as he was optimistic and wouldn't let it go until he'd had the chance to rule her out himself.

The sooner, the better.

The odor of livestock and sweat stewing with the constant din of braggadocious lowland males in rut gave me the hives.

Sticking two fingers in my mouth, I whistled, feeling an ugly little surge of satisfaction when my brother and several patrons winced and covered their ears. Others, including the waitress with flaming red hair, stared at them, perplexed.

She hadn't heard anything at all.

I aim a smug smile at my brother. "Ye were saying?"

"Just because she's *the heir* doesn't mean she has abilities, Kat."

His stating this like a foregone conclusion did little to comfort me.

We both glanced across the hall just in time to see one of the men clap her on the backside. Before Mark could launch himself out of his chair, the wench whirled and pinned the offending hand to the table with a meat fork. Smiling cheerfully, she whispered something that stole the color from his face.

"All right, so maybe this one's not *exactly* like the others," I admitted grudgingly.

My brother leaned forward, his huge body practically twitching with excitement. "Did ye see how fast she moved?"

"Aye, I said. "But there could be a million explanations for that. And most of them more likely than her being this werewolf heir you've been on about for over a century."

"The prophecy is real, Kat." For the first time that evening, he turned to give me his full attention. Though it's the very thing I've wanted, I felt an unexpected pang of sadness.

He's looking more like our father every year.

Prominent cheekbones. The brutal cliff of a jaw. Dark, watchful priest's eyes that could convince a person to do anything.

To believe anything.

Just as I had these many years.

"Let's say for just one minute that I still believe your ridiculous theory that there's some magical werewolf bloodline that has the power to restore order to the entire shifter kingdom and bring about a period of eternal peace and prosperity." I picked at a knot in the wood with the tip of my finger. "You're telling me that you honestly believe that fire-haired *ruadh* over there who just shoved an entire wedge of Brie in her mouth when she thought no one was looking is the one who's going to do it?"

A strange little smile curled the corners of my brother's lips as he watched her steal a second bite. "Yes."

My irritation receives a violent shove from mild to murderous. My brother may have inherited our father's looks, but I inherited Joseph Abernathy's temper.

"Ninety-three years you've dragged me from hell to Haaf Gruney, every single time insisting that this one was definitely the heir, and never *once* have you shared with me how you know," I said, slapping the table with my open palm. "Not to mention the various insults and injuries I've endured at the hands of these hussies."

"Ach, here we go." Mark crossed his arms over his broad chest like a barrier against my well-worn discontent.

"I've been stabbed—" I began.

"With a cockle fork," he countered.

"Shot at—"

"Her aim was nothin' to brag of."

"Vomited on—"

"She was possessed of a banshee."

"And baptized with a whole host of other bodily fluids I'd rather not call to mind, and after all this time, you *still* haven't found her."

My brother reached for his mug. "That's where you're wrong, Kat. I've been right every single time."

My mouth cracked open in a gape.

"They get to choose. The others have chosen—"

"To either try and murder us outright or flee you like the fecking plague."

Hurt flickers in the depths of his eerie eyes, transforming them into molten bronze. I can see him as he was when we were children for the briefest of seconds. Full of boyish enthusiasm and protective anger.

"How do you know this one will be any different?" I asked, placing both hands on the table before me. "How do you know that *any* of them will?"

Mark reached out and covered my hands with his. There's old comfort in the gesture despite the myriad crumbs stuck to my palms.

"The same way I know we need to do this together," he said. "We both have a role to play in finding the peace neither of us has ever had, Kat."

That *my* role was to traipse around on his coattails attempting to make sure some strawberry-headed tart got the chance to turn

497

down the offer of the kind of power I knew *I* could use to the good had officially begun to chap my arse.

But like most men of my acquaintance, my brother had never entertained the idea that if a female shifter of a royal bloodline was needed to restore order, that shifter might possibly be *me*.

"I don't want to do this anymore, Mark," I said. "I'm tired of searching for the heir."

"You could go back and marry Angus MacLeod," he teased. "Have yourself a whole pack of bairns with hair as black as the Earl of Hell's waistcoat."

The flippant suggestion is a bellows aimed straight at the seething rage at menfolk in general I've had a harder and harder time keeping concealed as of late. Perhaps it's a function of having crossed my first century on the planet, but I've begun to chafe under the bridle of their unquestioned rule. Their wars and weddings.

"What he'd have is a silver blade buried between his arse and his ballocks if he ever tried to bring that drooping meat sword near me."

My words vibrated with revulsion at the memory. Since we'd been children, Angus MacLeod had been flipping up his kilt to show off his exceedingly mediocre man tackle.

But it was more than that.

I'd known what I was before he and his slack-jawed brothers started calling me a *lass-licker*.

Once the betrothal contract between Angus and me had been set, I'd had no choice but to pluck up the courage to explain to my father I had no interest whatsoever in tupping with the male of the species after anguished years of keeping the truth to myself.

Joseph Abernathy had risen from his chair, placed a hand atop my two-and-twenty-year-old head, and told me not to worry. My relief had been remarkably short-lived when he followed his reassurance with the declaration that a man can just as easily sire a bairn on a woman who wants a chambermaid as he can on one who wants a Laird. That, if I played my cards right, Laird Angus MacLeod might actually enjoy watching me *with* a chambermaid.

And that had been the end of that.

Faced with marriage to Angus as the only other alternative, I had been all too eager to accompany Mark when he first proposed the idea of our leaving our ancestral home.

Not because I gave two shytes about this mysterious heir he was obsessed with. But because *I* was obsessed with the idea of freedom.

"Tell me how ye really feel, why dinny ye?" Mark said, drawing me out of the unpleasant fog of memory.

My words caught below a knot at the base of my throat. I'd harbored these feelings so long that I hadn't expected speaking them out loud to be this difficult.

"I'm through searching, Mark. I'm pure done in." I lean toward him to be heard over the din. "I'm not coming with ye this time."

All traces of levity evaporated from his features. "What would you do? Where would you go?"

"Dinnae ken." I shrugged. "I hadna really thought about it."

"You have." Mark pulled his hands away from mine. "And for a while, I'd wager."

He knew me that well.

"I've always wanted to see the Colonies," I said, tracing the ring's wet circle from Mark's stout mug.

"You hate sea voyages," he pointed out. "You couldn't sale from Aberdeen to Edinburgh without baptizing the mackerel the whole way."

"Aye," I said, lifting eyes of our mother's green to meet his. "Which is why I only intend to make the journey once."

A crease appeared in the center of my brother's broad forehead. "You mean not to come back."

"There's nothing for me here, Mark. Save our father's filthy reputation. I want to go somewhere I can make my own fortunes."

"Aye," he snorted. "Because nothing says fortunes like Puritanism."

I fixed him with a chilly look. "At least they see women as *spiritual* equals."

Mark studied his glass of muddy brown beer. "Nay," he said. "You'll not be going. It's oot the question."

I blinked at him, outrage, and rage-rage warring for supremacy within my corset-constricted chest. "Noo jist haud on," I said, my sharp tongue tripping back into our native dialect. "How's it ye think ye can tell me what to do?"

Mark leaned forward to rest his massive forearms on the table. "I'm your older brother. Failing our Da, isnae a county or country that wouldna put me in charge of ye."

Great gouts of heated blood sizzled into my veins, filling me with the bitterest of gall. Whatever my face might've been doing, it caused Mark's to soften.

"It isna safe for you to travel without me to protect ye."

"Protect me from who?" I challenged, folding my arms across my chest.

"Highwaymen. Thieves. Pirates," he ticked off on thick fingers.

"So, we agree that men are the problem, then?"

Lately, I'd been hoping for it. Inviting it, almost. The chance to defend myself rather than allowing Mark to do it for me. To see what I could do, permitted the full use of my teeth and claws.

"Aye," he allowed. "They're the problem, all right. And that's not like to change anytime soon."

He said this more as a pronouncement of inevitability than a lament.

I had my own ideas about remedying this but didn't dare speak them aloud.

Certain parts of myself had always been safer to keep hidden.

"I've already booked my passage, Mark." I turned my torso to reach into the leather satchel hanging on the back of my chair and pulled out the tattered piece of paper with elaborately looping script.

I held it out to him, not wanting to sully it with any mysterious substances smudging a table that probably hadn't seen a decent washing in a decade.

My brother's eyes moved quickly over the paper, the corners of his mouth tugging downward. His knuckles whitened, and for a moment, I feared I might have made a terrible mistake. He could tear it to shreds quicker than I could blink.

Or at least quicker than a human could blink.

"I assume you've already arranged transport to Liverpool?" he asked.

"Aye."

"When do ye leave?"

I looked at the wooden clock on the dingy wall beside the inn's main door. "Half an hour."

The noise and bustle of the inn died away as our gazes locked across the table. A reflection of the fire flickering from the hearth danced in my brother's eyes, merging with the memory of every blazing Yule log, every solstice fire. The years of our long lives lived in such proximity and were now destined to part.

"Kat, I—"

"Whit's like?" That damnable flame-haired wench asked, interrupting what might be their last chance for a tender moment as siblings.

Why hadn't I scented her? Or heard the approach of her footsteps? It wasn't like subtlety was her strong point.

"No bad, an' yourself?" Mark said, pouring on the brogue.

I pushed my still half-empty glass across the table. "I'll not have any more of that dragon pish," I said. "I'd sooner drink rainwater from the hog trough."

If the insult had landed, the serving wench gave no clue. "Might be an improvement, actually," she said with a little bounce that jiggled her ample cleavage. "Seeing as I'm responsible for feeding them. I make sure the hogs get a nice mix of fresh kitchen scraps, barley, and suet. Put a little burner under it, and you'll have a cracking soup. Speaking of, we have a lovely cock-a-leekie this evening if you'd care to try it." Cupping her hand to her downy cheek, she leaned conspiratorially toward us. "They make me say that as part of me job, but definitely don't try it. It's basically tattie water and sadness."

I narrowed my eyes at the wide green ones sparkling down at me.

Don't you fecking dare make me like you.

Wouldn't dream of it.

Wood scraped against grimy stone as I jerked back in my chair.

It happened like that sometimes. When I could pick a thought out of the air like a ripe plum.

But never involuntarily.

"I'd tell you about our other specials," she continued. "But they're just as bad. What isn't terrible is—"

"The cheese," Mark finished for her.

Her cheeks flushed at the broad smile my brother beamed up at her.

"It comes from a quaint little farm just beyond the forest outside town. A country idyl of green fields and misty mornings warmed by the sun—"

"Aye. Sounds lux. We'll take the cheese plate," I cut in to spare the wench the rest of her spiel. After all, I only had three and twenty minutes before I was supposed to meet my carriage.

"Excellent choice." The look she gave me held nothing but warmth and kindness.

Which pissed me right the hell off.

"I'll have that right out for ye," she said. "Can I bring ye more stout as well?"

"Please," Mark said. Their fingers brushed as she reached for his glass, and he tried to push it to her. The table jumped as he jerked upon contact. The smile evaporated from her moony face as they stared at each other.

Unable to contain my curiosity, I accidentally-on-purpose brushed the side of her palm as I reached for my napkin.

Nothing. Not one damn thing.

"What did you say your name was?" I asked.

"I didn't," she said, sounding hypnotized, her eyes fixed on my brother's.

"Hanna," Mark said. "Her name is Hanna."

The wench's eyelashes lowered to her lightly freckled cheeks. A single tear beaded below them and slipped down to the corner of her full lips. "How did you know?"

Because they've all been Hanna, I wanted to shriek at her. *You're nothing special. No different than the rest.*

My brother lifted her hand from the table and pressed it between his, deepening the strength of their connection. Speaking to part of her mind both private and primal.

"I know because you're the chosen werewolf heir who will unite the shifter kingdom and end our bitter battle with humans for all time, issuing in an era of peace and prosperity the likes of which the world has never known. You're the alpha, and I'm the Omega. We are the end and the beginning, and together, we'll complete the cycle."

The glazed look in her eye evaporated, and she shook her auburn head like a bird that had just run into a glass pane. The overwide grin returned to her features. "Has he been licking any toadstools that you know of?" she asked through the side of her mouth.

"All his life," I reported.

"Riiight," she said. "I'll be right back with that cheese."

Hanna sashayed away, bumping a table, and accidentally upending another wench's tray on her way to the bar.

"You ever thought that your delivery might be part of the problem?" I asked, massaging a tight spot on my temple.

My brother stared after her with an expression of such longing it almost brushed the desiccated petals of my cold, dead heart.

I'd seen this look before.

Five times to be exact.

This one wouldn't end any better than the others. And I had no intention of being here to see it.

Shifting in my rickety chair, I looked toward the door. I could get an early start, maybe. The road to Glasgow passed a well at the top of the hill. I could meet the carriage there. It would be easy to spot with the light of the almost-full moon.

So why wasn't I reaching for my cloak?

Why did my legs feel like they were welded to this stupid cheap splintery chair in this grease-coated people-pustule of a pub?

The answer was, as always, right in front of me.

My brother.

The boy who'd bloodied young Angus MacLeod's nose the first time he'd stuck a tree branch beneath my skirts, trying to get at me under things. The boy who had fought off a wild boar when I had insisted on taking a path through the forest he thought unsafe. The young man who told our father to go fuck himself with a fireplace poker when he had said that if I left, I would inherit nothing. The man whose unfailing belief in a magic solution to a terrible world had made me want to believe as well.

Once upon a time.

"I hope she's the one," I whispered.

Mark nodded, his unflinching gaze still fixed on his Hanna.

Trying to keep my movements as small as possible, I shimmied my arms into the sleeves of my traveling cloak and pulled the hood over my hair. I swung my knees to the side and gingerly lifted the satchel to my shoulder, careful not to bump the table as I stood and walked away from the table, unseen by my brother and everyone.

It was the one aspect of my mother's crimson-red cloak that hadn't made it into the secondhand story of how my parents met.

That, and the woodsman.

History was always eager to find a man to saddle with the credit. The idea that a fabled werewolf hunter like *Petit Rouge* would *decide* to shag the big bad wolf instead of bringing back his head on a pike just wasn't as sexy to the patriarchy.

Insufferable fuckwits.

The inn's heavy wood door squealed as I opened it, but only I heard.

The exterior was cool and damp beneath my palms as I shoved it closed without anyone being the wiser. I pulled in a deep breath, scented of rain and tender green spring.

I was invisible but all-seeing, I was silent but all hearing.

I was stealth itself. I was the night.

I was...very surprised by the razor-sharp tip of a silver arrow nocked directly at my neck.

CHAPTER 2

"*Y*ou know the cloak doesn't make you invisible, right?" Shadow swallowed the source of a voice both smoky and smooth. Neither masculine nor feminine but somehow embodying the best parts of both. Melodic. Lyrical. Seductive.

Mediterranean?

"Aye." My audible swallow drove the steely point further into my windpipe. "Of course, I know that. What kind of fool wouldn't?"

"The kind at the end of my arrow."

Why this sent a shiver down my spine, I had no idea.

"About that," I said. "If it's money you want—"

"It's not."

"Then what?"

"You," the voice said in a honeyed rasp.

"You don't."

"I do."

"No, but you really don't," I insisted.

"No, but I really do."

Exhaustion invaded my bones, turning them to lead. "This may be a good time to let you know that I am not, in fact, a human female."

"What kind of fool would I be if didn't know that?"

"The kind pointing an arrow at a creature who could cheerfully relieve you of your throat with a single jerk of its jaws," I said.

"I guess it's a good thing neither of us are fools, then."

Metallic acid ate at the base of my throat and glued my tongue to my teeth. "While we're on the topic of not being foolish, you should know I have no interest in being a receptacle for your cock."

The arrow's tip retracted from my neck with a creak I recognized as a bow losing tension.

"I don't have a cock."

Moonlight silvered cheekbones that could cut diamond as the face emerged from the shadows. A strong jaw, but not a masculine one. Dark brows, but not woolly. Not a chin cleft, but a single sunken dimple. Despite being cut short, the glossy feathers of inky hair revealed fine temples and a smooth brow.

No. Not a man.

A woman capable of frightening them.

"What do you want with me?"

"With you? Nothing. From you? Cooperation."

"Considering I could have summoned an entire pack of ravening wolves to my side by now, you can consider this cooperation," I said.

"Nice try, my lady." The flicker of a grin curled one corner of her lips. "Your pack can't stand you. Otherwise, you wouldn't be slipping away from your own brother."

My stomach somersaulted within my rib cage. "Who are you?"

The pointed tip of the arrow delicately brushed the underside of my jugular. "Someone who could kill you but is choosing not to."

"My eternal thanks," I drawled. "Should I throw my petticoat at you now? Or wait until we're in better light?"

Her mouth came near enough to my ear for me to *feel* her words. "You're not wearing a petticoat. You prefer to ride bareback and the fabric bunches."

Sand filled my throat. The longer I listened to that voice, the more I felt it winding itself around the base of my spine like a ribbon around a maypole. "Okay, now I *definitely* need to know who you are."

"In good time," she said. "You booked passage on the *Adventure*, correct?"

"How do you know that?"

"Anyone with half a wit in the pub would know it, the way you were flashing that letter around."

Whether the shock had worn off enough for me to recover my senses, or it finally occurred to me to notice details, I caught the subtle rubied glow of her coat. Cut not as a cloak, like mine, but fitted to her lean torso and hips. Generous hoods were the sole similarity.

"You're one of The Order," I said, several facts clicking into place.

Always spoken in hushed and reverent tones, the elite, highly-secretive, and mysterious organization of women had always intrigued me. Wearing blood-red cloaks and carrying baskets of gear suited to their covert purposes, they quietly wove the warp and weft of history.

I knew this because my mother had been part of it.

As witnessed by the crimson cloak she had given to me before her passing.

"Bold of you to wear this," my would-be abductress said. "Considering what your mother did."

"Determine her own destiny?"

"Betray her vows."

My heart dropped into my guts with a sickening splat. The oily stew I'd choked down mostly out of desperation began climbing the walls of my stomach.

She knew.

"We'll discuss that later," she said as if drinking in my thoughts. "For now, we need to ride."

"I appreciate the offer, but I've a coach to catch."

"No, you don't."

"Yes, I do."

"No, you don't." She lifted the arrow to the moonlight, and I noticed a faint dark gleam streaking its shaft. "Seeing as I just pulled this out of the driver's cranium."

I blinked at her, the first fingers of cold fear stealing into my rib cage as she shouldered her bow and gracefully tucked the arrow back into its quiver.

"Your driver had solid silver dagger tucked in the back of his breeches that he intended to drive straight into your silly heart."

My mind whirled with this new information. "How do I know *you're* not the one who intends to kill me?"

She took a step toward me. "Scent me."

All moisture suddenly evaporated from my mouth. "Pardon?"

The night glinted blue off her hair as she cocked her head. "You're meant to be an apex predator, aren't you? You ought to know a threat." The fine shoreline of her jaw lifted, exposing a smooth expanse of neck. I both saw and smelled the faint pulsing of her jugular vein. "Scent me."

My face turned to her like a flower to the sun and I dragged my nose over the warm silk of her skin. The scent receptors in my sinuses quadrupling as the primal part of me hunted to the surface.

She'd ridden through a rainstorm in a forest. Ozone and leather. Alder. Oak. Rowan. Wild cherry. Pollen and mold spores. The decadent spice of red wine.

Something else.

Deeper. Warmer. Like the freshly turned earth in autumn.

Arousal.

Quite of its own volition, my body matched its rhythms to hers. Breath for breath. Heartbeat for heartbeat. Every flutter, quiver, and clench she experienced, I experienced too.

Love at first...*scent?*

I lifted my lips and nose from her neck, our breaths in a cantilevered panting rhythm.

All at once, I *knew.*

She felt it, too. Saw what I saw. Smelled what I smelled.

It's how she had known I wasn't wearing a petticoat. And that I like to ride bareback. She could smell the horsehair on my naked thighs beneath the layers of my travelling dress and cloak.

The effect of this knowledge was even more devastating than her words had been.

"I'd like to rephrase my original question," I said, dizzy, and breathless.

"Yes?" Her voice was husky.

"*What* are you?"

Slim, surprisingly strong fingers closed over my throat as her eyes flared orange like glowing coals in the shadows. "Salvation."

I pulled my cloak tighter around me against the early spring chill. The rain was coming hard and fast.

The mysterious huntress stalked around the side of the pub, where a giant black mount was secured to the wooden fence post with a rope lead.

"Get on," she ordered, working at the coarse chords with deft, leather-gloved fingers.

I stared from her to the horse and felt a nib of fear growing roots in my belly. "I appreciate the offer, but I don't need to be saved."

She tossed the rope over the horse's thick neck and patted its flank. "Yes, you do."

I planted my feet on the cobblestones. "But I really don't, though."

"But you really do."

"From what, exactly?"

"*You*, to begin with." She bent to tighten the saddle straps. "I could have just ended your life. You practically walked into the tip of my arrow."

"But had you not been there, I could have followed the same trajectory and been none the worse. Which makes this a *you* problem."

She heaved a disgusted sigh. "Are you always this argumentative?"

"Usually, I'm worse," I reported proudly. "You might want to consider that before inviting me to accompany you."

Our eyes locked over the horse's back, and my stomach suddenly elected to turn arse over teakettle.

"What part of our encounter so far suggests to you that this is an invitation?"

"Look...you," I said, realizing I still had no idea what her name was. "I'm more than capable of making my own way to the *Adventure*. I would, however, appreciate it if you don't propel any more metal-tipped wood dowels through the heads of my chosen transport."

"You'd have preferred that I allowed him to stab you?" she asked.

"I have preferred the chance to fend him off myself."

"That wasn't a risk I could allow."

Maybe it was the presence of all that lean muscle, but I was having trouble arranging my thoughts into patterns that resembled common sense. "Did someone hire you to be my bodyguard?"

Bending to dip a wooden bucket in the water trough, she held it to the horse's muzzle while it slurpily drank.

The wire of tension around my rib cage eased incrementally.

No one kind to horses could be all bad.

"It's not your body I'm guarding."

"See, that makes me just a little confused. Because earlier, when I asked, "what do you want," you said 'you.' And if it's not my body..." I trailed off, allowing her to pick up the end of the implication.

"It's your *life*," she said. "Someone would like very much for you not to have one."

"How is that any different than guarding my body?" I asked.

"You're already making me regret taking this assignment," she grumbled, bending to pick a burr from the mount's belly.

I followed suit, idly picking one from its glossy mane. "But really, though. What is your name? I need something to pair with the insulting things I'm saying about you in my head."

"Salvation," she said.

"It's not that I don't appreciate the dramatic effect and all that, but it's really not working for me," I reported.

"That's my actual name. Salvation." She shooed me out of the way to buckle a leather saddle bag onto the horse. "You can call me Sal."

"Your mother named you Salvation?" I couldn't suppress a snort. "I guess it's a good thing she didn't go with Patience or Mercy, otherwise, you'd just be a walking contradiction, and wouldn't that be embarrassing?"

Sal allowed me a good wallow in my own cleverness before lowering the boom.

"I never knew my mother. As a baby, I was dropped off on the Order's doorstep in a picnic basket. Reverend Mother was the one who named me."

It was too early in the season for crickets to churr, but I heard them all the same.

"Well, don't I feel like a horse's shyte-chute?"

My own mother had never spoken of the Order much. Not how she'd become part of it or why she had decided to disobey when she met Joseph Abernathy—widely known as the Big Bad Wolf— that fateful day in the woods. In fact, the only time she'd ever brought it up directly was when she had called me to her side right before she died.

The night she had given me her cloak.

"*Anapnéo.*"

I thought Sal might be talking to me until she patted the horse, and it exhaled a long shuddery breath.

That sounded like—

"Greek."

Had she just—

"And, no, I didn't read your mind, you're just very predictable."

"I think it would be less annoying if you *had*," I said sourly. "No one likes a know-it-all."

"Then you must know a hell of a lot," Sal said without missing a beat. "Get on."

"Not until you tell me where we're going."

She held out a gloved hand to help me mount. "We're going to see the elves."

I actually felt surprised at the little frisson that leaped through my chest. I hadn't experienced any sort of excitement at the prospect of encountering a new creature since before I'd crossed the century mark. Elves were right up there with unicorns in terms of Others my parents had claimed existed, but I had never seen material evidence of.

Reaching into the pockets of my cloak to locate my riding gloves, I slipped them on before threading one hand into the horse's mane and hauling myself up without Sal's assistance.

Sal boosted herself onto the mount's back behind me using muscles I wasn't sure I even possessed. Her torso pressed against my shoulder blades and back as she retrieved the reins.

Sal clicked and gave the horse's flank a gentle nudge with the heel of her boot, and we pelted forward and into the night.

I had always loved to ride.

The rhythm of it. The speed. The way the world blurred, only the ground ahead mattered. How the beating of the horse's hooves sank me into a hypnotic fugue.

At present, it was an altogether different beat invading my thoughts. There was no way Sal didn't feel my heart thrashing around in my ribcage as our hips moved in tandem with the huge horse's powerful gait.

The night wind chilled my cheeks and nose as we thundered

over the hills and into the darkened tree line of the forest. I closed my eyes and let it fill my senses.

The enchantment lasted all of an hour until, predictably, the saddle began to chafe in ways that weren't helping my concentration.

"Can we stop?" I called back to Sal over the thundering of hooves.

"Why?"

"The saddle is killing me."

"Really?" Sal asked, the curious lilt in her voice. "You don't smell dead."

I glanced over my shoulder at her, the night wind whipping my hair into my eyes. "No, but you might if you don't let me get off and run on my own for a while."

My ears continued to ring after we'd slowed to a trot.

"How do I know I can trust you not to run away?" Sal asked.

For the most part, I tried to avoid showing off. I had grown up watching my brother and his friends engage in what seemed like the most ridiculous of contests to demonstrate their lupine prowess.

Even so, seeing Sal's eyes fly wide in surprise when I both dismounted and removed my cloak quicker than she could sneeze came with a stab of satisfaction.

"I'll let you hold this," I said, tossing the garment at her and reaching for the lacings in the back of my dress.

Sal carefully draped the crimson cloth over the saddle. "What do you think you're doing?"

"Undressing." I yanked my stays and took my first unfettered breath of fresh air, free of the crushing grip. "Oh God, that feels good."

"If you hate it so much, then why do you wear it?" Sal asked.

"Because as much as I despise it, I'm still required to transact in the human world, and a woman of my station apparently isn't acceptable unless my waist is the size of a gopher's arse."

I got as far as my shoulder blades, where even with my supernaturally elastic joints, I was unable to finish undoing the lacings. The more I wrestled with the fabric, the more vexed I became.

Mark never had this problem. Men's clothes were designed to be easy to get into and out of at all times. Hell, he could even allow his transformation to shred the garments from his body.

Whereas I, on the unfortunate occasions where I'd shifted without stripping and ended up cinched by the neck or rib cage, yelping as I fought with the cloth and whalebone prison.

"Let me."

I hadn't heard Sal dismount or sensed her behind me until her warm, gloved fingers lifted the dark skein of my hair over my shoulder. Her breath was warm on the back of my neck, raising chill bumps that flooded down my arms.

Three quick tugs and the knot fell free.

"You've done this before," I said.

"Yes."

The syllable moved through me like warm honey. "Does the Order no longer require a vow of chastity?" I asked.

"It does," she said. "But if everyone obeyed it, you'd not be here right now."

I raised my arms and allowed her to draw the garment up my body and over my head, taking my shift with it. Naked in the moonlight, I turned to face her.

Something I'd never dared done had my companion been male.

Sal's angular jaw flexed, her lips pressing together. The delicate nostrils flared on a long inhale as her eyes carved my shape against the dark cloth of the night.

She wanted me.

I could taste it in the air. Sweet as honeysuckle on a summer evening breeze.

"You're beautiful," she whispered.

"I know."

A fine mist of rain began to fall, laying a cool veil over my naked skin. My nipples tightened with the chill, and I didn't miss the flick of Sal's eyes moving to the tightened flesh. Heady, this draft was, settling heavy and warm behind my belly button.

"Can I watch you?" She asked in a voice that made fire lick my insides. "I've never seen anyone shift," she added.

This narrowed my options as to what she might be considerably.

"If you like," I said. Though I had done this more times and could be counted, it felt a sudden stab of trepidation. I'd certainly shifted near someone before, but never for the benefit of an attentive audience. It wasn't the most graceful of processes to watch, but as I'd begun in my formative years, the restructuring of matter separating my human body from my canine one required little pain.

I looked to the moon, finding it behind the clouds by sense alone, and offered up the part of myself connected by a million invisible strands of starlight.

I surrendered to the silvery flash that pulled me to all fours and rolled through me like the tide. The heat of my transformation exited me on a cloud of steam. The fragrant earth was my personal playground. The night was a poem in my nostrils.

"Dude," Sal said.

I cocked my head at her in acknowledgment, as I preferred not to speak in animal form. Not because it was particularly difficult, but there's something inherently ridiculous about a talking animal, and I intensely disliked being ridiculous.

Sitting back on my haunches, I watched Sal gently arrange my cloak and traveling dress across the saddle before securing them with a leather strap.

She swiftly mounted and clicked to the horse, taking off at a gallop.

Her mount neither spooked nor startled as I loped alongside, further narrowing my ruminations about her identity. Faster and faster, she galloped through the trees as I gave chase. Every pattern she set, I mimicked, no matter how complex.

We were no longer running but playing.

Dodging and weaving through the trees, setting in possible paces and challenges in the course until, at last, we reached a clearing and slowed near a massive oak with roots as thick as giants' fingers. I stared open-mawed as an owl hooted somewhere in the darkness, calling to its mate from further in the ominous-looking forest.

Sal dismounted and looped the reins over one of the low-hanging branches. "Might want to lose the fur," she said. "Elves aren't very keen on your kind."

I waited until she held out my dress to release the wolf back into the wild of my mind.

"I'll just have the cloak," I said, the idea of being strapped back into a corset sounding like a unique form of hell after my exhilarating run. "Presentable enough?" I asked.

The corner of her mouth curled upward as she tugged a twig from my hair and flicked it to our feet. "It's been stuck in your fur since the rock pass," she said, stepping around me. "I'd have pulled it out earlier but couldn't reach you from the saddle."

Had she been looking at me that closely all that time?

Such a strange sensation this was after barely drawing my brother's notice for longer than I could remember.

"Why are we here?" I asked.

"This is where we're staying tonight."

I glanced around at the dozens of glowing yellow eyes peering at us through the trees.

"Ye're oot yer mind if you think I'm sleeping out here." While I didn't fancy myself a princess, I had acquired a taste for certain creature comforts.

Like a roof.

"Not out here. In *there*." Approaching the tree's gigantic trunk, Sal considered the gnarly mass of knots climbing its base and pressed her finger firmly into the center of the largest.

"Secret door?" I asked.

Sal raised a dark eyebrow at me. "The doorbell."

Sure enough, a small section of the tree bark creaked inward. The creature who stared out in no way resembled the elegant beings

I had always pictured when elves were mentioned. Instead, with bulbous features, a lumpy red nose, and pointed ears sporting impressive white tufts of hair, the creature looked more like a story-book ogre in miniature than anything I'd envisioned as an elf.

"Password?" he rasped in a voice that suggested he might gargle glass.

Sal's lips flattened in annoyance. "Don't pull that shit with me, Brian. I know damn well there *is* no password."

"Is now," he said.

"If no one ever gave me the password, how am I supposed to give it to you?" Sal asked.

"If no one gave it to you, I'm guessing Ernie doesn't want you here." The door slammed shut with a crack that resounded across the meadow.

Sal glanced beyond her to where I stood, shivering beneath my cloak.

"He's such a cockbiscuit," she grumbled, jamming her finger into the bell again.

The door creaked open to reveal another elf with remarkably similar features and a pointy red hat atop his shiny skull.

"Password?" he croaked.

"You've got to be fucking kidding me," Sal said. "I've been here no less than seventy-eight times, David. You know who I am and why I'm here. Now let us in before I pull your nostrils over your head and hurl you like a bocce ball."

The elf's tiny pink tongue protruded from his mouth, his blunt, thick thumbs screwing into his oversized ears before the door slammed again.

"I can see they fear you," I said, my teeth chattering.

"Since when did werewolves have such a delicate constitution?" Sal shrugged out of her coat and draped it around my shoulders, belting it at my waist.

And that's when I saw her arms.

Long and draped with ropes of lean muscle, each covered with intricate designs I couldn't make out in the dark despite my typically acute vision. Sal reached behind her to shoulder her bow and knock an arrow, each perfectly shaped mounded swell standing out under the tension.

Moisture flooded my mouth as she turned her torso to aim the arrow's tip at the door and kicked it hard with the heel of her boot.

"Follow my lead," she said.

At that precise moment, I would have followed her to the very gates of hell.

When the door creaked open this time, she didn't wait to be asked the password, but booted the small figure through the opening.

I watched in horror as it bounced off something in the background and disappeared into the darkness.

"Did you?" I stammered. "Did you just kick an elf?"

"Everyone knows they bounce," she said. "This way." We both had to duck to get through the entrance.

Once again, my expectations were blown all to hell.

Far from the small, dank, cramped hovel I had expected, the space inside soared to cathedral height. In the center of the Great Hall, a courtyard with raised gardening beds and mature fruit trees surrounded the perimeter. Candles lined the lofty walls, illuminating portraits of women wearing the ubiquitous red hoods of the Order.

"What is this place?" I asked.

"Used to be one of the Order's strongholds," Sal said, pointing her arrow ahead. "They've been subletting to the elves since their numbers have dwindled."

"Werewolf hunting not as lucrative as it used to be?" I asked.

"Not as many of you to hunt," she said.

My stomach tightened at the implication.

We found our less-than-enthusiastic door attendant brushing flower petals from his coat in the squashed geranium bed where he must have landed after ricocheting off the fluted colonnade.

"The wolf stays with you," he grumbled, getting to his feet. "No one else will have her."

"Fine," Sal said, fishing a coin from her pocket and tossing it to him. "For my horse."

"Not fine," I insisted. "I barely even know this woman."

"You know them even less." Sal jerked her chin toward the cloisters surrounding the courtyard, where dozens of the gnome-like creatures were gathering to scorch me with withering glares.

"What about this place made you think I'd be safe here?" I asked from the side of my mouth.

"Because I'm with you."

And weirdly enough, I believed her.

We began walking down the corridor when a pearlescent glob hit the toe of my boot. "They're spitting at me."

"Don't take it too personally," Sal said. "A werewolf ate one of the line supervisors a fortnight ago."

"Line supervisors?" I asked, repeating the unfamiliar term.

No sooner had I asked than we reached a set of double doors emanating a bright white light.

Inside were three long banquet tables, each covered with a leather runner that rolled slowly and steadily down its length. The mechanism of its movement was readily apparent once I stood in the center of the doorway, where I could see the elf-operated cranks.

"Are those...picnic baskets?" I asked.

Sal plucked one from the end of the line and handed it to me. "For later," she said.

"I'm not hungry," I lied. I might have been tempted to bolt down one of the elves if I wasn't confident they'd give me worms.

"It's not food."

Peaking inside, I nearly sliced myself on the razor-sharp dagger secured to the lid. Additional contents included several wooden stakes, a leather sack of black salt, candles, a compass, rope, a small hatched, and a vial of glowing green elixir.

In short, a standard-issue monster-hunting kit.

"They make these for the Order in exchange for living here?" I asked.

"They pay the Order in exchange for living here," Sal said, resuming her long-legged stride toward a door at the back of the room. "These, they make out of duty."

"They pay the order for lodgings *and* put together these baskets for free?"

"Basically."

"This is wrong," I said, glancing at all the small, bedraggled faces. "You're being exploited. You know that, right? The Order is just using you as a source of cheap labor."

"Don't bother," Sal said, but I could scarcely contain my outrage.

"You could walk out of here right now, and there's not one thing they could do to you."

"Feck off, she-wolf," grunted the elf turning the crank nearest me. "I'm union. Three years more years, and I retire in a condo by Candy Lake."

Sal shot a smug glance over her shoulder. "Coming?"

I huffed out a disgusted sigh and jogged to catch up.

We passed additional rooms where various other groupings of workers assembled a stimying variety of items. Rocking horses, whirligigs, jumping ropes, shoes, boots, parasols, and sweets of all shapes, sizes, and flavors.

At last, we turned down a hallway off the main corridor and climbed three sets of stairs that had my thighs screaming after our extended sprint through the forest. Then, halfway down another long hall, a candle flickered in a wrought iron sconce next to a large wooden door.

Sal slowed in front of it and reached into the pocket of her leather vest to pull out an old brass key. The large lock clicked as it opened. She pushed the door out of the way and stood back, bowing slightly at the waist, and waving a hand in an exaggerated gesture of servitude.

"My lady Katherine, our quarters for the evening."

The contents were simple.

One brass bathtub. One old tapestry. One ragged brocade chair was seated next to the one window.

One bed.

My gulp was surely audible.

I jumped at the bracing knock on the other side of the large wooden door.

Sal opened it to reveal one of the elves holding the saddlebags that had been strapped to her mount in one hand and my dress slung over the other.

"Thanks, Bernie." Sal pulled a coin from her leather breaches and flicked it into the air. The elf caught it mid-flip, examining it with beady eyes in the crackling firelight.

"Draw me a bath?" Sal asked, already toeing out of her battered boots.

With one stubby finger, the elf traced the tub's shape in the air and blinked.

A pop, a flash, and steam began to rise from the copper tub.

Sal dropped another coin into Bernie's cupped palm before closing and bolting the door.

I set my satchel down next to the chair and gratefully sank into it. Supernatural constitution or no, weariness had officially set in.

"You want to go first?" she asked. "You look like you could use one."

I had to sit with that one for a moment. Wondering if Sal meant that I looked filthy —which I probably did— or exhausted, which I definitely was.

"You go ahead," I said, staring longingly at the tub. The steaming water looked like heaven, but the idea of sliding off my cloak and bathing under Sal's watchful eye made my head feel light and strange.

"Suit yourself," she shrugged.

With her back to me, she unbuttoned the leather vest and

slung it on the bed. Beneath it, the straps of a harness concealed an arsenal that made the basket look like an actual picnic. The buckle must have been in the front because Sal removed it in one piece, carefully hanging it over the footboard. Seeing all that gleaming metal held my attention until I saw the scars.

Two long thick purple gashes right over her shoulder blades. Mirror images of one another.

Wings.

"You're Fae."

I hadn't known I said it out loud until Sal stiffened.

"No," she said. I'm not.

"Yes," I insisted, "You are."

"No," she argued, "I'm not."

"But, your scars."

Her angular shoulders jerked upward in a shrug. "Had them since I was a babe," she said.

The idea of these kinds of wounds inflicted on one so young filled me with a flash flood of rage. "Haven't you ever wondered have you got them?"

"Seeing as I was left in a picnic basket full of weapons on the doorstep of the Order's fortress, not really."

"And your powers?" I asked.

The muscles of her lower back flexed as she leaned forward to undo her boot buckles. "I don't have any powers."

"Yes, you do."

"No, I don't."

"Yes, you really do."

"No, I really don't."

"How do you explain the fact that you knew I wasn't wearing petticoats?"

Sal turned to face me. My gaze helplessly drifted from her face to her breasts. Small but perfect, nipples hard and a dark auburn over the tawny globes. Below them, her ribcage was almost architectural in its graceful flare, narrowing into lean hips and the flat plane of a stomach interrupted by high-waisted trews.

"I could tell by how your hips moved beneath your skirt."

"Okay," I challenged. "What about knowing how I prefer to ride bareback?"

Sal heaved an exasperated sigh. "I've been following you for three days. When you and your brother arrived in town, his horse was saddled, and yours wasn't. He's not the kind of man who would make you ride without one if there was only one to share."

My heart clenched at her correct assessment as an inexplicable pang of homesickness washed over me.

I hadn't had a home in a very long time.

Home had become the area occupied by the sound of my brother's voice.

"And what about your eyes?" I continued.

Sal propped her foot on a trunk at the end of her bed and peeled back the cuff of her leather breeches to unstrap an additional dagger. "What about them?"

"They were glowing," I said. "Outside the inn, right before you took off your hood."

She folded her arms beneath her breasts. Seeing them in proximity to the elegantly drawn lines dancing over her forearms made it difficult to remember precisely what we were arguing about.

"Were they?" she asked. "Or were they reflecting yours?"

What annoyed me even more than the plausibility of her argument was how much I *wanted* her to be wrong. I wanted her to be something different.

Something like me.

Sal began peeling away her stockings. "You're more powerful than you know, my lady."

I leaned back on the bed and crossed my legs. "I insist all my abductors call me Kat."

Her dark brows drew together in her smooth forehead. "You've been abducted before?"

"Mad that someone beat you to it, are you?"

A wicked light gleamed in eyes that were more greenish than I'd originally thought. "If I were after any of your firsts, Kat, it wouldn't be that one."

I swallowed very, very hard as Sal stuck her thumbs in her breeches and wiggled them down her hips. My teeth sank into my lower lip, and I tore my eyes away before they reached the backs of her thighs.

"I don't mind," she said, smirking at me over her shoulder as kicked the pants aside she and stepped into the bath. Her moan elevated my temperature by several degrees as she sank to her slim, graceful neck.

The very last thing in the world I wanted to do was climb into bed with my skin feeling gritty and sweat salted, but damned if I could sit here, stewing in my own self-loathing for my martyrdom's sake while Sal emitted sexy sighs in her fragrant soaking tub.

Stomping across the room, I yanked my chemise from under my travel dress and tossed it on the bed. I stripped off my cloak without a second thought and pulled the undershirt over me before whipping back the coverlet and climbing in.

The bedding was annoyingly luxurious. An actual feather mattress pad, fine linen head sheet, and fur-lined blanket.

The exact kind of setup you don't want to climb into, feeling like something tumbled from the dustbin.

I wondered where my brother was at this precise moment.

Whether he and Hanna were dozing in a heap of tangled limbs and the glow of firelight.

Whether he'd found his happy ending at last.

A hot tear slipped down my cheek and soaked into the head sheet over the feather pillow. I wasn't even special enough to roll the shifter kingdom, yet someone still wanted me dead. The prospect of setting out on a new adventure with the wind of freedom in my sails ebbed further and further away as exhaustion pulled me down into a fitful, dreamless sleep.

CHAPTER 3

I woke in the middle of the night, disoriented, my head aching and my sweat-soaked chemise twisted about me. Blinking to clear my sleep-gritty eyes, the room made sense of itself. Hearth. Chair. Bed.

Sal.

Her breathing was even and deep, her naked back lovely in the moonlight.

I tried to roll over to face her and was somewhat confused when my head refused to cooperate. The tendons stood out on my neck as I tried—and failed—to lift it from the pillow.

All at once, my senses were invaded by a familiar scent.

Earthy and sweet with an undercurrent of vanilla.

A quick reconnaissance mission with my hands confirmed it.

Chocolate.

Encasing my hair in a hard, smooth disk and spreading out over my pillow.

Those little fuckers.

"Sal," I whispered.

No answer.

"Sal," I repeated.

"Mmm?"

"We have a problem." Flailing an arm, I caught her shoulder. "Wake *up*."

She sat bolt upright, a dagger flashing into her hand as she scanned the room.

"Unless you're planning on making pastry garnishes, I suggest you put that away and light the candles," I said.

Sal blinked at me in the dim light. "S'that?"

I grabbed her by the wrist and placed her hand atop my head.

"The fuck," she muttered groggily.

"Chocolate," I said. "One of those wee bastards came in and dumped chocolate on my hair while we were sleeping," I said. "And opened the window so it would harden."

Sal ejected herself from the bed and relatched the window before quickly rekindling the fire in the hearth, all the while muttering curses that would have made a sailor blush.

One by one, she lit the candles, setting the tallest on the table where her satchel sat. Then, she lifted the flap, reached in, and pulled out a bag several sizes larger than the one it had come from.

My neck strained as I craned to see. "You *are* magic."

"The *satchel* is magic," she explained, disappearing into the brocade fabric bag up to her shoulder. "I bought it from a woman in a pub in London. Carpet bags, she called them. *There* you are."

I caught the glint of copper in the candlelight as she dipped the kettle into the bathwater and crossed the room to set it among the fireplace's flames.

"You mean to melt it out of my hair?"

She crouched near the fire, using a poker to dig for any remaining coals. "You have a better idea?"

Currently, all my ideas were centered around the firelight worshipping the curved silhouette of Sal's ass through the thin linen braies loosely drawn at her waist.

"Don't you think you ought to put some clothes on before attempting this delicate operation?"

Sal flashed me a sideways grin. "I wouldn't have figured you for a prude."

"I'm not," I insisted. "I just don't think it's safe for you to be handling fireplace pokers with your tits out."

"Notice them, did you?"

"It's kind of hard not to with your nipples staring me in the face."

Sal rose and walked to the chair where she'd slung her breeches and leather vest.

"Better?" she asked, shrugging it on without fastening it.

No.

No, it was not.

Now, it was a deliciously maddening tease, revealing a tantalizing glimpse of her curved breasts every time the front gaped open.

The fact that I could feel something adjacent to arousal in my current state was a powerful testament to how astoundingly, mind-bendingly seductive this person was.

A loud crack from the fire caused me to jump, the chocolate's weight yanking at the roots of my hair. I sucked in a breath as pain flashed through my scalp.

Sal was at my side in an instant.

"Are you all right?

I tried to nod yes, which only made it worse. To my horror, I felt the familiar tightness at the base of my throat. The stinging at the corners of my eyes.

You will not cry in front of the hot assassin lady. You will not cry in front of the hot assassin lady. You will not—

I'd never been what one would call a pretty crier.

My face bunches like a drawn curtain. My nose tends to leak just as much as my eyes and can create snot bubbles if my shuddery, childish inhales catch the nose tears just right.

As luck—or the lack thereof—would have it, now was one of those times.

I felt the tickle at the end of my nostril, the tiny pocket of heat followed by the wet little pop, and then all hell broke loose.

The humiliation made me cry all the harder.

"Someone tried to make my head into a truffle, and now I've snot on my face. So, I'm going to go with nay. I am not alright."

Sal carefully sank down on the mattress beside me and fished inside her vest pocket for a handkerchief that she used to dry my tears before swiping it beneath my nose.

"That's absolutely disgusting," I sniffled. "I am so sorry."

"You want disgusting," she said, folding the damp cloth. "Try being on the business end of a Sigataur."

"I wouldn't even know which end was the business end of a Sigataur."

Picturing the man-headed, moose-horned, ponderously large Centaur-esque creatures fabled to roam the forests of the Hebrides, either end seemed like it could be a significant problem.

"Count yourself lucky. Let's just say the term cumbucket isn't hyperbole."

Suppressing a bark of laughter sent bubbles out of both nostrils this time.

Sal held the handkerchief to the end of my nose. "Blow."

I blew.

She gingerly dabbed my nose and lip before sliding the handkerchief back into her pocket.

"Who taught you to do this?" I asked, gazing up at her. "Take care of someone, that is."

Sal rose, crossing to the fire to check on the kettle. "It was part of my service to the Order. To care for the young ones who were... donated like me."

"They were lucky to have you," I said. "My mother passed when I was eight."

"I know," Sal said.

I blinked up at her. "How?"

"I grew up hearing stories of *Petit Rouge*. The villages she saved, the monsters she killed—"

"The one she married," I said, too tired to disguise the bitterness in my voice.

Sal fished the kettle from the fire with the fireplace poker and set it on the stones next to the copper tub. "So, what they say about him is true?"

"Aye," I said. "But it's my mother they always blamed."

In the cosseted confines of Caisteal Abernathy, I thought my father something like a king. Mainly because the visitors to our home treated him that way. The awakening I had received after Mark and I left hadn't just been rude. It had been brutal. However shifters within the xenophobic clan-based outpost of Scotland thought about my father, the rest of the world viewed him as the decadent, indulgent, philandering embarrassment to werewolf kind.

A traitor who mated with a woman famous for hunting among their numbers.

And I had committed the grievous sin of arriving on the planet looking exactly like her.

"I'll help you sit up, then we'll get you to the chair," Sal said.

I glanced toward the end of the bed. While I had been mining my memory, she'd moved it next to the tub. The prospect of making it even that far felt like an impossibility.

"Can't you just call Bernie or whatever his name was to magic this mess off me?" I asked, more out of desperation than anything.

"Seeing as it was probably magic that put it on you in the first place, I'm going to say no." She stood next to the bed, the flickering candlelight making the shapes on her arms seem to dance.

"What makes you think it was magic?" I asked.

"Because if one of them had physically been in the room, you'd have scented them."

I didn't have the heart to tell her that virtually all my heightened senses took their leave of me when I slept. Which I typically did with the conviction of a corpse.

Standing over me, her foxlike features took on a rabid edge. "I find out which of those shits did this, I'll have his heart for a hat."

"There!" I said excitedly. "Your eyes just did the thing again!"

"It was the candle," Sal said.

"Ballocks," I said. "I know what you're doing, and it's shyte."

Warm, strong fingers wrapped around my ankles, gently tugging my body toward the end of the bed. "What am I doing?"

"That thing what men do when they try to convince you that you didn't see what you actually saw or what you heard isn't what they said until you begin to think you've gone mad."

She leaned over me, the pillow beneath my neck shifting as she worked her hand beneath my skull. "Let me support your head."

Her face was closer to mine than it had been since we met outside the inn. Her lips parted on a warm breath that feathered my cheeks. "Ready?"

"Aye," I said, not meaning it in the slightest.

Sal lifted my head and neck as tenderly as I'd watched mothers scoop their bairns from a cradle, aided only marginally by efforts.

"There we are," she said. "Think you can stand?"

Now that at least my torso was vertical, the weight atop my head felt more manageable. "I think so," I said.

Sal's hand remained cupped at the back of my neck as her forearm banded beneath my shoulder blades and helped me to rise. We shuffled to the chair, and she eased me into the chair. "I'm going to lean you back over the tub."

Instant panic flared within my rib cage, and she must have seen it in my eyes.

"I've got you, Kat."

And she did.

Cradling my head with one hand, she poured the kettle's contents over the mass with the other, keeping the steaming stream well away from my scalp.

"I have good news and bad news," Sal said after several minutes. "Which would you prefer first?"

"Good," I said.

"The chocolate is coming away pretty easily," she said.

"And the bad?"

"There's caramel beneath it."

"Please tell me you jest."

"I jest not. If I sit the chair up, can you manage for a minute?" Sal asked. "I might be able to make some kind of solvent."

"Just cut it off," I said miserably.

"No," Sal said with enough vehemence to make me flinch. She brought the chair to all for legs and stalked over to the table.

"Why not?" I asked. "You think just because I'm not fae that I can't pull off a pixie cut as well as you can?"

"I'm not fae, and I didn't choose this style," she said. Rummaging through the bag, she set out an assortment of tiny bottles and pouches. "It was cut when I left the Order."

"Left the order?" I asked, admiring how the bathwater deepened the intensity of the linework on her arms. "But, your cloak...I thought anyone who left the Order was stripped of it."

"In that case, how did you get yours?" A flash of light and puff of smoke rose from the glass jar where she mixed the various contents.

"My mother gave it to me," I said after an extended beat of silence. "Right before she died in childbed."

The memory returned to me unbidden.

My mother's stomach was still a distended mound beneath sheets stained crimson in a circle spreading behind her. Her face was pallid as the chalky stones here along the Moors. Her dark hair tangled as kelp. All that power, all those battles, and the life dependent upon hers for survival had defeated her.

Which was why the Order demanded abstinence.

Not because anyone gave a damn whether they were virgins. But because sex required women to yield control of their sovereignty.

Nothing I had seen nor experienced in the course of my long life had proved anything different.

Sal returned with the glass jar, the swirling contents resembling a small, sparkling galaxy.

"Since you're *clearly* not magic, I suppose you're going to tell me that's stable dirt and horse piss?"

"Oil of the tea tree and coconut flesh."

"And what was the flash I saw?"

"Just a bit of black powder leftover from the fireworks I have brought from the far east. I thought you might appreciate it for dramatic effect."

My eyes searched the heavens. If karmic punishment was due, perhaps I could just get run down by a carriage next time?

"Hold this," Sal said, wedging the jar between my thighs.

"I do have hands, you know."

"The oil from the coconut flesh needs to stay warm to remain liquid," she said, snugging the glass against my sex. "Your body is warmer here."

I peered into the liquid, and she tipped the chair back to lean against the copper tub.

She dipped her fingers into the glass jar and began to massage the mixture into my scalp, her strong fingers needing the sore roots. When she had enough of it worked in for her hands to meet, she began kneading with both at once.

The long, relaxing strokes softened the tight muscles of my neck and rolled down my shoulders.

If I had been a cat, I'd have purred.

"What is this wizardry?" I asked.

"Just a little something I've picked up in the Levant," she said. "You've never had a massage?"

I considered this for a moment. Our mother would give us a cuddle now and again, and we had nannies who would rub our feet sometimes after we came in from the cold, but usually, they did it roughly enough to intimidate the blood back into our toes.

Sal's fingers now slid up the back of my neck and down to the tight triangular knots next to my shoulder blades.

She paused, her vest gapping to reveal the outline of her breast as she reached down into the jar to gather more salve.

Meanwhile, I had developed a curious pulse against the glass. If Sal kept this up much longer, I'd end up boiling the mixture.

My bare toes curled against the stone floor, and I let go of a helpless moan as she discovered a particularly stubborn knot toward the center of my spine.

I found myself wishing they'd covered me with twice as much confectionary gunk if it meant I could stay here with Sal's hands on my scalp and her half-bared breasts above my face.

"We're going to need to rinse you," she said, winding my hair into a thick coil and securing it atop my head. "I know the bath isn't terribly hot, but I can heat up a couple of kettles to make it bearable."

"You don't need to do that," I said. Not because a lukewarm bath didn't sound more pleasant than a chilly one, but because I thought the chilly one might serve to cool my ardor.

"If you're sure," she said.

"I'm sure," I said, rocking the chair up myself this time.

The bathwater looked like a brackish sinkhole but smelled like heaven.

Sal cleared her throat and turned her back to me.

"Such a gentleman," I said.

"Now there is a contradiction in terms," she muttered beneath her breath.

I couldn't say I disagreed.

I stripped and stepped into the tub, surprised that the water wasn't nearly as chilly as I'd expected, with the window open for as long as it had been.

Once again, I wondered if there was more to this huntress than met the eye.

"I'm in," I said, pleased that the cloudy water mostly concealed my body.

Sal pulled the chair around behind me. "Will you tilt your head back?"

I could and did.

She must have filled and warmed the kettle by the fire again because the water streamed over my scalp was warm enough to raise goose pimples on my chest and arms.

"I'm sorry," Sal said.

"That your little friends attempted to make me into an after-dinner sweet?"

"About your mother."

The place inside me her care had tenderized now began to ache with a dull, hollow thump.

"I'm sorry about yours," I said.

"I've no memory of being left on the Order's doorstep," she said. "That's something, I suppose."

"But I imagine you saw it happen to the young ones you cared for within the Order's walls."

Sal was silent a moment. "I did."

"Some part of you, however young, remembers."

The fingers coming through my hair slowed, resting on my shoulders. I lifted my hands from beneath the water and placed them over hers. "My apologies were for her."

The contact sizzled through my nerve endings like lightning.

Our eyes met in the mirror's reflection. An understanding was reached.

My hands fell away as hers slid over my collarbones. One remained pressed against my hammering heart as the other slid down my sternum to my quaking belly.

"You're shivering," she said. "We should get you out of here."

I didn't bother to tell her it had nothing to do with the water temperature as I used the tub's edge to steady myself and push to my feet.

Sal came to me with the towels she'd been warming by the fire, wrapping one around my shoulders and another around my hair.

And then, ridiculously, I was crying again. Big fat tears slipped slowly down my face.

Sal paused, her dark brows pinching together in the center of her forehead. "Does your head still hurt?"

I shook my head, my wet hair brushing against my bare back.

"Then what?"

"I... I'm not used to having someone take care of me like this. It's making me feel too many things, and I prefer *not* to feel things, so if you could maybe just stop doing that, I would be most appreciative."

Her long lashes lowered a fraction as she studied me. "No," she said.

Hugging the towel against me, I narrowed my streaming eyes at her. "What do you mean *no?*"

"I mean, no. I'm not going to stop taking care of you."

"But... why?" I asked.

"Because I like it."

Not because I needed it.

Not because it was her duty.

Not because the law required it.

Not because she'd been paid to.

I would have had a solid argument against any of those explanations. But this? I was utterly defenseless against.

"What if I don't like being taken care of?" I asked. "Doesn't that count for anything?"

"Of course," Sal replied. "Although, I would be curious as to the reason why something that makes you smile and sigh as you did earlier is so abhorrent to you."

Barefoot, she padded over to her bag and pulled out a small leather sack. She took an apple, a log of cured meat, and a wedge of hard cheese from it and began slicing them, laying them out on a wooden board that had also emerged from the bag's depths.

My salivary glands contracted painfully as the scent hit my nostrils.

Of all the times for me to argue that I did not enjoy having another creature see to my basic needs...

I hugged the towel tighter around myself and considered my options.

In sneaking away from my brother, I'd had to leave my luggage. The thought of slipping back into my sweat-soiled night shift made my skin crawl over my bones.

"Try these." Sal lobbed a ball of linen in my direction.

I caught them with one hand and identified the same kind of braies Sal wore, but with a matching top meant to go over my breasts.

I snorted at the small strip of cloth. "These might work for you, but there's no way under heaven my bosom will fit in here."

The corner of her mouth jerked upward in a pirate's grin. "Aye. I know."

With my back turned to her, I stepped into the bottoms and knotted the drawstring at the waist before shrugging the boneless stays over my head and shoulders. As predicted, it failed to cover the entirety of my breasts. Still, if the bottoms peeked out, it was at least better than hanging about topless or in a soiled shift.

My dissatisfaction with this situation lessened considerably when I saw the hungry look flicker into Sal's eyes as I approached and helped myself to an apple slice.

Since they were already cut up either way...

The bite was crisp and delicious, the cheese a perfect compliment.

While we ate, I talked. About Mark's search for the heir. My plans to visit the colonies. My profound lack of excitement for a ship journey. My desire to buy land and then farm it by myself until the end of my days, blissfully unbothered by the politics of the werewolf world.

"But then, even with the money Mark has saved back for me, there's no guarantee it'll last. A girl's got to keep a roof over her head at least," I said, gesturing to the trusses in the ceiling. "It's that or—"

Sal's hand flashed out to grab mine and pin it to the table. "You're driving me mad, Kat."

"Well, if you'd actually try to be a decent conversational partner, I'd not have to do all the talking," I fired back in frustration.

She shoved herself up from the chair and began to pace. "It's not your talking that's the problem."

"Then what?"

"I've been paid to see you safely to your destination. Already, you've been harmed on my watch—"

"I doona know about *harmed*," I said, running a hand through hair that had dried silkier than I'd ever felt it. "It was a pain in the arse, to be sure, but just look at it now."

"I *have*," she practically growled. "I can't *stop* looking at it. At *you*, Kat. And I can't afford to look at you because every time I do, all I can think about is how much I want to touch you."

The air between us vibrated with an elemental connection that, until this very moment, had remained unspoken. But now the words were out there, they couldn't be called back.

The breath evaporated from my lungs and was replaced with my heartbeat. Every single part of my body had been filled with it. That deep drumming below reason and thought.

"Then what are you doing all the way over there?" I asked.

Three purposeful strides saw Sal across the room. She didn't grab my face. Didn't attack my mouth with hers or crush me to her body, though any of those things I would have gladly submitted to.

Sal made love to me with her eyes first. Beginning at my hair, they drank me in with such intensity I would have believed that she'd memorized every strand she had spent so long freeing from the mess of confectionery. They moved next to my face. My forehead, cheekbones, nose, lips, and chin. They trailed down my neck to my collarbone, chest, stomach, hips, thighs, knees, and feet.

Almost as if she couldn't decide which part of me she wanted to touch first.

So I touched her instead.

My hands floated from my sides to mold themselves to her shoulders. I lightly trailed my fingers over the smooth, lean muscle all the way down to her elbows. "What do they mean?" I asked. "Your tattoos."

Even if this close proximity, I could pick out no shapes that resembled objects I recognized.

"I don't know," she said.

"How can you not know when you're the one that got them?"

"They're intuitive. The artist decides what wants to be tattooed there and then applies it."

"How long ago did you get them?" I asked.

"Two years," she said. "Right after I left the Order."

She rotated her arms to show me the undersides as my fingers reached her wrists.

"Interesting," I said.

"What's that?"

"This one connects to your lifeline," I said, thumbing the place where the delicate line connected to the crease of her roughened palm.

"Huh," she said. "I'd never noticed."

I looked at her from beneath my eyelashes. "You went to all the trouble to get these elaborate markings, and you never bothered looking closely enough at them to notice that they connected to your lifeline?"

Sal shrugged. "It was more like a trade, actually. The tattoos were how she paid me."

"Paid you for what?"

"Services," she said cryptically.

"What is it that you do exactly?" I asked.

Her dark eyes burned into mine. "You're asking this now?"

"I am," I said.

Sal's open palm closed around my wrist and curled me into her with my back to her front. "What is needed."

"Could you be any more specific than that?"

Her fingers splayed across my belly. "Not without compromising the confidentiality of my clients," she said, trailing fingertips just below the exposed under-curve of my breasts.

"Out of curiosity, what would have happened had I refused to come with you?" I asked before I was robbed of sanity entirely.

Her mouth nuzzled the sensitive shell of my ear, sending a shiver down my spine. "I would have persuaded you."

"How?"

"By any means necessary." Sal's lips were hot velvet against the curve of my neck, endlessly sampling. Nipping. Tickling. Her hands worked in concert, continuing their slow sensual exploration of the underside of my breasts only.

Somewhere deep in the recesses of my pleasure-fogged brain, I knew that I should continue this conversation. To stop Sal from distracting me and see it through.

But it felt *so* good.

So good to rest my weight against her and let my body become hers to manage. If only for tonight.

For now.

"Look," Sal said, directing my attention to the mirror.

I knew men found me beautiful. They'd made it abundantly apparent all my life whether I wanted them to or not. But, for my own purposes, I had never seen beauty as more than a commodity. A useful tool to get what I wanted.

What *Sal* wanted was for me to see myself.

To be turned on by my body under her touch.

Moving upward, she lifted the top until the barest edge of my nipple was visible, teasing the over-sensitized peak with fabric softened by contact with her body over time.

I ached to feel her there. Her fingertips. Her mouth. Her fecking elbow at this point.

The effect was the same whether she sensed this or simply couldn't keep her hands off me any longer. Sal filled her palms, relieving me of the weight of my breasts, gently brushing the hardened nipples with thumbs roughened by the hand that gripped her bow.

My teeth sank into my lower lip as wet heat gathered between my thighs. My hips arched into hers, and Sal lightly pinched the tender flesh, sending a flash of pleasure clear to my toes.

Suddenly, that one point of contact was no longer enough. I found Sal's mouth with mine, and we fused on a shared moan. Soft lips, demanding tongues, hot silken heat. She tasted of spice and smoke seasoned by mystery and deepened by what I knew was a terrible idea. As so many of mine had been.

And yet, had I done even one thing differently, I wouldn't find myself in this present moment. Helplessly dissolving into bliss.

Unable to bear it any longer, I turned in the circle of her arms and pressed my body to hers. Seeking every surface where my skin could make contact. Gluing our bellies together. Melding our mouths once more. Drinking her in with every one of my cells. For all the coming times when I'd be lonely.

What a cruel joke this was. To meet Salvation, to know she existed, but to have no more of her than I could take in one night. The thought made me greedier still, and I shifted my hips back from hers to wedge my hands between us. She caught me by the wrists and moved them upward.

My fingers memorized the ridges of her rib cage. The small swells of her breasts.

I pulled my mouth away from hers and brought it down her throat. It was the silkiest thing I had ever touched or tasted.

I couldn't get enough.

Sal's fingers threaded through my hair as I brought my lips to her nipple, gently testing it against the seam of my mouth before teasing it with the barest tip of my tongue. Her stomach contracted on an indrawn breath, her grip tightening, making the pressure on my scalp dance between pleasure and pain.

She tasted of leather, of salt. And of something that was all her own.

Gently drawing me upward by the hair, she walked me over to the bed and guided me to sit on the edge of it.

There, she helped me out of the top and traced the place on my shoulder where the straps had been.

I'd had my breasts fondled. Pinched. Squeezed and groped since they decided to bud before my eleventh birthday. They had never been the source of positive attention if I was honest.

To have Sal look at them in that worshipful way was amusing as it was disorienting.

"They're right pain to haul around," I said.

Sal lifted them in her cupped hands. "If you were mine, you'd not have to carry them another minute of your life," she said, brushing the turgid peak of one nipple.

"That would look a little odd, don't you think?" I asked. "You walking around behind me in the market holding up my tits while I stand in front of the fish case."

"Who cares how it would look?" Her eyes smoldered up at me as she breathed a warm current over my nipple. "Any man who dared insult you it soon be surrendering his tongue."

I was only about half sure she was jesting.

"We'd quickly run out of places to shop."

"Then I'd just have to bring the world to you." Her mouth closed over my nipple, and my back arched with pleasure the likes of which I had never known. Her tongue danced with my sensitive flesh in the hot, lush darkness until my entire body was one undulating wave.

"I could make you come this way," she said, arching a dark eyebrow at me.

"That would be a first," I panted.

"If you insist," she said with a wicked grin. Then she pushed my breasts together, took both my nipples at once, and I promptly lost myself in a detonation of lapping waves that rippled through my entire person.

When I'd strength enough to lift my head, I looked down at her with thunderous curiosity. "How did you?" I stammered. "But that's not even..."

Sal only pressed a finger against my lips and sank down on her knees before me.

My core contracted at the prospect.

I'd experienced the oral arts plenty and had a reliable list of lasses with equal parts skill and enthusiasm.

But Sal elevated the act to an art. She clearly knew of patterns and pressures but something else too.

Presence.

She spoke to me throughout. Anchoring her mind to mine in my mind to my body. She looked me in the eye. Asked me what I liked. Intuited what I didn't by a subtle shift of the hips or a gasped breath. She made it feel like something worth knowing.

The tension in my inner thighs had begun to spiral inward and upward, with regular little pulses, fluttering out their ancient warning. Sal moaned against my flesh as her fingers stroked the place she'd made slick.

She lifted her mouth and looked at me beneath hooded lids. "May I?" she asked.

"Yes, please," I half growled.

Then the same fingers that had drawn back her arrow were inside me. Filling me. Stretching me. Exploring me.

"Oh," I said, startled and a little curious about the strange sensation she was eliciting. "*Oh,*" I said louder as her fingertips curled to nudge a place that went made my eyes go crossed briefly.

A lazy cat smile stretched the corners of her mouth. "You like this, my lady?"

"It's Kat—"

The angle of the pressure changed, making my torso jerk as if someone had pulled marionette strings attached to it. "Never mind," I whined. "Call me whatever the feck you like as long as you keep doing *that*."

"*Whose* lady?" she asked, quickening the pace.

"Your lady," I sighed. "Yours, yours, yours."

Then she put her mouth on me in concert with her fingers, and... I died.

The sound that tore from my mouth was somewhere between animal and human and contained the rawest parts of both.

I fell back on the bed, limp as a boned fish, my breath sawing in and out of my lungs. "And you say you're not magic," I said. "What a load of pish."

Sal grinned up at me as she knelt between my knees. "That wasn't magic. That was technique."

"Fortunately, I can be taught," I said, rolling onto my side. I patted the bed beside me, somewhat rumpled by my body's enthusiastic spasms. Sal sat down but stopped me when I attempted to reach for her.

"Tonight was about you, Kat," she said, squeezing my hand before rising from the bed. She walked across the room and picked up one of the discarded towels. Retrieving the kettle from the hearth, she poured steaming water onto the towel and held it out to cool it down before bringing it back to me.

"Hot towel?" she asked with a little bow.

All I could do was stare at her, an ugly worm of doubt creeping in. Perhaps I wasn't to her liking. Perhaps my body didn't call to hers as hers did to me. "You don't want me to—"

"Of course I do." Sal sat beside me again and gently moved the warm, damp cloth over my face and neck. "But waiting for it. Dreaming about it. Fantasizing about it." A seductive smile spread over her face. "It only makes the experience sweeter when it comes."

My eyelids had fallen closed, sunken into the bliss of this simple sensation.

"It's not fair for me to take pleasure and give you none," I protested.

"Who gave you the idea that there's no pleasure in watching you receive it?"

I considered this for a moment. "Men, mostly." The towel had reached my breasts and felt like a bit of heaven, especially on the part of me she'd lit up like a flame.

"You've much to unlearn from having lived among them so long," Sal said, putting the cloth aside.

"Where do *you* live? When you're not completing dubious tasks for odd means of payment, that is?" I asked.

The crinkles at the corners of her eyes disappeared as the playful smile melted from her face. "Right here," she said.

Outside, the wind began to howl against the panes.

"At the fortress?" My mouth cracked open with a yawn.

Sal shook her head. "I mean, in this moment."

A profound and pleasant heaviness settled into my limbs. "It isna fair to melt my mind out of my skull and expect me to follow that kind of logic."

Her cheeks glowed amber as she stared at the hearth. "None of us live anywhere. Not really. Not even in our own bodies. Some have them longer than others. But the earth takes us all back eventually."

I cleared my throat. "Shyte and stardust," I said.

Sal turned to me. "How's that?"

"Something a friend of my father's used to say." I settled back against the pillows, allowing the memory to float into my mind. "He's a tailor and came to Caisteal Abernathy to make my wedding gown. I think he could tell I wasn't overly excited about the groom," I explained.

"I can't imagine why," she said with a smirk that scored a direct hit to my loins.

"He finished the gown, and it was the most beautiful thing I'd ever seen. His best work yet, he said. But no sooner than he'd put in the last stitch that he told me he hoped I'd never wear it," I continued. "Naturally, I was a mite confused and asked him why."

"A reasonable question," Sal allowed.

Shifting on the bed, I stretched my legs out next to hers. "'We're all made of shyte and stardust, my love. That being the case, you might as well please yourself,'" I said, attempting to capture his East End accent.

A crease had appeared in the center of Sal's forehead. "Does he live in Londinium?"

I raised an eyebrow at Sal. "He does. But, more importantly, did you just call London Londinium?" I asked.

"A slip of the tongue," she announced with a wave.

I traced one of the lines on her forearm through the complete circuit of a swirling vortex. "Strikes me that tongue doesn't do anything it doesn't mean to," I teased. "Why do you ask?"

"I think I've met him," she reported.

"Alan Ede?" I asked incredulously.

"That's him, all right. He's the one who turned my cloak into a coat," Sal said. "For a handsome fee, of course. He was pretty put out at my asking."

Knowing the adorably fussy tailor as long as I had, it wasn't hard to conjure his voice in my head.

What the 'eww 'ave you brought me 'ere? You know what the Order would do to me if they found out we've got one of their fancy capes?

"Can you tell me why that's such a big deal?" I asked. "My mother told me I was never to alter it but never gave me the reason why."

"Because the very first belonged to Mother Lillith," Sal explained. "And every cloak that is made contains a thread from hers. It is said to contain the outrage of every girl child, maid, mother, and crone who has ever lived."

A tiny light within me flickered with pleasure at this idea. "Aye. I know a bit about that."

Sal shifted on the bed to look me in the eye. "Haven't you ever wanted to see justice done upon those that harmed you?" she asked. "To be fairly compensated for what they took?"

I hugged my knees to my chest against the ache waking in my heart. "I just want my freedom," I said.

"Or what passes for it in their world." Her voice took on a bitter edge. "Assuming you make passage to the colonies safely, what will you do once you arrive?"

"I have money enough to survive for some time," I said.

"And what of the ones who don't? What of the ones like you who longed to be free but have been made mothers already? Who are bound to violent men, or servitude, or worse? The ones who, like us, would be in danger if their true nature was known. What of them?"

The fire in her words woke dormant coals long banked within me.

"What is it *you* would do?" I asked, already knowing the answer would matter more than it had a right to, given the brevity of our acquaintance.

"I would see them free, Kat." Sal pushed a lock of hair away from my face and molded her hand to my jawline. "I would see them *all* free. And I would have your help."

My heart began to speed within my chest. "What would I have to do?"

Sal laced her fingers with mine and brought them to her lips. "You'd have to trust me."

Even stranger than her saying this was realizing that I already did.

I squeezed her hand and brought it to my heart. "We ride at dawn."

Only we didn't.

We were woken from the most restful sleep of my life by a tap at the door. Squinting through the early dawn light, I recognized the elf Sal had called Bernie standing in the hallway in a rumpled nightcap. He whispered something to Sal that made her face go long.

There was much more whispered argument, and then finally, she nodded and shut the door.

"They bring us some shortbread to go with the mess they put on my head?" I mumbled sleepily.

Sal was silent until she sat down on the bed beside me. My stomach shrank into a small, cold ball when I saw the expression on her face.

"It's your brother," she said. "They said a red-haired witch has got him and is holding him prisoner in the woods."

As I launched myself out of bed, my brain unleashed a string of curses that was fairly impressive for that early in the day.

Hadn't I warned him? Hadn't I tried telling him this one would be no different?

I felt around for my underthings, or rather, Sal's underthings that I had absolutely no intention of returning. "He's going to get himself bloody killed."

"You don't mean to go help him?" Sal asked.

"Of course I do." I yanked my chemise over my head, grimacing a little at the scent of horse and road dust. Nothing for it at the moment.

"Is he also not one of the most powerful werewolves in all of Scotland?" Sal asked.

"In all the world, probably," I said. "But that's not the point. Mark won't use those powers against *her*."

Sal scrubbed a hand over her sleep-creased face. "Not even if she means to harm him?"

"Not even if she means to use his skull as a serving bowl."

Sal helped me into my traveling dress before pulling on her trews. "You realize this will mean you'll miss your ship."

Your ship.

That these words should hurt me even more than the idea of my brother within a witch's grasp surprised me.

Had she changed her mind during the night?

Unmade whatever plan she'd been making for us?

"Yes," I said, grabbing last night's towel and scrubbing my face with a clean bit. "*My* plans will just have to wait."

Using such a common tactic as passive wordplay to get my point across made me feel silly and shrewish. Neither served to improve my mood.

"It's a trap," Sal said, sinking down on the tub's edge.

I paused my ablutions. "What's that?"

"It's a trap." Her large, dark eyes didn't quite meet mine. "She doesn't want your brother, she wants you."

An army of insects marched down my spine. "How do you know that?" I asked.

Sal blew out a breath, deflating her shoulders. "Because I was supposed to bring you to her."

Cold seeped into my blood from the stone floor beneath my feet.

"So that's the kind of work you do." I sagged back against the table with the wash basin. "You were never going to help me get to my ship at all."

"Not in the beginning, no," she admitted. "But after last night—"

"Oh, please," I spat. "Next, you'll be telling me you meant what you said even though you had no intention of seeing it through."

Sal stood up. "I did mean what I said, Kat. All of it. But I also knew it was the best way to get you on that ship so you'd be safe."

I whirled on her, my temper rising like the tide. "How dare you speak of women being free when you held me unwitting captive through outright deception?"

Sal stared at the old stone floor like it might hold the answers to the Universe's riddles, offering no defense.

I grabbed the rest of my things and balled them up beneath my arm as I shoved my feet into boots. "You'd have thought I could smell a rat after a hundred years." I shook my head in disgust. "Some wolf I am."

"You don't have to go, Kat," Sal said, touching my arm.

"It's family," I said, shrugging her off. "I wouldn't expect you to understand."

CHAPTER 4

$\mathcal{F}$ucking cottages.

With their incessant need for coziness, the windows always invariably ended up being ridiculously small and almost impossible to see anything through.

And the flame-haired witch's *stunk*.

Stunk like a wet foot left too long in a boot. I blamed this fact alone for my inability to scent my brother despite the indelible genetic marker stamped on my very marrow.

As I hunkered below the ill-proportioned window, even the very walls seemed to sweat, filming my paws with oil every time I braced against it to glimpse the goings on.

And the goings-on were, in a word, pathetic.

Suspended from the ceiling beam of the disheveled hovel choking with mewling felines, an oversized cage containing my brother swung in a slow circle, turning him like a Yuletide goose.

I'd glimpse his lovelorn face with every rotation and lose it again as the cage turned.

Though I couldn't see the cursed wench, I tracked her position by his eyes as they followed her.

At last, a slim white hand came into view, followed by the rest of her.

Naked.

She gripped the cage's steel bars, bringing her face to the gap with a simpering smile.

Tear her throat out, I silently ordered him. *Turn into the wolf I know you are and break through your bonds.*

He didn't.

Only wrapped his hands over hers on the bars and said something that made her laugh uproariously.

My stomach turned. The vile submissiveness of it. The weak subservience.

I felt the animal rage rising in me and craved the release of an attack. If my brother wouldn't do it, I bloody well would.

I would wait until her attention was elsewhere. Creep down the chimney or break one of these stupid, ridiculously thin windows.

The witch's laugh rang against the panes as she pushed off the cottage floor, her feet lifting from the ground as the cage began a wild spin. I'd heard the term cackle before but always thought it an overstatement. The ecstatic glee with which this woman laughed...

It made me self-conscious. Maybe angry. It made me jealous.

When had I ever laughed like that? Even once in my life, had I been able to let go the way she had? To give myself over entirely to any one feeling? The answer came almost immediately.

I had. With Sal. I banished the thought, reminding myself she'd nearly sold me to this woman. That it might have been me in that cage instead of my brother.

Blessed anger coursed through me, feeding my grudge.

This witch would know my wrath. She would feel my rage. She would—benefit from about thirty fewer cats. I knew one thing. She would soon be down a one if the vile creature weaving through my legs didn't stop rubbing its disgusting little face on my flank.

I issued a warning growl. Making sure it knew in no uncertain terms what my intentions would be if it continued this unwelcome distribution of affection.

It only gazed up adoringly at me with pumpkin orange eyes, emitting a strangely comforting rumbling from its throat.

"Go away," I rasped in my deepest possible growl.

The filthy thing only began kneading my leg like a wad of dough. Its tiny paws pressing in a succession that proved oddly relaxing.

Unnatural beast.

"Leave me be, or I'll harm you most grievously," I threatened.

And then, do you know what that verminous skin sack did?

It rose on its hind legs and pressed its wet nose to mine. Then, quite against my will, an intensely maternal feeling overtook me. And instead of rending its innards out, I found myself speaking to it in an imbecilic voice.

Asking the inanest of questions and, worse, answering them.

"Who's a pretty girl? You are! You're a pretty girl Oh, yes you are!"

And so forth.

I had progressed to rolling on my side to mirror her adorable posture when a cleared throat brought me up short.

"I see you've met Grizelda?"

From my prone position, I looked up into eyes glowing a foul green.

The witch had donned a robe but wore nothing under it.

"You're here just in time. The moon is nearly full." A blinding red flash seared my eyes and filled my head with tremendous pain before the screens were lowered on my vision.

I woke with my entire body stiff and sore and a strange creaking in my ears. Glancing upward, I quickly discovered the source. I now hung in a cage beside Mark's. Perhaps it was the lack of sleep. Perhaps the ridiculousness of it. Whatever the case, I began to laugh. Hard enough that the soft body beneath the shift she must have dressed me in began to jiggle.

My brother didn't share my mirth.

"Are you mad, Kat?" he asked, all furrowed brow and discontent.

"Mad that my brother is such an idiot, maybe," I said unkindly. "I hope you're happy. Now we'll both be killed."

"But we won't be," he said with a gleam in his eye that struck me as particularly insane. "She's going to change her mind. I know it."

"You've said this every single time," I reminded him. "Every time. And every time, we are no closer to the heir than we were when we started. When will you see that if you could persuade her to your cause, you would be together by now?"

"You don't know her like I know her. This is it, Kat," Mark insisted. "I can feel it."

"That's the problem with feelings," I said, my own rising to the surface bearing Sal's face.

"She's the one, Kat." His eyes had turned molten bronze, and that's when I noticed the giant black holes of his pupils.

"Have you been licking toadstools for real? Or did that foul harpy slip something into your beer?"

"I slipped something into this beer."

From her position by the bubbling cauldron suspended above the crackling hearth, Hanna the witch shot me a triumphant look. "Can you honestly blame me? He nearly cost me one of my best hunting spots."

"Hunting spots?" I widened my eyes and regarded her with my very best naive expression. If there's one thing my father's foul friends had taught me, it's that not a single villainous bastard holds an exploit but that he loved to brag about it.

"Yes indeedy. How else am I supposed to keep this girlish figure?" She brought her hand to the waist of her green velvet cloak and tossed her head of russet curls.

"I've always found a diet of wild game improved my constitution considerably," Mark said in the lecturing tones that always made my eye twitch. "That and plenty of fresh air and exercise. If it be changing your shape you're after, you can always find stones of a proper size to heft about."

The witch and I fixed my brother with matching looks of vexation.

Though we were at cross purposes, we clearly shared an exasperation with the male of the species' tendency to believe that even hypothetical questions should and could be answered by them and them alone.

"That's not quite the diet I found to be most effective," the witch said, the corners of her mouth curling up in a mischievous smile. "But I certainly appreciate the effort. I do try to eat organic when I can get it."

Mark's thick eyebrows raised in confusion, and I wondered precisely what Hanna put in his potion.

"She means to eat you, you titanic git," I explained.

"Not all of you," Hanna clarified. "Just your soul."

I stared into Mark's eyes, trying to resurrect the ancestral connection that used to allow us to communicate without words. *Did you see where she put the keys to the cage?* I silently asked him.

I felt a sizzle of the old connection, and then his voice echoed inside my head.

Doesn't she look great in emerald green?

"Bleeding Christ." I stuck my leg through the bars and kicked his cage, which earned me a swift retaliation. We'd devolved to slapping each other between the bars when Hanna strolled over and whacked Mark's knuckles with the giant wooden spoon she'd been using to stir the bubbling cauldron. "Children," she said, "that's enough."

But it wasn't. Not by a long shot.

If I could get at my brother right now, I'd pin him down and wail on him as I had when we were children during the few times during my cycle I was able to overpower him.

I want him to see me. To hear me. For my opinion to hold as much weight in his world as his does in mine.

But it never has. And I'm beginning to understand it never will.

I can't blame him entirely. Raised in our father's home account among the kind of men that treated women like chattel, Mark was already considered a revolutionary merely for suggesting that I should be able to decide who I married. Implying that my opinion should carry weight equal to his in all realms might melt his mind right out of his head.

We're still poking at each other when Hanna returned with something clutched in her fist.

"I think you two could use a nap." Opening her pale palm, she blew sparkling dust at our cages.

The hurricane of sparkling filled my vision, and I was utterly mesmerized by the curtain of stars when my eyelids began to droop.

The cage's gentle listing carries me over gentle waves into a strange mist. And then I fell through memory and time.

I land at my mother's bedside and look into her pallid face. Her green eyes are as bright and beautiful as they had ever been, even more so if that's possible. There's a fierceness in them, an intensity that comes from almost being free of the body where she is imprisoned.

"In my chest, at the end of the bed," she says. "My red cloak. Bring it to me."

My spindly eight-year-old legs carry me to the giant trunk weathered by age and marred by a thousand dents and scratches. I return the cloak to my mother and gently lay it across her lap.

Red upon red.

"Do you remember what I told you about this cloak?" she asks, waxy fingers brushing over one of the gold buttons.

My throat aches, and my eyes sting, but I find the words.

"Red is the color of women's suffering," I recite. "It marks our entry into womanhood. It is the color of the portal through which life enters and exits the body. It is our birthright."

"That's right. That's what we are given. The power over life and death. To create. And to destroy. That sacred power is yours now." My mother's hand is cold and clammy as it lifts mine and places it over the cloak. She says something in French that's too quiet for me to hear. A slight sharp pain causes me to gasp, and I see a single ruby drop of blood well up on my fingertip. She presses it to the cloak, and it glows like a tiny star before disappearing.

"There now," she says. Her smile is even weaker than before. "Take the cloak and hide it somewhere your father won't find it. From this day forward, it will answer to you and you alone."

"And why would I need to hide it?" I ask.

"The same reason we hide what you are and what you can do." She strokes the back of my neck with fingers growing ever colder. "It's not always safe to own power in a world like this. But if you can use it at the right moment, you might just change everything."

The room grows darker as if filling with smoke.

My eyes opened, and I was again in the humid hovel.

Our hostess turned her back toward me, adding something to the cauldron that made a plume of green smoke rise from the bubbling brew. She tasted it and paused, tapping her chin with her finger. Then, reaching into her robe, she returned with a small blade.

What she did after that confounded me for the space of several moments.

Stepping to the side of the hearth, she shaved off a chunk of the wall and brought it to her lips to take a bite as she stared at her brew contemplatively.

How had I been so daft?

The cottage didn't smell like cheese.

The cottage *was* cheese.

"That smells delicious," I said, pressing my face to the bars.

Hanna's red hair tumbled over her shoulder as she glanced back at me. "You think?"

"Absolutely," I said. "The balance is so delicate. Nightshade. Agrimony. And adder's tongue is a far under-appreciated ingredient if you ask me."

Her expression brightened immediately. "Right!?"

"Everyone is always on about eye of newt and wool of bat like it's what actual witches use. It's ridiculous."

"So ridiculous," she agreed.

"I blame Shakespeare personally. It's bound to happen when men write witches."

Hanna heaves a disgusted sigh. "Don't even get me started. The Weird Sisters?"

"I *know*," I said. "For a woman to have that kind of power, she'd obviously have to be hideous."

"You know what I think? I think they just want to believe that they'll be able to recognize a witch when they see one, so they don't have to be afraid they'll inadvertently fuck one." Glowing green droplets fly from the spoon as she gestures toward the window representing the outside world.

"Because God knows how their tadgers would shrivel at the very thought," I added.

"Yes!" she agreed. "As if we couldn't make them see whatever we wanted anyhow." A sly smile lifts one corner of her mouth. "How old would you guess I am?"

I squinted my eyes at her, pretending to assess her features. "Not a day over twenty-and-three, I'd say."

By the beatific beam that lit her jade green eyes, I could see the number pleased her.

"Try sixty-and-seven."

"You're never." I shook my head emphatically. "That canna be so."

"It is sure enough."

"How's that possible?" I ask, dialing up the incredulity.

Her wooden spoon swung back toward the cauldron. "That's me beauty secret right there."

"But I've never seen a potion that can push back the very hands of time. You must be a powerful witch indeed if ye can brew a draught that can do that."

With her red hair and pointy nose, she looks as sly as a fox. "It's down to the secret ingredient." She nudged her chin toward the wall beside Mark's cage.

Within the gloomy shadow outside the fire's glow, I couldn't tell quite what I was looking at until a flare and the crackling fire through a warm glow over the wall.

"Are those—" I fought a gag "foreskins?"

Hanna pulled a face. "Of course not." She returned to her cauldron and resumed her stirring. "Those are belly buttons. I keep the foreskins in that drawer over there, she said, cutting her eyes toward an old wooden wardrobe covered with herb bundles.

I glanced at my brother, sleeping the sleep of the innocent.

Oh, to assume the world will always be exactly as you left it when you next lifted your eyelids.

The bitter words I'd spoken to Sal echoed in my head and heart.

It's a family thing. I wouldn't expect you to understand.

But my brother hadn't either. Else we'd not be here.

And *here* had some unique advantages.

I looked from her to the cauldron, window, and door. Then, slowly, an idea began to unfold in my mind.

"Could I try some, do you think?" I asked.

"You?" she asked. "But you've nary a wrinkle."

"You're off your nut. What do you call this?" I pointed next to my eye.

She leaned in to look, and I made my move.

Grabbing her cloak, I hauled her against the bars and grabbed the knife from her pocket. Our struggle was quiet and quick. She was surprisingly wiry but still susceptible to the persuasive powers of sharp steel. I managed to turn her around, the point of her blade at her throat as the cage swayed.

"Wake him up," I ordered.

Hanna booted the cage with the heel of her bare foot, and it crashed against the wall.

Mark snorted and jerked awake, looking around like he'd just arrived on the planet. His dark eyes quickly scanned the scene, and I watched rage take root in his features. He'd never looked more like our father than in that moment.

"Kat, what are ye doing?"

"I'm getting us out of here."

My brother holds his hands up, palms forward as if he's the one at knifepoint. "Hanna won't hurt us," he says in tones typically reserved for soothing wild mares.

"I most certainly will," Hanna says brightly. "But please know it's nothing personal. Quite a compliment, in fact. I'm exceptionally picky about my ingredients."

Mark's thick fingers clutched at the bars. "Ingredients?"

"She's brewing a youth potion, and she means to add us to it," I explained.

I felt Hanna swallow against the skin of my wrist.

"Oh no," she said. "Just you." Her eyes slid to the extreme side to meet mine.

"Me?"

"Well, of course," she said. "Everyone knows the female of the species is more potent. And with you being from one of the prominent bloodlines and all..."

"Not you, too," I grumbled.

Maybe Sal had been right. Perhaps they deserved each other.

"Don't get me wrong," Hanna said. "I'd have used him if he was all I could get. But now you're here, I'll definitely be using you."

The witch must have breathed too many of her own brew fumes.

"Seems like you might have trouble doing that now," I said.

"Nay," she insisted. "I'm only biding my time until you realize you have an arrow pointing at your pretty head. Heightens the suspense. Which makes the brew sweeter still."

Without releasing my grip, I craned my neck around toward the door. Sure enough, there stood Sal. Somehow even more stunningly lovely by the dim light.

"Let her go, Kat," Sal said in a voice that brooked no argument.

My heart gave an involuntary squeeze despite the circumstances, and I was most put out to know that I was glad to see her even now.

"And if I refuse?"

"That magic arrow of hers straight through your skull," Hanna answered for her.

"Magic, you say?" I asked, maintaining eye contact with Sal.

"Aye," Hanna said. "I'm the one who dipped it in the potion in the first place.

I must have made a noise of dismay because Hanna chuckled. "Oh, you thought *she* was magic." She reached behind her to pat my knee through the bars. "Don't feel bad. So many of the ladies she brings here say the same thing."

My teeth ground together painfully as white-hot rage rose in my gut. I'd been such a fool, such an idiot, to believe that she saw anything in me that she found unique or different. I was just one in a long line of many lasses that ended in her pointed tongue.

"Kat, let her go," Sal repeated, her bow creaking as she increased the tension on the arrow's shaft.

I looked over Hanna's curly head at my brother, whose pleading eyes beseeched me to comply. Even the cursed felines milling about the bottom of the witch's skirt had taken up a plaintiff chorus that assailed my sensitive ears like Hell's own choir. All but one. The small black and orange cat with pumpkin-colored eyes now sat on the windowsill, looking at me fondly.

At that moment, I saw why so many spinsters lived out their days with a beast such as this for company and all other beings at a healthy distance.

I released Hanna and shoved her away from the cage. Resigned to my fate.

No sooner than I did so, Sal's arrow swiveled from me to Hanna.

The witch's face creased in surprise. "What do you think you're doing?

Sal increased the tension on the bow. "I'm getting my lady the fuck out of here."

By the way she said this, I couldn't tell whether she was using my lady as a title word or endearment. A treacherous little spark of hope leaped into my chest, but Sal didn't make eye contact with me.

Hanna adjusted her cloak and righted herself just as one of her felines would have had it fallen from a high surface.

"Unlock Kat's cage," Sal ordered.

Hanna's chin lifted a notch, but she waved her hand, and the cage bottom disappeared from under me with the protest of rusty metal. I hit the floor hard and came away slightly oily from the sweating cheese. Parmesan, now that I had a closer look at it.

"Come here," Sal ordered. "Quickly."

I gained my feet but remained stationary. "I'll not be leaving without my brother.

The arrow's silvery tip bobbed as Sal's shoulder slumped.

"You said yourself he won't give up on her." Her eyes burned with the same intensity they'd had the night we met. A thousand questions churned in my mind, but the answers would have to wait.

"If you intend to leave, I'm guessing you'll want your navel back?" Hanna asked almost conversationally.

I looked at Sal. "Your navel?"

"Wickedly effective way of sealing a contract," Hanna explained. "As long as I have it in my collection, his owner is beholden to me."

My mind drifted back to the night before. To the way Sal had guided my hand away from her stomach.

"Unless" Hanna continued, "someone else's hold over them becomes stronger than their own will to live." Her eyes narrowed on me suspiciously. "It's a pity we couldn't be friends. We have so much in common."

One of the things we have in common cleared his throat.

Hanna's lips pursed as she considered him, then turned her attention to Sal. "I'll tell you what. The moon is nearly full, and I'm feeling generous."

I made a snorting sound, and Mark gave me a warning glare.

"If Kat can guess which one of navels is yours, I'll release her *and* her brother and allow the three of you to leave unharmed." The hem of her cloak rustled the bundles of dried herbs as she spun dramatically. "I'll even give her three guesses."

"What's the catch?" Sal asked, the point of her arrow tracking Hanna as she paced.

"She can't use any powers, and if she fails, I get to use her soul for my potion."

"Powers?" Mark asked from the cage. "What powers?"

"That's the part about what she said that concerns you?" I demanded.

Hanna placed a hand on her rounded hip and cocked her head at me. "Can it be your brother doesn't know you're a witch?"

Mark and I locked eyes for an extended moment and what he read in them told all.

"How could you hide something like this from me?" he growled between the bars. "All this time, and you never once thought this might be something I needed to know?"

"Whose business is it but my own what powers I have, or how I choose to use them?

"As if there wasn't already enough of a target on my back, you think father and his friends would have abided me had they known? Why do you think I want to go to the colonies. At least there, they believe in religious freedom."

"Blah blah blah," Hanna intoned, resuming her spot by the cauldron. "You two can finish your sibling spat if you live. Will you take my offer, or no?"

I looked to Sal, whose arrow was still trained on the witch. She shook her head, no, but I saw the fear behind the gesture.

"I will," I said. Golden light winked into existence and wove between us in figure 8, binding contract.

"Go ahead then," Hanna urged, slurping a sip of her soup.

Because the shift was loose enough, I left it on as I stepped into the beam of moonlight angling through the small cottage window.

The creature within me hunted to the surface with a savage burst of animal pleasure.

The world folded over on itself as I came to all fours and

watched my fingers shrink as glossy black claws appeared in place of the nails.

However awful I thought this place smelled before, it was multiplied a thousandfold once my transformation was complete.

My stomach lurched toward my mouth on a gag as my eyes began to water.

I took a moment to compose myself before continuing to the wall where at least a hundred shriveled skinfolds hung from iron nails.

"The outies are most unsettling, are they not?" Hanna said over her shoulder. "This is what happens when men try to be midwives."

On this topic, I could not disagree.

Resisting the urge to sink back into my rage, I focused on the task at hand. Or paw, anyway.

Hanna forbade me to use my powers, but fortunately, I'd the benefit of at least eight years with a mother who taught me how to operate them covertly.

Pondering the horrific sight before me, I selected one of the options that required the most negligible physical interaction.

Eenie, meanie, miny, mo, I spoke the sacred choosing spell to myself within my own mind. Catch a tiger by the...

Nice try. Hanna's voice overrode my own. *What next? Abracadabra?*

I don't know which annoyed me more. That the witch could so effortlessly invade my mind or that she'd been accurate about my choice of options.

I was attempting to think misleading thoughts when an altogether different presence arrived in my mind. With it, a scent memory that burst into my brain like an explosion of fireflies.

My heart beating beneath Sal's lips. The scent of her filling my lungs. The taste of her mouth. I could feel her within me. I could feel her on the very air.

Was this what Mark had always been yammering on about? This

undeniable connection neither asked for nor intentionally nurtured?

I opened myself to it. I yielded as much space as it wanted to occupy. And when I could sense Sal even in the space between breaths, I again turned my eyes to the board. They drifted down the road of puckered flesh, stopping when they reached one that was small, tawny, and taut.

I stared at it with my acute vision, enlarging it within my field of sight until I could see the faintest silvery scar crossing the top.

Sal's.

I lifted onto my hind legs, recoiling when the calloused pad of one toe inadvertently touched one of the other flesh knots. Stifling a gag, I gently pulled it from the nail before dropping it in Hanna's outstretched palm. Her hand closed over it, her knuckles whitening as they squeezed into a fist.

A ribbon of flame, like the one that had bound me to the witch, appeared between her and Sal, flaming a bright orange before disappearing in a puff of smoke.

"You're a cheat," Hanna ground out through tight lips.

"I won fair and square," I protested. "Now release my brother."

"A cheat," the witch repeated, stamping her foot.

"How did you know which one was hers?"

"I suppose I'm just lucky," I said with a shrug. "We had a deal. Release. My. Brother."

Hanna's eyes glowed a poison green when she lifted them to mine.

"Oh, I'll release him all right," she said. Her hair began to fly around her head, blown by winds that seemed to affect Hanna alone.

Which, I had learned long ago, was a very bad sign. An eerie quiet descended over us, and I leaped between Hanna and Mark just as a blinding green light erupted from her fingertips and filled the room.

A deafening shriek pierced my ears, and everything went black.

CHAPTER 5

*C*haos was the only word to describe the scene unfolding before me. Or rather, below me, as I seemed to be watching it from the rafters.

And I wasn't alone.

"Do my hips look that big when seen from the ground?"

A slightly transparent version of Hanna hovered beside me, a ghostly hand propped beneath her chin. I followed the direction of her gaze and gasped.

We lay on the floor in positions that suggested a violent trajectory, our faces smudged with smoke and limbs thrown in all directions.

Sal had covered my nude body with her coat and furiously dug through her satchel while Mark howled from his cage, threatening to remove Sal's entrails if she didn't get him out.

"Ask your precious heir to let you out," Sal sneered, nudging the witch's limp body with her bow.

"Oy," the witch's ghost protested.

"Touch her again, and I'll take your arm off," Mark said as if sensing Hanna's outrage.

Even now, his loyalty leaned toward the red-headed harpy.

"Not from in there, you won't," Sal shot back against the chorus of wailing cats darting across Hanna's limp form.

"You've bloody killed us both," I accused.

"Ballocks. I've only killed you," the witch insisted. "*You're* the one who killed me."

"Hog shyte," I retorted. "All I did was throw myself in front of my brother."

"Aye," she agreed. "And something within your heart deflected the spell back at me."

"Love?" I asked.

Hanna's spectral face wrinkled in disgust. "Feck no. Someone obviously put a shielding spell on your important bits."

"But who would have—"

My words were interrupted by the rising column of glacial blue growing upward toward the roof. I saw Sal kneeling over me, her palm pressed over my heart.

I watched in wonder as the lines on her arms began to fluoresce, running upward like silvery water in a stream until they burst out behind her in gigantic wings. More like a moth's than a butterflies, their spectral shape glimmered like the moon, deeply shimmering and luminescent.

"I *knew* it."

"Knew what?" Hanna asked.

"That she's not human."

"What was your first clue?" Hanna snorted.

The way she made me feel the second I looked into her eyes.

Having lived around humans far longer than humans ever had to live around themselves, I questioned whether their continued existence was altogether desirable. Whether their mess and their monarchies, greed, and gods might have more to do with consumption than creation. While remarkable creatures like Sal were mutilated for their own safety. Their powers concealed against craven and covetous eyes. And yet my brother damn near wept over a wench whose loss meant his precious peace with them might be within reach.

I had been angry at Sal merely for doing what any canny animal would. Knowing no law but that of the wild. Showing fealty only to those who had earned their place. Not been handed it by blood or by birthright.

"What on earth is she doing now?"

I extracted myself from my wrathful rhetoric and looked at Sal, who was no longer merely resting her hand on my chest but pushing on it in rhythmic pulses. Each time she did, blue light shot from my body's mouth, eyes, and ears.

"Oh my," Hannah said, her eyes glazing over as the lean muscles of Sal's arms flexed with each palm thrust. "I don't believe I've ever seen her without her coat off."

"Right?" I said distractedly.

Her skin glowed with a fine sheen of sweat as she muttered curses below her breath, ceasing the assault on my chest to lean over my face.

Her hand clamped over my nose, and I saw her draw in one giant breath before lowering her mouth to mine.

I felt a terrific sense of acceleration. Of being pulled through the fabric of the stars and spat out the other side.

I landed hard on my back with a rattling gasp and sucked in a lung full of air that made me cough and wheeze. Strong hands beneath my shoulders sat me up, and I coughed up a brimstone-flavored, bile-green substance that sizzled when it hit the floor.

"Kat," my brother's anguished voice called out. "Oh, thank God."

"No," I choked out. "Thank Sal."

For me, at that moment, they were one and the same.

Her skin shone as if coated in opal dust, an entire rainbow condensed into every whit of her being.

"You *are* fae," I whispered. "I knew it."

"No, you didn't," Sal said, pushing hair away from my clammy forehead.

"Yes, I did," I insisted.

"No, you really didn't."

"Yes, I really did."

Beside us, a wet gurgle followed by a gigantic sneeze broke what otherwise might have been a poignant moment.

"Bless ye," Mark said from his cage.

"Don't you dare, you daft wanker." Hanna held a hand to her head of wild curls as she slowly sat up and sucked in a breath. "Jaysus, but that hurts," she said, massaging her scalp. "Is that what I've been doing to people all this time? That's right unpleasant."

"Look at Karma doing her work," Sal said under her breath. Already, her glow had begun to diminish, her wings growing fainter until they disappeared back into her body with a whisp of smoke.

"Unpleasant? *Unpleasant*? You just attempted to steal my soul, and you use a word like unpleasant to describe what you have experienced?"

"I was trying to steal your brother's soul if we're being technical-like," Hanna pointed out.

Wrong or right, all the other times with all the other Hannas unspooled in my mind like a long, horrific loop. I'd often heard the phrase been *to Hell and back*, but this time, I felt it. I felt the full fury of the infernal regions attach itself to what remained of my soul.

Sitting up, I shoved my hands into the arms of Sal's coat and pulled it around me. "You know what? You two fecking deserve each other. You can sit there in your stupid cage and her stupid cheese cottage with her stupid cats and try to convince her of your stupid plan for her to fix the stupid shifter empire and make peace with the stupid humans. I am out. Done. Sick to death of cleaning up after the males of this line."

"Don't lump me in with him," the witch protested. "I didn't want him to sit there mooning at the inn, much less follow me back to my home."

"And you," I said, whirling on her. "One day, you and I will square for everything you've put me through. Every humiliation.

Every insult. Every slight and missed moment of my life. And when that day comes, you had better hope my brother is here to protect you."

Hanna yawned, bringing her hand to her mouth. "Some protection he is," she said, jerking her head at the cage.

I marched over to the wall of navels to grab the shift I'd slipped out of when I turned into a wolf. Then, stuffing it under my arm, I stomped toward the door. I wished I had some fine scalding rejoinder to level upon them, but I also knew the effect would be somewhat compromised by my arse flapping in the breeze.

Sal raced to open the door for me and slammed it with a satisfying jerk after I stomped through it.

"How very dare she?" Slipping out of the jacket, I grabbed my shift and clutched it to my chest.

"Can you believe that woman?"

"Kat—"

"There I was, showing her mercy, only asking for my freedom and a simple belly button—"

"Kat—"

"And she gets so pissed when I beat her at her own game that she decides to retaliate against my big, dumb, lovesick brother."

I heard the creak of wood behind me. Sal cleared her throat and looked over my shoulder.

Not just a horse but an entire carriage was parked at the ready, the driver's ears fairly glowing crimson in the moonlight.

"Oh," I said. "Sorry." I moved to put the shift over my head, but Sal stayed my hand. A secretive smile played on her lips as she walked to the carriage and opened the door.

"I took the liberty of retrieving your steamer trunk from the inn," she said. "I also had your gowns laundered."

Drifting forward, I opened the lid and was delighted to discover all of my dresses, several pairs of leather trews that Sal wore, and several sets of the same kind of undergarments I had stolen from her.

"Are we going to be one of those couples?" I asked, not realizing how presumptuous the question was until it had exited my mouth.

"What kind of couples?" she asked.

"The kind that dresses alike," I asked, holding a leather vest.

Sal made a rumbling noise low in her throat. "Better save that for when we get to our next stop." She leaned in close enough for her breath to tickle my ear. "I'm not sure the carriage can withstand what I want to do to you right now."

Liquid heat pooled low in my belly.

I selected a simple traveling gown and a loud sound to help let me put it on.

Just as before, Sal maneuvered the fabric with practiced ease. Punching her forearms beneath the skirt to hold open the bodice and shimmying it down my torso.

"Were you a ladies' maid in your last life?" I asked.

"I've been many things," she said.

Without my even asking, she laced up the stays of my corset and tugged them firmly but not tightly closed. The lack of pressure felt strangely unsettling.

"You can pull tighter," I said.

"But then it will be harder to get off you," Sal said, knotting the laces at my waist before she released me.

"Where to miss—es? The driver asked, his cheeks reddening to match his ears.

"We're bound for Liverpool," Sal said, offering her hand to help me into the carriage. "We have a ship to catch."

Her eyes met mine, and warmth suffused my being as I took her hand and stepped into the lushly appointed interior. Sal did the honors of lighting several tapers within the compartment, bathing us in a romantic amber glow.

The driver snapped the reins, and the horses began to move.

I waited to speak until we'd turned and were headed in the correct direction.

"Why did you come back?"

Sal's long lashes feathered her cheeks as she gazed at her lap and the hand she'd folded into them.

"For a very long time, I've answered only to myself. And this is the way I prefer to live."

The tender roots of hope in my heart froze their progress.

"But you," Sal continued, "feel like part of myself. The better part. And if I must answer to something, then I would have it be you."

Her golden eyes gleamed with emotion.

I moved from the seat across from hers and sat next to her.

"I would have us answer to no one. Not even each other. I would have us do as we like and be as we want. Running side by side as long as our chosen roads move in the same direction. Unbound by vows that become chains that we then grow to resent. Together, but free."

Sal slipped her hand into mine and squeezed.

"Together but free," she repeated.

Tugging me by the hand, she drew me in close.

Our mouths met and woke the fire in our blood, burning away the last wisps of sadness I felt in leaving my brother, my home, the only life I'd ever known behind.

Sal shifted on the bench, breaking the kiss with a mumbled curse. "What the—ouch!"

I peered behind the cushion she'd just leapt away from and was met with a pair of glowing, pumpkin-orange eyes.

"What on earth are you doing here?" I asked, as if the creature was capable of answering.

Grizelda marched out from behind her hiding place and claimed a spot on the seat between us. Her sonorous purr filled the carriage's cozy interior.

"Looks like someone has found her familiar," Sal said, scratching the cat behind one ear.

Grizelda flopped onto her side and rolled onto her back to expose the downy expanse of her orange and black belly.

"I know exactly how you feel," I said, sinking my hand into her silky fur.

"So, where in the colonies are we bound for?" Sal asked, turning her attentions from the cat to me.

"*Salem*?" I suggested.

"Aye," Sal said, lifting my chin to claim my lips. "That sounds like a good place to start."

ABOUT THE AUTHOR

Bestselling author Cynthia St. Aubin wrote her first play at age eight and made her brothers perform it for the admission price of gum wrappers. A steal, considering she provided the wrappers in advance. Though her early work debuted to mixed reviews, she never quite gave up on the writing thing, even while earning a mostly useless master's degree in art history and taking her turn as a cube monkey in the corporate warren.

Because the voices in her head kept talking to her, and they discourage drinking at work, she started writing instead. When she's not standing in front of the fridge eating cheese, she's hard at work figuring out which mythological, art historical, or paranormal friends to play with next. She lives in Texas with two surly cats.

Cynthia loves to hear from her readers! Visit her at http://www.cynthiastaubin.com

CPSIA information can be obtained
at www.ICGtesting.com
Printed in the USA
LVHW042134070623
749217LV00020B/188